PC

CW01654426

LLYFRGELL... SIROL
RHONDDA-CYNON-TAF
DISCARDED

Roscoe, Emily and all the Little Bastards

Roscoe, Emily and all the Little Bastards

JILL FENSON

ROBERT HALE · LONDON

© Jill Fenson 1999
First published in Great Britain 1999

ISBN 0 7090 6341 5

Robert Hale Limited
Clerkenwell House
Clerkenwell Green
London EC1R 0HT

The right of Jill Fenson to be identified as
author of this work has been asserted by her
in accordance with the Copyright, Designs and
Patents Act 1988.

2 4 6 8 10 9 7 5 3 1

Typeset in North Wales by
Derek Doyle & Associates, Mold, Flintshire.
Printed in Great Britain by
St Edmundsbury Press, Bury St Edmunds, Suffolk.
Bound by WBC Book Manufacturers Limited, Bridgend.

Contents

To
The Actors who first opened
Box Twenty-six

Roscoe and Emily once figured in a radio play of mine, broadcast by the SABC.
Some time later, the idea began to grow.

J.F.

A Box Full of Beans
1908–1919

Chapter One
1908

On August Bank Holiday, the sun shone bright over Hampstead Heath. The sights were garish, the smells heady and the many sorts of music in rousing conflict.

Emily Kilverston viewed the scene with the contempt of one wishing to be at least four years older. She had a blue ribbon in her hat and a handsome young man at her side whom she had decided to loathe like poison.

His name was Roscoe Summerfield and he was eighteen. Despite his style and elegance he was also penniless; current survival depended on his ability to sustain the interest of Emily's mother, whose passion for the stock market was rivalled only by her taste for young men. Younger with every passing year. Today, relegated to the duties of a nanny, Roscoe was sourly aware of the need to break new ground before he found himself put out to grass. He paid Emily as little attention as possible.

A short distance off, Flo Dibbins – known for occupational reasons as Florence Villiers de la Haye – nudged the loudly checked elbow of her companion.

'I seen one, Stanley! Sunny open face, dead young, pearl tie-pin. Sitter.'

Florence and Stanley were in the business of fleecing the unwary. Within their limits, they did quite well. They had come to the fair for a nice day out. Maybe the odd new prospect.

'Where?' Stanley's boots were pinching and he fancied a jar.

'Other side the hoop-la, coming this way. Him with the cross looking flapper in the sailor hat.' Florence adjusted her pink feather boa and steadied her diamanté eardrops.

The movement caught Emily's eye. She watched it catch Roscoe's as well. She seethed at being treated as the tiresome schoolgirl she undoubtedly was instead of an object of hopeless passion, as specified in the novels she favoured at present.

'Honestly, Roscoe,' she scolded shrilly. 'Have you gone deaf?'

Roscoe dragged his attention away from the twinkling ears. Bit early to risk complaints to Mamma. 'Sorry, Emily, what was that you said?'

They were outside a closed booth, where a grimy painted board proclaimed the credentials of Madame Zorilda, adviser to Crowned Heads. Emily sighed with extravagant patience.

'I want to know if Mamma will leave me millions, or squander everything on cads like you. Come on.'

'You'll get fleas!' he squinted after those eardrops.

Emily followed his gaze. She understood Roscoe and his motives far better than he imagined.

'What low tastes you have.'

'I've a good mind to stick you in the Lost Babies' Enclosure and tell your mother you absconded!'

Emily smirked. 'Much good that'll do you. You're on the way out, anyway. I know the signs.'

He looked at her in genuine surprise.

'You're too old!' she elucidated, 'Oh, I've watched them come and go, Roscoe dear. Whatever it is that makes Mamma behave so foolishly seems to have the effect on her that knickerbocker glories are still supposed to have on me. And *you've* been left out in the *sun*!' She delivered the insult with gusto.

'You deserve a damn good hiding, you brat!'

Emily's sulky little face lit up.

'Ooh, Roscoe, would you really? You'd see my drawers. They're threaded with blue ribbon like on my hat.' She winked at him with extreme sauciness and swept into the tent.

Roscoe was resigning himself to follow when Florence bore down on pink feather wings. 'Biffy!' she trilled ecstatically, 'Biffy Sopwith!' Where have you been hiding since Henley? Lady Pilkington thinks you've gone to Khartoum!'

Roscoe flung himself into similar action: 'What light through yonder Hoop-La breaks!' he declaimed. 'Believe me, lovely lady, how I wish I *were* Biffy Sopwith!'

Whereupon Florence blushed in bewitching confusion. 'Oh, stupid, stupid me,' she breathed. 'What must you *think*! I'm most *frightfully* sorry.' She inclined her head with finality.

As she pivoted slowly away, Roscoe moved faster and blocked her path.

'Don't go!' He raised his hat. 'Permit me. Roscoe Summerfield. And I've no pressing call to Khartoum. Unlike poor old Sopwith.'

'You know him?' Florence's eyebrow twitched.

'I believe we once shared a camel.'

She extended a gracious hand. 'Florence Villiers de la Haye.'

To Stanley, hovering at a discreet distance, Flo's performance was spot on, as always. He had to admire her technique, he did really. He observed Roscoe closely throughout the routine with mounting interest.

By the time his own cue came to move in, he was thinking that here might be an acquisition far exceeding Florence's shallow perceptions. After convivial introductions, he mentioned a small libation being in order. Would Roscoe care to join them? Jack Straw's Castle fit the bill?

Ruefully admitting to the afternoon's duties, Roscoe replied that he might look in later. 'When I've taken my kid sister home.'

Madame Zorilda, an unlaundered heap of coloured shawls and bangles with three teeth and a sparse beard, was in full spate over Emily's hand when Roscoe appeared in the tent.

'Long, long life wi' lovers a-plenty,' she was intoning. 'And Box Twenty-six, it'll follow you all the way. Remember Box Twenty-six...'

'Time to go, Emily.' Roscoe produced some coins.

Emily attempted to quell him with a look.

'Who says? How dare you listen to my fate!'

'I'm having to pay for it. How much, sixpence?'

'That's Mamma's money she gave you to amuse me with!'

'Bruvver an' little sister, are yer? ... Ah, no!' Zorilda amended hastily, seeing their faces, 'Linked by fate, that's it! I get that very strong.'

Roscoe put a shilling down and held his hand out for change.

She clamped it, palm up, to her unlovely nose. 'Thee'll go far, young man, far thee'll go,' she sucked her gums revoltingly. 'Over the water an' under the water an' beware Box Twenty-six, you too. Thassall.'

'Not much, what?' Roscoe pulled his hand away and wiped it fastidiously on his hanky.

'Wotcher expect for a tanner?' She scooped up the shilling.

Roscoe took Emily firmly by the arm and marched her out. There was no sign of his new acquaintances. About to write off the encounter, he glimpsed them strolling away towards the pub.

Emily found herself bundled into a cab and escorted home to Fitzjohn's Avenue. It was ten past five. She maintained an outraged silence all the way. She knew exactly what Roscoe had in mind. But for his cavalier treatment of her, she would have been glad to assist. She told herself he was unbelievably stupid not to recognize the valuable ally he might have had. It was too late now. She would get even with Roscoe Summerfield, one fine day.

On arrival, he handed her out with a flourish. She stepped down, stony-faced, just as a youth of about sixteen emerged rather furtively from her house and scuttled away down the hill.

'Who's Galloping Acne, then?' Roscoe enquired. 'Little friend of yours?'

'Probably your successor in Mamma's string of favourites,' Emily informed him with devastating hauteur.

The sound of the front door violently re-opening caused Emily's mother to pour herself a slow, stiff whisky in aid of her composure. Amaryllis Kilverston was thirty-four. She had married Emily's father for the dual purpose of improving her own material situation and learning to play the stock market. In all other respects he bored her mightily until he obliged her by succumbing to a massive coronary some five years back. A pleasant enough life had ensued, based equally on her flair for making money and her penchant for malleable young men wishing to bask in the sunshine of her smile. She was actually beginning to find Roscoe a shade too assured these days.

The image of those younger, softer liquid eyes into which she had so lately gazed with gentle wisdom faded abruptly at the sight of Emily with a face like thunder.

'You're very early home,' she said. 'Didn't you enjoy the treat Roscoe and I arranged for you?'

Emily pouted. 'He had a business appointment.'

Her mother stiffened. Roscoe had no business having business appointments. She, Amaryllis, was his sole support until such time as she, Amaryllis, should decide otherwise.

None of this was lost on Emily, who shrugged. 'There were two dreadful people on the Heath. I think they were friends of his and he didn't want me to know. I say, you're a bit windblown, aren't you?'

Amaryllis shot a glance at the mirror over the fireplace. Was Titian Beauty becoming Faded Redhead? Not yet. Not quite. She patted the odd stray tendril. 'I've been on the river at Richmond, actually,' she explained casually.

The idea of her mother taking up outdoor pursuits was a novel one. 'What on earth for?'

'The vicar wished his son to learn how to punt.'

'If that was him leaving just now, he looked pretty thoroughly taught,' Emily commented. She waited defiantly to be told that children should be seen and not heard. Instead, she found herself being regarded speculatively.

Amaryllis studied her daughter's burgeoning figure with grudging approval. My God, she was thinking, the child's unusually perceptive for thirteen. She's growing up. And she's going to be a beauty. What am I going to do about that? Well, one can't ignore it entirely…

Philosophically, she returned to the subject of the vicar's son: 'It's one's Christian duty to succour the young. As I said to his father the vicar.'

'Did his father the vicar agree with you?'

'His father the vicar appeared more inclined for a little succouring himself.'

'Ah,' said Emily.

Amaryllis found but scant reassurance in the thought that Emily would soon be back at school in Saltdean.

In the saloon bar at Jack Straw's Castle, Stanley Jellybean nursed his second pint and watched the door. The lad might not turn up, of course. On the other hand, he might. If he did, Stanley was ready for him, having despatched Florence homeward.

Bit of a set-to there, he'd had. After all, she'd spotted the mug in the first place. Stanley had to insist very forcefully that this was no ordinary punter; that a man-to-man assessment was needed here. In the end, she departed with a fairly bad grace, because she knew that Stanley's hunches were liable to be right.

The partnership of Jellybean and Villiers de la Haye was one of diverse activity. Profits from boxing promotion, off-course betting and the escort service – more Flo's department, that – all came home to the flat in Camden Town, above the gaming club which they ran with cheerful disregard for legalities and the Inland Revenue.

When Roscoe duly strolled into the bar looking young, keen and engagingly frank, Stanley sensed a goldmine in that appearance alone, never mind the toff accent. His judgement was not misplaced. As the interview developed, Roscoe blossomed in response to Stanley's persuasive interest. He found it rather agreeable to tell the truth for a change. Or at least, more of it than usual.

'So what's your old man do for a living?' Stanley asked confidentially when they were both comfortably mellow. 'Duke?'

'Brilliant actor. When not pissed,' Roscoe replied, adding: 'He's dead, y'know.' Tears welled up with a nice warm glow at doing the tatty old bastard such credit.

Stanley also learned that his new young friend would likely need lodgings before long. He was able to recommend some rooms in Camden Town. 'Nothing fancy, mind. But handy if you're looking to increase your scope.'

By the end of the evening, Stanley Jellybean and Roscoe Summerfield were business associates. Stanley began to envisage heights hitherto undreamed of.

Chapter Two
1911

On an afternoon in early October, Sir Redvers Grinling sat behind his monolithic desk, gazing morosely at his eighteen-year-old daughter. After six months in Switzerland, Kate was still convex and tubular with the sex appeal of a blanched leek. His ideas for a Christmas Dance of vast magnificence, here in London, to signal her next year's debut and improve his own standing with the nobs, were losing a bit of edge somehow.

'I shan't know what to say to anybody,' she whined, 'and anyway, I hate dancing. People tread on my feet.'

Her father, contemplating her pale scowl and ungainly demeanour, thought: God, what's anything for...?

From modest beginnings, Redvers Grinling had, with cheerful ruthlessness, amassed a gigantic fortune from the railway system. Marriage to the excessively plain sister of an earl, at thirty-eight, had eased his way to a baronetcy. Although considered parvenu himself, his wife's position could scarcely be ignored. Neither could his enormous house in Hampstead or, indeed, the Hampshire estate with its model home-farm, private zoo and rapidly growing art collection.

Now fifty-nine, he was damned if he was going to be done out of founding a nice little dynasty. His daughter, however depressing she might be, was still a hell of a catch for some blue-blooded buck. His son, now, young Teddy, was much more the ticket. Pity the lad was so short. Sir Redvers himself was rather short. His women had all the height. Well, Kate had to be brought up to scratch. He would be setting the wheels in motion, whatever she might feel about it.

That very evening, he requested his wife to enrol the child somewhere local but reliable for deportment classes. Lady Priscilla Grinling assented with pallid resignation. She was in the grip of one of her frequent migraines and in no mind to converse with her husband, let alone oppose him.

For twenty years now, the whole business of marriage to Redvers Grinling and motherhood to Kate and Teddy had been one of dogged endurance. Preferable, maybe, to the penury brought on by her noble family's excesses, although she sometimes wondered.

When Redvers first appeared in her life, barnstorming his way into the local hunt, Priscilla had been a gawky spinster of thirty-four. His declared intentions brought much jocularity about new blood and fresh vigour from her degenerate younger brother the earl. Priscilla had little say in the matter. Always happier in gumboots and jodhpurs than frocks, she would have been perfectly content as a farm hand, had such a thing been possible. Instead, she found herself bartered as a job lot with Heatherley Castle, the mouldering family seat.

Staying on as mistress of Heatherley was a bonus, certainly. Redvers restored it way beyond any former glory and her tiresome brother departed for good, to indulge his decadent preferences in Italy.

Often, she told herself she had much to be thankful for. Her pervading melancholy stemmed less from aversion to Redvers than a deep disinclination for marriage to anyone.

These days, she took refuge in ill-health, particularly when they spent time at the Hampstead house. She detested London. Lying on the sofa in her upstairs sitting-room, she listened dolefully to Redvers' notions for a spot of Christmas cheer.

With a damp white face-cloth rolled like a sausage across the bridge of her prominent nose and a plaid rug over her angular knees, she reminded him of a steeplechaser with colic. He doubted if their mutual filly would ever make the parade ring, but kept going anyway. They eventually reached a dispirited decision on the Adelaide Road Finishing Academy for Young Ladies, in case St John's Wood might succeed where Lausanne had failed.

Kate herself had been counting on her performance in Switzerland to browbeat her parents into letting her do what she wanted: namely, retreat to Heatherley and work in the zoo. She was always completely happy amongst the assortment of small exotic fauna her father kept there. Especially the reptiles, whose cool disregard for social intercourse she found deeply impressive.

No such luck. Here she was, a 'new girl' all over again, stumbling about with a book on her head. The academy was pretty harmless on the whole. The tutors were far less demanding than the Swiss ones and the other students tended to leave her alone, since she had so little to say for herself. It was just all such an awful waste of time.

Then it became apparent that clouds do sometimes have silver linings. In class, she sat next to a girl whose personality she found quite dazzling. When Emily Kilverston turned out to be friendly as well, the world began to seem slightly less rotten.

Emily was vaguely sorry for the poor creature. She also had a keen eye to the main chance. A best friend with Kate's social connections was not to be sneezed at. Emily was her mother's daughter, however much she might sometimes wish otherwise.

At present, she was livid with her mother. Just seventeen, she assumed without question that she would be given a season next year. Amaryllis stunned her by declaring that one came out at eighteen and not a second earlier. There were towering scenes, with Emily threatening to snuff out her own blighted life, but Amaryllis would not be budged. She insisted that a deferred debut would only heighten impact. Of course they both knew she was damned if she would invite public scrutiny as a back number until she absolutely had to.

Emily poured all her outrage and frustration into Kate's receptive ear. It was heartening to have a captive audience of such uncritical disposition.

Although Kate thought Amaryllis extremely glamorous and a joyous contrast to her own mother, she thought Emily extremely glamorous, too. It certainly seemed jolly unfair to keep Emily away from dances if dances were what Emily wanted. It was also deliciously shocking to listen to scathing indictments of someone else's own Mamma.

'She'll be younger than *me* before she's much older!' Emily growled after a particularly colourful piece of slander. Kate thought this incredibly witty.

As the Christmas holidays drew near, Emily, in her turn, was required to listen at length to Kate's misgivings at being forced into society. 'I'm a ninny, I know I am, but I can't help it,' Kate confided sadly, 'I never know what to say to boys and I bore them and my brother says I dance like a kangaroo.'

Emily was unable to disagree with any of this and simply sat there, grinding with silent envy. Then, Kate had an inspiration:

'Oh, Emily, if only you could come! It wouldn't be nearly so bad if you were there...' Resolve grew as the idea bit, 'I know! I'll organize an invitation for your Mamma, and I'll get *my* Mamma to put in a special note about *you*!'

For Emily, her mother's intransigence suddenly lost its teeth. Amaryllis would be irresistibly trumped.

Ten days before Christmas, in the vast modern house overlooking the Heath – built in 1893 with every convenience – the ballroom vibrated for most of the night to the sweated labour of two full orchestras. One bore the dancers away on a tide of massed strings rendering Strauss, Offenbach and tunes from Gilbert & Sullivan and the other, rather racy, thumped out strange new transatlantic rhythms with names like 'Ragtime' and 'Cakewalk'. It was, without doubt, a thoroughly significant occasion.

Lady Priscilla Grinling presided with a smile like a plaster lemon. As soon as decently possible, she intended to retire upstairs with a hot-water bottle. Kate stood about awkwardly, shoulders hunched with embarrassment, in a terrifying dress composed entirely of peach frills. Sir Redvers, determined to make the most of his own hospitality, got other pre-debs to teach him the Bunny Hug.

Emily Kilverston, pretending to be twenty, was having the evening of her life. Chestnut hair piled high for the very first time, dressed in a floating dream of cinnamon chiffon piped with satin and set off by her mother's topaz necklace, she whirled between boys and their fathers with ethereal ease; a firefly, spiking the banked clouds of debutante white.

Prevented from joining 'em, why not try and beat 'em?

Amaryllis had to concede the point with grudging admiration. Emily was certainly taking hold with both hands. She felt a sudden pang of guilt regarding her own contribution to Emily's grasp of the facts of life. Well, one could only hope Dibbins the Housemaid had been worth her keep...

... About fourteen years earlier, in answer to an advertisement in *The Lady* for a housemaid, a small round person with a buttoned-up face had presented herself and nearly pulverized Amaryllis with ferocious emanations of rectitude. She had, she said, in tones that brooked no argument, Been A Mother. No excuse for the termination of this office was forthcoming and Amaryllis felt no pressing need to seek one. About to reject the grim little being with the desperate eyes, however, she was hit by a swift intuitive flash regarding Emily, then aged three.

This woman might prove an absolute find, she realized. Those cast-iron standards as a basis for ... well, whatever instruction is required in the course of time would provide an excellent balance for her own! How truly enlightened Emily's upbringing would be!

Dibbins the Housemaid had been an integral part of the household ever since. As to Emily's state of readiness for life's rich tapestry now, Amaryllis could only hope for the best...

With sparkling eyes and glowing cheeks, panting charmingly after an energetic Turkey-trot, her daughter was returned to her, champagne-cup in hand, by Teddy Grinling.

'You're much too young to be doing all this...' Amaryllis murmured severely, '...so well.' Her eyes devoured Teddy.

'I learnt from a mistress.' Emily's tone was ambiguously respectful.

Amaryllis asked Teddy if he played Bridge. He replied that he'd be jolly keen to learn.

Equably, she surveyed the scene. Across the room, Kate was blushing furiously beside her mother. A tall young man was bending over Lady Priscilla's hand.

'I'm sure I know that back,' said Amaryllis.

Emily craned to see and when she did, stifled a gasp of astonishment. 'I don't think *that* back would interest you, Mother,' she stated briskly. 'That back is positively middle-aged!' Her attention switched to Kate, who, it appeared, was being swept not only onto the floor but off her feet. It was hard to believe, but it looked as if she might be engaging in animated conversation as well. Emily noted the aristocratic tilt of the young man's head, the romantically un-English style of his hair, the cut of his beard...

What the blazes did Roscoe Summerfield think he was up to?

Her dance card, almost full, showed the next waltz to be free. 'Excuse me, Mother,' she got up, 'I'm a little warm.'

She ducked prettily past a hovering Teddy Grinling and made her way to the ladies retiring room. She felt in definite need of a dab round the temples with cold water. Roscoe had been out of their lives for years now. The sight of him was having an effect on her that she was unable quite to analyse. And why was he got up like the Prisoner of Zenda?

When Emily returned to the ballroom, the waltz was ending. Dancers were leaving the floor. She spotted Kate and her partner and stood watching, from a point in their direct path. 'Twas thus, she thought poetically, the primordial pussy-cat looked when cows invented cream. Roscoe must have been working overtime.

Was it Roscoe? At second glance, Emily was less positive. The overall impression was quite different. As they drew near, she waved. Kate immediately turned glowingly to her partner.

'You must meet my friend Emily Kilverston!' she exclaimed. 'Emily, may I present Comte Etienne du Couteau?'

Chapter Three

1912

The interests of Jellybean, de la Haye and Summerfield had expanded greatly over the last few years. There was now a pleasing range of jewellery, small *objets d'art* and paintings to be fenced; pickings from country house-parties, dances and the like, to which Roscoe's looks and manner gained him ready access. Right from the start, it was a tribute to his projected image that mothers of daughters never doubted his accounts of himself. His effect on them was such that they were disinclined even to compare notes with each other.

As need to guard against over-exposure increased, targets became more selective. Roscoe Summerfield took judicious breaks from the social whirl. These were diligently spent developing a valuable stock of aliases. A natural actor to his bones, Roscoe perfected his unique ability to change character convincingly without need of grease paint. Between the three of them, an operation was maintained at maximum risk and maximum profit.

One afternoon in late January, Florence sat in her plushy living room doing a spot of cashing up. Every so often, she glanced at the ormolu clock on the chenille-swagged mantel.

The day before yesterday, Roscoe had set off for a hunt ball at Heatherley Castle in Hampshire, equipped with a copy of the Dutch master which hung in the hall there.

The forgery was a nice bit of work, Flo told herself. Sure to be. Not that she'd seen it, mind, but what would she know? Stanley's area, that was. Cost a packet, it did. To be recouped in multiples, just as long as Roscoe avoided getting nabbed.

Heatherley Castle had been on the agenda for some time now. Preliminaries had included Roscoe's low-key attendance, less than two months back, at a Christmas Dance in Hampstead. 'Low key' being the agreed brief. All the same, Flo couldn't help feeling it was all going a bit quick.

The pressing invitation to the hunt ball from the daughter of the house was seen as a bonus by all concerned except Flo. It seemed that Kate Grinling was hopelessly in thrall to one Comte Etienne du Couteau, heir to vast unspecified tracts of France and over here to polish up his *Anglais*. Roscoe's translation of his favourite alter ego as 'Steve the Knife' enchanted Stanley.

Flo still fretted, for no good reason, She looked again at the clock. He ought to been back by now! Even if he's gone off somewhere, he ought to been back to report!

She said as much to Stanley when he came in from the Dogs.

'He done the job, that's for sure,' Stanley replied. 'Then the careless little bleeder goes and hangs it back up all wonky. Look what it says here!' He handed her the evening paper.

The front page reported theft by substitution of a Dutch masterpiece from Heatherley Castle, country home of Sir Redvers Grinling, after the Heatherley hunt ball. The switch had been discovered when the painting slipped from the wall and dislocated the neck of a housemaid dusting the table underneath.

The criminal had not yet been apprehended.

'They'll be after him, though! Get us all done, he will!' Flo's pent-up misgivings about this whole set-up were threatening to boil over.

'Nah,' Stanley soothed her. 'Who's after Roscoe Summerfield? Steve the Knife, now, he might get 'em thinking, with his ritzy French accent and his poncey little beard. Anyway, we're not sitting here to be nicked. I got plans.'

'Eh?' She was in no state to be traumatized further.

'Now, you make a nice pot o'tea, and you lace it with a nice slug o' gin, and then you have a read of this other little item in the paper here, and you tell me you don't fancy a trip to America!'

'Eh?'

'I'll have us all on the high seas before we're much older, you see if I don't.' He slapped her bottom. 'In the clear, an' all. Like I say, who's looking for Roscoe Summerfield?'

*

Who, indeed? At this precise moment, Roscoe was taking tea with Emily Kilverston.

Face to face with Comte Etienne du Couteau in the Hampstead ballroom before Christmas, Emily had found herself at an unaccustomed loss, so flawless was the performance.

Smiling with genuine pleasure at a new and delightful acquaintance; brushing her gloved hand with his subtly waxed little moustache; murmuring '*Enchanté, m'selle*', this courtly stranger, upper-crust French through and through, convinced her only of bearing a strong resemblance to someone she used to know.

As the evening wore on, she became too much in demand to follow up the encounter. It was some time before she realized that Kate and her Count were nowhere to be seen. Although still mightily intrigued, she transferred her attentions to Teddy and set about dismissing Roscoe Sommerfield from her mind.

The following day, the Grinlings left for the country.

Teddy Grinling returned on Boxing Day. He preferred town for the rest of the holidays, especially with Emily there. Kate stayed on at Heatherley. She wrote inviting Emily down for the hunt ball at the end of January, but Amaryllis decreed that Adelaide Road must take priority. Emily retaliated by cultivating Teddy Grinling with marked success.

Emily was displeased with her mother to the extent of wondering how best to kill her. She was also organizing a pleasant enough unofficial season of her own. Acting as her mother's social secretary, with access to the diary, she was able to plan her own life quite agreeably, with no shortage of beaux; her mother's dedication to male youth had its uses. Arrangements went pretty smoothly on the whole, though Amaryllis might wonder from time to time why Teddy Grinling missed a bridge lesson.

Coming upon Roscoe's address in the diary gave rise to an audaciously stimulating idea which would, Emily soon realized, serve more than one purpose rather beguilingly. Not only would it be gripping to see him again and compare him to Kate's Christmas *chevalier*, there was also an irksome situation which had lately arisen.

Although Emily considered herself unusually sophisticated, areas existed about which she was still extremely hazy. Her mother had always neatly avoided any passing on of basics. After all, what was Dibbins for? At school, due to a studied attitude of advanced worldly wisdom, most of the crucial secrets whispered in the dormitory at night got missed out on and at home, budding curiosity had been dealt with less than capably, had Amaryllis but known.

Dibbins' earliest account of herself to Emily as a 'poor orphan' had struck infant ears as 'Poor Awful'. For Emily, so she remained. At eleven or so, leading questions were nervously parried with vague but vivid warnings of the 'Curse of Eve' and its effects –which, in Dibbins' case, had apparently brought shame and disaster. In spellbound confusion, Emily heard tales about the feckless lion-tamer who, in his carnal frenzies, ruined Dibbins and left her with twins.

'Both gone to the bad long since, Florrie and Ivy did. Both no better than they should be, neether. Come to think of it, you put me in mind of Ivy, you do. Better keep yourself to yourself, you did.' All of which left Emily little the wiser, wondering like mad about carnal frenzies and how to spot them.

Dibbins was also given to cheering herself up with frequent sessions at a drab shack in Chalk Farm she referred to as Chapel, where they sang bloodcurdling hymns and listened to gut-wrenching threats from a furious preacher.

Emily was taken along, too, as soon as she turned four. It scared the wits out of her and left indelible images of smiting, blighting and fighting between plucked-out eyes and teeth. She cried and clung to Dibbins, who shushed her and whispered to take heed, because Mr Jellybean was only speaking for her own good.

Jellybean? How could such a merry name be so nasty?

How could Dibbins and Emily know that really and truly, Mr Jellybean was raving against his son, Stanley, for scarpering off when he was twelve and never coming back.

Emily's association with Teddy Grinling consisted mainly of matinées at the Music Hall and *thé dansants* at the Trocadero. One afternoon however, in a cab from Shaftesbury Avenue to Hampstead, Teddy grew alarmingly ardent. He was, he declared, frightfully keen on her. In fact she was the most topping girl he'd known in all his sixteen years. He couldn't sleep for thinking of her. He would quite like to eat her. Or at least find out if she wore garters. Emily, considering this a new and essential aspect of her education, allowed him to do so. She also allowed him to guide her hand into exploring the state of his own underwear. The experience left her slightly baffled, but with a disquieting suspicion that Kate might become an aunt before Michaelmas.

Emily was quite fond of Teddy, but as a long-term prospect he filled her with acute dismay. For one thing, he only came up to her ear. She intended therefore, with Roscoe's unwitting assistance, to remedy the matter. There was also a score to settle from some three years back.

Emily Kilverston sent an unsigned, printed card inviting Roscoe Summerfield to tea.

On receipt of the formally worded invitation, Roscoe had assumed it to be from Amaryllis. He accepted on the principle of always keeping his options open; to which end Amaryllis had long been furnished with a poste restante address.

After the hunt ball and all it involved, Etienne du Couteau boarded the train at Much Heatherley and repaired immediately to the first-class toilet facilities, where sporty continental breeches and belted jacket gave way to unmistakably English city suit. The pointed beard was regretfully and rather hazardously dispensed with against the motion of the train. Roscoe Summerfield emerged at Paddington with an unsevered jugular and only one small cut on his chin.

On presenting himself at Fitzjohn's Avenue, he was extremely surprised to find Amaryllis absent and pleasure of his company apparently being sought by Emily.

'One lump or two?'

'Three, please.'

'What a sweet tooth you have.'

'I always did. I must say, Emily, you're looking quite tremendously toothsome.'

There was no doubt that Emily was a stunner. After forty-eight hours' professional effort in the company of Kate Grinling, Roscoe's vigour began to re-tingle. He accepted a tiny cucumber sandwich and wondered where it was all going to lead.

Emily had no doubt whatever. She giggled enchantingly.

'I find it warm for January, don't you?'

'We may be in for an early spring.'

'It's *so* nice to see you again, Roscoe,' Emily spoke with flattering warmth, 'What are you doing with yourself these days?'

'Oh ... all manner of things. The, er, the organization I'm with has multiple interests.'

Emily looked impressed. 'Is it a very big organization?'

'Quite small, actually. I'm one of the directors.'

'And you so young!' She sighed with admiration.

'Twenty-two,' he confirmed with an apologetic laugh, 'I doubt if your mother would think so.'

'My mother didn't ask you to tea.' Emily patted the sofa beside her, 'Won't you come and sit here? You look lonely.'

In a mounting state of agreeable confusion, he obeyed. 'I – I thought you hated me, Emily. You even said so once or twice, if I remember.'

'That was a long time ago. I was a brat.'

'You're a corker now.'

'Do you think so? Really?' Emily guided his hand first to her knee, then slightly further up. She patted it into place.

Roscoe transferred hers to his thigh. 'Can't you tell?'

She obliged with a little gentle massage. 'That's to prove I'm not a brat any more,' she said. 'And to make you feel warm.'

Roscoe was feeling very warm indeed.

With her free hand, Emily reached over the back of the sofa to the gramophone, ready wound up on the table behind. She lifted the rotator arm and held it poised over the turntable.

'Now,' she invited. 'Tell me all about your work.'

'Well...' Roscoe's composure was disintegrating fast. He could feel the sweat trickling down his back. 'I, er, travel about a bit, dontcher-know . . . . What are you *doing*, Emily!'

'Don't you like it?'

'I can only say that the early spring we mentioned is ... is coming up like thunder...!'

' "Out of China 'crost the bay"? Rudyard Kipling.'

He made a feeble last stand. 'So it is! D'you like Kipling?'

'I've never been kippled.' She lowered long, long lashes over brilliant eyes. 'That's a music hall joke, did you know?'

'I didn't think young ladies went to music halls.'

'This one had time to kill. I mean, *you* weren't about...'

Had she gone too far, too fast? It couldn't be helped. She was getting cramp in her gramophone arm. She let the needle fall at random on 'Gems From Beethoven'. The Ninth Symphony burst uncertainly on the air.

'Roscoe,' she murmured. 'Do you remember once, you said you'd like to give me a damn good hiding? And I said my drawers were threaded with blue ribbon? Roscoe, would you like to see what colour ribbon my drawers are threaded with now...?'

He was lost. Utterly and completely.

Clothing flew in all directions.

They climaxed gloriously to a rather tinny rendition of *Ode To Joy*.

Emily's reasons for engineering this occasion having proved groundless, her enjoyment of it was reckless indeed.

Florence had read the item in the evening paper several times and was feeling very insecure. It was unsettling enough seeing their nice little network in danger of blowing apart. What with Stanley carrying on about crossing the Atlantic in style, she didn't know if she was coming or going. The tea had long gone cold in the pot. They were on the gin. Stanley was waxing very verbose but Flo still needed convincing.

'Bit out of our class, innit? Anyway, it'll be booked solid.'

'Don't I keep telling you I got contacts?' Stanley sighed. 'As for class, who's worrying about class with young Roscoe along? With Roscoe along, I tell you, we'll be in clover!'

At which point, young Roscoe walked in with a rolled-up newspaper under his arm and a daft smile on his face.

Florence, in her overwrought state, erupted all over him: 'Where d'you think you been, you horrible boy? Strolling in here like Burlington Bleeding Bertie with Scotland Bleeding Yard on your tail! Oh, never mind us, cornered like sinking rats!'

She might have gone on indefinitely without a little lung-power diplomacy from Stanley. When calm was restored, he enquired as to the fate of the bleeding Dutch bleeding master.

Roscoe unrolled his newspaper. Inside was a dark rectangle of roughly sixteen inches by twelve. Stiff with age and varnish, horizontal cracks bearing witness to undignified transit, the corners had to be weighted down with the teapot, the gin bottle and two bags of Flo's takings before it could be considered.

'I had to unfasten it from the stretcher and swop it with the fake in the dark,' he explained. 'Bit of a fiddle, what? I was in a bit of a hurry, too, dontcherknow. I expect that's why it fell off the wall.'

Stanley and Florence gazed upon it, lost for words. They knew that it was an object of untold value; that, properly implemented, it would be their passport to a life of beer and skittles. They could not, for the life of them, imagine why.

It was mostly tobacco-coloured murk. Just discernible was the figure of a bad-tempered, toothless female person clutching a grubby red sock.

'Well, there she is,' Roscoe said proudly. '*Old Woman with Stocking*.'

'No accounting for tastes, is there?' Flo observed. It didn't seem right, doing stir for a mouldy thing like that.

'Bit of an uproar, I'm afraid, yes,' Roscoe admitted. 'Sorry and so on. Luck of the game. What happens next?'

While he stared at the dingy work of art, something was nagging in Stanley's brain. Not until Roscoe finished speaking did he realize what it was.

'Here,' he said, as puzzlement hit. 'That fake, it was a Sammy Viner. How come they rumbled the switch so quick? Even if it did fall down? Sammy Viner, he'd be an old master himself if he could keep off the bottle. Frigging genius, Sammy Viner is.'

'Was,' Roscoe corrected. 'He's dead.' Well, it had to come out sooner or later.

They were struck dumb, both of them. Eventually, Florence said indignantly, 'He's thirty-seven!'

'He's still dead,' Roscoe took a deep breath. In for a penny and so forth. '*I* painted *Old Woman with Stocking*,' he announced with modest pride. 'The copy, that is. I painted it myself.'

You could have heard a pin drop. Then Stanley started going a very funny colour. He took Roscoe by the lapels and lowered him with vigorous accuracy onto a chair.

'Right, Mr Roscoe Bleedin' Summerfield. Right. I'm waiting. Don't waste my time.'

'I think you'd both better sit down too,' Roscoe advised.

The talents of the late Mr Viner might indeed have contributed to artistic heritage, had he not been a committed member of the criminal classes, a slave to alcohol and a priceless asset to the likes of Stanley Jellybean.

Stanley himself had dropped in frequently during the construction of Viner's final masterpiece and been duly satisfied. Roscoe had been put in charge of its collection and ultimate destination.

'I took along a bottle of Scotch,' Roscoe began.

'He's kept off, he can't work else!' Stanley shouted.

'He'd been off! He'd done the job! It was only fair,' Roscoe protested. 'Then he wrapped himself round half the bottle without so much as offering me a snifter!'

'You knew he was a drunk!'

'I didn't know he was a fighting drunk!'

It appeared that Sammy Viner had become very emotional about the abuse of his divine gift as a tool for knaves: ' "Mocking up copies for confidence tricksters" – his exact words,' Roscoe related. 'At least, that's what he meant, but it came out garbled and it made him very angry.' A violent palette knife attack on *Old Woman with Stocking* followed, with Roscoe leaping to her defence. 'I got the canvas away from Sammy,' he recalled, 'but he kneed me in the stomach and I dropped it. Then he put his foot through it, slipped on the wet paint and hit his head on the fender.'

'W-where is he now?' Florence asked uncertainly.

'Lying on his back with his head impaled on a nasty brass spike at the corner of his fender.'

'You left him there?'

'I had an assignment,' Roscoe reminded her virtuously. 'I grabbed another canvas and did the job myself. It took all night. Then I left the studio and got on with the operation as planned. I'm not the sort of fellow to leave a thing half done.'

Stanley cut to essentials. 'Anybody see you?'

'Not a soul,' Roscoe assured him. '*And* I locked up after me. Here's the key.' He laid it on the table and studied the ill-gotten gain displayed there. 'I like mine better, actually.'

Florence fingered the key warily. 'Still in there, is he?'

'Want to pop round an' look?' Stanley enquired.

'I wouldn't fancy it, he's a week old.' She pushed it away.

'Shut up and listen, the pair of you!' Stanley could always think quickly when need be. He outlined a few new proposals.

Roscoe's mind began to wander. He seriously suspected himself of having fallen dizzily in love. 'What is Love, 'tis not hereafter…', ran his errant fancy, 'Present mirth hath present laughter...' Emily was present in every fibre of his being. Emily was mirth; Emily was laughter. Oh, Emily Kilverston, what have you done to me!

'I'm talking to you an' all, young Roscoe!' Stanley's grating reminder broke through the swirling glory.

'I know, I know!' Roscoe pulled himself together. No point in diversifying at a moment like this. It did begin to look as if he would have to remove Emily from his immediate hereafter. He listened with mixed feelings.

'... so you see, my lad,' Stanley concluded, 'what happens next is, you lie low. You lie very low indeed. For about two months and a bit!'

Chapter Four

With a little expert attention, Kate Grinling could have been acceptably pale and interesting. In Emily's view, this sunny morning in mid-March, she was simply peaky and glum. She stood with Emily in the flower room at the Academy, working on a spring arrangement for the entrance hall. Her fair hair was lank; her eyes and nose faintly pink.

Emily thought she looked like an anaemic flamingo. She was also beginning to find endless speculations on the whereabouts of Etienne du Couteau more than a touch tedious.

'I can't understand it, after all we were to each other!' Kate was agonizing. 'Now, I'm beginning to wonder if he's joined the Foreign Legion.'

Emily stifled a yawn. 'Why would he do that?'

'Well ... for love of me?' This was hazarded with threadbare hope. 'And of course, there's all that fuss about the beastly painting. It's nearly two months now and they still haven't found the thief. Etienne might have joined the Foreign Legion to prove his innocence.'

'Or escape the consequences of his guilt?' Emily found the idea rather diverting.

'How can you, Emily! You wouldn't say such things if you'd met him!'

'I did.'

'Only just. But if you *knew* him .... So aristocratic! So romantic ....' And once again, Emily was forcibly regaled with a blow by blow review of the primrose path to peaks of careless rapture at the Heatherley hunt ball. '... he was terribly interested in my collection of china cottages, you see, so I invited him to my room, and ... oh,

Emily!' A graphic description of Etienne's most intimate charms followed, with the new addition of the acorn mark on his left buttock.

Emily's attention sharpened very swiftly.

Kate was becoming tearful again: 'He would only say "Au Revoir" at the station,' she recalled, 'not Goodbye. Oh, I can see him now, so elegant with his gorgeous little pointy beard!'

Emily remembered a small cut on Roscoe's chin and a slight rawness about his freshly shaven jaw. She placed an iris with close attention, softly humming *Ode To Joy*.

'It's frightfully important to get in touch with him,' Kate was droning, 'he's simply got to come to my dance. He's simply absolutely got to!'

There was to be yet another Grinling dance in about three weeks' time, again in respect of Kate's coming out. Once having embarked on a strategy, her father was not a man who did things by halves. This one would be held at Heatherley, to present her formally to the county.

'What's the point of a dance without Etienne there?' Kate mooned on. 'I don't care about anything since he went away. Besides, I don't feel well. It must be all this pining I'm doing. We're sending out the invitations this weekend. You're getting one. I did miss you at the hunt ball, Emily. You could have got to know Etienne better. Do you think your Mamma will let you come this time?'

Wild horses, Emily promised, would not keep her away. She had reached a kind of armed truce with her mother; agreeing to an official debut next year, provided Amaryllis was flexible about endeavours to amuse herself meanwhile. In view of one thing and another, Amaryllis was disposed to be reasonable.

'You could come and stay!' Kate suggested. 'That would be really ripping!'

Emily agreed. Amaryllis wouldn't have a leg to stand on. Besides, this would be a gathering to gladden any mother's aspirations.

Suddenly, Kate lurched forward, almost knocking their floral pyramid into the sluice. 'I ... I must go to the cloakroom,' she muttered, 'I think I'm going to be sick!'

Left alone, Emily grew reflective. She had not seen Roscoe since that riotous January afternoon. But over the past fortnight it had become clear, with the help of some informative reading, that she must proceed with her contingency plan.

She was sorry for Kate, languishing after a shadow. Jolly bad luck. But the pass she now found herself in was less than pretty. She could do with the ace she had just been handed.

It would serve Roscoe right. All of it. Besides, she knew perfectly well, deep down, that she and Roscoe were made for each other.

Emily arrived home as her mother was preparing to leave. The forthcoming dance at Heatherley presented no problems when mentioned. Amaryllis clearly had other fish to fry. A taxi-cab was waiting outside.

'I may be late-ish back, darling. I'm doing a musical appreciation class for Viscount Montglebe. So talented, he is. So sensitive. One cannot grudge a little extra time.' She was pinning her hat at a provoking angle.

'Is he talented and sensitive enough to warm your lonely twilight years?' Emily asked with sudden kind concern, envisaging her own imminent departure from the nest.

She was rewarded with an indulgent laugh. 'He's seventeen! He'll be the catch of the season next year. See how I keep your interests at heart? Must rush, poppet. See you later.'

Emily thought Pongo Montglebe a genetic disaster, but only smiled benignly. Amaryllis swept out of the house on a cloud of Parma Violet.

The taxi was directed to the Savoy Hotel, where she was to meet not Viscount Montglebe, but Sir Redvers Grinling, who had expressed a need to learn some of these modern dances and wished to make arrangements for tuition. Amaryllis had not entered the appointment in the diary, nor did she see any reason to mention it to her daughter.

When Roscoe called at the poste restante and found Emily's invitation to tea at the Trocadero, his heart annoyed him by leaping most irresponsibly. He had obeyed orders and lain low for over six weeks now, but her image would keep rising unbidden to his mind, despite his certain knowledge regarding her extreme lack of principles. Or, perhaps, because of it. The confidences enjoyed on that apocalyptic afternoon in January had left him in no doubt whatever as so the delectable amorality of her soul.

His colleagues reacted neurotically to his proposal of a private West End sortie. Understandable really, *Old Woman with Stocking* being wedged behind the pianola until she could be let loose on the fine arts underworld of New York.

He offered to wear dark glasses and even side-whiskers if it would make them feel better. He added that he intended to keep the appointment, whether they liked it or not.

It was a truly delightful setting, Emily thought, for what she had to say. The orchestra played and lovers swayed on the dance floor. Besides, thanks to Teddy Grinling, she had the added confidence of being on familiar ground.

She and Roscoe faced each other over chocolate éclairs at a discreet table behind a potted palm. She was very intrigued by the sideburns and tinted spectacles.

'Spot of conjunctivitis, dontcherknow,' he muttered.

'It's the people you mix with.' She told him about the forthcoming Grinling dance. 'Why don't you come?' she suggested. 'I'm sure I could get you invited. Of course, poor Kate's own beau won't be there. He's joined the Foreign Legion.'

'Oh. Has he?'

'He's French, and very highly born. His people have a French Chateau in the Ardennes.'

'Have they?'

'The Ardennes are in Belgium.'

'Are they?'

'The police are looking for him. The Grinlings lost a valuable painting when he was staying with them.'

'Did they?'

Emily laid her hand on his. 'Roscoe, do you remember when you came to tea at our house that day when Mamma was out? And you took advantage of me?'

'You invited me *because* she was out, Emily!' he snatched his hand away. 'You said so. And you seduced me.'

She was quite unmoved by this cravenly righteous attitude. 'You always were a boor, Roscoe,' she observed sweetly. 'Now, you're to become a father as well.'

Denial, counter-accusation, refusal to become any such thing – all were fruitless. Emily was in supreme command. 'By the way, how *is* the fine arts world these days?'

Roscoe looked at her, taken totally unawares.

'The Grinlings still haven't got their painting back,' she went on conversationally, 'we know them quite well.'

'Look, Emily,' he attempted a confidential laugh, 'I admit the baby might be mine. On the other hand, from what I gathered of your premature private debut it might not.'

As an argument, that impressed Emily not one bit. 'You're looking awfully peaky behind all that hair,' she said. 'It must be pretty boring laying low like Brer Fox.'

Roscoe was actually feeling rather faint.

'You're in disgrace with your shady friends, aren't you?' Emily went on, 'because you can't even pull off a simple art robbery without messing it up.' She paused and regarded him pleasantly. 'You look as if you'd been hit on the head with a blunt instrument. And I bet you're broke again.'

'B-bit pushed...' Not remotely true, but it seemed a tactical admission to make.

'I've not told Mother yet,' Emily said. 'We needn't upset her with scandal. You shall simply ask for my hand. I'm sure she'll be pleased, really. She won't have to give me a season after all.' She studied his discomfiture with amusement and added: 'She's doing very well on the stock market, you know. Very well indeed.'

Roscoe swiftly re-arranged his viewpoint. He took her hand again with a rueful, affectionate grin. 'What's done's done. I've decided, sweetheart, to be the happiest chap in the world!'

'Splendid! We'll go to Mamma together.'

'No, Emily,' he sounded unexpectedly, thrillingly strong, 'I'm no shirker, I'll approach your mother myself. Say nothing.'

Emily almost wondered if she might have misjudged him.

When Amaryllis received two dozen roses, accompanied by a note from Roscoe requesting permission to call upon her in confidence, her curiosity took wing. The memory of that 'familiar back' at the Hampstead dance had returned to tease her more than once, in spite of newer, fresher conquests. She graciously invited him to take elevenses with her one morning whilst Emily was occupied at Adelaide Road. The thought of seeing him again, rascal that he was, sent quite a *frisson* right through her.

Seeing the engagement in the diary, Emily said she wanted to be there too. On being told it was none of her concern, she smiled enigmatically.

When Roscoe presented himself on the appointed day, the front door was opened, as always, by the boot-faced Dibbins. Had he realized he was bidding good morning to Florence's mother, he would have been suitably astounded. So would Florence.

From behind her tea-table, Amaryllis regarded Roscoe in his chair by the window. With his bright hair lit by the morning sun, his face still so very appealing, his eyes meeting hers with candid admiration, she felt her heartstrings tugging as they had four years ago.

'Well, my dear,' she said, 'to what do I owe this pleasure?'

'I – I need your help, Amaryllis,' he blurted, with all the boyish sincerity he could muster. 'To put it bluntly, I need to leave the country.'

She immediately stiffened, as he knew she would. 'You're not in trouble with the law, I trust?'

'Of course not!' he laughed. 'Only with your daughter. You see, dearest Amaryllis,' he plunged on recklessly, 'Emily has conceived—'

'What?!'

'— a passion for me. Of embarrassing proportions.'

This was certainly something of a surprise to Amaryllis. 'She's a schoolgirl! Not even out yet!'

Roscoe described how, after an accidental reunion in the street, he had treated Emily to an ice-cream soda for old times' sake. 'And that was the beginning,' he spread his hands wide, 'I've been – I hate to say this, Amaryllis – hounded ever since!' He went on to tell of letters, violent declarations and the like, 'She even discovered where my rooms are, in ... in ... off Bond Street,' he improvised rather wildly. 'She keeps on turning up. I – I felt that you, as her mother, should know. I count myself a family friend,' he finished, soberly meeting her gaze, which struck him as disconcertingly level.

To her credit, Amaryllis was not so easily rattled. She knew Roscoe of old. She began to wonder about his motives.

'I appreciate your concern, my dear,' she said coolly, 'but surely a man of the world such as you can deal with a childish crush?'

'I'm afraid it's more than that. She's threatening to kill herself unless I elope with her.'

'Dear me. What do you suggest?'

He became very earnest. 'I've given the matter careful thought. It seems to me that a clean break is indicated here. The young are resilient. She'll recover quickly enough if I'm simply not about.'

'How wise you are,' she murmured. 'It's all a question of equilibrium.' Quite unconvinced by his trumped up verbiage, she nevertheless felt a familiar tingle as she looked at him.

He pounced on it. 'I behold your exquisite features offset by the Rockingham china, dear Amaryllis, and my own equilibrium is in imminent danger of collapse. May I sit beside you?'

About twenty minutes later, he returned to his purpose in literary vein. He mentioned being much taken of late with Mr Rudyard Kipling. 'Do you know Rudyard Kipling?'

'He's a little old for me.'

'I'm referring to his poems.' One in particular, evidently, urging a young man to the other side of the world, where he was overdue because the Red Gods were calling to him, had fired Roscoe with profound enthusiasm for a new life in the Americas.

Amaryllis took his point. It would be in everyone's interests for Roscoe to disport himself elsewhere. She agreed to finance his departure. 'How we shall miss you, my dear,' she breathed, with warm but resolute finality.

Spring in his step and a cheque in his pocket, Roscoe went to keep tryst with Emily.

Under the impression that they were out to choose a ring, Emily was mystified to be ushered into the Army & Navy Stores Leather Goods department.

'Nobody who's anybody would be seen dead on board ship without decent luggage,' Roscoe explained loftily. 'The only valise I have does up with fuse wire.'

Emily instantly envisaged a honeymoon cruise of exotic delight. 'Oo, Roscoe! *Darling*! Oh, *how* I love surprises!'

'That's good,' he said absently, surveying the elegant displays of pigskin, calf and crocodile.

'Where are we going? And what about my ring?'

He looked at her, then. She had asked for this and she was going to get it. 'Not we. Me,' he corrected, very bright. 'I'm going away to make my fortune, Emily. When I come back … well, *if* I come back, we'll choose your ring.'

Being out-manoeuvred was not within Emily's experience. She stared at him blankly. The full implication took a while to penetrate. Then, she felt herself gripped by hot, rising panic. 'I'll – I'll tell Mamma!' she stammered, momentarily weak.

'Will you, Emily?' he raised a debonair eyebrow, 'And risk the scorn she'll pour upon her careless little girl? I don't doubt there are others you can trick more easily than me.'

Emily looked away. The panic dissolved into a far more practical and rather stimulating surge of cold, implacable, murderous fury. When she faced him again and said quietly, 'I'll kill you, Roscoe', she meant it.

The naked steel in her eyes reminded Roscoe that discretion is the better part of absolutely everything. He tipped his hat, murmured 'Toodle-oo, old girl', and was gone.

Emily stood rooted to the spot, gazing fixedly at nothing.

After what might have been twenty seconds or a century, a voice filtered into her frozen consciousness:

'If it's not little Emily Kilverston!'

She turned slowly, breathing deep to re-align her wits. She was looking into the beaming face of Sir Redvers Grinling, which was on a level with her own.

Emily liked Sir Redvers. He was prosperous, expansive and jolly. She often wondered how he came to have such a drip of a daughter and supposed it was due to his boring wife. His son had inherited all the family enterprise. She shook hands and even managed a smile.

He was carrying a small round woven basket with a fitted lid. She admired it and asked what it was for.

He was delighted to tell her. 'Imported specially for me. Lid's a perfect fit. Has to be, what?' He was bound for Regent's Park Zoo now, he said, to pick up a new addition to the Heatherley reptile collection. 'Indian swamp adder,' he glowed with pride. 'Queen of my crop, she'll be. Small, mark you. Delicate. Very, very regal.'

'Lethal?' Emily enquired, life-force re-kindling.

'One little nip from Her Majesty,' his voice dropped in respectful emphasis, 'you wouldn't stand a chance, m'dear. Not a chance!'

Emily was deeply interested. It put her in mind, she said, of one of the exploits of Sherlock Holmes, which she had recently much enjoyed.

'Ah, yes, *The Speckled Band*!' Sir Redvers happily approved her erudition. 'Yes, by Jove, that was a swamp adder, too! Introduced into the victim's bedroom down a bell rope, as I recall. Very neat. Splendid yarn.'

They left the department together and walked out to the street. The London Zoo, he told her, had been holding the snake for several weeks. 'Had to wait, y'see, for her royal equipage.' He patted his little basket. 'Now that she can be transported in fitting manner, I shall escort her home.'

His motor was waiting at the kerbside. 'Would you care for a ride?' he offered. 'My man can take you on after he drops me at the zoo. Better still, come with me, what? I've an appointment with your charming mother afterwards.'

Emily was surprised. Wasn't he out of the usual range?

'On account of this dance of Katie's comin' up,' he went on cosily, 'your charming mother has kindly agreed to teach me some Ragtime dancing. Must keep up with the times, what? You've been invited, what?'

Emily assured him she had, but declined the lift with regretful thanks, pleading a prior engagement. She had a great deal to think about.

After he had gone, she treated herself to tea and walnut cake at Fullers and then walked home. It was a long way, but the day was mild and she took it leisurely. By the time she reached Fitzjohn's Avenue, a plan of considerable artistry was forming in her mind.

Strains of 'The Black Bottom' filled the drawing room. Sir Redvers, ever sporting, thumped gamely round the floor with more enthusiasm than grace, his nostrils dilating to Amaryllis's Parma Violet. During one spasmodic hug, just as the gramophone was beginning to run down, the cameo brooch at her cleavage caught on his fob chain and they collapsed in a tangled heap on the sofa. The music ground to a halt.

'Could you, perhaps, do a little unpinning? My stupid brooch?' Amaryllis was appealingly mortified. 'Dear Sir Redvers, I'm so sorry...'

He applied himself to her bosom. ' "Redvers", m'dear, surely? After all, at this range...'

'Well...' a little, breathless laugh, 'proximity does tend towards informality, doesn't it? May I offer you a drink?'

'Indeed you may, dear lady. A whisky would be a great relief.' He was still mildly winded. 'Katie, she's set on this jungle music. Have to keep up with the young, what?'

Knowing Kate, Amaryllis could only salute such stubborn wishfulness. He put her in mind of a Jack Russell with its jaws locked in the wrong quarry. She handed him his glass with compassion.

'Are you joining me, m'dear?' he asked rather wistfully.

'I've poured myself a glass of sherry, yes.'

'Then don't be a stranger. Come and drink it beside me, here on the sofa.'

She went to fetch it. 'I believe that would be very relaxing, Redvers.' She sat down.

'Won't you call me "Red", m'dear Amaryllis?'

Her hand brushed his as if by accident. 'My goodness, that does sound ... vigorous. Your very good health.'

'Oh, it is,' he beamed at her, '*very* good. M'health. Now I've got m' breath back from all that jumpin' about. Except, lookin' at you takes it away again. M'breath.'

'How gallant you are. Red.'

'And you, Amaryllis, you're a damn fine-looking woman, by Jove.' His voice grew husky. 'Damn fine...'

The dancing lesson was progressing very agreeably.

Emily stood in the hall, listening to their voices through the closed doors of the drawing room. About time, too, she thought. He's much better for her than all those pimply sprigs. I wonder what she'll say when I tell her ... whatever I tell her? Anyway, she's only got herself to thank. If she hadn't been so selfish and vain it might never have happened.

She lifted the lid of the basket on the table. The Indian Queen was curled in a deep dream of peace. After replacing the lid, Emily went slowly upstairs.

When Sir Redvers had gone she re-appeared, thumbing through the diary. 'So it was this morning that Roscoe called on you, was it?' she remarked casually.

'Yes, that's right.' Her mother watched her intently.

'Hm. As a matter of fact, I was quite surprised when he suddenly wrote to you. He disappeared ages ago. Actually, I thought he was dead.'

Amaryllis stifled a sigh of vast relief. 'I believe he lives in Camden Town, which is practically the same thing,' she said. 'It's aged him dreadfully.'

The 'Bond Street rooms' had been Roscoe's undoing.

'I expect he'll come to a sticky end one of these days,' Emily commented. 'He deserves to, in my opinion.'

'He's emigrating to America soon,' her mother said casually.

'Oh, really? When?'

Amaryllis told her. It was the day after Kate's dance.

Chapter Five

Mr Jennings was not a Well Man. His mother's all-purpose declaration, 'I am not a Well Woman', had so permeated his early life, he rather grew up with the idea that it was an enviable condition. Ever since she died, during his first year as errand boy at the Army & Navy Stores, he had upheld family tradition as a superior type of person who keeps himself to himself, both in the Battersea Guest House where he lived and in his career.

Lately promoted to junior assistant in Leather Goods, His manner was that of someone born aged forty-nine, with a cold. In fact, he was nineteen.

Nobody knew his name was Wilfrid. Nobody ever asked.

One day early in April, he was called over by Mr Reece the Floorwalker to assist a customer interested in a thirty-piece set of matched pigskin luggage. Mr Jennings remembered the young gentleman from yesterday. Mr Jennings remembered thinking he looked a proper blade, probably a bit of a bounder. He geared himself to open cases, demonstrate locking devices, expound on the many and various design features of each item, only to be told that the customer had already made up his mind.

It was a cash transaction too, which bore out Mr Jennings's initial judgement. Respected customers at the Army & Navy Stores had accounts. When arrangements turned out to include delivery to an address in Camden Town, Mr Jennings's opinions hardened. Respected customers at the Army & Navy Stores lived in the colonies or in the country, with an acceptable London address. Mr Jennings permitted himself a small, silent, derogatory sigh. Still, all in the day's work, as they say…

Roscoe Summerfield left the shop mightily pleased with his purchases. The sun was shining and he fancied a stroll along the Embankment, but mindful of Stanley's warnings about keeping out of sight, he took a cab home instead. It would be boneheaded to take risks now, with everything going so swimmingly. He did have the odd twinge about Emily. Quite sharp at times, actually. But needs must, and so forth...

Emily herself had, in fact, just completed a piece of detection on her own account which she reckoned worthy of Sherlock Holmes himself. The previous day, seeing Roscoe's eye light upon the pigskin display, she had felt pretty certain he would return for it as soon as possible. She intended to watch the place until he did. Seated in a teashop opposite the main entrance the very next morning, it was pleasing to have her vigil rewarded almost before it had begun. When Roscoe's cab moved off, she went into action.

Mr Jennings was just beginning to dismantle the edifice when a soft voice behind him said, 'Excuse me...'

Well, fancy! It was the young lady who'd come in with the bounder yesterday, then stayed on and left with Sir Redvers Grinling. Sir Redvers being a very respected customer, Mr Jennings switched immediately to full attention. 'Why, certainly, madam. In what way may I be of assistance?'

'I believe my fiancé was here,' she said, with a trace of coyness. 'Choosing our valises for the ... the honeymoon.'

'The gentleman just left, madam,' Mr Jennings confirmed. 'The pigskin, was it?'

Emily nodded. She and Mr Jennings both knew the pigskin verged on the ostentatious. 'He thinks that as I like bright things, bless him...' she giggled indulgently. 'Now, I want you, if you will, to keep a secret for me.'

With shining eyes, she divulged her entrancing little scheme. She wished to present her fiancé with an assortment of cravats. 'So, I wonder if I could take the cravat case with me now,' she said, 'and give it to him separately, as a surprise?'

Mr Jennings felt a dilemma coming on. It was most irregular. He sneezed, as discreetly as possible.

Emily was equal to that. 'And I do believe I'll take a matching wallet as well,' she said, 'as an extra.'

Mr Jennings had the makings of an excellent salesman despite his constipated demeanour. He agreed to connive with his charming customer, thereby achieving another cash transaction.

Upstairs in Gentlemens' Haberdashery, Emily chose six very handsome cravats.

Amid potted equatorial vegetation, the Indian Queen lay torpid in the simulated Indian warmth of her enclosure in the reptile house at Heatherley. She was comfortable and regularly fed; staying alive required no effort whatever; there was no reason to move about.

Kate, watching her through the glass, envied her insouciance and sighed aloud: 'If only I were you.'

Fruitless yearning was rudely interrupted by a pang of acute hunger. Kate realized she was in urgent need of cold bread-and-butter pudding. There was sure to be some in the servants' hall. Yes, cold bread-and-butter pudding with tomato chutney.

Striding hungrily down the kitchen garden path, she ran into her mother. Inside the castle, preparations for the dance were at zenith level. In Lady Priscilla's experience, the staff were well able to cope without her and she was happy to do them the courtesy of keeping out of the way. Apparelled as she preferred to be, in an antiquated fairisle jersey and corduroys from her brother's youth, she was carrying an empty swill bucket.

'Pigs,' she said, by way of greeting.

'How's Tulip?' Kate enquired.

'Not outstandingly maternal,' her mother replied. 'She's squashed two now. We may have to take them away. If you're going back to the house, here's the bucket.'

'I got hungry. I'm on my way to find something to eat.'

'It's chaos in there.'

'It doesn't matter. I'll help myself. As long as there's cold bread-and-butter pudding.'

Her mother ran a critical eye over her. 'You're starting to show.'

Unlike her glamorous London friend, Kate Grinling had no illusions whatever about the general ins and outs of procreation, having grown up in its midst on the Heatherley estate. All too aware of her condition for two months now, she was miserably uncertain what to do about it. Not being a complete fool, her expectations of seeing Etienne again were becoming rapidly eclipsed by those of his lasting memento. She had told no one, not even Emily. She had put off approaching her mother, for fear of being the cause of some kind of health crisis. Priscilla's self-protective myth had become effective enough, over the years, to shield her from practically any demands on her attention.

In the face of this almost casual observation, Kate stood dumbfounded, not knowing whether to be relieved or violently sick. She eyed the swill bucket.

'Certainly not,' her mother held it firmly out of reach, 'into the long grass, if you must, but I think bread-and-butter pudding's probably the answer. I'll come with you.'

They walked slowly past the rows of early spring vegetables. 'I suppose it was the Ruritanian rotter,' Priscilla remarked.

Kate bit back tears. 'Don't call him that! Even if he is!'

'Too mild, I agree. I wonder what he did with the painting?'

'I never even liked *Old Woman with Stocking*,' Kate muttered, still obscurely defensive.

'We'll have to make a plan,' Priscilla went on. 'Austria, perhaps, or some unfashionable corner of France. At least it'll save a good deal of nonsensical capering this summer.'

Greatly confused, Kate said, 'You mean you're not going to have the vapours and throw me out?'

Priscilla snorted. 'I don't suppose your father will be frightfully thrilled. He has a tiresome streak of middle-class morality. Still, cheer up. In our family, the bastards often turn out best. Any idea who this counter-jumper is?'

'A – a French nobleman?' Kate offered. It sounded rather lame even as she said it.

'I only ask in case I come across him. And find I have the luxury of killing him.' Priscilla spoke with understated relish.

Kate began to see her mother in quite a new light. And Emily would be here tomorrow. She could tell Emily all about it. She was one up on Emily now. Perhaps things weren't so bad after all.

At the selfsame moment, Emily was in the potting shed of the long narrow garden at Fitzjohn's Avenue, watching Teddy Grinling prepare to bore holes in a pigskin cravat case.

Teddy was down from Harrow for Easter. He and his father would be driving to Heatherley tomorrow for the dance on Tuesday, taking Emily with them, which she thought a most excellent arrangement. She was to stay two nights with Kate.

Better still, to her pleasant surprise, her mother was content to remain in London. Emily had no idea the main reason was to avoid an encounter with Lady Priscilla Grinling.

Teddy fiddled with the cravat case, reluctant to attack such a handsome object. 'It's brand new, isn't it?' he protested. 'Who wants to make holes in a brand new piece of luggage?'

Emily explained patiently that far from being new, it had belonged to her father. 'He just never used it. He's been dead ten years, so he doesn't need it. And I've promised it to the little brother of a friend of mine who wants to take his hamster to the seaside.'

Teddy was suitably impressed. Emily really was a pretty wonderful girl. He aimed the gimlet at the lid.

'No, no!' she caught his wrist. 'There's no need to deface it! Put them round the side, near the base where they won't show. And, Teddy…'

He looked up, catching the new note in her voice.

'Yes, Emily?'

'When you've finished, you can look at my garters again.'

He applied himself rigorously to the task in hand. Much to his delight, he found that his reward far exceeded mere garters.

To Emily this was a tactic of simple prudence. It struck her that having Teddy in place might not come amiss.

The drive down from London on Monday afternoon in Sir Redvers' Hispano Suiza was sheer delight. Kate's new ball dress, which they brought with them, diverted attention from Emily's own suitcase, unusually large for two nights.

After the full paraphernalia of formal afternoon tea, Emily was taken round the zoo. She looked with appreciation at the Indian Queen and the other snakes. Kate won her unqualified admiration by demonstrating a practised technique in the handling of them.

When at last the girls were alone in Kate's room, Emily felt it was time her monstrous scheme for the destruction of Roscoe Summerfield entered its final phase. Sitting on the bed, watching Kate brush her hair, she commented:

'Welcome to the boat.'

'What boat?'

'The one we're both in. And, indeed, the one Roscoe Summerfield and Etienne du Couteau will be in, next Wednesday.'

Kate swallowed. 'I don't know what you're talking about.'

'You are pregnant, aren't you?'

Kate nodded miserably. 'Two months. How did you know?'

'It would be quite difficult not to. So am I.'

'What?' Kate was truly shocked. 'But – but you're still supposed to be in the schoolroom!'

'Only because my damn mother is desperately trying to pretend I'm seven. Anyway, I floundered into the same corner as you.' Emily embarked on an edited version of events leading to her own predicament. 'I have every reason to believe,' she concluded. 'That the scoundrel who deflowered me also deflowered you.'

'You and Etienne?' Kate looked as if she might pass out.

'No! It's not like that. Just listen.' Emily described enough of Roscoe's attributes and general versatility to convince poor Kate that they had both been victims of an unscrupulous confidence trickster. 'I am going to kill him,' Emily finished up with impressively quiet resolve. 'He fully deserves it.'

'I do believe my mother would agree with you,' Kate said slowly, wading through this forest of new perceptions. 'Only yesterday, she used almost those words. She meant it, too.'

Emily had always steered fairly clear of Lady Priscilla. Now, she digested the unexpected titbit with approval. 'That's very good to know,' she said, 'but we can save her the bother.'

'We?'

'Well, I need your help.'

'I believe this is all too much for me,' Kate quavered.

'Buck up, Katie. Think how awkward I could make things for you. I mean, how are you going to convince anyone you didn't help him with switching those pictures?'

Kate's mouth dropped open. 'Y-you wouldn't, Emily. You wouldn't!'

'No, I don't expect I would. But you're in up to your neck. Anyway, this is what I want you to do…'

*

The gaming club in Camden Town was closed, the flat upstairs empty, the rent outstanding. In Stanley Jellybean's philosophy that was the landlord's worry, not his. The consortium of Jellybean, de la Haye and Summerfield had stolen away like Arabs without lingering to fold their tents. Stanley believed in travelling light.

For the past fortnight, Stanley and Florence had been occupying modest rooms in Southampton, virtuously paid for in advance to cover the period up to sailing date. They were known there as Mr and Mrs Morgan; identities for the voyage picked at random by Stanley from a race-card. When the landlady enquired with hushed excitement if he was related to the owner of the great liner, he could have kicked himself at the unwanted attention but decided not to disabuse her. Instead, he drew her into a mild conspiracy of silence regarding confidential business reasons for the extremely low profile he had to keep.

Roscoe, on the other hand, was installed at one of the classier hotels under his own name, since it had survived unsullied thus far. He awaited embarkation in manner befitting his first-class accommodation on board, which entailed a great deal of impeccably matched luggage that filled his room to the point of claustrophobia. He escaped its glossy vigilance on his final evening and set off with coat collar well up, trilby well down, three bottles of champagne under each arm, for a few hours' slumming with Stanley and Flo.

Despite his recent enforced retirement from commerce, Roscoe Summerfield could be described as very comfortably placed. Over the last three years and more, his achievements in respect of personal gain had been considerable. The judicious bouts of absence from the social scene had served not only to increase his repertoire of personae through direct observational study, but also lined his pocket by means of card games on the *Train Bleu*, escort duties around the promenades of the Riviera, the spas of Baden Baden, the canals of Venice. All of which might have earned Emily Kilverston's unstinted esteem had she known. One commodity Roscoe could not afford, however, was regret. Emily must now belong to the past. The future resounded with the call of the Red Gods much too loudly to be ignored.

The modest lodgings of Mr and Mrs Morgan resounded that last evening, too. It was a merry gathering. Stanley's connections had come up with a nicely comprehensive casing of the entire floating prospect which, he was confident, would yield a very handsome dower to establish them in the Land of the Free.

'I'll be masterminding you, don't forget,' he pontificated. 'I'll be working my own patch very nice, an' all. So I don't expect no slacking from you, Florence my lovely, queening it in second-class, see? You got a free hand, understand me?'

Florence understood him. Apprehensions long overcome, she was Diana, sniffing the hunt.

'Where will you be then, Stanley?' Roscoe asked.

Stanley winked and tapped the side of his nose. 'Never you mind. Just you remember I've got me seaman's ticket!'

Stanley had often regaled them with his turbulent youth in the China Seas. They were never sure whether to believe him.

He thumped Roscoe on the back. 'The form you was showing in them playgrounds o' Europe, my son, you'll bloody clean out this sea-girt mausoleum. I mean Coliseum.'

Florence said what the hell did it matter which he meant, she was that impressed with his classical knowledge.

They cracked another bottle.

Kate Grinling's dance was a brilliant success for everyone except Kate Grinling, who felt ghastly. She took it amiss that pregnancy seemed to inconvenience Emily hardly at all. On top of everything else, the terrible thing she had undertaken to do weighed dreadfully on her mind. But as Emily had pointed out, she had little alternative.

Emily enjoyed herself immensely, this time a vision in aquamarine. She was proud, too, that Kate looked much less of a sore thumb than at Christmas. Emily had taken her in hand properly over the last two weeks, overseeing her choice of material and accompanying her to fittings.

Although Kate had said nothing of her condition at the time, Emily – now an authority on the subject – had strongly suspected it. Kate's long, willowy form was encased in a cleverly draped confection of grey silk shot with pink, which warmed her pale complexion and gave her elegance. Lady Priscilla, having doubted the wisdom of allowing the girls to save her a trip to London, was pleasantly surprised at the result.

About three o'clock on the morning of Wednesday, April 10th,

Emily and Kate checked on the comfort of the Indian Queen, now coiled on a pile of silk cravats in a pigskin case commensurate with her station, equipped with some dead flies and a cleverly wedged bottle which would drip sufficient water into a shallow dish for four to five days.

The case was then securely closed and gently slid under Emily's bed. Kate had completed her mission in the reptile house without a hitch. Emily said she had the makings of a first-class cat burglar. Kate tried to ignore the praise, but the exercise had, in fact, done wonders for her metabolism.

Later on, in a silence punctuated by Kate's rhythmic breathing, Emily was attacked for the first time during this escapade by tidal panic at the enormity of what she was doing. It had all been rather a lark so far, in spite of the white-hot rage which had initiated it. Now, slowly and steadily, a sticky sort of cold crept over the surface of her skin and enveloped her from the roots of her hair to the soles of her feet. Her mouth dried up. Her throat tightened. She began to shiver uncontrollably.

Did she really want to kill Roscoe? Something in the nature of a silent howl, either from a long way off or deep inside her own mind cried, '*No-o-o…!*' She kicked and struggled in the sheets like someone drowning; someone intent on suicide having second thoughts. '*Do I want to destroy myself?*'

For an endless moment the question hung almost tangibly, like a dark prism dangling in a storm-cloud, before fading itself away. The shivering eased, inch by inch; arms and legs relaxed. Emily lay on her back, eyes wide open, staring up at an oblong patch of moonlight on the ceiling, vaguely surprised to find herself safe in bed.

Like after a nightmare, she thought. That's it. It was a nightmare. A dream. I was asleep. I'm awake now, though. And I'm faced with a choice of carrying this thing through or running away. Does Roscoe sail off scot-free after treating me like that? And then Kate, too?

How dare he even look at Kate after me!

Do we face the rest of our lives as ruined creatures, coping unavenged with the results of Roscoe Summerfield's selfish, cruel philandering?

Images of the preacher at Dibbins' Chalk Farm chapel came slamming across the moonlit screen overhead. Pale eyes blazing with sadistic fervour, whipcord veins blue on quivering neck, the Reverend Mr Jellybean's rantings about steadfastness of purpose in the cause of vengeance echoed down from far-off Sunday afternoons, with Poor Awful trying to dispel the terror by saying it was for Emily's own good.

Well, steadfastness of purpose had got her to this point, hadn't it? And vengeance was about to strike on behalf of all other hapless women who would have suffered in a future that Roscoe Summerfield no longer deserved.

Also organized was a trip for the following day. At Emily's request, both girls were to be driven down to Southampton to watch the great liner, whose construction had been closely followed in the newspapers for months, leave on her maiden voyage to America. It was too late to back out.

Too late to back *right* out…

In response to a half-formed glimmer, Emily rolled softly to the floor. Her hands groped beneath the bed. There was a way, her sleep-addled brain insisted, of carrying the plan to a neat conclusion without an irreversible climax of cold-blooded murder. It was risky and disagreeable, but it must be taken if she were ever again to enjoy a night's untroubled slumber.

She made contact with the cravat case. Very carefully, she drew it out and stood up. Tucking it under one arm, she crept to the window sill where Kate had left the gauntlets for handling the snakes. Managing to wedge them under the other arm and leave both hands free, she eased open the door and slipped through.

Barefoot down the carpeted stairs, too light and swift to invite a creak, she was across the hall, through the baize swing-door into the service passage and out the side entrance in seconds. The early April pre-dawn air was very cold, but Emily scarcely noticed. Like a shadow she sped along the straight paths of the kitchen garden to the reptile house.

The light inside was dim but constant, like the temperature. Emily stopped briefly to get her bearings. The Indian Queen's enclosure was tenanted now by one of the half-dozen snakes from the one next to it which, according to Kate, were all harmless.

Emily studied it through the glass. It looked the same to her as any other snake of that size. The same as the Indian Queen, in fact. She wondered anyone could tell the difference. Unless, of course, they got bitten.

Honestly, how could a person actually *like* snakes and not mind *touching* them? With a nasty jolt, Emily realized she was going to have to overcome an unsuspected natural aversion and get on with it.

Setting down the case, she put on the gauntlets and pressed open the catch, holding the lid shut with her right hand. Then she pushed the sliding trap in the glass open a few inches with her left, at the same time flicking up the cravat-case lid and grasping the contents with her eyes involuntarily screwed tight shut. Blindly, she thrust the wriggling object through the opening and rammed the trap shut again.

Gorged on a picnic intended to last four days, the Indian Queen was extremely sleepy, otherwise she would doubtless have made a bee-line for her uninvited room-mate. As it was, she slithered comatosely away about six inches and subsided, basking in the glow of the overhead heating. The other snake, alarmed at the disturbance, shot forward from behind a frond.

When Emily looked again, she saw two small snakes about a foot apart. To her untutored eye, they were indistinguishable.

There was no time to waste. She forced herself to ease a gauntleted hand through the trap again and grab the nearest. It must be the harmless one. It had got to be the harmless one, after all her trouble! She pushed it into the case, secured the lid and fled.

With sweat prickling her spine and her heart pounding in her ears, she stumbled recklessly away across the vegetable sets, too scared and desperate to go round by any path.

Amongst rows of vigorous bean-shoots, she stopped dead.

She hadn't slid the trap shut! Whichever snake was in the enclosure now could escape and be a lethal danger at large! And it was the Indian Queen, of course it was, because she, Emily, had done the switch correctly, hadn't she? Oh, corks!

It couldn't be helped. She wasn't going in there again. Her short-cut home became a wild bravado of bouncing leaps over the sturdy new lines of growth.

Safely back upstairs, she returned the cravat case to its hiding place and crawled into bed. Kate slept on, oblivious of the entire operation.

At breakfast next morning, not only did Teddy announce his intention of coming to Southampton as well; he also insisted on showing Emily round the stables before they all set off. There was no way of raising objections to either notion without attracting undue attention. Inspection of the stables proved interminable. Teddy was bosom chums with all the grooms and all the lads and apparently had a great deal to discuss with each of them in turn.

When at last Emily got back to the house, it was almost time to leave. She hared upstairs to find that the maids had been in to do the room and the cravat case was now on the window sill. Frantically, she grabbed the gauntlets. She would force herself to look inside. By morning light, she would surely be able to verify that the snake now there was the harmless one.

Before she had a chance, Teddy appeared at the open doorway to tell her the motor was waiting.

Emily had no choice but slip the unopened cravat case into its brown paper carrier and hope for the best.

Chapter Six

Oh, the utter, soaring wonder of this stateroom! And all for me!

Roscoe basked within the softly tapestried walls – or were they bulkheads? They looked like flock-papered walls to Roscoe. What with the brass bedstead, the marble washstand, the sofa, armchairs – even a fan in the ceiling – it seemed barely credible that this Ultimatum from Xanadu was about to travel all the way to New York. Life certainly held promise.

Outside, the bunting fluttered gently, adding to the atmosphere of festive notability. It would be fitting, he thought, to take a short stroll and look his last on shores which he was departing without regret. Well, almost without regret. Emily Kilverston's form would keep clouding his mind's eye.

Resolutely, he turned to the open door. Emily Kilverston was standing there. He rubbed his face in disbelief.

She enjoyed his shock to the full. 'I decided to wish you well, after all,' she said. 'I mean, this is quite a step you're taking. No hard feelings?'

Roscoe all but felt like the heel he was. He wondered how the devil she'd found out but didn't have the nerve to ask. 'R-really?' he stammered.

'Really.' She gave him an open, comradely smile. 'I must say, I've never seen so much exclusive looking luggage. However many pieces are there?'

Roscoe's scruples diffused in pride of ownership. 'Thirty altogether,' he said. 'The four biggest are in the hold. I've twenty-five in here with me.'

'That only makes twenty-nine,' Emily observed.

'Yes, well, they delivered the set without the cravat case,' he explained, 'But I … er … I didn't want to kick up a fuss, dontcherknow.' He had, in fact, wanted to kick up a hell of a fuss but Stanley had put his foot down.

'So, you've got twenty-five boxes in this room?'

'That's right.'

She produced a package from behind her back and removed its brown paper wrapping. 'Box Twenty-six,' she said.

Roscoe stared at it. 'Emily! How did you … I mean, how did you…'

'I guessed!' She was delighted at his astonishment. 'There are some jolly nice cravats in it, too. However, I do have one condition to impose.'

Roscoe was looking sheepish, to put it mildly. 'Anything,' he responded. 'Anything, Emily.'

'I think you'd better ring for your cabin steward,' she announced mysteriously.

A discreetly uniformed minion with a jaunty air appeared in impressively swift answer to the summons. 'Something we require, sir?' It was Stanley Jellybean.

His face struck Emily oddly as being vaguely familiar, but she was quite unable to place him. 'One moment, if you'd be so kind,' she smiled, ushering him through the door and out of earshot. 'This little present for my brother,' she passed him the cravat case, 'it's a surprise, you understand? I want you to keep it until you're well under way. After perhaps four days, he'll be needing some fresh neckwear. That's when you produce it, with my farewell gift inside. Thank you so much. Now, what did you say your name was?' She squeezed his hand round two crisp fivers. He was her slave.

When she returned to the stateroom, she took a tiny key from her reticule and handed it to Roscoe. 'Morgan – that's his name, by the way – Morgan will bring the box when the moment is right and not before,' she said. 'I know you can't be trusted an inch, so I've arranged a little commemoration. *Well and truly out at sea; think of ties and think of me*! I made that up. Don't you think it's neat?'

For once in his life, Roscoe could find nothing to say.

A blast came from the hooter. An amplified voice could be heard asking relatives and well-wishers kindly to disembark now. A ragged cheer went up from spectators on the dockside.

'*Bon voyage*, then, Roscoe.' Emily held out her hand.

As he took it, his heart disconcerted him by lurching violently. If only things could have been otherwise.

Emily caught her breath. For a moment, she seemed on the verge of some kind of significant utterance. Roscoe waited, wondering what it would be; wondering whether or not he wanted to hear.

Eventually, she merely said, 'Well, toodle-oo.'

'Toodle-oo, old bean.'

Walking down the gangway, Emily glowed with the satisfaction of a plan carried out flawlessly. She had quite convinced herself by now that her intrepid nocturnal swoop had resulted in retribution apt but not drastic. Even a harmless snake would probably be in a pretty filthy temper when the moment came. Roscoe would get the fright of his life. Less than he deserved, of course. Serve him right if it *had* been the Indian Queen!

Kate was not at all happy. She had carried out Emily's instructions to the letter, including the one about not asking questions. She knew this was for her own protection. A very small part of her, never before suspected, wanted to be there on board, passing sentence on the despicable villain without whom the world would be a better place. Mostly, though, she fought back waves of nausea at the wickedness of the crime she was helping to commit. She had no idea where Emily was. They had become separated in the crowd, either by accident or by Emily's design.

'Where d'you think she's got to?' Teddy jumped in an effort to see over heads. 'You don't suppose she's been abducted or something, do you?'

'No, I don't,' Kate replied crossly, 'and I wish you'd shut up!'

Teddy was an added complication. The idea approved by Lady Priscilla was an 'educational expedition' for the girls to watch the historic departure of the new, much-vaunted maritime giant. The chauffeur had driven them down and would bring Kate home. But arrangements had been made, on the telephone to Amaryllis, for Emily's return to London by rail from Southampton. All perfectly splendid until Teddy elected to muscle in with a ripping wheeze for escorting Emily back to town on the train.

Kate was even uncertain as to whether they had actually brought the cravat case with them at all. The brown paper package Emily carried could have been anything. There had been no chance to find out, with Teddy in the motor car.

People were leaving the ship now. Suddenly, Emily was there again. Kate nearly fainted with relief. 'Where have you been?'

'Where I said I'd be,' Emily replied briskly. 'Teddy, why don't you go and find us some ices? It's hot in this crowd and there's a man selling them over there.'

Obediently, Teddy took off.

'Well?' asked Kate.

'Well,' said Emily, 'I've sent Roscoe Summerfield and Etienne du Couteau on their wicked ways with a most original present.'

Kate gasped. 'So it *was* the cravat case you had with you!' She went even paler than usual. 'Oh, Emily, this is a terrible, terrible thing we've done!'

'Six nice cravats? I think it's pretty generous.'

'Six cravats *and*...'

'And what?'

'W-what about the Indian Queen?'

Emily took a deep breath before lightly imparting what she could only hope was the truth: 'In her enclosure at Heatherley, I imagine. Where I put her while you were asleep.'

This took a little time for Kate to grasp. 'You mean ... you put her back?' She very nearly keeled over with relief.

Emily caught her arm and steadied her. 'You don't honestly think I'd involve you in something like that, do you, Katie?'

'I – I did everything you said,' Kate mumbled, having more or less lost her bearings.

'Yes, and look how you enjoyed it! The excitement did you a world of good!' Emily laughed reassuringly, 'It was a game, Katie. To take your mind off your tummy. Like a treasure hunt, or a paper chase. And we won!'

'We're still pregnant.'

'We still won. Believe me.' Her airy confidence was not quite as genuine as she could have wished.

'What happens now?'

'I suppose we apply ourselves to the more practical aspects of our tiresome situations. And life, as they say, will go on.' For Emily, one way or another, the mission was completed.

Teddy came back with ice-cream cornets.

Hooters and streamers and music. The three of them were caught up in the thick of carnival, that April noon, as the *S.S. Titanic* pulled majestically away from the quayside.

On the train to Waterloo, Teddy asked Emily to marry him.

He was a thoroughly likeable little chap. 'Teddy, old thing, you're sixteen,' she pointed out reasonably.

'Seventeen!' he corrected with vigour. 'Birthday last term.'

'People don't usually get married while they're still at school, all the same.'

'What I really mean is, will you wait for me, Emily?' he persisted. 'I shall be down for good in July. I'm too dim for university, so it'll probably be the Army. That'll do, won't it?'

'It'll do splendidly,' she was truly touched. 'But I do think we ought to wait and see how things turn out, don't you?'

'I know how things'll turn out. I'll be dotty about you for the rest of my life.'

'Now listen, Teddy,' Emily spoke with the assumed wisdom of millennia, 'your life hasn't begun yet. You have to give it a chance. Come to that, so do I.'

With tenacity worthy of his father, he played a valuable card. 'I'm going to be an earl,' he said. It was true. His Uncle Hereward, Priscilla's younger brother, was not of an inclination liable to produce heirs. 'You'd like that, wouldn't you?'

Emily reflected that her mother would certainly like it very much indeed. But despite her present inconvenience, she was not at all sure she herself wanted to be swept into that sole objective of her peers, an early marriage, however brilliant it might be. The uncharted future beckoned. She was disposed to explore it on her own terms. The prospect of taking a child along with her had in no way dented her outlook so far. Still, it was nice to listen to Teddy's aspirations. She wondered how long they would last. He might be a great asset one day. 'Let's just wait and see, shall we, old chap?' she said.

When Kate got back to Heatherley Castle, she hurried off immediately to the reptile house.

Oh, what an imagination Emily has! she marvelled to herself as she went, what an exceedingly clever diversion! Really quite frightening at times, too. Looking back, that only added to its attractions.

She was a touch anxious now, though, that the Indian Queen might have eaten the poor little snake she herself had popped in on impulse as a cover.

She could only stand and stare, foolishly, at the open trap in the glass. On closer inspection, the enclosure proved to be quite definitely, absolutely, empty.

Amaryllis Kilverston was beside herself. Dibbins had quite clearly been a total waste of time for nearly fifteen years. Not only was Emily devoid of the moral rectitude Dibbins was supposed to have instilled, she was also – or appeared to have been – woefully ill-informed.

Now, Emily had let the side down too appallingly. Blind rage, having already encompassed the wretched Dibbins, was still erupting over Emily, with little sign of abatement.

'The brazenness of it!' she spluttered. 'The bare-faced deception! To say nothing of the carelessness!'

Having been reasonably truthful concerning what Amaryllis was pleased to call her downfall, Emily felt justified in giving as good as she got. 'It's your own fault!'

Amaryllis stared, momentarily speechless.

'You left me to be brought up by Poor Awful, who couldn't even look after herself, let alone anybody else, because you couldn't be bothered, then you behave as if I'm still in rompers when I should be in society, and you turn a blind eye to whatever I may be getting up to from my sheer natural frustration! You're a terrible, terrible mother, Mother! And I've learnt what not to do with my own progeny when it arrives!' As she spoke, Emily realized for the first time – with a bit of a shock – that somebody *was* going to arrive. Somebody who would look to her and no one else. It needed thought. Later.

Amaryllis returned to the attack. 'On top of everything, you wait until four days – *four days* – after that foreign scoundrel has left the country before breathing a word about your disgusting condition! Why?'

Somehow unable to admit to her lover's true identity, Emily had presented him as Kate's French Lothario of criminal intent. She thought quickly, 'To make sure you wouldn't contact the ship by radio-telephone and have him hauled back here!' she retorted.

'Even though you're ruined?'

'I certainly should be if you had!' Emily replied with conviction. 'I wouldn't marry him if he were the last man on earth! So what do you propose? Apart from becoming a grandmother, that is?'

Amaryllis was in no state for clear thought. 'It can't be born here,' she fretted, 'and the London season just about to start, it's too bad of you, it really is.'

'What season?' Emily enquired sweetly. 'I don't come out till next year, thanks to your vanity.'

'Oh, be quiet!' Amaryllis snapped.

Kate was sobbing weakly.

Her father, grey in the face for many reasons of which she was yet one more, tried not to frighten her with too much wrath. 'Stop snivellin' gel,' he blustered. 'What possessed you? Well brought-up filly like you?'

'Etienne du Couteau, Daddy,' Kate snuffled. 'He possessed me very thoroughly indeed, I'm afraid.'

'I'll horsewhip the bounder. Where is he?'

'He left the country. Four days ago.'

Sir Redvers would remember this year as the worst of his life. Priceless work of art stolen, police still with no lead, useless blighters; lethal swamp adder at large in Heatherley Park, '... and to top it all, m'daughter put in the puddin' club by some Frog!'

'Etienne du Couteau is not just "some Frog", Daddy,' Kate pulled together shreds of distinction. 'I have reason to believe he may be an international criminal.'

If Emily's plan had been real, Etienne would be dead by now.

'Our tails, Mr Summerfield, sir. In anticipation of this evening's assorted jollity. Sponged, pressed and ready.'

'Come off it, Stanley!'

'Begging your pardon, sir, I take my calling very serious.'

There was no doubt that Stanley Jellybean set a standard for cabin stewards; his praises rang the length and breadth of three decks and his duties led to his being unusually well-informed as to the potential of any passenger worth a light, which was no less than his intention.

For four nights, Roscoe had been in clover; charming and being charmed. Although not officially acquainted with Flo, he had noted her budding attachment to a distinguished white-haired American who seemed encumbered by a bony female of indeterminate age with buck teeth, whose eye Roscoe had sensed upon him more than once and taken steps to avoid.

Stanley arranged the evening suit with polished expertise. 'Going to pull our finger out soon, are we, sir?'

'What's that supposed to mean?'

Relentlessly in character, Stanley expounded on Florence's sterling spade work. 'Got going very nice with the father, sir, Florence has. Wasted no time, unlike some I could name. Left you a clear field, sir.'

'You mean that – that *horse* is the old boy's *daughter*?'

'Sitting duck for you, sir. Fitton's Fitness Breakfast Bars. Cleaned up solid on the capacities of the toasted oat, sir.'

Roscoe's ears pricked. 'Fitton? The old boy is Randolph Fitton?'

'The very same, sir.' Stanley's unctuousness knew no bounds. 'And there's his nice daughter up for grabs I don't doubt, sir, for them as knows which side their oats are toasted, sir.'

Roscoe groaned. 'I was enjoying myself.'

'We are not put here to enjoy ourselves, sir.'

Roscoe wanted to hit him. 'I see you've brought the cravat case,' he remarked, changing the subject.

'We shall be needing fresh neckwear come the morrow, sir, just like the young lady said. The young lady who referred to you as her brother, sir.'

'The young lady is an accomplished liar, Stanley. I've no doubt, though, she'd approve the way you've heeded her orders.'

'She was a very generous young lady, sir. It wouldn't be proper, else.'

Roscoe pulled out his key-ring. 'Right, let's have a dekko, what?'

'By all means, sir.'

Roscoe unlocked the cravat case. Stanley lifted the lid.

A small, lithe shape shot forth with the speed of fork lightning, slithered over Stanley's wrist, down the counterpane and under the bed before either of them had time to move.

'What the blazes was that?' Roscoe whispered.

Colour drained from Stanley's face. He clutched his wrist. 'It bit me,

Roscoe! Bit me it did! I wouldn't swear, but I think it's a swamp adder, I seen 'em in India. Get a doctor!'

Unversed in snake lore, Roscoe scrabbled about frantically on all fours, muttering, 'Little devil! You're going to pay for this!' in respect of both Emily and her exceedingly unfunny jape. Behind him, Stanley was groaning. Hell of a fuss over a slight nip. 'Do shut up, there's a good chap, help me find the bugger!'

Stanley's groans changed key and moderated into gibbers. The word 'doctor' became a strangled splutter. With a superhuman effort he reached for the bell rope, missed it and collapsed silently forward, spread-eagled on the bed.

Exasperated, Roscoe clambered to his feet. 'Look here, Stanley, it's all very well poncing about as a chambermaid, but there *are* limi—' His voice died away. He approached the still form on the bed. Gingerly, he turned it over. Stanley's eyes, wide open, fixed him with a terrified glare. Stanley's mouth, also wide open, seemed about to say something fairly urgent. Stanley's face was blue.

Roscoe forced himself to feel Stanley's pulse. Then he staggered to the marble washstand and was very, very sick.

White and shivering, he tried to get a grip on himself. A lethal reptile was loose somewhere in this room. A cabin steward, with whom he was precluded from claiming any closer acquaintance, was dead on his bed. What to do?

A stiff drink. A very stiff drink indeed was indicated. He finished dressing. Fortunately, Stanley's final throes had managed to avoid his evening togs. He would deal with it later, with proper support.

Meanwhile, the night and the music called.

'A' Deck foyer was a noble setting indeed with its oak panelling, its marble-tiled floor, its wrought ironwork on the balustrades of the magnificent staircase. Gertrude Fitton sat alone in an elegantly informal wicker armchair beneath the enormous glass dome, watching the world go by.

She had already seen her father stroll past on his way to a card game; that expensive looking floosie he seemed so taken with clinging to his arm and making him laugh.

À chacun son goût, she reflected wryly. The trouble was, her own *goût* was too selective by half. She was thirty-three and knew herself to be possessed of features not generally recognized as beautiful. In fact, she knew she had a face like the back of a bus.

She could have married several times over. From West Point to Washington, via Harvard and the Board of the Pennsylvania Railroad, there had been no lack of suitors. But Gertrude was too well aware that the image dazzling their hungry eyes was no more than a toasted oat. She was damned if she was going to settle for a life of conceding infidelity rights, just for the privilege of owning a husband.

She did not, however, intend the Fitton line to end here; nor did she wish to clutter it with any untried, undeserving name. She was rich enough, old enough and certainly intelligent enough to do whatever she pleased.

What Gertrude Fitton needed was a stud.

She looked up at the fantastic wall clock, flanked by its two bronze nymphs. It was a little after half-past eleven. Perhaps she would go to the lounge for a nightcap. Perhaps the tall young man with bright hair and merry eyes would be there. If not, she would take a stroll through every likely venue until she found him.

Roscoe leaned on the bar in the smoking room, nursing his fourth brandy. His mind was becoming fuzzier and fuzzier with assorted plans of action.

The thing to do, he decided, was to go to his stateroom, discover Stanley there, raise the alarm. Nothing to it. First though, he had to nerve himself to walk in and see that dreadful face again. To say nothing of risking a fatal snakebite. He swallowed his drink and ordered another.

'Good evening there.'

He turned his head to find himself blearily face to face with the very teeth he was supposed to be cultivating. Inebriated as he was, they seemed double the usual quantity.

In fuddled tribute to Stanley, he did his best to pull himself together. He bowed with raffish gallantry. 'Good evening to you, ma'am.'

'I saw you from the promenade. You looked worried.' She surveyed him critically. 'How about some fresh air?'

It seemed wise to clear his head for the ordeal before him. Besides, anything to put it off a bit longer, what? 'Splennid, ma'am,' he said. 'Splennid idea!'

The movement of the ship, so slight as to be unnoticeable, was nevertheless ever present. Everyone on board had become accustomed to it without realizing. As Roscoe turned away from the bar, he lurched violently against it again.

Annoyed, he steadied himself. Not good enough. He could hold his liquor better than this. Get a grip, Summerfield!

Then he noticed that the bony American woman, too, had a hand on the bar. People at the tables were looking up, vaguely puzzled. After a moment, someone said, 'Why have we stopped?'

When official news of the situation first filtered through, it made little more impact on the evening's pursuits than had the initial jarring. A few minutes after midnight, the call came to muster the passengers. Roscoe and the bony American made for the boat deck. Finding his own escape hindered by the admonition, 'Women and children,' he returned to the lounge for another drink. The orchestra was playing there and it seemed sensible.

At the sound of the first rocket, he became aware of a commotion outside. It was Flo, thumping Randolph Fitton in the chest and shrieking. As soon as she saw Roscoe, she hurled herself at him instead.

'Stanley!' she yelled. 'I want Stanley! Where is he!'

Roscoe grabbed her, assured the startled Fitton that his daughter was safe and unceremoniously bundled Flo off to the nearest clutch of waiting women. She was fairly drunk and kept up a stream of strenuous objections and wailings for Stanley.

'Stop messing about, Florence!' he ordered sharply. He shoved her into the arms of the nearest crew member and fled, all his attention now turning to himself.

He swooped down on wings of self-preservation to Flo's saloon deck cabin and ransacked her hanging space, but most of the garments appeared to require a corset, which was out of the question. Then he spotted a heavily frilled nightgown near the back. He pulled at it.

It came off its hanger to reveal a rolled canvas propped behind. Roscoe assumed immediate ownership. If ever there was a case of true entitlement . . . . He straightened the painting roughly and pushed one end down the front of his trousers and the other under his starched collar. *Old Woman with Stocking* and Flo's nightdress combined gave him quite a convincing bustline.

He could hear more rockets going up. It was an outboard cabin and he peered through the porthole. There was a great deal of activity in the water. Since his life and future probably depended on this masquerade however, he forced himself not to rush. He worked with practised professional thoroughness.

Eventually, with an excellent make-up on his face and a Chinese shawl over his head, he was ready to join the rest of the weaker sex. Then, the ship began to list more steeply. The bow took a nose dive.

Not for Roscoe the quiet dignity of waiting his turn. The moment had definitely come. He scrambled outside and across the deck, clambered over the rail and jumped.

He surfaced, gasping and shocked with cold. He could hear cries and sobbing on the air. The huge ship, now at a sickening angle in the water, lay behind his left shoulder; lights still blazed the length of her. He grabbed a deck chair as it floated past him and clung to it.

All this, he thought, really is extremely nasty. Not to mention what he must look like with his mascara running. He divested himself of the shawl and the nightie, his stiffening fingers undoing every little tiny satin-covered button he had so meticulously made himself do up. He pushed *Old Woman with Stocking* further into his trousers and kicked out towards a boat he could see ahead in the mist, even though it seemed full to overflowing. It was the only one in his direct line of vision, but he felt unequal to turning round.

What a way to sober up, Roscoe thought, propelling himself with weakening legs towards a refuge that would keep moving away. How many hours, weeks, years had he been pursuing the thing? He'd lost count. He just kept on and on doing it.

It was icy in the water. A not unpleasant numbness began to creep over him. Then he heard a shout of 'Roscoe!'

It was Flo. The lifeboat slowed down. Painfully, Roscoe caught up with it. 'Thanks for keeping me a place, Flo. Bit chilly down here!' He tried to drag himself over the side.

Some woman screamed, 'Stop him! He's capsizing us!'

'Leave off, Roscoe!' Florence shouted. 'The boat's full, can't you see? You'll have to stay there till we get rescued!'

Roscoe appeared not to hear. 'Just give me a hand so I can … hitch m'self over . . . . Thanks.'

He pulled himself in. Florence screamed loud and long as he catapulted her out in the process. It was unintentional, of course. He was fond of Flo. He collapsed in a heap, more dead than alive, just conscious of a faint voice hollering, 'I can't swim! Roscoe, I can't swim...!'

From time to time, for the rest of his life, he would hear that cry and be sorry.

'Woman overboard!' somebody shouted. But no one acted on the information. Too much else was going on.

Roscoe felt himself being shaken. His eyelids fluttered. An elderly woman was glaring at him. 'You deliberately pulled that poor creature into the water!' she hissed.

'I did no such thing, madam. She fell.' Roscoe fainted.

'Someone else go save her!' Gertrude Fitton suggested in commanding tones, pushing Roscoe's accuser aside. 'Let me by, if you please. This young man needs help.'

Chapter Seven

May

There was the sound of weeping. Emily heard it through the ceiling as she crossed the landing to her room after being sick. Pregnancy was catching up with her. Gone were the challenge of crime, the excitement of conspiracy. Roscoe was dead; her own contribution to his end swamped by the scale of the disaster during which he probably met it.

Grounded, gated, hidden away like a freak, Emily's social dealings were confined now to snatched telephone conversations with Kate when Amaryllis was out. One of these had convinced her that she would indeed have been responsible for Roscoe's death had the sea not intervened, which made her feel even worse. And Kate was to leave next week with her mother for Switzerland. Teddy was back at school. Life was utter, utter hell.

So who was it making that noise upstairs? Heartbroken, tearing sobs? Emily mentally ticked off each of the servants. Hardly Fred the bootboy. And she had just been watching Cook mix a cake and scraped out the bowl. Annie the tweeny perhaps? In the same fix as herself? Whoever it was, they were dreadfully unhappy. Emily climbed up to the attic floor to see.

Gripped by helpless embarrassment, she stood at a door that was not quite closed, beyond which Dibbins was racking herself to pieces. Poor Awful! Oh, poor, poor old Awful! I can't let her go on like that but what can I say, what can I do?

Dibbins had been the ultimate authority of Emily's early years. Listening to authority in such abject despair was disconcerting in the extreme. Had somebody died? Stop hanging about eavesdropping, Emily! She pushed the door and walked in.

Huddled face downwards on the bed, shapeless grey cardigan dragged round heaving shoulders, afternoon uniform billowing over ample backside, Dibbins presented a silhouette not unlike that of an afflicted porpoise. Emily sat down and tentatively patted the nearest bit. 'It's only me,' she said, 'only Emily.'

The quivering mass continued to quiver, but with a marked effort at control. 'It's nothing, miss,' a muffled hiss came fiercely from its depths. 'You run along now.'

'I shan't move,' Emily responded, 'until you tell me what's the matter.'

Little by little, Dibbins complied. Until this moment, Poor Awful had simply been part of the bricks and mortar of Emily's childhood, taken for granted along with the sound the front door made when it was damp and the gradient of the hill outside the gate. The stories of Poor Awful's past experiences had been … well, stories. Looking at the shiny, waterlogged face with its red button nose, framed in greying, wispy hair spiking out from a tightly twisted bun, Emily could see that once, this might have been a creature of soft, plump prettiness.

'Pretty face don't get you nothing but trouble!' The refrain which used to meet most of Emily's questions took on heightened meaning as she heard again the order of Dibbins' surrender to the man who ravished her and left her, so many years ago.

'The muscles in his thighs, they rippled. Rippled, they did,' Dibbins smiled damply, side-tracked as she always had been from present issues to past glories, a faraway gleam in her bloodshot china-blue eyes, 'Watching him in the ring with them big cats, it was better than the Battle of Jericho!'

'And the walls come tumbling down an' there was Florrie'n Ivy?' Emily picked up her cue from long practise.

'Fodder for Sodom and Gomorrah, them two,' Dibbins rejoined with traditional gloom and went on to itemize her failures as a mother. Out came the sorry tale rooted in the depths of ignorance which had made her one in the first place. Drawn from the orphanage by the glamour of the circus in general, the lion-tamer in particular, then dumped. Casual labour to support two remnants of shame single handed; eventual succour from the Association for Fallen Women. 'I was saved, miss. Saved I was. To bring them up righteous. But they wasn't!' Run rings round her, they did. Truancy from poor school, secret auditionings at the music halls, rites of passage from the chorus to respective lives of debauchery. 'Ivy, she comes back that time, flauntin' her fine feathers. Then off she goes with her protector an' I never see her no more. Fifteen, she was, then. Shockin'.'

'And Florrie?'

'Oh, Florrie, she kep' in touch right enough. Pressin' me with the wages of sin! Not a penny I'd accept from 'er. Not one! Took up with a spawn of the devil, she did. In the underground.'

'Underworld,' Emily corrected gently, keeping her on track. At least talking prevented Poor Awful from collapsing back into that harrowing uproar.

'Then she says she's goin' to America,' Dibbins continued. 'Says she'll write an' send me a ticket to join 'er...'

Emily listened more closely. This was news. 'So you made it up with her? Splendid! She's really fond of you, isn't she?'

Poor Awful's face began to disintegrate again. 'I'll never know, miss. She's at the bottom of the sea.'

Florrie had been on the...? Oh, no! Oh, crumbs!

'Didn't I used to tell you, miss? Didn't I used to try and shield you from Sodom and Gomorrah? But would you listen?'

The truth was, Emily had never had much idea what Poor Awful was on about when she hit that tack, which she so repeatedly did. Looking now with helpless pity at this liquifying pillar of salt, she was getting more than a glimmer. Amaryllis's lazy caprice of investing Dibbins with sole responsibility for a child's natural development had put the blind in charge of the sightless. Dibbins had done her best. Emily knew for a fact that her mother had never felt moved to intervene. 'It's not your fault!' she asserted firmly. 'What's happened to me is not your fault. It's entirely mine!'

'Your mamma, she don't think so. Sent packing, I've bin.'

So that was it! How dare Amaryllis! How dare she! Emily's contempt for her mother's shallowness knew no bounds. A month ago, when the news of the *Titanic*'s fate first broke, Amaryllis had reacted with, 'Only last night, darling, and we're reading about it already! What a wonderful invention the wireless telegraph is!' Now this!

'Cheer up!' Emily kissed the startled Dibbins on the nose, 'Cheer up, now, d'you hear?' Suddenly, she felt a great deal better. There were things to do, plans to make, obstacles to be knocked out of the way. She marched downstairs to see what her mother was up to and, if at all possible, spoil it.

A certain amount of moving and shaking was taking place on the sofa.

'Ah, Red,' Amaryllis breathed, 'you're so masterful!' With the house full of people, she felt he was getting a little out of hand. She pushed him away.

He looked very disappointed. 'You make me feel young again, Amaryllis!' he protested. 'You make me forget what a disagreeable time I'm havin' lately. Oh, Amaryllis…' He lunged again.

'Not now, Red! Emily might come in.'

'Pretty gel her age mopin' about at home? Ought to be out gallivantin', what?'

'She's *been* out gallivanting,' Amaryllis said tightly. 'Too much. I'm thinking of continuing her education in Europe.'

'That so?' Sir Redvers' interest quickened. He himself would be giving the London season a miss this year, he told her.

Amaryllis was genuinely surprised. 'I thought Kate was to make her debut!'

Lady Priscilla, it appeared, was unequal to the strain. 'Very poor health, m'wife enjoys. Very poor. She and Kate, they're off to Switzerland.'

'Very bracing, I'm sure. And you?'

His gaze slid over her bosom with undisguised relish. 'I feel no pressing need to become more braced than I am at present. In a month or so perhaps, I may repair with m'son Teddy to Monte. Meanwhile…' His hand touched her neck and moved downward.

The door was flung open. Emily walked in with an air of imminent purpose.

'Why, good afternoon, Sir Redvers,' she said, 'how delightful to see you. How is Kate? I do hope she's stopped feeling sick now. They say the first three months are the worst. Speaking for myself, I've been quite lucky on the whole. A little nausea, to be sure, but I expect it to fade quite soon. You do know, of course, that the same scoundrel ruined us both within a few days of each other? You'll be glad to hear that he no doubt received his just desserts when the *Titanic* went down.

Rough justice, would you say? *I* would. What I really came in to suggest, mother, is this. Since Kate is leaving next week, is there any reason why I shouldn't leave as well? You could follow later. I know you can't face Switzerland, so why not send me to Monte Carlo with Dibbins? Dibbins, Sir Redvers, has looked after me all my life. She is the best possible person to look after me now, in these unfortunate circumstances. I shall be suitably chaperoned, and out of the way. Do try and make mother see what an admirable notion that is. Well, I must get back to my books. It's been so awfully nice talking to you, Sir Redvers. Excuse me, Mamma.'

She sketched a charming little curtsey to them both, smiled shyly and left the room.

Amaryllis and Sir Redvers sat in silence for quite a few moments. A hurricane had engulfed them, capturing them in the deceptive stillness of its eye. Now it had passed, they were left with quite a choice of debris to put together.

In Utica, New York State, it was pouring with rain. Roscoe sat in the Mens' Room at the railroad station, listening to the water hit the windowpane. Scrutinizing his Baedeker for evidence of a crock of gold in this vicinity, he noted that not only had he stumbled upon the headquarters of the American cheese trade, but the State Lunatic Asylum was only a short distance to the west.

Is this, he wondered, the end of my rainbow? The contents of his pockets tended to suggest so. Fleeced to the bone on the train from Buffalo, he had slithered off it here while he still had the clothes he stood up in.

Little more than a month back, life had looked so good. Picked up by the *Carpathia* that dreadful night in April, treated with utmost kindness and taken under the wing of Gertrude Fitton, the lines: '*Bring me your poor, your huddled masses...*' seemed redolent of distinctly personal, limitless invitation. Except that Roscoe, once dried out, felt neither poor nor huddled.

He liked Gertrude Fitton and seriously considered succumbing to her fancy for a gigolo, who might in due course supply her with a good-looking heir. But he really liked her. He incurred her respect by telling her so, as a good reason for declining the offer before she quite got to the point of making it. Besides, this was to be a clean slate, a new beginning, a fresh start.

Instead, he accepted a loan and kitted himself out handsomely at Lord & Taylor. He also bought a carpet bag with several compartments, into one of which he slid *Old Woman with Stocking*; now the extent of his capital, badly done over though she might be.

Feeling ready to take on the entire United States, Roscoe invested twenty-five dollars with the New York & Hudson River Railroad for a ticket to Chicago, via Buffalo and Detroit.

Standing on the observation platform at Falls View, appreciating the spectacle, he came to the conclusion that it was a pretty splendid way to see the world. 'Ah, the glory of Niagara!' he remarked, to no one in particular. He felt totally exhilarated, both by the general scenic wonder and the fact that last evening he had emerged with outstanding profit from a poker game on board. His appearance, his accent, his form on the Paris-Lyon-Marseilles and the Orient Express – unknown this side of the Atlantic – were serving him well.

At Detroit, he astounded himself by returning Gertrude Fitton's loan. Way out of character, he reflected as he bought the money order. But she was one exceptional dame. Enjoying the easy slide into local vernacular, he mailed it before giving himself a chance to reconsider.

In Chicago, after a month or so, his luck sprang a leak. It became apparent that the native operators were resentful of being challenged by a smooth limey. Indeed, the smooth limey was rapidly becoming putty in their hands.

Reviewing the state of his exchequer in the opulence of his room at the Hotel La Salle, Roscoe realized with a nasty jolt that it fell significantly short of covering his bill. He left by the service entrance with his carpet bag, never to return.

New York! he thought, as he walked to Illinois Central Station. New York, that's what! I might even get a proper job and earn an honest living, who knows? I'm an actor, dammit, a brilliant one. With enough experience to busk myself into anything on Broadway. New York, here I come!

The fare depleted his funds alarmingly. Not wanting to arrive destitute, he took steps to recoup between Detroit and Buffalo.

Things looked up. After Buffalo, they looked down again. On the approach to Utica, he left the game for a call of nature, managed to lift a wallet from a jacket on his way out, retrieved his precious carpet bag from the box-car and decamped discreetly to this exceedingly dismal platform.

He looked through the wallet he had picked on the train. It was full of IOUs. Grimly, he surveyed his assets: Fifteen dollars thirty-five cents; three shirts; a change of underwear; Stetson hat; suit and shoes that would soon have seen better days – and Gertrude Fitton's card.

August

It was very warm in Monte Carlo. The breeze, no more than a stirring of the air, scarcely touched the sails of the yachts at anchor. Heads lifted, hands raised in greeting as *La Belle Anglaise* and her duenna walked slowly along to the café where they took tea every afternoon at this time. After three months, they were a familiar sight. Other visitors might come and go, but *La P'tite Veuve*, so bravely carrying her loss and her expanding burden, was on more than nodding terms with residents of every degree. Pregnancy, even at this cumbersome stage, was no detriment to Emily's looks. Her hair shone, her eyes sparkled. Not for a moment did she forget how wonderful it was to be away from Fitzjohn's Avenue.

When they first arrived, she had eagerly explored this enchanted place, dragging poor Dibbins up winding hills and over cobbles. Now, progress was perforce more circumspect. It was pleasant enough just to sit and watch the world go by, when the world was so delightful.

It had certainly transformed Dibbins. From the grimy brimstone cocoon of the chapel at Chalk Farm, where Emily's childish nightmares had their roots, a butterfly – well, a stoutish moth emerged. In an amazingly short time, Lily Dibbins remembered how to giggle again. Her appreciation of the passing scene got saucier and saucier.

They took seats at an outside table under the awning and Emily ordered what the French liked to call '*le feef o'clock*'. She herself strongly fancied a fair amount of *patisserie* as well. 'What about you, Lily?'

On the Channel ferry, Emily had announced her intention of addressing Poor Awful henceforth by her given name. She was well rewarded by the resultant jubilant blooming. Today, though, Lily seemed down in the mouth. She wasn't of a mind for them cakes, she said, perhaps just boiled water might be more the thing.

'Something you ate?' Emily asked.

'Dunno reely. Maybe just this heat. I feel sorter tight across my middle. An' I've a pain somewhere. It'll pass.'

'A sip of tea won't hurt,' Emily coaxed. 'When we get back to the *pension*, I'll ask Madame about a doctor.'

'I don't want no fuss. Go on now, eat up your tea.'

As she demolished a substantial *tarte aux framboises*, Emily watched Lily Dibbins with mounting anxiety. There was a pudgy pallor about the round face which usually glowed with pronounced high colour. Beads of perspiration stood out on the upper lip of a mouth clamped tight in discomfort.

Emily summoned the waiter and paid the bill. 'Come along Lily,' she said briskly, snapping her reticule shut, 'I'm taking charge. We're going home now and I'm going to find you a doctor.'

Getting no reaction, she looked up. Lily was sitting stock still in her chair, staring as if mesmerized at something across the street. Emily followed her gaze.

A carriage stood outside the Hotel de Paris. Stepping down from it was an exquisite creature of immense grandeur and sophistication, whose diaphanous parasol vied for size with the sweep of her magnificent hat. A sound escaped Dibbins, somewhere between a sob, a gasp and a wheeze. A strange shade of magenta began to suffuse her neck.

'What is it? What is it, Lily?' Emily grabbed her arm and shook it, really frightened now.

Lily's breathing became shallow and strained all at once. She seemed under some unbearable stress, yet wanting to speak. Eventually, she managed to mutter thickly: 'It's Ivy! It's Ivy Dibbins! That's what it is!' Whereupon, to the intense dismay of Emily and everyone else nearby, Lily Dibbins pitched forward to the ground.

The doctor called by M'sieu le Proprietaire would have been ready to settle for heart failure. The lady was overweight and *entre les deux ages*, to put it kindly.

Emily wanted more attention for her old friend than that. Genuinely devastated, badly shaken, she sobbed piteously and allowed herself to faint, causing great consternation in the café. On being brought round, she proclaimed her fears that Mademoiselle had suffered food poisoning. In order to avoid a miscarriage on his premises, M'sieu le Proprietaire advocated a post-mortem which, to his relief, revealed a burst appendix.

Emily found herself required to give answers regarding funeral arrangements and next of kin. No one but herself had heard Dibbins's final utterance. No one else knew of the chance recognition which had caused it. She took the bull by the horns.

'I can tell you with truth, messieurs,' she said, 'Miss Dibbins had no relatives. Her only home has been with my family for as long as I can remember. She owned no property. Any final arrangements would rest with my husband, were he within reach. Since I am a widow, I believe the responsibility is mine.'

Emily's condition, her dignity of bearing and her air of quiet authority combined to bring local officialdom to its knees. No one presumed to question her account of herself, or seek to verify her age and true legal status.

When it came to the funeral, she relied on a mixture of judgement and imagination. She was well aware of Dibbins's views on 'Them Cathy Licks, carryings-on with beads'n candles'n smells'. She doubted both the likelihood and the value of locating a French equivalent to the threadbare savagery of Chalk Farm. So she requested a non-denominational private cremation with as little religious bias as possible. Miss Dibbins had been a Free-thinking Pantheist, she said.

With true Gallic *sang-froid*, they respected the wishes of the departed as best they legally could.

After it was over, Emily asked to be rowed out to sea a little way. She dropped the urn over the side and watched it spiral gracefully away through the clear blue of the Mediterranean.

This, she knew, would please Lily most; to stay in the place where she had learned how to enjoy herself again.

According to her last letter, Amaryllis would be arriving, like it or not, within a fortnight or so, accompanied by Sir Redvers; and possibly Teddy as well. In any event, Emily was instructed to leave Dibbins in the *pension* and join them at the Riviera Palace.

Resigning herself to the inevitable, Emily set about composing a telegram.

*

'So tell me, Mr Summerfield, what have you been doing with yourself since we last deteriorated together in an open boat?'

Amid the splendour of the lounge in the Waldorf Astoria, Roscoe found Miss Fitton's choice of words beguiling. At her invitation, they faced each other across a low table bearing the quaint accoutrements of English afternoon tea. A string quartet provided selections from *Florodora*. It was all very pleasant.

'Oh, this and that, dontcherknow. I thought I should see something of your great and beautiful country. So I bought a railroad ticket and ... drifted a little.'

'I admire the spirit of adventure in a man.'

He grew bolder. 'I hope it won't shock you that I got into a few poker games on the way?'

'Why should it? I hope you won?'

'When I contacted you from Utica, I wasn't about to arrive back cap-in-hand,' Roscoe assured her, adding quickly, 'I trust you didn't mind my writing?'

'Would I have given you my card if I were going to mind?' Her face softened. 'When I opened your earlier letter and a money order fell out, it was one helluva surprise, but did I mind?'

'Sometimes, there is honour among thieves,' Roscoe murmured with portentous humility, then feared he might have overdone it.

Gertrude changed the subject. 'I watched you on board the *Titanic*,' she said. 'And that flashy doll with you. The one you pushed into the sea.'

He went cold. 'It was a tragic accident!' he maintained strenuously, 'I scarcely knew her. She was—'

'She was keeping your place in the lifeboat,' Gertrude cut in, 'whether she knew it or not. Partners, were you?'

He could think of nothing to say.

She shrugged. 'Water under the propellors, huh?'

Roscoe wondered what the hell game she was playing with him. 'In my darkest moments, dear Miss Fitton,' he confided with floundering technique, 'I recalled the bright glow in your eyes and the warm ring of your voice...'

'Balls.'

His mouth hung open.

''S the kinda thing young men like you say to frumps like me when they're after something. Beautiful girls don't need it.'

Roscoe rebuked himself for underestimating her. 'I meant it when I said you were fascinating!' he protested more truthfully. 'Even drenched and shivering in that bloody lifeboat.'

'And it made me feel real good. You see, Mr Sum— why don't I call you Roscoe?'

'I wish you would. Gertrude.'

'Sure. You see, Roscoe, I'm going on thirty-four. And as my old man didn't have my luck on April fifteenth last, I own the controlling interest in Fittons Fitness Breakfast Bars, which is quite some empire. I have buck teeth, round shoulders and flat feet. I could go on a physical training programme. I could have my teeth straightened. The hell with it! I can buy what I want.'

'You have a keen mind. That's beyond price.'

'And you, sir, a silver tongue. I wouldn't want you getting yourself on the wrong side of the law, here in the U. S. of A.'

'I appreciate your interest in my welfare, Miss F— Gertrude.'

Her eyes glinted. 'I need an interest, don't I? Imagine how dull life can be when you're ugly and rich with no interests. You don't even get the stimulation of struggling to exist.'

'I see your point.'

'I knew you would.' She studied him speculatively. 'Ever think of going into movies? You've the looks of an actor.'

Roscoe's ears pricked. Here was a new twist. Unexpected, but by no means unwelcome. 'You mean the bioscope? As a matter of fact, acting is … er, did run in my family, but the bioscope?' he laughed. 'Isn't it just an amusing stunt?'

It was a vast new industry, she told him forcefully. Big already here in the States and getting bigger. 'I got to thinking it's a whole lot more fun than breakfast food.'

'Now you mention it, I did see a moving picture once,' Roscoe said, 'at a fair in England. It was called *Rescued by Rover*. Rather neat, I thought, at the time.'

Emily had dragged him into a smelly tent to watch it. On a sunny day when the world was young. Before he spotted Florence's diamanté earrings; before life had taken a dangerous spiral spin.

'Ever hear of David Wark Griffith?'

She might not have spoken. Roscoe was sauntering across Hampstead Heath in the company of a precocious, oddly bewitching moppet of thirteen.

Gertrude picked up a teaspoon and banged it against the cup. 'Or Granville Warwick, maybe? Ever hear of those names?'

Roscoe re-focused with difficulty on the present. He shook his head. 'Should I? Who are they?'

'Movie-makers,' she replied, 'I'll have you meet.'

Roscoe's ambitions quivered. 'You know them?'

'Not yet. Who argues with money?'

Chapter Eight

September

'*Vingt-six. Noir.*'

Chips raked up or slid across the table; gleams flickering in or out of eyes in carefully blank faces; lighters flaring, skirts rustling, fans swishing.

'You've lost again, mother,' said Emily.

'It will change soon. It must. I'm using Sir Redvers' system.'

Emily took a deep breath, which somehow failed to fill her lungs as it should. 'I saw him go out to the terrace less than ten minutes ago, with a face like parchment.' The effort of speaking left her oddly exhausted.

Amaryllis got up. 'I might join him for a moment. I could do with some fresh air.'

'I don't think there is any. Even outside.' Emily got up too, awkward now and heavy. 'I think I'll go back to the hotel. I feel rather peculiar.'

Amaryllis glanced at her sharply. 'You do look a little strange. Are you all right? Could it be...?'

'Not for three weeks,' Emily sighed. 'It's heat, that's all. I'll get Teddy to walk me home. I think he's about somewhere.'

Amaryllis knew, she just *knew* that her system was on the point of proving itself. 'Very well, dear,' she smiled with glad relief, 'better go straight up to the room and lie down.'

Redvers Grinling's knuckles stood out white and shiny. He looked down at them, displayed like a row of pearl onions along the tops of his fists, clenched so tightly on the balustrade. Funny they should suddenly strike him like that, he thought, when he wouldn't be seeing them again.

He felt cold, even in this balmy soft air. Cold and shivering. Hey up, Redvers – sod 'Redvers'! Hey up, Herbert Grinling. You've had a good innings. The rest of 'em, they'll have to make out as best they can. No point hangin' on when the game's over, what?

Slowly, he unclenched one fist, willing the hand not to shake as he moved it round to where the handle of his revolver protruded from the top of his cummerbund, beneath his tail coat. God knows why he'd brought the thing with him tonight. Some sixth sense? He had been a gambler all his life. Win some, lose some.

Winnings had become self-perpetuating for over twenty years, when he thought about it. Sailed pretty close to the wind once or twice in the early days, oh, yes. But then, the deals that held! The investments that grew! The wife ... poor old Priscilla, eh? Still, it'd been a bargain for her, as well. And for himself, the prestige, the power, the fun ... Oh, fuck. So much for that, now, too, what? Curtains, eh?

A soft finger tickled the back of his neck. 'Why, there you are, you elusive Red, you! Are you having a good run tonight?'

He very nearly shot her by sheer reflex. 'I've known some excellent runs, Amaryllis, but not tonight.' Leaning rather heavily on the balustrade, he turned to face her.

'And I've been using your system!' she pouted, prettily.

'My system is flawed, Amaryllis. Fatally flawed.'

'But you told me how, in the past, you—'

'Before I evolved my system. My system does not work.'

'You will have your little joke...'

Redvers' right hand hung down casually at his side; index finger touching trigger, thumb on safety catch. 'I assure you, dear lady, it's no joke. It's Heatherley. The estate, the zoo, the pack o' hounds, my art collection ... gone. All gone. In the attempt to prove my system. I'm ruined, Amaryllis.'

Like any challenge of real moment, serious problems faced by others had to be avoided. Subconsciously, automatically, her mind would wipe them away as they threatened to appear. She had greeted the news of Lily Dibbins' passing with: 'At least it was no bother. The French are so *practical*, aren't they?'

Now, the ring of truthful finality in Redvers' unemphatic statement passed wilfully unheeded. 'You must just keep playing,' she said lightly, 'I'm sure dear Teddy will lend you some chips.'

'Teddy's gone, too.'

'You've gambled away your son? How did you manage that?'

'If he hasn't left Monte already, he very soon will. To escape the stigma of a bankrupt father. Foreign Legion, if he's sensible. All that's left to him now.'

'What a waste of a good bridge player! I think, actually, he's walking Emily back to the Riviera Palace. Shall we follow?'

Redvers seemed not to hear. 'Fine fellers in the Legion,' he mused. 'Bit on the short side, Teddy. Got guts, though.'

On arrival in Monte Carlo with his father, the sight of Emily had been something of a facer for Teddy Grinling. No one had given him any idea of her predicament. No one had mentioned it. No one had prepared him.

Although down from Harrow for good, he was not yet eighteen. Uneasily, he noted the polite fiction, carefully built up by Dibbins over three months, of *la belle p'tite Anglaise* so tragically widowed on her honeymoon. It was quite bad enough, Kate and Mother having to exile themselves to Switzerland on account of some bounder of a foreign crook. Now Emily, too? The memory of that afternoon in the potting shed at Fitzjohn's Avenue swept across his mind again and again in nightmare proportions.

To be absolutely honest, he really didn't feel ready to be a married man. Let alone a father. He wanted to do what other chaps did for a bit. Play the field, travel, sow some wildish oats maybe. Somewhere else. Without fear of retribution.

It perplexed him still more that Emily, in all her bow-fronted glory, behaved towards him as though her condition did not exist. She was cheerful, friendly, pleasant. But something in her manner made it impossible for him to broach the subject of parenthood. Until this evening.

Walking her slowly, very slowly, through the chiffon velvet Monte Carlo night towards the lights of home, twinkling in concert all over the huge frontage of the Riviera Palace Hotel, Teddy could not ignore the agitation of Emily's breathing.

In front of the main entrance, she suddenly stopped, clapped both hands to the small of her back and said: 'Ow!'

'What's the matter, old girl?' Teddy was struck by an impending threat of inadequacy.

'Well, I've just had a griping pain somewhere round my pelvis and I'm all wet,' Emily replied, as calmly as possible in the circumstances. 'I think I might be about to have a baby.'

'Porter!' Teddy shouted as loud as he could, waving his arms. 'Porter!' He turned to Emily and whispered frantically, 'Is it mine?'

'You don't really want to know, Teddy dear. AaaHOW!'

The Head Porter and two bellboys rushed down the wide steps just in time to catch her. Anxious, out of his depth and intensely curious, Teddy followed. They bore her into the foyer and lowered her on to a *chaise-longue*, which was partially hidden from public view by two enormous potted fronds.

Resourceful to a legendary degree, the Head Porter rapped out cool, quiet, French instructions to the bellboys. At the speed of lightning, three folding screens swiftly converted Emily's corner into a makeshift private suite, inside which the Head Porter proceeded to remove her lower garments with dispatch.

Teddy found himself on the outside, wondering what to do. The receptionist was on the telephone to the hotel doctor; one bellboy had been sent to find the housekeeper and request her immediate presence with hot water and towels, the other was under orders to fetch Amaryllis from the casino. Such guests as were aware what was afoot, studiously pretended not to be.

Teddy felt at something of a loss in all this activity. He sensed that any attempt at participation the other side of the screens would be *de trop* from every point of view including his own.

'*M'sieu Grinling! Par ici, M'sieu Grinling, s'il vous plait!*' The receptionist had finished on the telephone. She was trying to get his attention.

He crossed the foyer, hoping to be directed into doing something vaguely useful.

She handed him an envelope. '*C'est pour vous, M'sieu. Milor' votre père*, 'e leave it here for you.'

It was bulky. Obviously quite a few sheets, folded tight. His name on the outside was in his father's writing.

Amaryllis waited expectantly for Redvers to respond to her suggestion of returning to the hotel. He seemed not to notice her head tilted at what she knew to be a charming angle. He just stood there, staring at nothing.

Perhaps he didn't hear me, she concluded. Well, he's having a run of bad luck, bless his heart. I'll offer my support. What are friends for, after all? '*I'll* lend you some chips,' she announced gaily. 'You've been such a dear to Emily and me.'

Dragging himself back from a great distance, he looked at her in bewilderment, as though surprised to find her still there. Slowly, he shook his head. 'Thank you, Amaryllis, but I fear it would be good money after bad. No. I have been reckless. I must face the consequences.'

She really had no idea what he was talking about. 'Well, if you're sure … I ought to be getting back to the hotel. Emily was feeling the heat.'

'Before you go, Amaryllis, I – I feel I must touch on a somewhat delicate subject…'

Alarm bells clanged in her head. He's not interested in chips, she thought. He wants me to lend him money! 'Your luck having taken the turn it has, dear Red,' she murmured gently, 'I fear I couldn't possibly consider it.'

He in turn was puzzled. 'You misunderstand, madam. I was referring to your daughter's condition.'

She stiffened. Where was this leading? 'In my enjoyment of your company, Sir Redvers, I was perhaps less than circumspect. It was not our intention to cause you embarrassment.'

'It's immaterial now,' he said dully. 'I was only about to observe that my son and I were alone in the knowledge that Emily's single state is not due, as generally supposed, to tragic early widowhood.'

She drew herself up with quiet dignity. 'In view of your own daughter in Switzerland, sir, I felt sure you could be relied upon.' She paused briefly, then awarded him a conspiratorial smile. 'I'm still prepared to lend you some chips.' She squeezed his hand warmly.

He stared at her with dawning comprehension. 'You … you thought I was about to blackmail you into backing me at the tables?'

'It did just cross my mind.'

He studied her in silence for a long moment. 'Rest assured, dear lady,' he said wearily, 'I was merely about to remark that with Teddy gone, I am the sole remaining witness to your situation. And that my presence, too, will shortly cease to trouble you.'

She was nonplussed. 'Oh. Are you leaving?'

'Yes. Yes, I am.'

'Oh. Well,' re-arranging her manner accordingly, she gushed: 'I do hope we'll be seeing something of you before you disappear?'

'Goodbye, Mrs Kilverston,' he went on as if she had not spoken. 'I am about to do, not the decent thing, but the only thing. Priscilla and Kate will have to manage as best they can.'

'I don't in the least understand what you're talking about, my dear,' Amaryllis said, 'but I'm sure you know best. Gentlemen always do. Now, if you'll excuse me, I must get back to Emily.'

She turned and left.

Monte Carlo was a most pleasant place indeed, she reflected as she strolled homeward. Look up, and there are those exotic palms in silhouette, majestically stirring against a clear, starlit sky. The fleeting appreciation of such natural beauty made her feel both agreeably profound and free to pass from nature to artifice; to enjoy wedding-cake buildings ablaze with lights; myriad snatches of music from countless orchestras blending on the night air. Poor Sir Redvers, he did seem a touch down in the mouth. Still, he's staying on to do the only thing. Quite right. Any moment now, his number is sure to be up.

As she came within sight of the *porte-cochère* at the Riviera Palace, the drifts of music were fragmented by a sharp report from the direction of the casino. Amaryllis paused, startled. A pistol shot? Never. More likely a backfiring from a motor car.

The echo died. She went on her way.

A small figure hurled itself out of the hotel and made straight towards her at breakneck speed. It was one of the bellboys. With athletic gestures, he stopped her in her tracks. '*Madame Kilverston? Madame! Venez, Madame! Venez vite! Vite!*'

Resisting a twinge of alarm, Amaryllis followed him.

At the top of the steps, she found her way blocked by Teddy Grinling, with a letter in his hand. His eyes held stark terror and he was white as a sheet.

'Have you seen my father, Mrs Kilverston?' he almost shouted.

She thought his manner excessively brusque. 'I left him at the casino, dear,' she replied a tad sharply, 'I'm sure you'll find him on the terrace there.'

He sprinted away without a word.

Really, too casual! She looked about. What was the matter with everyone? Total strangers, scattered round the foyer, all seemed focused on one corner of it which appeared to be screened off. The bellboy started dragging her towards it.

She was about to pull free and reprimand him in no uncertain terms, when the air was rent by an ear splitting, full-throated female howl.

A second or two of silence. Then another; incredulous, outraged. And another. And another.

The onlookers quivered with suppressed excitement. No one moved. The bellboy redoubled his efforts at getting Amaryllis into the midst of whatever was in progress behind the screens.

Oh, God, must I? Not having been conscious at her own confinement, what authority decreed that she be harrowed in minutest detail by each successive biological *tableau vivant* presented at her daughter's?

Another blistering roar.

The world went mud-coloured for Amaryllis. She swayed. Her knees buckled. Just as she was about to sink into grateful oblivion, she felt herself caught under one armpit. Her face was firmly slapped.

'Don't be idiotic, woman!' the contemptuous hiss came in an oddly indefinable accent. 'This is an event more stylish, far, than any middle-eastern stable! Pull yourself together!'

Amaryllis had the impression of an eagle's face looming above her. Bony, garishly painted like a ship's figurehead, surmounted by an upswept pile of blinding red hair. The eyes, glittering with a raptor's zeal, pierced her awake.

One more earth-shaking bellow.

Amaryllis was pushed through the screens just in time to witness a small, purple male creature draw breath and, without waiting for the customary slap on the back, offer promising competition.

October

Bells ringing, from churches in the town or cows on the hills behind; clocks striking, with or without cuckoos leaping out at the same time; cannon, celebrating some historic landmark for the lakeside town of Neuchatel ... none of these, even in unison, had much chance against the indigestion of Bunty Grinling after twelve and a half days of life.

Kate walked up and down, up and down. Bouncing, patting, back-rubbing. All at once, her daughter surprised her by puking down her shoulder-blade and instantly falling asleep.

'Into your cot, Bunty. There. Please, please don't wake up for a little while, could you?' Kate pulled up the coverlet and crept through the arch to the living-room of the tiny apartment at the back of the town.

Last week, they had been at the Hotel du Lac. Bunty was six days old when the wire came from Teddy. Priscilla's immediate reaction was to get them into somewhere more befitting their abrupt, unsettling, undeniably real transition to the ranks of the underprivileged.

'I've simply got to sit down,' Kate moaned, sinking onto an uncushioned pine window-seat.

'A young thing like you? How do you suppose *I* feel?' her mother managed to sound both pained and brusque.

'I've really no idea. Except that you didn't have a baby less than a fortnight ago.'

'No! I was widowed instead! By a feckless gambler who shot himself rather than face his responsibilities!' Priscilla made no pretence at grief. She saw no reason to. In her view, she had been ruthlessly exploited by the males of her family all her life. What this upstart had done was the final straw. 'Did he think of me? Did he consider for a second that this might kill me, too?'

'Perhaps he relied on you enjoying your ill-health too much to let it,' Kate replied with unaccustomed irony.

Teddy had risen to the occasion with remarkable capability, considering his age. He even surprised himself. In the general ghastliness of the circumstances, though, it was helpful to have so much to do. It did take a little time to absorb the diverse aspects of the disaster. The implications of the situation as a whole came in a series of waves, each one alone being more than enough to undermine any administrative skill and general balance in someone rather young to have acquired much of either.

The facts outlined in Redvers Grinling's letter to his son were clear. Income and investments gambled away; credit raised on property and capital assets, gone too. That final evening, there was to be one last swing against the odds. As the old rascal said, he'd done it before, he just might do it again. If not, his London lawyers already held instructions as to the honouring of debts incurred; Priscilla and Kate were hereby returned to the stewardship of the Heatherleys; Teddy was urged to make a career in the Foreign Legion. He himself would be taking the remaining way out. A note to the French authorities, requesting a funeral both minimal and unattended, was enclosed. Bloody good luck to you all.

Teddy confirmed the bleakness of the outlook with a call to the lawyers by radio-telephone. The hotel bill had been settled up to and including the night after the tragedy. He would have to leave the following morning. To bypass his father's wishes and attend the funeral had been made wellnigh impossible. What remained of his monthly allowance would buy him a ticket to … Marseilles? To enlist in the Foreign Legion? In shock, he tried to consider the idea. The suggestion was practical, certainly. Food, lodging, uniform, all found. Bit like school, really, with bullets.

He mentioned it to Emily when he called in to say goodbye. She was sitting up in bed, looking absolutely radiant, with Hugo in her arms. Teddy was still wondering if perhaps he was responsible for Hugo as well.

Something in Emily's eyes warned him against asking. Her views on the Foreign Legion were given instead: 'You're not a coward, old thing, are you?'

'What do you mean? The Foreign Legion is a sort of garlic-flavoured blood-bath!'

'Very handy for losing yourself in. And your mother and your sister on a Swiss lake in a boat with no paddle? Not to mention little Pushface, when it arrives. Buck up, Teddy, do!'

Before leaving for Neuchatel, he took steps to locate his Uncle Hereward, Earl of Heatherley. Twenty years back, after exchanging his sister and his family seat for a large capital sum and a handsome annuity from his brother-in-law, Hereward settled in Italy. Teddy had never met him. A telephone call to the villa at Fiesole yielded the information that *Il Signore e La Contessa* were from home, sojourning at the Hotel de Paris, Monte Carlo.

The allusion to 'La Contessa' was a complete surprise to Teddy, who had grown up with the idea that his uncle was not the marrying kind. Neither did his father's letter refer to her. The London lawyers, however, had requested the present whereabouts of the Earl as a matter of urgency. Teddy notified them by cable. Next, he composed a letter to his uncle, with help from Amaryllis – who, he must admit, was being a real brick.

As the last person to see Sir Redvers alive, Amaryllis was the centre of considerable attention, which she found by no means disagreeable. However, she did feel regret to a depth that sorely stretched her capacities. Going over that final conversation in her mind, she realized how grievously she had misunderstood the poor man. The recollection was not a comfortable one. Nor could it be spoken of. The least she could do now was be a tower of as much strength as she could muster.

She offered to take Teddy's letter to the Hotel de Paris. A bellboy was sent with her card and a note to the Earl requesting leave to call on behalf of his nephew. A courteous invitation was returned. She set off, agog to meet Lady Heatherley.

The Earl received her in the drawing room of his suite. Her prevailing impression was that he and his sister should have been the other way round. He was in the early forties, of fragile, graceful build. In soft-lit halls of evening, he might well look ten years younger. But this was midday. Light brown hair, a little too uniformly burnished; carefully smooth face, shadows discreetly dusted out; long dark lashes framing bruised violet eyes, all presented an image that should, more acceptably, have been Priscilla's.

Amaryllis touched the limp hand. She murmured the kind of condolences suitable, she hoped, to a trusted family friend of his brother-in-law. She wondered why on earth he was married. She had gathered from Teddy that it was most likely a fairly recent arrangement, but even so. Her speculations were interrupted by the arrival of his wife, full of breathless, charming apologies for having been waylaid in the foyer.

A credit to Monsieur Worth, Lady Heatherley was anything between twenty-six and forty. Amaryllis had expected an Italian grandee. Fascination at the seductively pitched, unmistakably English voice only increased when a few seconds' polite exchange pegged the expensive vision – addressed by her husband as 'Ivy' – to origins somewhere in the drabber reaches of London.

Amaryllis estimated, fairly accurately as it happened, that the Earl must have had pressing reasons. However decorative an accessory for a gentleman of means in European society Ivy might be, the Heatherley title was a bargaining counter of some weight. The facts of the matter were that Lord Heatherley had been barred from every casino from Biarritz to Rapallo. In order to gamble at all, he needed a personal agent, over whom he had legal control.

Amaryllis handed over Teddy's note and accepted a glass of champagne. She outlined to the Earl, as kindly and briefly as she could, the manner of his brother-in-law's death. It soon became apparent that some communication from Sir Redvers' lawyers had already been received and was causing a measure of acute domestic tension. Reluctantly, she took her leave.

As the door closed behind her, all hell was let loose.

Ivy had seen this marriage – her first – both as a triumphant passage from *demi* to *haute monde* and an insurance certificate. The deal was clinched on the assumption that income and property, as well as title, were Hereward's by right. To Ivy, it seemed a hard-earned reward for all the insecurities of a long and uncertain career.

Not to mention school fees for her fifteen-year-old daughter, of whom Hereward was unaware.

Little Joyce, the result of a regrettably careless encounter, had always been kept so far in Ivy's background as to be invisible. Respectably farmed out in Kent as a baby; now maturing anonymously in a private establishment for girls near Tunbridge Wells, Joyce was another ongoing expense for which Ivy had foreseen automatic coverage.

'Now it comes out you're a bloody remittance man!' she screeched in the unconfined accents of Mornington Crescent. 'It's bloody misrepresentation, that's what it is! You're a bloody con, that's what you are. As well as a bloody fairy.'

'You're still the Countess of Heatherley.'

'I'll divorce you! For non-consummation! And *still* be the Countess of Heatherley!'

'Much good it'll do you. I'm wiped out.'

Quite true. Ivy, however, was not. Ivy had represented Hereward at the tables with practised aptitude; breaking even, winning regularly enough to keep him satisfied. She had also looked after herself. While Redvers Grinling lost, Ivy – more often than Hereward imagined – had won.

Teddy was touchingly grateful to Amaryllis for her efforts. It would have been rotten, he said, to meet his uncle for the first, maybe the only time, as bearer of tidings to the effect that not only would the annuity cease forthwith, but the Fiesole villa was to be sold too, along with all other Grinling assets, to cover the accumulated losses of the past few weeks.

Three days later, the *Menton & Monte Carlo News* reported that the honeymoon visit of the Earl and Countess of Heatherley to Monaco had been mysteriously cut short.

Emily questioned her mother again about Lady Heatherley's appearance. 'Did you say her name was Ivy?'

'It seemed to be. I can't imagine why you're so interested. I thought her rather common, actually.'

Teddy was going to have to sleep on the floor. Kate had the bed; Priscilla the sofa. It was a nice little apartment for one, which would be beyond their means next week.

'Don't we still have the Pimlico house? Where Grandmother lived till they took her away?' Kate asked. Now that Teddy was here, she felt she might have some constructive support.

'It's a slum,' her mother growled. As the only prospect open to them, the idea depressed her unutterably.

'Didn't the Civic Health or somebody go in and clean it out?' Teddy said. 'Didn't you come storming in that time and say so? Don't you remember?'

Priscilla remembered only too well. The old Countess of Heatherley, autocratic battleaxe of daunting obstinacy, had declined all proposed retirement care in favour of her verminous haven in the one remaining family property near Victoria Station. Public authority and the Salvation Army combined could not move her. Nor could her relatives. She despised her son-in-law as a vulgar little nobody and flatly refused any assistance from him. She preferred not even to acknowledge him as a legal attachment of her daughter's.

Eccentric to the end, her remains were eventually carried out in the wing chair she had occupied, without moving for any purpose whatever, for at least two years. The Westminster Borough Council fumigated the place from top to bottom.

'And it's still ours, isn't it?' Teddy said.

'It's too damn big!' Priscilla objected. 'We're destitute! We have no proper idea what the word means, but that's what we are.'

'Perhaps ... perhaps we could take in lodgers?' Kate suggested vaguely, having no idea how one went about such a thing.

Chapter Nine
1913

February

The cavalryman flung back his head, arching in the saddle as the first Sioux bullet ripped into his left kidney. The second, straight between the shoulder-blades to the heart, caused him to topple slowly from his horse with a graceful undulating motion, his dying face side-lit with dramatic effect by the rays of the southern Californian sun.

He rolled over and lay, gazing upwards, in the dust, well aware of the camera lingering closely upon him before the touring car on which it was mounted passed on to keep abreast of the battle still raging down the valley…

'… Cut! And we will print that.'

With relief, the cavalryman sat up and loosened the tight collar of his uniform tunic. He was black and blue all over. Never much of a horseman, he wondered just how he'd managed to survive nearly a week of such unremitting carnage at three dollars a day. The title of the epic was *Slaughter*. Roscoe Summerfield felt well and truly slaughtered.

This, he supposed, was known as 'learning the business'. Even though Gertrude Fitton had money in the project, privileged treatment of her protégé was by no means part of the deal. An introduction to Granville Warwick, its creator, was as far as her personal sponsorship inclined to go.

That suited Roscoe well enough. He was no one's pet. The relationship with Gertrude, as it had developed over the past few months, was one of mutual self-help. It was also, to his amusement, a source of speculation to a widening circle of influence, both in New York and here at the raw, exciting hub of a new industry whose aspirations and potential seemed daily to outstrip its own limits.

When he first arrived in the United States, the idea of moving pictures as a significant branch of the entertainment business had been outside Roscoe's perception. They belonged in the penny arcade; they were side-shows, fairground novelties. Now, after two months on the West Coast as an 'extra', involved in a different film almost every other week, he was beginning to see the boundless scope of the new dream factories, rapidly evolving in a fast-growing suburb of Los Angeles called Hollywood.

The afternoon's shooting was over. It was the final day's work on this film, as well. Hot, dusty and bruised, an assorted mixture of US Cavalry, half-naked Indians and half-scalped civilians made their way toward the coaches waiting to take them back to base. Before getting on board they filed in a ragged line past where the unit manager sat behind a trestle table, to collect the day's pay.

The touring car was parked nearby. The cameraman's assistant was packing the camera away in the trunk. Granville Warwick, the director, was talking to the cameraman, his gaze casually skimming the queue.

Roscoe looked at the two of them, standing there like a pair of Egyptian slave-masters. Come to think of it, he'd been an Egyptian slave himself, the week before last. On the whole, he reckoned he'd had enough.

This is a mug's game, he decided, this weary shuffle at the end of a fourteen-hour assault-course to pick up twelve bob. I'll go back to New York. Try my luck as a proper actor. I've done my stint as beefcake on the hoof.

As he signed for his pay-packet, he realized he was the object of their discussion. He found himself tacitly invited to join them. He went over, antennae alert.

Granville Warwick shook his hand. 'Mr Summerfield, sir? Am I right?' He had the manner of an old-style Southern gentleman.

'Quite right, sir.'

Roscoe was given to understand that he would be required in New York in due course for some studio inserts. 'That dying sequence just now. It was a sight too good a moment to waste. I've a mind to back it with new plot to point it up some. You're free, I hope? My office will be in touch when we get back east.'

A sullen February light seeped through the heavily leaded windows of the headmistress's parlour at the Pembury Residential Establishment for Girls, where the Countess of Heatherley faced Miss Selina Frinton across the headmistress's desk.

As far as Miss Frinton was aware, she was receiving 'Mrs de la Haye', an impression which Ivy had no intention of updating. Answering to the name again made her feel quite nostalgic. Ivy and Florence Dibbins had appeared on the music halls as 'The de la Haye Sisters' when they first left home at fourteen.

We could shake our bustles at that Marie Lloyd, an' all, Ivy recalled silently, smiling graciously at Miss Frinton the while. Till we went our separate ways and lost touch. I wonder what Flo's up to these days...

With an effort, she jerked her mind back to the job in hand. This interview was likely to be an awkward one unless she stayed in complete control of it.

Divorce proceedings were under way; it was an uncontested suit. No money was involved because Hereward had none. In a few months time, Ivy would be free to marry again. Provided, of course, no awkward questions were raised about a daughter of sixteen at school in Kent.

There was no reason why they should be, but Ivy was taking no chances. Marriage, she had decided, was to be her future from now on. With her title, her looks and a flexibility of image cultivated over twenty years, she felt equipped to achieve a nicely profitable one. As long as the problem of Little Joyce was handled with utmost discretion.

So far, it had been. Miss Frinton had no idea that Ivy was the girl's mother. She knew 'Mrs de la Haye' merely as the philanthropic guardian whose munificence had funded Joyce's upbringing. Joyce herself was no wiser.

The situation this afternoon was intricate. Ivy wished to discuss with Miss Frinton the possibility of a post for Joyce as a nursery governess. Or even, perhaps, an agreement to stay on here as a junior teacher in return for her keep. Fees were a burden Ivy now felt it timely to shed. Such funds as she had were about to be called upon in respect of her own survival.

Miss Frinton, on the other hand, wished to discuss the matter of her pupil's behaviour. Little Joyce, it seemed, was a handful. Her influence on the other girls was not in line with the aims of this institution, not at all. There had been the business of the gardener's boy, resulting in the wretched youth's dismissal. Subsequently, there had been the business of the gardener. Twenty-seven but a little simple, the poor man had become upsettingly infatuated. His wife, understandably put out, had stormed into this very room with demands for 'that wicked young doxy' to be kept out of reach. Despite all Miss Frinton's efforts at charitable diplomacy, Little Joyce emerged as a fledgling strumpet of marked dedication.

Considering Little Joyce's father and herself, Ivy was less than surprised. Motherhood had never figured in her agenda. Faced with it, her instinct had been to get it over with as quickly as possible and resume her materially rewarding career. Though family ties meant nothing to her, she yet chose expensive foster care and residential education rather than adoption. It had seemed the kindest solution for them both. Until now.

Well, it'd caught up with her now, hadn't it?

'Can you tell me, Miss Frinton,' she said carefully, 'which subjects in her school work my ward prefers? In which – er – direction her abilities appear to lead?'

Miss Frinton sighed with a suggestion of frost. She would have thought that was fairly clear by now. In a final, weary attempt at fair play, she admitted that Joyce showed a definite talent in the performing field. 'Not something we encourage here. We prepare our girls for lives of service.' With masterly forbearance, she omitted to add that Joyce was at present under corrective discipline for having slipped out undetected on a succession of Saturday nights to sing at a public house in Tunbridge Wells.

'It might be an idea for us to meet. I wonder if you'd be kind enough to send for her?' Ivy could see no easy alternative.

At the sight of her daughter, she barely suppressed a gasp. Small, dainty, curvaceously pretty; golden curls, dimples, tip-tilted nose and rosebud mouth, Little Joyce duplicated Ivy's earliest memory of her own mother; almost. Except for the limpid gleam of the huge blue eyes. In Lily Dibbins's face, they would have held bewildered panic. There was no resemblance to Ivy herself. The dark allure of the de la

Haye sisters derived entirely from a forgotten lion-tamer.

As Joyce bobbed her curtsies and answered questions with due meekness, Ivy reached an accurate and bothersome conclusion:

The child was pure natural crumpet. Without another idea in her head. To place this smouldering bundle in some worthy household as a nanny and expect it to subside would be to invite mayhem. Clearly, the nettle would have to be grasped and rendered self-supporting.

Ivy's own immediate plans entailed crossing the Atlantic with a recent and ardent admirer; a French merchant banker of diverse interests, some of which were in New York. To do with the film business, if Ivy was not mistaken. She had already agreed to accompany him on the *Olympic* when the summons from Miss Frinton arrived. Now, she realized that Franz-Clovis de Lavalle-Fontaine's reputation as a ladies' man might be turned to distinct advantage.

America, Ivy felt confident, would prove more responsive to the impact of Lady Heatherley than London or Europe. With lightning clarity, it occurred to her that America might also offer plenty of scope for Lady Heatherley's talented young protégée to make her professional debut and plenty of space for her to consolidate it at a suitable distance.

To Joyce Dibbins, Mrs de la Haye was no more than a shadowy but accepted fact of her life; the faceless name responsible for her education and upbringing. At school, she was by no means an exception; most of the girls there were funded by absentee benefactors. Her basic disposition was placid, almost bovine. Her main goal so far, despite all obstacles, had been to achieve and revel in the attentions she seemed to attract from men of every age and kind. It was easy. It made her feel nice.

Suddenly to be sitting in a hired Daimler on the way to an unknown, brightly beckoning future after the thick fog of pious disapproval and perpetual censure was a heady turn of events indeed. The vastly elegant lady opposite seemed friendly enough, if disinclined to converse. That was all right. Joyce was quite content to look out of the window and take things as they came.

For Ivy, conversation was not a priority. She felt no pressing need to acknowledge any relationship to this unruly young person. At least, certainly not yet. The opening of a few doors as a matter of mutual interest was, at present, the extent of her resolve. Whether or not some latent bond would develop remained to be seen. Somehow, Ivy doubted it.

There was plenty to look at as they drove through the south-eastern regions of London. The sheer volume of activity! Trams and taxicabs, street vendors, shops, markets, people in a hurry. Joyce had never seen so much life on the move all at the same time before.

In Camberwell, a tyre blew. They got out to stretch their legs while the chauffeur changed it. A tall, reddish building, implacably grim even for this part of London, glowered at them across the street, a board attached to the iron railings in front proclaiming: South Camberwell Hospital for Women.

'Enough to put you off being one, isn't it?' Joyce remarked.

Ivy was regarding it with an indefinable expression. 'It's where you were born,' she said.

Joyce looked at her curiously. 'Did Miss Frinton tell you?'

'Come along, he's finished the wheel.'

April

With the mounting popularity of the films, a star system like that of the theatre was developing. Certain players were becoming familiar, certain faces were drawing bigger audiences. The new medium was giving rise to new celebrities. Within the past year or so, even established stage-artists were being tempted to the screen. The power of the studios was beginning to stir. Film companies in competition with each other were signing up actors for exclusive promotion, vying for public favour.

The plot of *Slaughter*, as far as Roscoe had been able to make out, concerned a family of settlers caught up in a battle between Indians and Cavalry. The colonel was in love with the settler's daughter, who was held hostage by the Sioux Chief's son. After an action-packed and bloody skirmish, the colonel and the settler's daughter were the only two left alive. Fade out.

On his return to New York, Roscoe was duly contacted by the front office of Polyscope Films. It appeared that the settler's daughter had now acquired a younger sister, whose heart belonged to a simple cavalryman. Seeing her lover fall, she would hurl herself, shrieking, upon his lifeless corpse, only to be finished off with an arrow in the back. This sequence, as well as other, tender scenes before the battle, were to be added in close-up at the studios in the Bronx.

Roscoe was offered a contract for *Slaughter* as a featured player, with a three-year option depending on how he made out.

'You must have made out pretty good,' Gertrude remarked.

'I died. That's all, on the whole,' Roscoe replied with modesty. 'Perhaps I died rather well.'

'And played around, I guess. Who with? The leading lady?'

He bristled virtuously. 'Certainly not!' The girl playing the part of the settler's daughter had been spoken for by the cavalry colonel. As a lowly extra, Roscoe had been in no position to make any headway. Disinclined to involve himself with rank and file, his behaviour had in fact been exemplary.

Gertrude grinned philosophically. 'You will now,' she said. 'Play around. Sure to. That's okay. Just so long as you don't rag yourself out. We have an understanding, remember? Now pour me a Scotch.'

The additional scenes were a definite asset to the finished product. Polyscope took up the option. Roscoe's career looked like blossoming very satisfactorily indeed.

So, it seemed, did that of the new discovery who had been cast as the younger sister. An English girl of tender years and angelic appearance, she was signed up for three more titles in quick succession, yet to be written. In all of them she would be cast opposite 'Roscoe Somerville', as the studio wished to call him.

Roscoe objected to none of it. They could call him anything they liked. It was spring in New York and life was wonderful.

They were marketing his co-star simply as 'Little Joyce'.

'It will be spring in London soon,' Amaryllis observed, 'I ought to think about opening up the house.'

'Don't let me stop you,' Emily replied.

'Is that supposed to imply that I should leave you here?'

'I was here for over three months before you arrived.'

'That was different. You were chaperoned.'

'Poor Awful a chaperone? I had to be got out of the way.'

'As far as London knows, you were continuing your studies.'

'That's one way of putting it. What had you in mind now?'

The truth was, Amaryllis was getting restless; feeling the pull of London life and her own congenial place in it. She was also finding the relentless presence of an ebullient baby more and more tiresome. The truth was, she wanted to go home.

All things considered, she had wintered pleasantly enough in Monte Carlo. After Redvers Grinling's unsettling death and the departure of Teddy however, the Riviera Palace Hotel was perhaps a touch excessive. An apartment in the town seemed altogether more suitable. Amaryllis and Emily, with the addition of Hugo and a nursemaid, blended harmoniously into English Riviera living.

Canny and moderate at the casino, Amaryllis used her winnings to play the bourse as she did the English stock market, continuing to turn a natural penchant for gambling into a profitable occupation.

Emily, having absorbed more than she might care to admit from her mother's undoubted proficiency, began to do the same. Severally, neither of the Kilverston ladies was in foreseeable danger of suffering from material deprivation. Together, they existed in a state of armed truce.

'You're my daughter. You're still only eighteen. There's a season to be thought of.'

In Amaryllis's view, this was a pronouncement of extreme benevolence after Emily's unseemly conduct. Also, on reflection, she was beginning to enjoy the image of herself as a gracious lady presenting her chick to the fashionable world. Having shot her little bolt, she smiled with uncertain chumminess.

Emily stared at her in blank astonishment for a moment before hooting with incredulous mirth. 'And are you planning to deck Hugo out in Prince of Wales feathers as well as me?' she enquired. 'I'm sure he'll be the dish of the day at fork luncheons!'

Amaryllis looked uncomfortable. 'Actually, poppet, I wasn't thinking of taking Hugo.'

'I beg your pardon?' Emily's tone held warning.

'I've given it a great deal of thought,' Amaryllis ploughed straight on without meeting her eye. 'And I've come to the conclusion that you've been through a very difficult time, very bravely. Now, it's over. Even the poor dear Grinlings are out of the way. No one need ever suspect. I thought perhaps … well, you know – adoption?'

Emily hit the roof. The tirade that broke and continued, remorseless and unabated, until its subject matter was thoroughly exhausted several times over, reduced Amaryllis to a sobbing, shaking wreck, huddled in the corner of the sofa. Emily turned on her heel and left the room.

Five minutes later, she re-appeared with a cup of tea. She set it down on a small table beside her mother. Then she seated herself opposite and waited.

Eventually, a fragile hand emerged and weakly lifted the cup. 'Did you put any gin in this?'

'Yes, I did.'

After a few restorative sips, Amaryllis felt strong enough to salvage her shredded character. 'How could you say those things to me?' she whispered brokenly. 'How *could* you! I'm your *mother*!'

'And I'm Hugo's. And don't you forget it.'

Emily had never had the slightest intention of returning to Fitzjohn's Avenue, with or without her son. Everything had just been made a good deal easier for her. Thanks to groundwork by Lily Dibbins, she was already established here as a young widow by the time Amaryllis arrived. As to chaperonage now, there was the Comtesse de Lavalle-Fontaine.

An eccentric lady of wealth, imposing both in years and demeanour, the Comtesse had been a member of the entranced audience on the occasion of Hugo's birth. It was she who, when Amaryllis threatened to steal Emily's thunder by fainting and knocking down one of the screens, slapped her awake and told her not to be idiotic. The Comtesse had taken to Emily strongly, adored Hugo, thought Amaryllis a fool of a woman and put her way out of her depth with a kind of vague courtesy just short of insult. Amaryllis responded with wary dislike, but could hardly object to her daughter being taken under so highly placed a wing.

July

Slaughter was released to immense acclaim, playing to huge audiences in 'legitimate' theatres the length and breadth of the country. New movie theatres, too, were springing up everywhere. The film industry was taking hold.

The management of Polyscope had already foreseen the combination of Roscoe Somerville and Little Joyce as a box-office sensation. By the end of June, there were three new titles ready to meet public demand when it arose.

Little Joyce's face was a gift to the camera, as was Roscoe Somerville's. Granville Warwick's innovative genius with new angles and lighting in the advancement of visual dramatic effect excelled itself, particularly when it came to close-up. It was just as well, since the third storyline had to be shot almost entirely in close-up, due to the fact that Little Joyce was pregnant.

'So whaddya have to give to that doll-faced liddle broad you ain't got to give to me?!' Gertrude raged. She was on whisky sours and getting coarser with every one. Athletic, too. She had already hurled three Waterford decanters and a Ming vase across the patio.

The bricks and mortar of the Fitton residence at Remsenburg, Long Island had better watch out, Roscoe reflected wearily, ducking yet again as a tree of fire-irons skimmed past his ear. The act of flinging it had thrown her off balance and sent her reeling into a couch. He shot forward and clamped her there in a half-nelson. It was the only remedy when she got this way, which she tended to, from time to time. He did his best, he honestly did. Was it his fault if she was so damn tense she didn't give herself a chance?

'You're hurting me, you creep!' she hissed thickly.

'I'll let you go if you promise to stop murdering me.'

'Okay.' The fight was out of her. She just looked sad and sloshed. He put a cushion behind her head, lifted her feet and pulled off her shoes.

'You want out?' she mumbled.

He perched beside her and took her hand. 'Don't be a stupid lady and listen. Little Joyce is pregnant, true. Little Joyce is *very* pregnant. I gather the baby is expected in early October. It is now July. I have been working with Little Joyce for less than three months.'

He sat back and waited for it to sink in. Of course he'd laid Little Joyce. So had most of the unit. Her forthcoming production, however, owed its origins to a Kentish garden boy, a Kentish gardener, or any of the regulars at the Ploughman's Firkin in Tunbridge Wells.

Be that as it might, Roscoe was first choice amongst opinion in general and the Polyscope press office in particular.

'The tiresome thing is,' he went on, when he judged Gertrude ready for it, 'the studio wants to marry us off.'

Gertrude stared stupidly. 'You and me?'

'Me and Little Joyce. In the Fall. The idea is to get the baby adopted at birth, then run a big romance for publicity. I was trying to explain but you wouldn't listen.'

She giggled. It grew and turned into a belly laugh.

He joined in with almost hysterical relief. Gertrude could always be relied on to see the funny side of anything.

'You want that?' she cackled. 'As a career move?'

'I'd rather die.'

'Maybe you should,' she nodded. 'Maybe you should go back home and join the army. They reckon on having a war in Europe before too long.'

October

Little Joyce registered the baby as 'Edith Dibbins'.

Discharging herself from hospital a day early, she took a taxi to the Park Avenue apartment of the former benefactress she now knew as the Countess of Heatherley. Contact had dropped away entirely since fame and fortune claimed her.

This evening was a triumph for the wayfarer who had begun as Ivy Dibbins. The gathering in her drawing-room set the very air humming with fashion and money. And all of them here to help her celebrate her engagement to Franz-Clovis de Lavalle-Fontaine.

'Fitz', as he liked her to call him. Standing at his side, Ivy fingered the unique gold-link bracelet he had given her. Set round her wrist with no clasp; never to be removed.

Silently, she toasted the de la Haye Sisters across all the long, hard years. She was almost tempted to break into '*Don't Peep Under My Pinny Sir Please!*' with soft-shoe.

When the butler announced the arrival of Little Joyce, the atmosphere became positively electric. To the guests, it was the cherry on an already fascinating cake. Little Joyce had more impact at present than Pearl White, Lilian Gish and Mary Pickford rolled into one. Her actual entrance caused even more of a stir as she stepped into their midst, tiny and ethereally fragile, with a lace-wrapped bundle clasped in her arms.

After presenting her daughter of three weeks, Little Joyce withdrew to the library on the pretext of 'feeding time'. Ivy followed as quickly as she could in search of an explanation.

There was no sign of Little Joyce.

Little Edith was still there, a warmed bottle tucked into her shawl, preparing to let it be known that she was hungry. According to the Hall Porter, the lady had left by motor car not five minutes back. With Franz-Clovis de Lavalle-Fontaine at the wheel.

Chapter Ten
1916

Monte Carlo

The Comtesse de Lavalle-Fontaine poured herself a pink gin as an aid to rolling bandages. It was very pleasant here on her terrace, looking out from the hillside clean over Monte Carlo to the sea. As she sipped and rolled, she reflected that fate was indeed smiling more than kindly on a lady of seventy-six. At an age when many of her contemporaries were in care, incapacitated or dead, Magda de Lavalle-Fontaine revelled in a personal renaissance with the distinct advantage that her public image, arresting enough on its own, was now reinforced with the warm glow of heroism.

She had brought her beautiful villa into combat duty as an unofficial convalescent home for officers, a therapeutic staging post between the crudities of field hospitals and either return to the firing line or medical discharge. Surrounded by charming young men with impeccable manners – French, British, Austrian, German – Magda was a law unto herself concerning the conduct of this war.

Austrian by birth, widow of a French aristocrat, she had the space, the money and the wish to be part of the action. She was not disposed to discriminate between nationals, provided they were persons of civilized bearing. She ran a unique operation. Each of her guests responded to both the ambience and their hostess by recovering up to and sometimes beyond the extent of whatever limits their injuries might have prescribed.

Brilliant red hair piled high, dressed for preference in the style of

1880, which she had always felt became her best, Madame la Comtesse presided over her extraordinary oasis of cultivated truce with immense enjoyment.

A piercing shriek of '*Tante Mag! Regarde-moi*, *Tante Mag!*' interrupted her daydreaming. A small boy hurtled out of an open glass door on a yellow tricycle. Hugo Kilverston, quite big for four, had come for his cocktail lesson.

'Stop him, Magda, before he goes over the parapet, would you?' Emily called, following just out of reach. Magda caught the back of the saddle. Hugo squealed and wriggled off. He handed her a rose which had narrowly survived the ride.

'Maman says for you. From Hugo.'

'Good boy!' Emily beamed approval at her son. At twenty-one she was an undoubted knock-out. She and Hugo were enduring this war very agreeably. Her arguments against a return to Fitzjohn's Avenue three years ago had prevailed with her mother most effectively, one way and another…

… To Amaryllis, the surplus baggage of an unscheduled infant had been out of the question. All things considered, it was a definite relief to get her inexpedient daughter and her even more inexpedient grandson off her hands. There was certain *cachet*, too, in having an address on the Riviera as a modish retreat.

She had found it pleasant to visit for the Christmas of 1913 and return to London life the following April. When August signalled restriction of movement and Emily elected to stay in Monaco, which was to preserve a measure of neutrality, Amaryllis breathed another sigh of relief and regaled her London circle of acquaintance with half-truths about her daughter's war work in France. It suited them both very well…

… Hugo was displaying decided aptitude as a barman. Fortified by a *citron pressé* of his own in a long glass with a straw, he was totally absorbed in helping Magda prepare the trolley to be wheeled through the *salon*. Olives black and green, cherries, lacy thin slices of orange and lemon in glass dishes, twists of peel, all arranged with earnest care as an artistic setting for the ice-bucket, massed bottles and gleaming shakers.

'One for Manhattans,' Hugo counted them off, 'one for Sidecars, one for Martinis, one for White Ladies. Makes four!'

Magda applauded. '*Bravo, mon p'tit!* A gentleman is never too young to learn.'

When the display of hospitality met with his approval, the three of them formed up and the Sundowner Cavalcade advanced.

There were some new faces this evening. One in particular struck Emily with the oddest sense of *déja vu*, although she was certain they had never met. The man was older by far than most of the others; forty-five at least, maybe more. Tall, painfully thin and pale, with dark rings round his eyes and a sporadic, dry cough, he lay full length on a garden recliner.

Emily was some distance away when she spotted him. Laughing and flirting, mixing the drinks, she racked her brains. Who *did* he remind her of…?

Magda caught her questioning eye. 'He's dying without help from any war, that one,' she said, 'but he would go and carry stretchers. It's Heatherley.'

Emily realized then. He was so like Kate.

He had no idea who Emily was, of course. At Hugo's orders, he chose a Sidecar and was suitably impressed with the expertise that went into its mixing. Magda swept by and took Hugo and the trolley away. Emily sat down and asked, 'Do you know Teddy Grinling, by any chance?'

Hereward was able to tell her that he and Teddy had both been blasted by the same shell. 'No idea he was any relation till afterwards,' he said. 'There he was in no-mans-land, lying about. There I was with my stretcher. Then boom, what?'

'Was he badly hurt?'

'It depends what you mean, dear. He shot himself in the foot.'

Ridiculous though it sounded, it seemed that Corporal E. Grinling had tripped in a rut whilst obeying the order to advance with rifle cocked. His rifle discharged itself as he fell, immobilizing him as target practise for snipers.

'I saw it happen, y'see,' Hereward explained. 'He wasn't far from the trench. So we nipped out to retrieve him. Then this bloody great whizzbang comes at us and knocks us silly. Finished off my other stretcher-bearer, I'm afraid. But I managed to drag young Teddy in. He'll be fine.'

'He's not here, is he?' Emily asked doubtfully. Teddy's modest rank made it unlikely, but one never knew.

Hereward grinned. 'He might well have been. In fact, I suggested it. But he preferred the idea of Blighty with his nurse. Rather taken with his nurse, you might say. Obstinate little beggar.'

Emily agreed. It was good to know Teddy was all right. It was good to know he had a nice nurse.

The following day, when Emily and Hugo arrived for cocktail duty, Magda told her that Hereward had died that morning. 'He wasn't inclined to wake up, you know? They call it pneumonia, but between us, my dear, I think he was just played out. He was at the mercy of any passing germ at all. There was no resistance, you see.'

'Didn't I hear somewhere that he was married?'

Magda lifted an eyebrow. 'I do believe, for reasons of his own . . . . Some truly dreadful person. It was of no consequence.'

In response to Emily's interest, however, she was delighted to expand upon the general ghastliness of Ivy Heatherley. 'Goodness knows where she came from, or what she was called. "Courtesan" by some, no doubt. By me – "Trollop"! Rubbish, *cherie* Trash! Left poor Heatherley, of course, as soon as he was ruined. And then, would you believe, my dear, took up with my own son!'

Emily was agog. 'You never mentioned you had a son!'

'He's unmentionable, *liebchen*!' To Emily's delight, Magda was now in full spate and not to be stopped. 'I've told him so for years. His poor little wife had to die to get away from him. I believe that unspeakable creature of Heatherley's even considered herself engaged to him, before the war. Nothing came of *that*, of course. He ran off with a film star. He is *tout-à-fait* disgusting, Franz-Clovis!'

To Emily, this was far, far better than all the raciest novels from the English library put together. 'Where is your son now?' she asked with acute interest.

Magda shrugged. 'Who knows? Berlin? London? Paris? And who with? Ach, he was always a womanizer, that one. It used to be the films, but now of course it's armaments, *n'est-ce-pas?*'

'Er ... for which side?' Knowing Magda's intriguing lineage, Emily felt it was a pertinent question.

Her friend seemed a little surprised at her naivete. 'Why, for all the sides, *ma p'tite*,' she replied with some amusement. 'Franz-Clovis will be making far too much money from this war, I promise you!'

And Teddy Grinling, thought Emily, is the Earl of Heatherley. Jolly good luck to him, too!

London

26 Claverton Street, Pimlico, the last remaining bastion of the Heatherleys, stood no bloodier, on the whole, than its stately companions and certainly no less unbowed.

Return in the autumn of 1912, to a future for which their combined life-experience had done little to prepare them, was a drastic plunge indeed for the Grinling family. They survived it with considerable ingenuity.

The house was put to work. The onslaught by the council at the demise of the old Countess, whose obstinacy had begotten a five-storey health hazard, left a hygienic shell bereft of all hangings and upholstery, but with plumbing, wiring and a quantity of indestructible and priceless furniture intact.

Priscilla Grinling began by renting it out room by room for tuition. Sewing classes, shorthand and typewriting, trainee upholsterers were the first priority. She advertised for teachers in need of premises and found no shortage of takers. The huge kitchen, with its ranges and equipment designed for hosting banquets, was taken over by a college for apprentice chefs.

After a year, the house was re-supplied with soft furnishings, Kate had secretarial skills and the food was a source of unfailing interest.

Teddy got a job with a racehorse trainer. From earliest childhood, he had found complete satisfaction helping out in the stables at Heatherley. Anything to do with horses delighted him, but the racing world in general and jockeys in particular seemed to him the epitome of glamour.

He had always assumed that his future would involve a commission in a cavalry regiment and that was fine. It was just that he would rather have been a professional jockey, had it been possible. He had the build, the weight and the talent.

By the summer of 1914, E. Grinling was a newcomer worth watching.

August that year brought far-reaching changes. In the course of things, tenancy of the kitchens passed to the catering corps; Priscilla Grinling became landlady to a succession of officers in London for short periods; Kate took a typing job in Whitehall. E. Grinling joined the 7th London Regiment as a private soldier.

Priscilla and Kate, with Bunty – very vigorous for four – stood at the open front door scanning the street, waiting to welcome Teddy home. On being told he was a casualty at Ypres, their relief had been boundless. For over two years, he had somehow avoided getting killed. Now, he was coming back for good. He had written from hospital in France to say that he would be arriving in the charge of his nurse.

Taxis kept on going past. Eventually, the right one appeared and drew up. Looking fairly normal, except for one unwieldy leg, Teddy was helped out by an attractive girl with dark hair and brown eyes.

After the acceptably joyous display of pecking his mother and sister on the cheek and flinging his niece round by the heels, he presented his companion.

'I'd like you all to meet Wendy,' he said, 'my wife.'

With the inbred habit of never showing the smallest tinge from the spectrum of human feeling, Lady Priscilla cordially shook hands with her new daughter-in-law, studying her closely the while. She saw a capable young woman with little nonsense about her and thought: I shall find her a frightful bore. Still, they may not be here for long...

Wendy looked back equably. She was already pregnant. That was why she had been able to accompany Teddy. The war was over for both of them.

'I wonder if you'll be able to get up the stairs to the top floor?' Kate cast a doubtful glance at his foot. 'That's where we all sleep, you see.'

'I did rather hope you'd be fit enough to manage it,' his mother said, 'The thing is, there's a Mr Jennings coming this afternoon to look at the first floor front. He works at the Army & Navy Stores. He might turn out to be a long-term tenant.'

Teddy managed it.

The following spring, Maudie Grinling was born.

1918

Monte Carlo

'Now, my Hugo, *wunderbar* it will be! The films, they will come from America! The film stars, too! The war is over and we shall have lots and lots of swops!'

The Comtesse de Lavalle-Fontaine and her six-year-old friend were pursuing an important hobby: namely, their growing collection of glossy postcards depicting idols of the silver screen. Supplies from Hollywood had been at a premium for a long time now, almost black market commodities. An avid film fan, Magda tried not to cheat. But Hugo made it difficult because he valued his well-connected source and egged her on shamelessly.

'I'll give you Lew Cody for Little Joyce,' he offered, knowing what she held in her hand.

'Done!' the swap was made. She crowed with triumph. 'Who wants Little Joyce? Flash in the pan, *ça*!'

'What's a flash in the pan?'

'Something gone quick, *poof*! before it starts.'

'Little Joyce is *très jolie*.'

'But gone *poof*! She hasn't been heard of for years.'

'I still think she's pretty. Would you like Bobby Harron for Roscoe Somerville?'

'No. I keep Roscoe Somerville.'

Emily came out to the terrace just in time to hear. 'What was that?'

'The heart-throb of all time, my dear!' Magda informed her. 'But you think the movies are only for shop girls, you snob, you. And so you wouldn't care.'

'Show me.'

Magda passed her the hand-tinted photograph.

The ground beneath Emily's feet suddenly seemed unsteady as she beheld Roscoe, grinning toothily up at her from a shiny piece of card.

1919

England

Prospects of one day riding a Derby winner were no longer an option for ex-Corporal Teddy Grinling, Earl of Heatherley, thanks to his marksmanship at Ypres. Acutely aware that he was lucky to be alive at all, he settled for the next best thing, took his wife and baby daughter back to his ex-ancestral home and went into business with Barkworth, the Head Groom, as a racehorse trainer.

He also decided against using the title. Since the castle now belonged to a Girls' school, much of the land to property developers and the contents of the zoo to Whipsnade, there was precious little to justify it. Nevertheless, word of the partnership filtering through the racing world was no hindrance.

The Heatherley Stable was set to flourish. Joshua Barkworth, Head Lad, along with Ed Heatherley could face the future with optimism.

In London, the epidemic of Spanish 'flu swept through 26 Claverton Street. Bunty picked it up from school; Kate from the typing pool at the Home Office. Three of the eight paying guests succumbed. Lady Priscilla and Mr Jennings – now a fixture in the first-floor front – each convinced of certain doom in view of their constitutional frailties, found themselves nursing most of the household and emerging totally unscathed.

Kate was the only one there who died.

Table of Kindling in Proximity

A Box Full of Beans

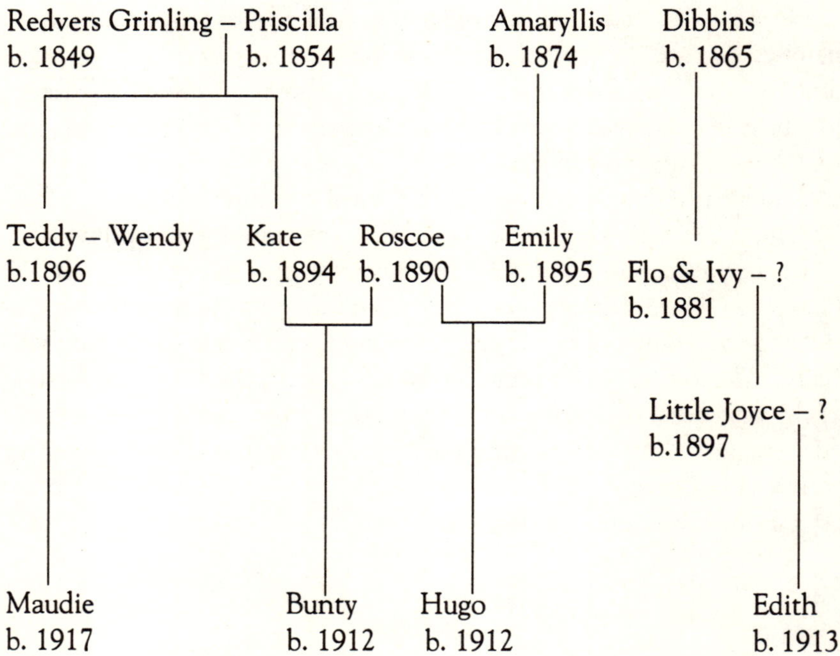

Jumping About

1921–1934

Chapter Eleven
1921

New York

Tilly Krantz was a lucky girl. She liked to think of herself as smart, but 'lucky' was nearer the mark.

In 1893, ten years before she was born, her Uncle Siggy Lubin – Momma's big brother – had arrived in America from Hamburg, aged twenty, with the clothes he stood up in and a pair of tailor's shears. Being a first-class cutter, he was not long in gaining a foothold, whence he developed latent entrepreneurial talents. Soon, he was able to send for his mother and sister, thus firmly re-settling the family in the New World. Within five years, he had an American wife, two American children and several clothing stores. He married off his dull little sister to Nathan Krantz, his area manager, and looked round for new horizons.

By this time, he was bored with the rag trade. He sensed vast potential in the 'flickers' that drew crowds to the penny arcades. He toyed with the idea of buying a theatre for the sole purpose of showing moving pictures, but dropped it in favour of actually making them.

He put Nathan Krantz in charge of the tailoring businesses and himself embarked on a new career as a film producer. In 1910, with some like-minded friends, he set up a company which he called Polyscope.

Nathan was quite without his brother-in-law's vision. He and his unremarkable, rather colourless wife were reasonably content in their modest Brooklyn apartment; the main nag in their placid existence was what best to do about their daughter.

Tilly was a bit of a puzzlement. For one thing, they could neither of them imagine where she could have got her looks. As she grew more and more dazzling, more and more discontented with the confines of her life at home, they both wished she were plainer and easier to manage.

As for Tilly, she thought school tedious and her parents stifling. At seventeen, she eloped with a trumpet player, who turned out to be violent when he got drunk, which was often. When he left her and went off on tour, she clung to her risky freedom, insisting that somehow, she'd make out fine on her own.

Since she had no training and no skills, she was lucky to be endowed with red-gold hair, dark-lashed green eyes, a rosebud mouth and the figure of a sylph. She was also lucky not to be pregnant. She went to the night-club where her trumpeter had played and asked for a job. She auditioned, disastrously, as a singer. They would have taken a chance on her as a showgirl, but she didn't really fancy stripping. Instead, she settled for the hat-check counter and the cigarette tray. She quite enjoyed it.

Her parents sighed a little, but if that was what she wanted, it was easier to leave her alone. At home, she had been raucous in her disdain. Life was much more peaceful without her. Her mother was even given to saying, with forlorn hope, that one never knew, she might yet find a nice respectable boy to marry.

When the night-club management entered Tilly for a beauty contest, however, Nathan got in touch with his brother-in-law. Perhaps, after all, there was a direction for that appearance of Tilly's. A direction which, it was increasingly evident, Tilly was a sight too dim-witted to achieve for herself.

Uncle Siggy Lubin, far removed from the clothing trade these days, long out of touch with the rest of the family, was unimpressed by the reported charms of an errant niece he didn't know. He grudgingly said he 'might send a scout along' to the event. When it came to the point, prodded by a residual sense of family obligation, he went himself.

The sun was setting on Park Avenue. The latest issue of *Picture Show* magazine, picked up by Gertrude Fitton on her way home from the doctor's, lay open at the page of advance publicity for Roscoe Somerville's next film, to be made in the summer.

'Some day this is!' she called, just in case he was there to answer. Her voice rolled round the apartment and came back to her in pieces.

So? Who keeps who on a leash round here? He'll pitch. He always does. Meanwhile, let's start celebrating. Scotch? Champagne? Scotch, definitely. Last fling. From now on, I'll have to watch it.

When Roscoe finally did pitch, she was still on her first. Very much weaker than usual, too, although her manner suggested otherwise. 'You've arrived, Roscoebaby! You seen this?' She brandished *Picture Show*.

He had. 'Aren't you starting a little early? If you don't give it a rest, you'll pass out before nine.'

She knew the wary note in his voice too well. It was amusing to add fuel, just for the hell of it. 'What if I do? Will you be here to see? Or will you be dining 'n' dancing your next co-star for the benefit of the goppis-camel-coroners? Gossip-column cameras?' Lay it on thick. Serve him right.

Roscoe groaned silently. Was he in for another bout of pugnacity? He spoke with care: 'It's a studio directive, old dear. It's in my contract. Is that my fault?'

Her glance slid to the open page and the dewey features of Roscoe's new leading lady. 'Sure is a looker. And see what it says underneath? "Hollywood's most eligible bachelor . . . . When *Ashes of Lavender* hits our screens, shall we detect romance at last?" '

Roscoe poured himself a drink. It seemed practical. 'I've asked you to marry me more than once. If you were my wife, it would be different.'

She brayed with laughter. 'What gusset-coral-calumner wants to see a forty-year-old broad with buck teeth, round shoulders'n flat feet? Who is also pregnant?'

He almost dropped his glass. 'What?'

'That's right.'

Roscoe knocked back half his Scotch in one. His mind was spinning. He owed everything to Gertrude. From his first American suit of clothes to international celebrity. After eight years, the relationship had settled into more of a resigned habit than anything. What now?

He took a very deep breath. 'Er ... is it mine?'

'The gentlemen callers who might be lining my driveway tend to get discouraged when they reflect to themselves that all the resources of Fitton's Fitness Breakfast Bars are being poured into promoting Roscoe Somerville to world status. Whose else would it be?'

'Sorry.' He took her hand. 'Gertrude, old thing, what can I say? It's amazing news. Amazing! And here I'm supposed to be collecting some studio doll at seven-thirty!'

'Not just some studio doll. *Ashes of Lavender*.' Gertrude's finger jabbed the page.

'I'll call them. I'll cancel.' Roscoe picked up the phone.

She pulled it out of his hands. 'You'll do no such thing. You'll go. And don't bother to come back.'

He stared at her, not understanding.

'I don't need you any more, get it? And you don't need me.'

A glimmer of incredulous hope winked in the recesses of his brain. He tried to keep it out of his eyes. 'Y-you mean you don't want to get married? Not even now?'

'Hah!' Raucous and reckless, she poured herself a second, really stiff one. 'Least of all now! I got what I need, don't I? And my baby's surname will be Fitton! *Gesundheit*! Move it, sweetheart. You don't want to keep Miss Rosa Delaney waiting.'

Roscoe eyed her glass anxiously. He was still under the impression that she'd been tanking up. Now she was talking about someone he'd never even heard of. 'Who?'

'The chick you'll be making *Ashes of Lavender* with.'

'I was introduced to her as Tilly Krantz.'

'They changed it this afternoon. She's Rosa Delaney now.'

'How do you know?'

'I know everything. Oh, and you're sailing for Europe in a coupla weeks. She's going along too.'

Roscoe glanced at the clock. The studio car would be here any moment. Either Gertrude was away with the fairies or she was a good deal less drunk than he had supposed. 'What else do you know?' He'd been told nothing of this by the press office.

The press office had withheld it at Gertrude's request. Now, she reeled off the schedule: '*Aquitania* to Cherbourg, railroad to Marseilles. On to the Aga Khan's yacht, cruise along the Côte d'Azur. Juan, Cannes, Nice, Monte Carlo. Seems the French are crazy for Roscoe

Somerville. When they see him in person they'll go crazier yet. And it'll build up Tilly Kr— Rosa Delaney and *Ashes of Lavender* before she even hits the cameras.'

The prospect was gilt-edged. His last film, *Phantom of the Box* had already reached cult status in America. The Riviera, it seemed, was following suit. 'Even with the captions in Frog!' as Gertrude enthused.

For the fans, the eye-patch worn throughout by the Phantom had proved titillating to the point of hysteria. To inflame them further as to whether or not it would be shed, *Ashes of Lavender* was planned as a sequel with a new co-star.

Miss Krantz's face had the luminous magic of a Christmas rose about to open; her figure the fluid grace of a naiad; her voice the cadences of an over-excited road drill. Vocal quality was not a prerequisite for film acting. Yet.

'The babe needs to be kept mute,' Gertrude concluded.

It occurred to Roscoe that to unleash Polyscope's newest acquisition, as yet untried by camera, upon potential audiences, was bold strategy to put it mildly. He could only surmise that as it was France, the press office had settled for vision in favour of sound. Still, the lady must be dissuaded at all costs from opening her mouth in public. He would have to keep her under close personal supervision. In view of her other attributes, who was he to complain? Went with the job, what?

Gertrude watched his face as the train of thought took shape. He was so transparent. 'It'll be work, buster. Don't you forget it!'

With a start, he met her eye. 'Absolutely not,' he asserted firmly, 'absolutely! I shall treat it as a diplomatic mission!' Then he remembered there was another matter of some importance to be addressed. He fixed her with the keen, perceptive, narrowed gaze which turned knees to water in darkened movie theatres across middle America. 'But you, old bean. What about you?'

She looked back at him for a moment, then slowly raised her glass. 'I'm letting you off the hook. Hit the road, Roscoebaby. Gertrude Fitton says so long.'

Gertrude Fitton always meant exactly what she said. She had already booked him into the Algonquin Hotel. The studio cadillac had to wait while he changed and packed.

Left alone, Gertrude up-ended her untouched drink into the ice-bucket. To cry would be easy. Rather pleasant, in fact. But pointless. She laughed instead. I made a plan, she reminded herself. it came together. I'm in movies. I'm going to be a mother. And Roscoe and me, we're still friends . . . .

Monte Carlo

It was nearly nine years since Emily had last seen England. After the Armistice, her mother had resumed visits to Monaco and Emily was happy to stay there. She had a circle of delightful friends; Hugo was growing up bilingual; life was pleasant.

She could have married, could still marry, any one of a fine collection of admirers. She chose not to. From time to time she asked herself why. Her mind refused to come up with an answer.

There were pressures, of course, not least from Magda de Lavalle-Fontaine, whose pipe-dream it was to have Emily as a daughter-in-law and Hugo as a step-grandson. 'If you will only marry my wicked Franz-Clovis, *chère Emilie*, what would he need with the Mafia? How happy we all should be.'

Emily would smile and change the subject.

In spite of resisting such blandishments, she was by no means averse to the occasional elegant fling. And Franz-Clovis de Lavalle-Fontaine was, without doubt, very attractive. 'Fitz', as he liked her to call him.

If not born to the purple, then certainly to the mulled claret of the Almanach de Gotha – the irreversible decline of whose listed tribes these turbulent days bothered him not a jot – Franz-Clovis combined talents both for ruthless banditry from the founding fathers of his line and stylish intrigue from its mothers, with a bearing acquired from generations of personal magnetism. He manipulated money and people for the fun of it.

Women adored him. At their peril, they fell helplessly in thrall to him. As his own mother once remarked to Emily, his wife had to die to escape him; the truth being that childbirth proved too much for her, so debilitated was she by his robust appetites and general behaviour once the novelty of marriage palled. Their son, raised by the Austrian side of the family, was now a diplomat of promise.

For twenty years, Franz-Clovis had avoided any legalized repetition.

Excused, in his own estimation, from further dynastic requirements, he preferred the excitement of pursuit, the thrill of conquest, the exhilaration of freedom regained. Occasionally, as part of a particularly amusing pattern, he got engaged, but never with a view to permanency; and his parting settlements were far too lavish to risk anything as messy as litigation by the ladies in question.

The game could sometimes be expensive. Just before the war, for instance, an exceptionally ill-judged interlude had divested him of funds which he had to work quite hard during the next four years to recoup. Entirely his own fault, as he admitted to Emily one blissful afternoon in his apartments at Magda's villa.

Emily was positively basking in her affair with Franz-Clovis. Long intrigued by the infamy of his reputation as presented by his mother, she was enchanted to meet him when he actually arrived to spend Christmas in Monte Carlo. He was everything Magda had said and more. He was also superb in bed.

He, for his part, found Emily a challenge rarely before encountered in his long experience as an accomplished libertine. After a romantic liaison of nearly three months, her gaze was still clear of the lurking anxiety which, as soon as it appeared in the eyes of his *amoureuses* – as it invariably did sooner or later – was his signal for strategic withdrawal. An exception had been Ivy Heatherley, mistakenly believing herself in control.

But Emily was disconcertingly carefree. He even found himself wondering whether marriage to Emily Kilverston might, at this late stage in his career, be a serious consideration.

Emily wondered no such thing. She revelled in his ardour and responded to his passion with flattering enthusiasm. But nothing, for her, would ever quite eclipse a certain riotous afternoon at Hampstead in the January of 1912, which the far reaches of her memory persisted in failing to expunge.

Anyway, she had no need to be married to anyone. She also sensed instinctively that whilst Franz-Clovis relished duelling for domination with women, he had no real regard for them.

Besides, at fifty-two, he was old enough to be her father.

Most of all, she enjoyed drawing him out in conversation; delighting in stories of his amorous triumphs, wheedling from him reminiscences of a most ungentlemanly nature. Somewhat to his surprise, she appeared to find the catalogue of misdemeanour hugely entertaining.

'Tell me about Little Joyce, go on,' she coaxed. 'Wasn't she a film star?' In view of the hobby her own son shared with Franz-Clovis's mother, it would have been difficult to overlook the links between Little Joyce and Roscoe Somerville. Thereby must hang tales of potency indeed.

'Film star? Hardly. A scrap of raw material in the initial stages of manufacture.' After delivering which gem of pomposity, Franz-Clovis became unusually reticent. 'It was years ago anyway. Before the war,' he mumbled.

'Never mind that,' Emily persisted, 'she ran off with you, didn't she? I want to hear all about it.'

He was conscious of the faintest twinge, heavily diluted by time, of something akin to guilt. Little Joyce was not an episode he liked remembering. To whisk away, on a whim, a neon-lit juvenile delinquent from under the noses of the Tinsel Empire-builders of the Bronx was, for him, out of character, being an act of intentional kindness. Superficial, no doubt. Also impulsive and unpremeditated.

Brought to his attention by his *soi-disant* fiancée, the child was no more to Franz-Clovis than a business commodity, whose promotion in the field of his current financial activities had looked set to show some promising returns.

On the evening of Ivy's dreadful, contrived engagement party, he was standing immobile, glazed with ennui and distaste at the situation he had so carelessly allowed to develop, when it was suddenly enlivened by the entrance of Little Joyce with her little bundle.

Only too glad of the diversion, he himself conducted her to the library. Once there, she activated his ever-precarious susceptibilities by dissolving in piteous tears. Overcome with dismay at the prospect of motherhood, bruised and rattled by the speeding glitter of this brash new world, she announced her intention of bequeathing her daughter to the grown-ups and removing herself forthwith.

She was vulnerable, fairylike and very, very appealing. In a blinding flash, Franz-Clovis saw a way out for them all.

Once the heady mists of daring flight and new delights had cleared, he found himself in Paris, in sole charge of a daintily tinted, exquisitely moulded handful of plasticine without the brains it was born with.

This had definitely been, he realized, one of his sillier impulses.

Conciliation of Ivy cost him dear, too, in the form of a substantial income for life and a trust fund for the baby. As to Joyce, his patient attempts at eliciting any future aspirations she might have were finally rewarded by wistful memories of a son of the Kentish soil with green fingers: 'He had nice strong arms,' she said, 'I used to like watching him lift parsnips.'

A few discreet enquiries located the youth, by now an under-gardener at Hever Castle. He, it turned out, was by no means averse to Joyce, either. The broken blossom was touchingly grateful at being handed over to an expert well qualified to salvage its roots.

Capital further diminished by a handsome settlement and the purchase of a market garden business, Franz-Clovis closed the door on the entire débâcle with profound relief.

'What a sweetly pretty story,' Emily commented with a glint in her eye. 'You sound like a cross between Santa Claus and Cupid. I bet there's more to it than that.'

In the edited version, Franz-Clovis did indeed emerge as a philanthropic uncle of unimpeachable honour. Also untouched upon was the *récoupage* of his losses, which involved a shift of his commercial interests from fields of entertainment to those of conflict. Ambivalence as to which side was which rivalled his mother's; his end-products and her services offering a graphic illustration of the laws of cause and effect.

Unconcerned with any of that, Emily's curiosity was by no means satisfied. 'Was Little Joyce any relation to Lady Heatherley?' she asked, with casual interest.

He looked at her blankly. No such possibility had ever occurred to him. 'Not as far as I know. Merely a protégée. From an orphanage she took an interest in. Ivy's unsuspected charitable side, you might say.'

'I suppose you might.' Emily was thoughtful. 'What was Little Joyce's real name?'

' "Dibbins", I believe. Not noticeably distinguished.'

'Not noticeably,' Emily agreed.

AM VERY UNWELL STOP FEAR SPANISH FLU STOP CONFINED TO BED STOP HIGH FEVER STOP TRY NOT TO WORRY STOP YOUR LOVING MOTHER

As Emily read the telegram, a chill streaked through the March sunshine. The automatic jab of irritation brought on by most of her mother's pronouncements splintered into uncertainty.

The likelihood of Amaryllis succumbing, two years later, to the dreaded strain which had killed people in their hundreds just after the war was remote. But perfectly possible, of course. Emily would have to go and find out for herself.

It would mean leaving Hugo with Magda. No doubt that would delight them both, but Emily was not entirely happy about it. He would be thoroughly spoiled, but it was more than that. At eighty-two, Magda was becoming more and more eccentric. Emily was beginning to fear that her affection for Hugo bordered on the obsessive. Still, it wouldn't be for long.

Franz-Clovis offered to fly her over in his Curtiss R-6 biplane. He had to pretend not to be vexed at her polite refusal.

Tempting though it was, she felt a natural reluctance to risk her neck so far off the ground in such a little machine for such a long way. Hugo was, she said, on the young side to be left motherless. But the main, undisclosed reason was a strong disinclination to put herself under any obligation to anyone ever, no matter who.

'Anyway, you wouldn't get on with my mother,' she told him.

'Don't you be too sure,' he countered, half serious. He found Emily's independence of spirit inappropriate at times. 'She might be more *sympathique* than you. *Belle dame sans merci, toi!*'

With disarming honesty, Emily agreed it was very likely.

He gave her a charming present: a gold-link bracelet of most unusual design, engraved with his name and the date. He wanted to have it fitted round her wrist without a clasp.

To Emily, that smacked a little too much of being shackled. She thanked him prettily; and travelled by wagon-lit and ferry.

Unaccustomed to brush-offs, however friendly, Franz-Clovis packed up his troubles in his calfhide grip and flew himself to Croydon.

Chapter Twelve

April

London

Roscoe was battling through what he had hoped was going to be a well-earned holiday. Management had agreed his request to sail to Southampton instead of Cherbourg, a week earlier than scheduled. Management had also reiterated the clause in his contract which required Rosa Delaney to be with him at all times in public. Polyscope was not prepared to let its lately acquired filly loose, supervised only by studio officials little better versed in the ways of Europe than she was.

Confidence in Roscoe Somerville's native diplomatic skills had not so far been misplaced; neither had his holiday so far materialized. Conducting Rosa round London was like being in charge of a Bisto Kid at a state banquet, voraciously hungry and baffled by the menu. She had marvelled ear-splittingly at the Tower, pitying the warders for their enforced diet of beef; imagined Nelson's Column to be the gossip page in *The London Times*; was enchanted to discover, when ushered into what she referred to as 'Fort Numbs', that it was not some Ancient British prototype for Fort Knox.

She was meltingly lovely, Roscoe had to admit, except for the appalling voice which he never minded reducing to a sated, breathless sigh, although there were limits as to where this could be achieved. It was not her fault she was plumb ignorant. Hadn't she been signed up after winning a 'Miss Hat-Check' contest in Brooklyn, or some such? The boys from Polyscope's press office who accompanied them on the *Mauretania* had gone on to France. After five unrelieved days of Rosa

Delaney, due to that damn clause, Roscoe felt in definite need of a spot of recuperation.

In a calculated bid for some respite, he took her on the town. Discarding the protective beard and glasses, now essential to unhindered movement in public places, Roscoe Somerville had no difficulty entering a succession of the most fashionable venues in the West End.

The evening began sedately with cocktails in the Savoy bar, followed by dinner at the Café de Paris, where heads turned as Rosa shimmied down the double staircase to the dance floor; turned again when Roscoe Somerville and his dazzling companion took their seats in the orchestra stalls at the Pavilion Theatre for the current C.B. Cochran Revue.

After supper at Romano's, they went night-clubbing – the newest, most piquant activity of Mayfair's gilded youth. Impudent baby phoenixes rising from a burnt-out wartime Defence of the Realm Act for the regulation of drinking hours, these exclusive, smoke-filled cellars with chic decor and dim-lit, miniscule dance floors were *the* places between midnight and 5 a.m. To be caught in one during a police raid was the smartest thing that could possibly happen, but Roscoe and Rosa were out of luck there. Both the 'Kit-Cat Club' and Kate Meyrick's recently opened '43' in Gerrard Street had been descended upon the week before.

'The Embassy' in Bond Street, however, offered diamond-studded compensation. Rosa's ongoing query, 'When do I get to see the King?' was as good as answered with the arrival of a party which included Freda Dudley Ward, the just-married Mountbattens, and the Prince of Wales, who admitted to having much enjoyed *The Phantom of the Box*.

Awash with enough champagne to float the Cowes Regatta, Rosa was eventually decanted into her bed at the Savoy Hotel about 6.30 next morning. Roscoe retreated thankfully to his own, via the communicating door, which he locked with firmness and relief.

Looking very good for fifty-one, Amaryllis lay on a chaise-longue in her drawing-room at Fitzjohn's Avenue, clad in polka-dotted georgette pyjamas and feeling sorry for herself. It would serve Emily right if I *had* got Spanish 'flu, she thought. There's still a lot of it about. Well, perhaps not Spanish, with people dropping like ninepins ... those poor Grinlings, so badly hit in 1919, too tragic.

In her weakened state, Amaryllis felt quite affected at the notion of Lady Priscilla battling alone to run that rooming house (or whatever it was) and bring up a granddaughter into the bargain. She dabbed her eyes and took a sip of revitalizing port. It's all very well, she told herself, to feel deeply for others, but I mustn't get upset and have a set-back. Not with Emily waiting to take me to Monte Carlo as soon as I'm fit to travel. It's too bad of Emily to go out and leave me on my own all day. It would serve her right to come home and find me in a state of collapse.

She contemplated the idea briefly, then decided it would be more amusing to stay alert this afternoon and receive the visitor she had invited for tea. The visitor she was able to invite only because Emily was out. She topped up her port.

On arriving a fortnight ago, to find her mother over the worst of something between a nasty cold and mild influenza, Emily's relief was genuine but brusque. She had agreed to stay on until Amaryllis was strong enough to face convalescence in Monte Carlo, which she considered pretty fair.

Meanwhile, it was good to have a day to herself. Blood might be thicker than water, but a little still went a long way. She had been invited to 26, Claverton Street for tea. Feelings at renewing acquaintance with Lady Priscilla Grinling were mixed, to be sure. But she had been truly sorry at the news of Kate's death two years earlier. Back in London after so long, she had felt an obscure sort of obligation to make contact.

Standing now in Fitzjohn's Avenue, she decided against turning left to Swiss Cottage and thence to the West End by bus. It was only just after midday and her invitation was for half-past four. Until then, her time was her own.

It was the Tuesday after Easter. The Bank Holiday fair would still be running. Feeling like a child out of school, Emily turned right and began the uphill trek towards Hampstead Heath.

Rose Delaney was snoring. In Roscoe's opinion, this was vastly preferable to her talking. For one so young, she could certainly put away a remarkable amount of liquor. At a guess, she would be out for the rest of the day.

Roscoe pinned a note to the neighbouring pillow saying he had an important appointment and if she woke up peckish, to call room service. Having been unusually circumspect in his own drinking during the night-long marathon, Roscoe himself had woken fresh and keen at eleven, with a wonderful sense of freedom.

It was the Tuesday after Easter. The fair on Hampstead Heath would still be running. For Auld Lang Syne, what better? Prudently equipped with specs and beard, Roscoe stepped out into The Strand.

Any observant passenger on top of the bus travelling north from Baker Street, who took the soignée woman and the bewitching child for mother and daughter would have been wrong. Edith Dibbins, aged eight, was on a day out with her grandmother. Her face was an elfin reflection of Ivy's own; her rich auburn hair, despite much contentious guesswork, the probable legacy of the pub pianist at The Ploughman's Firkin in Tunbridge Wells.

In transit between Paris and Los Angeles, Ivy was stopping off in London over the Easter holidays. Partly on a whim to indulge her sense of occasion in respect of yet another watershed in her life; and partly as a treat for Edith. Where Ivy went, Edith went, too.

Ivy was genuinely devoted to Edith. Making up, as it were, for an absence of such customary instincts in the case of Edith's mother. Fury in the best hell-beating tradition at the joint departure of Edith's mother and Ivy's own fiancé had taken a lot of assuaging. And the resulting financial arrangements had set Ivy and Edith up very comfortably indeed.

Eight years on, Ivy Heatherley was a woman of affairs; business chiefly, other designations when inclined. Now forty-three, she was about to merge both interests by collecting a new title and opening a ferociously exclusive restaurant on Hollywood Boulevard. What with pre-war property investments rocketing and shrewdly deployed shares booming, Ivy was riding high.

Her attentions had lately become focused on a powerfully attractive Parisian cab driver who turned out to be a White Russian emigré. Entranced by his impeccable lineage – which she discreetly had verified – unconcerned that he was penniless and dispossessed, Ivy was in the process of carrying him away to a glorious *renaissance* in California, where he would preside as authentic aristocrat *Mâitre* of the 'Prince Nikolai', whose Gala Opening she was already planning for the Fall.

The wedding was to be at Marylebone tomorrow. Today, His Highness Prince Nikolai Vishnevski was in charge of his own amusement. Today belonged to Edith Dibbins. And Edith Dibbins was off to Hampstead Heath with her granny.

Not considering herself prone to hysterical fancies, Emily rather resented having to hang on to the back of a municipal park bench to prevent her knees buckling. From her position on North End Way, over the road from Jack Straw's Castle, she could see right across the Vale of Health, where a dizzying time-warp worthy of H.G. Wells was presenting itself.

I'd know that back anywhere! Roscoe Summerfield, walking away from me, goggling at that woman just beyond the Hoop-la! Where's the pink feather boa? And those twinkling eardrops to stop him in his silly tracks? She was wearing them just now .... In Emily's careening subconscious memory she herself, aged thirteen, was already in the fortune-teller's tent ... *Where's the man with the loud check suit who's really a steward on the* Titanic*? I'll have to give him a ten-pound tip...*

Strolling between the booths, Roscoe was thinking: *It's all the same! Exactly the same as – when was it, 1908? '08, yes. The year I took up with Stanley and Flo. The Heath's the same, the fair's the same, the noises, the music, the smells, the people.*

There was Flo, just the other side of the Hoop-La. *But I thought she was dead! And I thought I was the one who'd .... This is incredible! Wonderful! She's a little older maybe. Well, so am I, aren't we all...? She's looking terrific, though, what? Has she seen me? No, not yet...*

He started forward on a sort of bound.

The woman with Flo's face, Flo's hair, dressed with a taste Flo had never known, caught the movement and looked straight into his eyes behind their tinted glasses. With no recognition...

... Emily blinked, shook her head, got a grip on herself. It was Roscoe all right. And it was Ivy, wasn't it? Ivy Dibbins. Ivy, Countess of Heatherley. Ivy, Comtesse de Lavalle-Fontaine *manquée*. On Hampstead Heath with Little Joyce's little bundle. Well, well, well.

She watched the scene unfold. She could feel Roscoe's shock from the set of his back as he stopped and then leaped forward. She could see that Ivy had never clapped eyes on him before.

In the split second it took to realize that he was mistaken, Roscoe slowed his pace and passed casually by. He noticed the unusually good-looking child the woman had with her. He left them playing the hoop-la and strolled off, taking a wide circle so as not to meet them again.

Emily could sense his turmoil as he moved away. '... *And the walls come tumbling down and there was Florrie 'n Ivy...*', she recalled. The one in the pink feather boa must have been Florrie, of course. With the '*spawn of the devil she'd took up with in the Underground*'. I wonder what Lily Dibbins would make of this afternoon. I wonder if she's here watching. I hope so. She learnt how to enjoy things, with me. I hope she's enjoying this. What an exceedingly odd thing coincidence can be.

Roscoe wandered aimlessly, no longer seeing the sights, smelling the smells, hearing the music. They did say, didn't they, that everyone has a double somewhere? Well, here was living proof. He thought of Flo and was sorry. He was always sorry, helplessly sorry, when he thought of Flo. For that reason, he thought of her as little as possible. This encounter, it had left him properly shaken. Could Flo perhaps have had a sister? She'd never mentioned one. He needed a drink. Jack Straw's Castle. Why not! Stanley Jellybean's double was very likely there already, what?

He turned and started up towards the pub.

Emily saw the beard and glasses for the first time. My God, he looks ridiculous, she thought. Exactly the same as he did that day at the Trocadero when I told him I was pregnant.

Stanley Jellybean, now, *he's* dead, poor old sod, Roscoe reflected sadly as he trudged upwards, eyes on the ground. No doubt whatever, there. And all on account of that unprincipled little minx.

Emily found herself being buffeted alarmingly by a tidal wave of vaulting, conflicting tumults.

That, she said to herself, that ... is Hugo's father! How dare he, how dare anyone treat me the way he treated me and expect to live! Roscoe Summerfield deserves to be dead. How *dare* he not be at the bottom of the sea!

The white-hot anger whirling through her brain became part of a mad orchestra tuning up all over the rest of her; trumpets and cymbals clamouring for him, drums throbbing for him, strings yearning for him, tenor-saxes screaming for him...

Poor old Stanley, poor old Flo, Roscoe's thoughts beat a rhythm as foot by foot, he made the last few pulls to the top of the hill. Come to think of it, the only double missing round here this afternoon is probably Emily Kilverston's.

He reached North End Way and lifted his head to find himself face to face with Emily Kilverston, separated only by a municipal park bench.

'Unspeakable, unmitigated bastard,' she said quietly.

'Psychopathic baggage,' he responded.

There was a taxi rank near Whitestone Ponds. With no further conversational exchange, they walked along and got into one.

'Savoy Hotel,' Roscoe directed.

Then he removed the beard and glasses.

Ivy bought a coloured ice for Edith, and wondered idly if the man with the false beard who'd stared was a Bolshevik spy. Or perhaps some film actor incognito. There'd been an air about him.

Ivy's wrath would prove far-reaching indeed when, in the fullness of time, she discovered that he was none other than Roscoe bloody Somerville who, amid sizzling conjecture, had been a leading candidate for having put her daughter in the club.

Franz-Clovis de Lavalle-Fontaine accepted a second cup of tea. Studying him, Amaryllis had to admit to herself that he was devastatingly attractive, if considerably more mature than her accepted circle of admirers. Escorts these days tended to be somewhere between twenty-three and twenty-nine.

Emily had mentioned Franz-Clovis casually in letters, of course. But Amaryllis, who felt perpetually slighted by his mother, had paid scant attention. She was surprised and somewhat intrigued however, soon after Emily's arrival, to receive his note from the Ritz Hotel, requesting permission to call. Some sixth sense prompted her to set a day when she would be strong enough to suggest that Emily might safely arrange to make calls of her own.

'I had no idea,' he was saying, 'that Emily's Mamma would be so absolutely delectable. Almost, I have been bewitched by the reflection, when here sits the reality.'

On the point of drastically re-arranging all pre-conceived opinions of middle-aged Austro-French bankers, the word 'almost' echoed back to Amaryllis:

I'm 'almost' as bewitching as Emily, is that what he's saying? Yes, it is.

She was nothing if not a realist. With a philosophic little inward sigh, she regarded him with warm, enquiring attention.

Since Emily, with such filial despatch, had hurried to her mother's bedside in time of sickness, he had availed himself of this opportunity, he said, to seek the honour of meeting Madame Kilverston for himself.

Before making a formal proposal of marriage to her daughter.

Gracefully assuming the role of a charmingly world-weary back number, Amaryllis inclined her head in acknowledgement at the correctness of his approach. She laughed with a trace of self-deprecation.

'I'm so happy at your coming to see me, M'sieu le Comte,' she murmured, 'it's truly delightful to meet you. But I very much doubt if Emily would feel obliged to ask approval from me for any intended step of her own, however momentous. She would probably consider a *fait accompli* perfectly adequate.'

'I know,' Franz-Clovis smiled with disarming candour, 'it was a ruse, Madame, on my part. A way of confirming what I had hopefully suspected – that as *belle-mère*, you will be an acquisition most unique. Not run-of-the-mill at all…'

He's good, Amaryllis thought. Almost good enough to make me

want to be a mother-in-law. She realized he was still talking:

'... I'm aware, naturally, that Emily was already once a married woman...'

Are you, indeed?!

'... most tragic, to be widowed so immediately. So sensible to revert to her maiden name...'

Amaryllis forcibly restrained her eyebrows from meeting her hairline.

'... "Fibstock" would be a burden indeed for a boy...'

So that's what she told you?

'... Hugo, he is a splendid chap...'

Precocious little lounge-lizard needs the hell kicking out of him on a rugby field.

'... Looking at you now, *chère Madame*, I want to know, what do you say to becoming *en famille* at last?'

Looking back at Franz-Clovis, Amaryllis indulged a frivolous passing guess as to who in this hypothetical *famille* would be matched with whom and for how long. Idle fancies polish long spoons, she rebuked herself.

'Dear Franz-Clovis,' she smiled a smile to dazzle the young and vigorous, 'what a thoroughly delightful notion. You could have asked Emily yourself, this very afternoon. If she hadn't gone out to tea.'

'I would be most happy for you to call me "Fitz",' he said.

Every fibre in Emily's body was a live wire. Vibrating as though the lot had been bunched together and crammed into an open wall-socket, she stood in the middle of Roscoe's room at the Savoy as he began methodically to undress her. Neither of them had spoken a word in the taxi from Hampstead. There was too much to say. Or possibly too little. Either way, speech in the present situation was entirely superfluous.

He had unclipped her amber beads and was just beginning on the buttons down the front of her chiffon blouse when the door between this room and the next burst open. The communicating door which he had locked so thankfully last night. So carefully.

'*WAATHcaow!!*' The piercing outcry of startled indignation split Emily's nervous system into shivering fragments.

Roscoe's curdled to junket. Now, he remembered that after pinning the note to Rosa's pillow this morning, he had left her room by its main door and forgotten all about the other one. The vision before them was stark naked; tousled curls bouncing, huge eyes welling with tears.

'I wuz *hungwee!*' it complained at banshee pitch. 'Hooza dame?'

Roscoe cast about for something – anything – to say.

He was forestalled by Emily. 'Mr … Somerville is a chance acquaintance,' her voice was husky with cracking ice, 'he has just been gallant enough to repair my necklace.' Steadying one hand with the other, she looked at her watch. 'My goodness, is that the time? I shall be late for tea at Victoria.'

'Wid da *Queeyun?*' Rosa's brush with high society was addling her hangover.

Emily turned away and retrieved her beads from the wall bracket where Roscoe had just artistically, sensuously draped them. At the same time, she did up the two top buttons of her blouse, which were as far as he had got with what might have become a prelude to unimaginable glory.

She turned back again, with iron control gamely striving to answer its emergency summons. One eyebrow very slightly raised, she surveyed the unveiled charms of Miss Delaney. Her gaze travelled at discomfitting leisure over every single one of them, before coming to rest on Roscoe.

She looked him in the eye for a longish moment. Then, with a barely discernible lift of the chin, walked out of the room.

'Please take your lacrosse stick out of the fender, Bunty, and go and finish the holiday work I know you haven't started. It's school again tomorrow.'

Emily watched the graceless, rather lumpy eight-year-old sidle annoyingly across the floor, each long step punctuated by a half skip.

'And please hurry up,' Priscilla Grinling added, on a fatally plaintive note, 'I haven't seen Miss Kilverston for a very long time and we have such a lot to talk about.'

'Was Miss Kilverston friends with Mummy?'

'Yes, I was,' Emily said.

'Then why can't I stay?'

Emily wished she had kept quiet. She looked apologetically at her hostess.

Priscilla sighed. 'Because you have a geography test tomorrow, and a map of the world to colour in. Now go along.'

'Why can't we have hockey tests and lacrosse tests?'

'It's more important to improve your geography marks.'

'Why? Geography's dull. I hate geography.'

'All the more reason to...' Conscious of Emily's attention, Priscilla stopped pleading. 'I'm not going to argue with you, Bunty. I have a guest and you're being very rude. Now go and get on with that homework, do you hear me?'

'All right!' Straddling the lacrosse stick like a hobby-horse, Bunty cantered slowly to the door.

'And say goodbye to Miss Kilverston!'

'Goodbymskilstn.' With which glowering mumble, the odious child mercifully left the room.

Until Bunty came in from Brownies, the reunion had been something of an ordeal for Emily. Pulling herself together, after the day's events so far, was proving exceptionally difficult.

Before the war, Lady Priscilla had been a remote figure, to say the least. Now, she was equally remote in a different way. Emily had the impression of a fighting spirit very early crushed, then suddenly required in the interests of sheer naked survival. Having risen to the occasion, it was still pretending years later, from long habit, not really to be there.

It was good to know that Teddy and his wife were prospering down at Heatherley. 'Teddy's getting quite famous, I hear.'

'We don't see a lot of them. Her name's Wendy,' Priscilla said dismissively, as if that explained why.

'Haven't they got a daughter?'

'Oh, Maudie's splendid,' a swift gleam of animation, 'four now. Thinks she's a horse.'

On the subject of Kate, there seemed little to say. Kate had died in the 'flu epidemic and that was that. Then Emily's attempts at affectionate reminiscence brought an outburst of unexpected eloquence:

'She wanted to go. People usually do what they ultimately want, don't they? Except me, it seems. And Kate wanted to go. She had no taste for life, you see. No enthusiasm, no interest. Not even in her daughter.'

It was enough to jerk Emily out of her self-absorbed coma. She remembered Kate's pale disinclination for pretty well everything.

'I really believe you're right,' she agreed, with dawning comprehension. 'It used to puzzle me.'

'When that foreign gangster put her in the family way I was quite pleased, y'know,' Priscilla went on. 'Thought it might buck her up. No such luck.'

'She was madly in love with him, I thought.'

Priscilla shrugged. 'Brief glimmer of a low light. I'd kill him, naturally, if I ever ran across him. On principle. Not that Kate would have cared one way or the other in the long run.'

There was no mention of Hugo. Priscilla seemed to have forgotten, if indeed she had ever known, that Emily was the 'foreign gangster's' other moll. Emily decided against reminding her.

After Bunty had come and gone, Emily was conscious of a surge of pity for the old girl, now a leathery sixty-five, still denying her own staying power; still convinced of being an invalid, chronic but unsung.

'I don't think you ought to let Bunty bully you,' she said.

Priscilla sighed heavily again. 'Bunty's mother disliked her. One tries to make up.'

It was very clear to Emily that Bunty's grandmother disliked her as well.

Chapter Thirteen

May

Monte Carlo

Hugo Kilverston was in love. At eight-and-three-quarters, he was completely soppy about Rosa Delaney, who was to star opposite his other idol, Roscoe Somerville, in a new film called *Ashes of Lavender*. Hugo thought this a perfectly spiffing title, whatever it was supposed to mean. He was familiar enough with the lavender fields of Provence; acres and acres of pungent green and mauve. He was also much taken up at present with tales of war, full of clashing sabres and smoking cannon. On the whole, he rather hoped *Ashes of Lavender* would be about scorched earth, with Rosa Delaney in a Cossack hat.

He was in love with Rosa Delaney because he had met her. Actually *met* her. She was here in Monte Carlo with Roscoe Somerville on a personal appearance tour. Tante Mag, the Comtesse de Lavalle-Fontaine, was to host a gala reception for them at the Hotel de Paris. She had taken Hugo to greet them on the yacht where they were staying. Maman hadn't wanted to come.

Hugo had a marvellous time. The crew made a fuss of him and he was introduced to Roscoe Somerville by Tante Mag as 'My grandson soon, I hope,' with no further explanation.

Did that mean Maman was going to marry Effcee? Hugo quite liked Effcee, but only quite. The name had evolved by mutual consent; 'M'sieu le Comte' being too formal, 'Franz-Clovis' too familiar, 'Uncle' plain ridiculous. 'Fitz' was by invitation only. Hugo hadn't been invited.

Effcee was all right in the realm of pocket money and so on, of course. And he was always coming up with ideas to please Hugo. Sometimes it got downright embarrassing. If Maman went and married Effcee, she'd be raving mad, in Hugo's opinion.

He himself, on the other hand, would be delighted to marry Rosa Delaney. She was quite the prettiest person he had ever seen. And when the casino was pointed out to her from the yacht, she shrieked like a train whistle. That showed real appreciation. She hadn't made a film yet, of course. She was here so that she'd be famous by the time she did. Very sensible.

Meanwhile, *Phantom of the Box* was showing at the cinema yet again. Hugo and Tante Mag had seen it at least twice before.

When Franz-Clovis de Lavalle-Fontaine astounded himself by asking Emily Kilverston to marry him, her reply to the effect that she would consider it astounded him more. It was not at all the kind of reception which proposals to other ladies had led him to expect. Besides, this time he meant it. The more he dwelt upon her calm response, the more he meant it. He was almost convinced that marrying Emily would even mark the end of his buccaneering.

Why did he find her so mightily intriguing, this opinionated young woman of not yet twenty-seven, widowed on her honeymoon? 'Mrs Peregrine Fibstock'? Come, come. Franz-Clovis had not been born yesterday. Still, if Emily wished to perpetuate such a nonsense. His own view of it had been well borne out when he tried it on Amaryllis – who, one must admit, was by no means without attraction herself. For an idle moment, Franz-Clovis toyed with the piquancy of Amaryllis as mother-in-law…

Doucement, doucement! To conquer Emily was the priority. To make of her a wife, the supreme aspiration. Only think how it would please Magda! What son doesn't want to please his dear old mother? And Emily had said she would consider it.

Emily was, in fact, considering it quite seriously. She had been badly shaken by her own behaviour on seeing Roscoe again in London, less than a month ago. Had she been out of her mind? Undoubtedly. Nothing like that must ever happen again.

He hadn't changed, had he. Still having his cake and eating it all over the world. It was just as well, on reflection, that they had both been too consumed by fires of unreason to begin catching up on their respective activities over the past nine years. Roscoe knew nothing about her life here in Monaco; nothing of Hugo. He'd have quite forgotten, Emily was sure, that he was supposed to have fathered any baby of hers, anyway. He hadn't taken the idea seriously, even at the time. He would certainly have no inkling of the daughter, sulking her way through childhood in Pimlico.

With a revelationary twinge, Emily acknowledged that she was a mine of information; a guardian of secrets unlimited.

It might be very sensible, she reasoned, to put myself out of reach, once and for all, by marrying Franz-Clovis. We get on famously, don't we? It would give Hugo a distinguished father-figure. It would delight Magda. And I would have a powerful shield against the world, not to mention a resounding title.

Emily, Comtesse de Lavalle-Fontaine. One in the eye for Ivy Dibbins? What an absurd notion. Ivy Dibbins and she had never met, nor likely to. Somehow, though, it seemed like a point scored for poor old Lily. Did she really want to marry anyone? That was the question. Odd, too, that Amaryllis struck her as less enthusiastic than one might have expected.

Tonight, now, was going to be a problem. Magda's gala at the Hotel de Paris. It was the grand finale of the promotion tour. So far, Emily had managed to avoid any crossing of paths. It had been easy enough to foster the myth, for Magda, of having no interest in either the 'flickers' or their celluloid gods and goddesses.

No amount of imaginative dissembling, however, would get her out of tonight. Magda was to preside with the film people over a party to be completed by Franz-Clovis, Amaryllis, Emily and Hugo. Hugo had pleaded; Magda had pronounced. It was all highly unsuitable, but Emily had found herself put on the spot. She would simply have to play this evening by ear.

The following day, Roscoe Somerville and Rosa Delaney were to leave for Paris by train. Magda and the reception committee had arranged to have Polyscope's private coupé decorated with motifs from *Phantom of the Box*.

As no information on the forthcoming *Ashes of Lavender* existed, the script being as yet unwritten, an inventive touch would be added in the form of a silver incense-burner, stuffed with lavender heads packed round a coiled wick, to be lighted in time to fill the air with fragrance as the train moved off.

This device had been put together at the Lavalle-Fontaine villa. Hugo, who was allowed to help, wanted to present it himself to Miss Delaney. Magda and Polyscope applauded the notion: Magda, because Hugo's every wish was her command; the publicity boys because they saw the chance of some very saleable pictures. Emily, when approached later, reluctantly agreed that Hugo might go, adding that she herself had no interest whatever in joining the delegation.

Tonight was the peak of Hugo's career so far. Aglow with pride, he gazed at the new, miniature tail suit, laid out on his bed. His first grown-up evening out, and with Rosa Delaney! Tonight, he had no doubt, would be an occasion to remember.

Already an adept helper at cocktail parties, Hugo was no stranger to *ambiences élégantes*. He could mix a mean martini, hand round canapés and converse very articulately, even when idiotic ladies cooed at him. He was in great demand with Tante Mag's circle and enjoyed it on the whole, although he did sense that Maman would like to ease him out of it.

These days, he felt a bit the same himself, although he hadn't said so. He was very fond of Tante Mag, naturally. She had been part of his life ever since he could remember. From her, he had learnt things other boys his age had no concept of.

Lately, though, he found himself wishing she wouldn't keep looking at him with a gleam in her eye which an observer would recognize as predatory. Only this morning, she'd said: 'Soon, you will truly belong to me, *mon p'tit*. Your mother will present you to me as her wedding dower, *n'est-ce-pas*!'

What did she mean? He tried not to feel uneasy at her apparent need to have him by her always, like a sort of pet.

'It's disgusting, Emily! That grotesque, enamelled old witch, turning your son – my grandson – into a … mannequin! A creature! Something from a depraved medieval masque!'

Three weeks' convalescence in the April Mediterranean sun had restored Amaryllis to fighting form. Attired for the evening in the best that Fenwick's of Bond Street had to offer and looking pretty splendid in it, Amaryllis loomed over Emily who, sitting at her dressing-table, was trying to put the finishing touches to her own appearance.

'Are you even aware of it?' Amaryllis's long cigarette-holder skimmed the top of her daughter's ear. 'Is that what you want for him?'

Emily was aware of it. She did not want it.

'Do stop exaggerating, Mother. If I hadn't come tearing over because you said you were dying, Magda wouldn't have got so obsessive. She's well over eighty now, and she's obviously getting more peculiar than I thought. One doesn't want to hurt her feelings. Hugo's very fond of her and he's a perfectly normal little boy.'

'For how long, I ask myself? This absurd indulgence of a set of tails at eight! What are you thinking of?'

'Magda gave them to him.' Emily knew her mother was right and hated admitting it, 'How could I disappoint him? Anyway, he's got a terrific crush on Rosa Delaney.'

'I suppose that indicates a measure of normality,' Amaryllis conceded. 'Still, the sooner he's safely incarcerated at St Oswald's, the better.'

Amaryllis was hell-bent at present on extolling the merits of English public school over the present effete preparation for life's knocks to which, in her opinion, Hugo was becoming far too well accustomed. It was beginning to wear Emily down.

'I've told you, yes! In time! He's only eight!' She was struggling with an earring.

'Nine in September, if my memory serves me. You don't really want to raise a pooftah do you?'

'That's thoroughly nasty, Mother.'

'And being exhibited like a trophy at geriatric covens is nice? Speaking as your mother, Emily, I can't help feeling it's a good thing I'm here at this altogether sensitive time.'

In spite of herself, Emily was inclined to agree. She said casually: 'I'm not going to marry Franz-Clovis, by the way.'

Amaryllis relaxed visibly, with a faint glimmer of approval. 'I never did take you for a *complete* fool.'

There was also Roscoe to be faced in about half an hour. Not to mention his little bit of klaxon stardust. At least Amaryllis had no idea of the encounter three weeks ago in London. Or of the fact that he was Hugo's father. Emily paid silent tribute to the eponymous Etienne du Couteau.

'I wonder if Roscoe will remember us, now he's so famous,' she said, 'after all this time?'

*

Roscoe and Rosa Delaney were spending their final night in Monte Carlo at the Hotel de Paris, for organizational reasons. Before leaving the safety of Suite 26, Roscoe – well equal to the evening's demands, given no undue hindrance – briefed his little colleague for the umpteenth time:

'You have acute laryngitis, remember? All you do is bat your eyelashes, look booful, and stay shut up.'

'I beeyun thut up! Cain't I even thay Hi?'

'If you do, this exercise is likely to be all ashes and no lavender. Now, come on.'

The assembly was glittering, the emphasis on elegant informality. Instead of a full dinner, Magda and the Polyscope publicity men had settled for a lavish buffet. Waiters flew unobtrusively about, filling glasses. The atmosphere was a delicious blend of old-world sophistication and burgeoning Hollywood glitz. Tables bordered a dance floor, the orchestra alternated hits from *The Belle of New York* with Charleston, foxtrot and tango; guests were encouraged to circulate.

Franz-Clovis retreated from the centre of his mother's party to its perimeter, for a more objective view of its members. Standing there, he reached two very forcible conclusions: namely, that Roscoe Somerville (or whatever his real name might be) was the father of Hugo; and that the unique light in Emily Kilverston's eyes, which he himself now so earnestly anticipated, would never be forthcoming whilst the damned popinjay lived.

His mother, enjoying the limelight with shameless gusto, was in full sail. 'You already know my little Hugo, *chèrs amis*,' she was proclaiming, 'but here now is my dear, dear friend Miss Emily Kilverston. And her mamma,' subtly demoting Amaryllis at a stroke, 'for chaperone, *n'est-ce-pas?*' Head cocked, parrot-like, her gimlet eyes flicked over each of them in turn. 'Ah, but I see you have already met…?'

Roscoe and Emily stood motionless, their faces devoid of all expression. After what seemed to Franz-Clovis an eternity, Roscoe's gaze slid to Hugo, then back to Emily.

'Why, Roscoe!' rang forth from Amaryllis. 'What a delightful vindication! I always sensed you had the stuff of greatness in you.' She extended a hand for him to kiss. He complied with the suspicion of a wink.

Before Magda had time to react, Franz-Clovis accosted Rosa, with a click of the heels: 'Franz-Clovis de Lavalle-Fontaine.' He bowed over her hand, murmuring, '*Enchanté de faire votre connaissance*, most beautiful lady,' with an appreciative glint in his eye. 'This is your first visit to my country?'

Rosa drew breath to reply.

'You must please forgive Miss Delaney,' Roscoe was smoothly apologetic, 'she has been forbidden by her doctors to speak this evening. A severe throat infection, dontcherknow?'

Rosa shrugged and nodded, managing to look daggers at Roscoe at the same time.

Almost immediately, Roscoe was submerged in a tide of vociferously female high fashion. Rosa was suddenly surrounded by their escorts. Normally, she would have relished that sort of attention. Now, under such exacting orders, she looked about rather wildly for a directive from somewhere. Franz-Clovis, in the face of so much noisy competition, allowed himself to become separated in the crush. Magda, out of reach now, was talking to the mayor.

Suddenly, Rosa spotted Orville from Publicity, on the edge of the crowd.

'*Aowervayul!*' she squawked, *in extremis*.

'Excusez-me, fellas,' Orville pushed his way in, 'Miss Delaney can't speak ce soir. She has a mal in the gorge. Pardon moi, s'il vous plait!'

Hugo, not to be outdone, wriggled through a forest of legs and popped up in front of her. 'Shall we dance?'

He was rewarded with an unscheduled screech of gratitude. 'Sure! Hey, y're saow cute!'

'A turn on the terrace? Madame Fibstock?' Franz-Clovis offered Emily his arm.

'Not at the moment, thank you,' said Emily.

'I am finding the atmosphere in here a trifle oppressive. You will perhaps excuse me?' He bowed.

'Of course,' said Emily.

Franz-Clovis disappeared into the throng. A few moments later, unnoticed, he left the reception.

Roscoe and Amaryllis reached the dance floor to find spectators lining the edge, clapping in rhythm. In the centre, to the robust strains of 'I Wonder Does My Baby Do The Charleston?', Rosa Delaney and Hugo were giving an extremely competent exhibition.

'Handsome little blighter, what?' Roscoe said.

'Ought to be tucked up in bed at his age,' Amaryllis replied a shade waspishly. Then added, on unconsidered impulse: 'He's my grandson.'

Having been introduced by the Comtesse simply to 'My little Hugo,' Roscoe stared at her, a welter of questions rising from long untickled reaches of his memory like demented trout.

Eventually, he said, 'You must be very proud of Emily. She's Madame de Lavalle-Fontaine these days, then, is she?'

Amaryllis contemplated him briefly. Should old acquaintance be forgot? Or not? She came to a swift decision.

'My daughter was ravished and abandoned,' she asserted unequivocally, looking him straight in the eye, 'at a very early age, by an unprincipled cad of a foreigner with a criminal record.' Until now, there had been no way of testing Emily's original story. She waited with some interest for his reaction.

Roscoe allowed some pent breath to escape silently. 'Poor child. What ... er, what happened to the bounder?'

'I'm told he went to America. On the *Titanic*.'

'Is that so? Me, too.'

'Yes, I know.'

'Of course you do!' he assured her hastily, 'and can I ever forget your generosity? But tell me about the scoundrel who enticed Emily; was that the end of him?'

'It would seem so. Better than he deserved.'

'Quite.'

Franz-Clovis walked out of the hotel, got into his Buick and drove unhurriedly up the hill to the Lavalle-Fontaine villa.

Emily was dancing with Roscoe. There was no way she could have avoided it without causing comment.

Rosa Delaney's unmistakable cackle challenged the violins. Roscoe glanced over to where she and Hugo sat, eating ice-cream. All efforts to gag her had clearly been demolished by Hugo's undoubted enterprise.

'Chip off the old block,' Roscoe remarked casually.

'I beg your pardon?' Emily's face was a mask of neutrality.

They waltzed sedately for a while before he said, 'If I'd fancied a girl at that age, I'd have done the same. I'm proud of the lad.'

'If that's supposed to be a gesture of recognition, it's a little late.'

'I've never ceased to regret that circumstances prevented—'

'Please spare me!' she cut in tightly. 'I seem to remember you chivalrously implying that I'd been caught with a by-blow from any one of a numberless wanton encounters.'

'I was in a difficult situation.'

'And I wasn't?'

He swung her into a stately turn. 'Water under the bridge now, though, what?'

'Oh, yes. Definitely.'

He whirled her faster as the music gathered momentum. 'A son to be proud of, all the same.'

'Certainly.'

The dance finished. He offered an arm. 'Mine?'

'Mine.' She allowed him to lead her from the floor.

Emily woke up next morning feeling vaguely uneasy. For a moment, she wondered why, then remembered she had given Hugo permission to go with Magda to wave the Hollywood circus on its way. That had been before the Hotel de Paris, with Hugo drawing so much attention to himself. Her mother was right. He was becoming spoilt and precocious. She would have to do something about it.

But what? Tell him he couldn't go to the station after all, without giving a reason? Some mothers might, but to Emily it seemed unnecessarily harsh. He'd enjoyed himself so much last night. His undisguised crush on that ghastly Delaney creature was harmless enough, if left to fade without comment. His behaviour hadn't been excessive, either; just naturally exuberant. No one had objected. On the contrary, he had been encouraged.

That was it, of course. At his age, it wouldn't do, not any longer. She had allowed Magda to indulge him far too much. Now it must stop. She realized, with less regret than she might have expected, that she must remove her son from the caressing, insidiously soothing air of this artificial haven and introduce him to the real world.

Perhaps the three weeks back in London had something to do with her rapidly stiffening resolve? Or could it be that Franz-Clovis was expecting an answer to his proposal over lunch today?

In any event, the time had definitely come. Hugo could go to the train this morning. I'll go down there too, she decided. Later. On my own. And stay well out of the way. But I'll be on hand to collect him when all this nonsense is over. And after that, we'll start on a few momentous changes.

Fans milled around the station to watch the film stars leave. Reporters were out in force. Attention was focused on a small group clustered by the open door of coupé twenty-six.

When the good-looking little boy handed Rosa Delaney an ornate silver ball swinging on a chain, she looked at it in utter bewilderment. Until the extraordinary old lady, wearing a purple satin bustle and a huge hat perched on a pile of bright red hair, explained it to her.

With an ecstatic shriek, Rosa Delaney kissed the little boy on both cheeks and struck an instant pose, knee bent in, hip thrust out, chain and bauble poised for a *vodeo-doh*.

Flash bulbs popped, cameras clicked, pencils scribbled.

The Station Master looked at his fob. With jocular haste, the film stars and their minders were urged into *coupé numéro vingt-six*.

Doors slammed along the length of the train. The guard raised his flag. Magda de Lavalle-Fontaine started blowing kisses.

With incredulous distaste, Roscoe gazed round the carriage. It was hung with a bunting of domino masks and eye-patches, against a draped banner bearing the legend, *The Phantom of Box Twenty-Six*.

'Will you look at this!' he exclaimed.

'The guys already got their shots,' Orville from publicity assured him keenly, 'we let them in ahead, okay?'

'What I mean is, how nauseating!'

'Now, you don't mean that, Roscoe, hon!' Orville was hurt, 'It's great public relations!'

'Damn all relations!' Roscoe turned away and slid the window down for a breath of fresh air.

Cameras clicked in his face again. The bizarre Magda swooped forward, still blowing kisses. Hugo backed away uncertainly, grinning and waving as if the train had already begun to move. Then, Roscoe thought he spotted Emily, hovering beyond the barrier on the outside edge of the crowd.

A wave of unexpected, furiously proprietorial indignation surged over him: She's got to get that child off this mindless merry-go-round! She's got to get him away from that barmy old harridan. And keep him away, if he's to have any sort of chance. Dammit, I'll tell her so. I'll tell her now!

He opened the door, jumped down, pushed past the lot of them and sprinted back along the platform. He was unaware that, just for the fun of it, Hugo was running after him.

Emily saw them both. She moved quickly out of Roscoe's line of vision. Keeping a screen of people between them, she plunged forward, scooped up the startled Hugo and beat the fastest retreat of her life.

'Roscoe! Quit horsin', willya! Come back, willya!'

Waving frantically from the carriage window, Orville went into overdrive: 'Hold the train! Hold the star! Kill the cameras! Cut!'

The guard froze, his whistle half an inch from his mouth.

Inside the carriage, Rosa was absorbed with her new toy. 'I gotta flame da wick, okay?' She applied a cigarette lighter to the protuberance at the top of the censer.

Roscoe had almost reached the barrier when there was an almighty explosion. Section twenty-six of the train blew sky high. The blast knocked him off his feet. He lay there, half-stunned, for some minutes. When he picked himself up, there was no sign of Emily.

From his corner table in Monte Carlo's most fashionable restaurant, Franz-Clovis listened to the reverberation. The echoes rolled on and on, mixed with shouts and wails. He heard the approaching ambulances, fire-engines, police cars.

The girl had been good to look at, certainly, he reflected. Still, what of her chances when the talking pictures came in? It was a kindness, really, to extinguish her now. He did feel a swift pang of remorse for his mother and the boy, if they had been caught as well. But what would you? To warn them had simply not been a viability. They were unlucky pawns, no more, in the white-hot intensity of his present game; expendable means to an end which was now most surely achieved. The coxcomb of last night, whom he had recognized as a hitherto unsuspected adversary, had been wiped clean from the board.

He ordered a second Pernod and checked his watch. Emily was late. It was unlike her. He trusted this would not become a habit now that they were about to be formally engaged. He had no doubt as to what her answer would be, no doubt whatever. She was simply exercising her prerogative and making him wait.

He adjusted the position of the small package on the place setting opposite. He looked forward to watching her face as she opened it and saw the splendour of the ring inside. He began to imagine what would follow. Today, tomorrow … even, perhaps, for the rest of his life.

Franz-Clovis de Lavalle-Fontaine could not, at this supreme moment, imagine himself ever tiring of Emily Kilverston.

'*M'sieu le Comte?*' The head waiter was bowing beside the table.

'*Oui?*' Franz-Clovis dragged himself reluctantly back from the promising vistas of his reverie.

The waiter presented a salver, on which was an envelope.

Franz-Clovis saw that it was addressed in Emily's hand.

Of course, the tragedy caused a sensation in the press. Investigations showed that it had been an act of considered violence; why, to what end, or by whom, was impossible to determine. All that really remained in the way of tangible evidence were traces of explosive in a blackened, buckled silver incense-burner, and a mangled red wig, attached to an enormous purple hat.

Chapter Fourteen
1926

Bunty. January.

Dear Dairy,
I have never had a diarey before, but as this was a Christmas Present I suppose I must perforce become a Dareist like Samuel Peyps. I must look at the front to make sure which way round the a and the i go, spelling is not my strongest suite, It is a very handsome DIARY with a padlock. I therefore intend to pour my girlish heart into it for the next five years if I live that long, as it is a Five Year Dairy. In five years I shall be 18. Yippee.

Today is new Years Day. It is very boring. There was a party last night. Mr Jennings brought in some paper hats. I think he got them from the Army and Navy. He is very senior there now, Gramps says. He still calls Gramps LADY PRISCILLA and makes it sound like LEEDI. He's been in the first floor front so long now I wonder he dose'nt call her Priss. It might cheer her up. Everybody else calls her Mrs Grinling anyway. Mr Jennings danced with me and kissed me under the missal-toe. I am nearly as tall as him now. He said I am becoming well-grown and patted my chest. It was a bit creepy, actaully, not like kissing in books. I wonder if it will always be creepy, being kissed I mean. I long for it to be romantic like in Elinor Glyn or Dornford Yates. I wish I was a Dornford Yates Heroin. I HATE BEING THIRTEEN!!! I'll be 14 in October. That might be worse.

Scool next week. I HATE SHOOL!! (exept for games and PT) Well Dear Diary thats all for now.

*

Lady Priscilla Grinling faced the New Year with her usual absence of enthusiasm, coupled with a sort of leathery assumption that although nothing remotely pleasant was in the least likely to happen, it must all be got on with.

This year, she would be sixty-eight. When she thought about it, she was vaguely surprised still to be walking the earth. The fiction of being martyr to a frail constitution, adopted long, long ago in self-defence was now so deeply ingrained that anyone in more than two minutes' conversation with her would get the impression she was living on borrowed time.

For many years now, 26 Claverton Street had been a going concern. Priscilla still presided, from the office downstairs, over a small but highly efficient staff. The place was something between an exclusive boarding-house and a small block of service apartments; a uniquely select address for a lucky few.

Mr Jennings of the Army & Navy Stores had been a fixture in the first-floor front for the past ten years. When he first arrived, catarrhally refined, in 1916, Priscilla was glad enough of his clearly respectable custom, but thought him deeply depressing and hoped it wouldn't be long before his cold cleared up so that he could join the army. But he failed the medical on grounds of a heart murmur and pursued his career at the Army & Navy instead.

Since then, he had proved himself a tower of strength more than once in times of crisis. Not least, during the 'flu outbreak just after the war, when people dropped like flies and Kate died, leaving her mother single-handed with a houseful of sick guests and a fatherless granddaughter of seven. Priscilla and Mr Jennings worked shoulder to shoulder, doing what had to be done with the exchange of no more than a few polite civilities. These days, they still maintained a relationship of warmish formality. It was easier.

'Ay thought you might fancy a cup of tea, Leedi Priscilla, so Ay took the liberty.' The tray was gently placed on the desk beside the open ledger. New Year's Day might be a holiday for most, but Priscilla was in the office pulling the books into shape.

'How extremely kind of you, Mr Jennings. Are you joining me?'

'Thenk you, but no. Ay have a few little tasks before the hurly-burly sets in again.'

'Ah.'

'Ay thought of asking young Bunty if she'd care for a turn in Battersea Park. It's quaite pleasant for January.'

'You could try her.' Priscilla sounded discouragingly doubtful, as she did about more or less everything.

'Ay will.'

'Wrap up, or it'll get to your chest. Don't let her run you off your feet.'

'Ay won't. Bay-bay for now.' He took himself off.

Why does Jennings always have to speak like a strangled whippet when he talks to me? she wondered. He sounds fairly reasonable with anybody else. You'd think he'd have grown out of it by now. If he really wants to go thumping round Battersea Park with Bunty, good luck to him. I wouldn't. She poured her tea.

Bunty's a problem, of course. Such a lump, for one thing. And really, if one's absolutely honest, most awfully tiresome about the place in the holidays. No interest in anything. Like her mother. Poor Kate. Well, Kate got out of it, didn't she? And left me to pick up the pieces. In my state of health.

I wonder if Jennings will up and get married one of these days? He's been middle-aged all his life, of course, but that doesn't alter the fact that he's only thirty-three. I wonder if he'll go and do something ghastly like falling in love?

On the whole, Priscilla hoped not. She would miss him.

At the party last night, she remembered, he seemed to be looking at Bunty in a rather unexpected manner. Like a very normal kind of man. Big for her age, Bunty, very. She could be taken for sixteen. But of course Jennings knows better. Anyway, she'll be back at Nunsfield next week. Buried in Berkshire. And things will calm down again.

Always unsettling, Christmas. People forced to sit and look at each other whether they want to or not. At least Teddy and his smug little wife have pushed off back to Heatherley. I like that daughter of theirs. That Maudie. Not a bit like Bunty when she was nine. Maudie, now, I could really take to. And I'll most probably never have the chance to get to know her better. I'm stuck with the wrong grandchild. Bloody unfair, life, isn't it?

Hugo. February.

St Oswald's College
Hells Teeth
The Inferno.

Très Chère Maman and Gramaryllis,

I greet you both from my durance vile which you kept on telling me would get better in my second year, well, I'm nearly halfway through that now and it hasn't yet. I seriously considered a) killing myself or b) running away and joining the Foreign Legion which would probably amount to the same thing, but I fear they might refuse me on account of my age, even though I am five foot nine-and-a-half. We were measured after gym yesterday.

Otherwise I am well. I hope you are too. Please send more marmalade. I derive much comfort from it. Coopers Oxford, also a chocolate cake from Fullers as we are badly starved by the authorities in this place and it might come in handy for bribes. This term I am fagging for one of the prefects. His name is Wrigley, he is fairly decent but I cant say I am devoted to cleaning his shoes. I dont know if his father makes chewing gum.

Your languishing hier,
Hugo

'Poor little blighter! If I were him, I'd run away and join a circus,' said Emily, subconsciously picking a choice of escape direct from Lily Dibbins's nursery cliffhangers.

Amaryllis sniffed. 'At least he seems intelligent enough to realize that kind of behaviour wouldn't get him very far. I'm surprised he's spelt "heir" wrong. It's not like him.'

'*Hier* is French for yesterday,' Emily observed with some disquiet.

' "Your languishing Yesterday"? How too absurd! Anyone can make spelling mistakes.'

Emily hoped her mother was right, but doubted it. For a boy of thirteen really to feel like that would be a sad thing. Well, he'd have to grow out of it. People do tend to melodrama at that age. And other people could only do their best. Taking action as circumstances dictated.

When Emily snatched her son off the station platform at Monte Carlo seconds before half the train blew up, she carted him straight out to a waiting taxi which contained her mother and three suitcases.

Throughout that fateful morning four years ago, she had had a sense of impending menace. Also, a galloping conviction that the sooner the Kilverstons shook the sunspots of the Côte d'Azur from their collective brain, the better. All at once, it seemed, her feelings for both Magda and Franz-Clovis de Lavalle-Fontaine had undergone a transformation from uneasy, vaguely obligatory affection and a sense of imminent and inevitable surrender to clear-headed outrage and revulsion. It was like suddenly shaking off a pervasive infection.

They took the taxi all the way to Nice, where they boarded a less explosive train for Paris. Two days later, Hugo had his first sight of the cliffs of Dover. By which time, Amaryllis was wondering apprehensively how long the hospitality of Fitzjohn's Avenue would be required in the process of her daughter and her grandson re-establishing themselves.

Not long, as it turned out. Emily was by no means destitute, thanks to a combination of her own undoubted flair for the stock market and her instinct as to which of Franz-Clovis's many tips to follow. Tips offered, she now considered, in a sickeningly condescending manner.

She took a flat in Walton Mansions: a new, thoroughly modern block just off Knightsbridge, ideal both for the park and Harrods. Hugo went to a prep school in Chelsea. She feared that to send him off somewhere as a boarder right away would be altogether too drastic.

She was certainly right on that score. The contrast between the relatively mild disciplines of Chelsea and the fleshpots of Monaco were almost more than Hugo could take at first. But after three years there, Emily judged him ready, at twelve, to be exposed to the rigours of St Oswald's – which, Amaryllis insisted, must be far better than Eton, Harrow or Winchester, since it had produced her own father.

Emily knew very little about her maternal grandfather except that he had met a cloudy end in South Africa, following an argument with Cecil Rhodes, or Barney Barnato, or both.

Bunty. June.

Dear Diary

I see I have not opened you since January 1st. Well there wasnt anything worth writing about on the hole. Just schol and boring Easter holidys and more school.

Until now, Dear Dairy, until now. I AM IN LOVE!!! Also I have been punching tickets on a Greenline Coach. It was the Number 26 rout.

All this has transpired, Dear Diray, because of the Strike. Suddenly the persons who keep everything running stopped doing so, and the persons they are supposed to keep things running for had to do it themselves. It was a great lark when Nunsfield joined in and formed us into squads with prefects in charge to deliver newspapers and letters. At the GPO in town there was this green line coach at the bus stop. One of the masters from St Oswalds was driving it. Nobody was watching so I hopped on to see where it was going, I was fed up sorting mail. It was going to London. A St Oswalds boy was punching tickets and took me on as assistant. We punched tickets all the way to Victoria Coach Station and back again. His name is Hugo. He looks 16 at least. Our seniors somtimes know St O's boys, St O's being so near and yet so far from Nunsfield. Me too now so hard cheese to THEM!! I thought I hated boys but O Dear Diary I will now nurse my passion from this moment on. Tomorrow I am in goal for Lacrosse form matches. I will keep gaol for Hugo and the Lower Fifth will win even if we never meet again. I dont know his last name. Thas all for now so Goodnight dear Dairy.

Chapter Fifteen
1930

London

July

Rumblings from Wall Street echoed heavily back across the Atlantic. Since the day when billions of paper profits were lost on the floor of the New York Stock Exchange, an inexorable economic depression had spread steadily across America and was now making itself felt in the coalfields of South Wales and the shipyards of Jarrow.

Life in London – at least, the life led by the Kilverston ladies – went on much as usual. With unerring instinct, however, Amaryllis began to explore the possibilities of deriving additional income in ways other than from stocks and shares.

Emily's flat, at 26 Walton Mansions, was central, spacious and ideally placed for some chic and exclusive enterprise or other. One that could make money in an altogether congenial manner. Reluctantly at first, then with growing recognition of the practical expediencies, Emily listened to her mother's proposals for a private Bridge and Social Club.

When Hugo came home after his final term at St Oswald's, he found the place positively humming. The hall had become a cocktail bar, the drawing-room a 'card lounge' and the dining-room a kind of understated, unofficial casino. His mother, it seemed, took to the position of *Madame la Patronne* with consummate enjoyment. As for his grandmother, she would sweep in from Hampstead whenever the mood took her, hold court and make certain the wheel was being fixed as often as necessary.

Hugo disapproved intensely. During the last four years, he had resigned himself to school because there was no alternative. He submitted to being flattened in rugger scrums; argued half-heartedly in the debating society; achieved in his final exams substantial passes which were still a long way short of distinctions; and, on the whole, emerged as an average example of what the place usually turned out, with better than average looks. The relief of St Oswald's and of Hugo at their being done with each other was perfectly mutual.

He would be going up to Cambridge in September, just after his eighteenth birthday. Meanwhile, there was summer in London to be enjoyed. Hugo could see little prospect of enjoyment in the frenetic decadence that appeared now to have engulfed his home and found the behaviour of his senior relatives nothing short of deeply reprehensible.

Amaryllis shrugged and said it was a phase; he would grow out of it. Emily, after a few attempts to engage his interest as a trainee croupier or a barman, reached the dampening conclusion that her son was well on the way to becoming a thoroughly pompous young man.

Perhaps Cambridge would cure him. She hoped so. Until then, the outlook was fairly depressing. It seemed way beyond his toffee-nosed comprehension at present to acknowledge that, thus far in his pristine life, material resources had been provided entirely by his female support-base.

August

For more than fourteen years, Mr Jennings had been secure in his position of increasing seniority and trust at the Army & Navy Stores. Floor Manager now, he was. With three departments under his jurisdiction.

His security reflected itself in his private life at Claverton Street, where he indulged in quiet enjoyment of his love affair with the nobility. Nobility in decline, be that as it may, but nobility nonetheless. Lady Priscilla Grinling was Lady Priscilla, from the great and proud house of Heatherley, even though the name these days attached itself to the racing fraternity. Leedi Priscilla was still Leedi Priscilla in her own raight, even though she was known by everyone except Wilfrid Jennings as Mrs Grinling.

In appearance, Wilfrid Jennings was ageless, sand-coloured, dapper and correct. As he had been ever since his mother used repeatedly to stress, in his formative years, the importance of being of a correct appearance and manner at all times.

Bunty was home from Nunsfield for good. At seventeen, turning eighteen in October, she was a good deal more robust in build than Mr Jennings. He thought her simply magnificent. Just the idea of her. All that blue blood! What was she going to do with herself? He had listened to her ambitions of being a games mistress at some really progressive school. Now, he caught himself wondering how – and if – he could forestall them.

To Bunty, no doubt, he must still appear as a sort of uncle. In spite of little intimations to the contrary, which he had given now and then, in the process of watching her lollop towards dauntingly athletic womanhood.

Thirty-six and seventeen? Well, almost eighteen. Well, not far off thirty-seven. Pull yourself together, Wilfrid Jennings! On the other hand, Wilfrid Jennings, 'faint heart ne'er won fair lady…'

On August Bank Holiday Monday, he invited her to go for a picnic. He would have preferred to take her to a nice restaurant, but aware of her opinions on expensive and unhealthy over-eating in artificial surroundings, he rightly decided that such an outlay would be entirely wasted. The way to Bunty's heart, should there be one, more likely lay in fresh air and exercise.

They lugged a hamper to Battersea Park. So, it seemed, had the rest of the population of London. After a good deal of tramping about, they found a measure of seclusion on one side of a rhododendron clump. The other side was playing host to a family party with at least five children under eight, but it was the best they were going to get. It was quite a large clump.

'We can make believe we're in the shrubbery of our own rolling acres,' he beamed at her, 'with our own stately towers rising behind.'

'*You* can if you like, I suppose,' Bunty screwed up her face in perplexity, 'but I know perfectly well we're in Battersea Park and it's the power station.'

She was, however, encouragingly hungry. It was quite a nice day, although there had been rain on and off ever since St Swithin's and the grass was inclined to be damp. Mr Jennings spread out both their macs, covering them with a motoring rug and a three-ply paper tablecloth from 'Stationery & Sundries'.

Then, he unpacked the hamper. It was an impressive array, he thought. Egg-and-cress, ham, chicken-and-lettuce in white bread and brown; apple turnovers and a thermos of tea for afters. Ready-mixed with milk and sugar. That could wait. With a flourish, he produced the *piéce de resistance*: the bottle of sweet Sauternes with which he intended to breach her defences.

It was a bit warm, after incarceration beside the thermos under the sandwiches, rolled in party paper serviettes. For a terrible moment, he thought the corkscrew was missing, but found he'd wedged it inside the green and yellow Bakelite cups.

She protested that she didn't like the taste of wine and hadn't they brought any lemon squash? By nefarious design they hadn't. And the Sauternes prevailed, because she was thirsty.

When the sandwiches and the apple turnovers had been reduced to scattered crumbs, the thermos of tea was still untouched. The Sauternes was not yet quite finished.

'It grows on you,' Bunty pronounced.

'I wonder…' he up-ended the bottle into her proffered beaker, 'I wonder, if by a miracle, I might, er … hope to do likewise? Miss Bunty?'

'Pardon?' Her face stretched unbecomingly in grossly overdone amazement.

Emotionally earnest, he ploughed on: 'I cherish feelings for you, Mitch White … I mean, which might … come as a surprise,' he floundered. Having got this far, though, he was damned if he would retire without a fight to death or glory. 'Even should you laugh me to scorn, Miss Bunty, I insist that you listen to how loud my heart is beating for you.' He had never said such a thing before in his life.

She was staring at him a touch myopically, with her mouth hanging open. Then, she started to giggle.

'Why on earth are you calling me "Miss Bunty"? You've called me Young Bunty ever since I would walk, nearly. "Miss Bunty" …!' Whereupon she dissolved in a bout of mirth which was clearly beyond her control. Tears squeezed themselves from the outside corners of her eyes.

He was alarmed. Had he overdone the tiddly? Was she going to be ill? No matter! As Confucius he say, *carpe diem*.

'I love you, Bunty!' he hollered to her contused, creased-up face, 'I want to marrish you!' This announcement was made with an authority which, on occasion, might have been heard in the staff canteen at the Army & Navy. 'I mean I want to ravvy you!' Words were becoming dangerously entangled with unaccustomed urges.

All of a sudden, Bunty stopped shaking and opened her eyes wide. 'Why don't you, then?' she demanded, loud and lucid. 'It's about time somebody did.'

On the other side of the rhododendrons, ears were flapping. Four pairs of adult hands forcibly restrained a junior task force from mounting an instant recce.

It was Mr Jennings's turn to stare. Had he heard her right? The Sauternes did seem to be pounding somewhat in his ears. He, too, was unused to alcoholic beverages. In a state of suspended animation, he watched her bounce across the rug towards him on her bottom, making her skirt ride up until stocking-tops; suspenders and peach celanese knickers were in full view.

His own legs were stretched out, ankles crossed. With a final hefty kangaroo leap, she cleared the polished toe-caps of his white and brown holiday shoes and landed like a hundredweight bag of warm silage athwart his solar plexus. He could only sit there, pinioned and gasping.

'Come on, team!' she rallied, as if he were a hockey eleven. 'Let's go for a goal!' She dug him in the ribs, which winded him further, then started unbuttoning his shirt.

On the other side of the bushes, Mum, Dad, Auntie Iris and Uncle Norman gave up on the physical control of their young and contented themselves with fiercely mimed commands of silence.

For the protagonists, the ensuing onslaught was a classic endeavour of mutual discovery. Until now, Wilfrid Jennings had managed without getting himself involved in 'that kind of thing'. Bunty had never had the chance. After a certain amount of trial and error the object was achieved, leaving them both more than a little battered.

When the excitement was over, an army of feet, large as well as small, retreated whence it had come with cracking twigs, muted squeaks and shushings. It had been much too good to miss.

Neither of the star attractions was aware of having provided a show which beat Punch and Judy hollow, any day of the week.

'Well,' said Bunty. 'They never taught us that at Nunsfield, Mr Jennings.'

'Won't you call me Wilfrid?'

After waiting some time for an answer, he wondered if she had gone to sleep. She was still on top of him and his right leg certainly had. Then she shifted her weight to his left, bringing intense if short-lived relief.

A foggy mumble tickled his ear: 'If it's all the same to you, I don't see you as a Wilfrid somehow, Mr Jennings.'

He began to ease himself from under a bulk which by now had collected a cocoon of two macs, a heavy-duty motoring rug and a three-ply paper party-tablecloth. The only reaction was a snore.

He became conscious of a rising ground chill, stealthily permeating the length and breadth of his back.

Hugo Kilverston had had enough. As he had told himself often over the last few weeks, with mounting chagrin now approaching crisis point, he couldn't turn his key in the front door without wondering who would be in his bed, how many and how long for. Now, after what he considered to be selfless attempts at making himself agreeable to the members and supporting his mother's disreputable enterprise, he was telling her, too.

'... and let me say that I heartily abhor your way of life. *And* Gramaryllis's. There's no room for me here.'

Emily was torn between active dislike and cutting disappointment at not having raised a kindred spirit.

'Really, Hugo, I never thought you'd grow up to be a prig.'

'I am not a prig. I'm fed up with being turned out of my own bed. I take less and less kindly to sleeping on the sofa, and when I find that occupied too, I drop off the end of my tether!'

Emily's patience fractured. 'Whippersnappers your age don't *have* tethers to reach the end of, drop off the end of, or threaten their elders and betters with in any way at all! Let me tell you, young man, that the Kilverston women have raised you, educated you, and are about to launch you up to Cambridge by their own fortitude and wit, untrammelled by any generally accepted safeguards of society such as marriage—'

'And jolly embarrassing too!' he cut in. 'I had a rotten time at school, trying to explain my "people" to other chaps.'

His mother looked at him oddly, he thought.

'I wouldn't go into that, if I were you,' she said. 'Quite a few of the chaps, as they grew up, rather enjoyed finding out for themselves. I remember a charming boy called Wrigley, not so long ago.'

Hugo, suffused with shock and outrage, was unable to react immediately. Eventually, he said: 'They never told *me*!'

'Why should they?' Emily poured herself a drink.

'There you go again,' he pointed an accusing finger at the soda siphon, 'and it's not even lunchtime!'

'Do be quiet,' you tiresome boy. Or is there some obscure advantage in seeing your mother as a pointless soak instead of a rather successful business woman?'

'It's just all so unsuitable,' he grumbled. 'Other chaps' mothers and grandmothers meet for lunch at the Berkeley and take their dogs for walks in Shropshire. Other chaps have fathers.'

The heel of his shoe scuffed a circle in the carpet.

Very deliberately, Emily took a black and gold cigarette from the box on the table and fixed it into a long holder.

'Look on the sunny side,' she said lightly, 'other chaps are occasionally known to loathe their fathers like poison.'

'At least they know who they are.'

From her seat on the sofa, his mother looked across at him, standing there scowling in the middle of the room. Six foot one, with light brown hair and blue-green eyes, he certainly had an air of Roscoe, but she thought, hoped, he favoured her more.

'Was it Effcee?' the question zinged through the air like a blow-dart.

The sudden use of Hugo's own old nickname for Franz-Clovis caught her off-balance. Without thinking, she laughed with frank amusement. 'Don't be ridiculous! I didn't meet him till you were seven.' Then she wished she'd held her tongue, or closed the discussion, but it was too late.

'Then it was Roscoe Somerville.' He faced her, daring her to laugh again.

'What on earth makes you think that?'

'Even at eight, a person isn't necessarily blind or stupid,' he replied. 'In my case, I recall, I was unusually bright. I saw the way he looked at you, the night before the flit. I saw the way he looked at me. I didn't make much of it at the time.' He paused, then fired another broadside. 'Why was I got up like Pinocchio? And egged on to show off at parties? Why did we run away like criminals?'

Emily groaned inwardly. It was such old history. The ins and outs of it all had never been gone into at the time, true enough. Hugo's questions had been neatly deflected, the whole episode discounted and left to evaporate.

'Why did you grab me off that platform under Somerville's nose?' Hugo persisted grimly.

'To save you getting blown up, you little idiot.'

'So you knew!'

'I did not! And I don't propose to discuss it any further. It's none of your business.'

'That's the most unreasonable thing you've ever said to me.'

Emily flicked the lighter. She was not disposed to chew over Roscoe's motives for attempting to murder his own son. That was a score to be settled in due course. In her own way.

Hugo coughed at her cigarette, 'Utterly depraved! I shan't stay under this roof a moment longer than I have to.'

Emily inhaled deep and blew the smoke out very slowly. 'How do you intend to live? Until, at my expense, you go up to Cambridge?'

'I shall get a job.'

'You had a job here. You were very bad at it.'

'It's too humiliating. Now you tell me I'm liable to bump into half St Oswald's.' He slammed out of the flat.

Battersea Park went straight to Mr Jennings' chest. Within three days he had a very nasty cold which quickly settled there. He made light of it, not wishing to tarnish, as he hoped, his newfound status as a romantic hero in the eyes of his beloved. He did not, as had always been his custom before, take a week off work and go to bed with Vick and a hot-water bottle. Instead, he soldiered on with hardly any voice and a progressively sinister cough.

He saw very little of Bunty. She seemed to go in and out of the house too quickly for him to catch her, even in the hall. Eventually, wondering how best to establish his proprietorial interest in her without, as it were, jumping the gun, he bearded Priscilla in the office on the pretext of discussing his holiday.

Every year, Mr Jennings spent the last two weeks of August at the Palm Gardens Hotel, Saltdean. It was modest but nice and comfortable, near enough to Brighton for the entertainments and far enough away to avoid the flashiness and attendant unnecessary expense. They knew him there, welcomed him warmly and he had no wish ever to try anywhere else. He always kept his room on at Claverton Street, budgeting carefully, in earlier days, to balance his rent *in absentia* with his holiday bonus. There was no longer the need for that kind of accounting, but the arrangements still suited him excellently.

On the way downstairs to see Priscilla, he found himself wondering with a small ripple of excitement how Bunty would take to the Palm Gardens for a honeymoon, then stopped the thought in infancy. One thing at a time. Besides, he really was feeling exceedingly unwell just at present.

In the office, after confirming this year's dates – 15th to 29th – he enquired, carefully casual, after Bunty.

'She's joined a health club in Roehampton,' Priscilla replied, looking surprised that he wanted to know, 'a sort of "Strength Through Joy" outfit. Pretty tiresome really. At least it'll keep her occupied until she starts at Physical Training College in September.'

All this was news to Mr Jennings. He stared at her in silence across the desk, with a turmoil of black dots chasing each other round and round behind his eyes. Why had he not been told? Why had Bunty not told him herself? Why had she made a point of avoiding him, after all they had been to each other? Really, it all made him quite hot under the collar. Extremely hot. In fact, his collar itself was becoming so tight, he feared his head might burst. The ceiling swooped down on top of him; the floor swooped up to meet it. Quite suddenly, he knew no more.

Priscilla regarded his recumbent form, face downwards on her Tabriz rug, with dismay. What was she supposed to do about *that*, in her state of health? Pick him up and carry him to his room? Nevertheless, she managed to get him under the armpits and heave him on to the couch, after which she poured herself a large medicinal brandy and telephoned the doctor.

It was a severe attack of pleurisy. Mr Jennings had quite a high temperature. There was to be no question of returning to work for some time, unless he wanted to risk pneumonia. He was to stay in bed until told he could get up. The doctor would call each morning, for as long as necessary.

A great deal of barley water was drunk, aspirin swallowed, Friars Balsam inhaled. After four days, his temperature dropped. After a week, his chest cleared and he was allowed into a chair with a rug over his knees. On August 12th he ventured out, pale and a little wobbly, for a breath of fresh air.

He mentioned to the doctor that he was due to leave for Saltdean very shortly, that long-standing arrangements had been made. 'I would be most reluctant to cancel, Doctor,' he averred, weakly querulous. 'They take very superior care of me.'

'Do they, now?' The doctor looked thoughtful. He could see that to forbid the trip might cause a relapse. If Jennings could make the journey, a spot of sea air might be just the thing. Also, he was beginning to find his patient a bit of a bore. 'Two weeks is not enough,' he pronounced. 'In my opinion, you need at least six.'

Not only did Mr Jennings see the wisdom of this edict, he was too debilitated to argue. He was under doctors' orders, and that was that. Besides, what chance would he have with Bunty unless he built himself up?

He telephoned the Palm Gardens Hotel and was much heartened to be told that although almost full, they were prepared to take steps, to re-arrange other bookings to accommodate him for the six weeks required, '... seeing it's you, Mr Jennings.' It made him feel much better already. Also quite influential.

Of course, there was the question of expense. Although Mr Jennings was no pauper these days, extravagance was anathema to him. 'Maight Ay suggest, Leedi Priscilla,' he proposed, in tones denoting a keen business sense, 'that a short let on may room could be beneficial to us bewth?'

She saw the point. She could charge at least double.

'Neturally, Ay would clear drawers and cupboards. Ay should be returning the fourth week in September.'

Within half an hour, using her title, Lady Priscilla had placed an advertisement in the *Evening News*.

Mr Jennings treated himself to the luxury of booking a hire-car at the huge sum of fifteen shillings, to avoid the buffetings of a journey by rail.

Bunty brought him up a cup of tea while he was packing. 'I think Saltdean sounds a very good idea for you, Mr Jennings,' she said, 'heaps of bracing seaweed.'

Although she had fetched and carried strenuously during his illness, changing his hot-water bottles and bringing up fresh barley water, Wilfrid Jennings was somehow made to feel that the picnic in Battersea Park had never taken place. And he considered himself engaged to her!

'I shall miss you, Bunty,' he said, sidling towards her round the bed, 'madly!' He hoped that sounded as thrilling as he meant it to.

She backed away with a breathy giggle, shifting her weight awkwardly from one foot to the other. 'Oh, I don't expect so. You'll soon be enjoying yourself far too much!'

'Not without you, Bunty, not at all. I shall be working hard at getting fit for my return to you, that's what I'll be doing. After all, we're engaged, aren't we?'

By this time, Bunty had backed herself almost out of the window. 'Sorry, I didn't quite catch—'

'Engaged. You and me. Unofficially at present, but as soon as I come back, we'll—'

'Oh, I don't think so, Mr Jennings.' It was a sort of frantic blurt. He stopped short.

'But, Bunty! After Battersea Park! After all that happened there…'

She swallowed. 'Oh, it was very informative, I did so much appreciate it,' she flashed him a rather wild grin, 'but, you see … oh, I know this sounds soppy, but, well, I love another.'

He was stunned. Wordless, he stared at the unprepossessing, basically arrogant person he had always known she would become. His dream of joining the serried ranks of the aristocracy, lately so amazingly, gloriously attainable, dwindled to dust.

'I have done since I was thirteen,' she said. 'I'm sort of, well, saving myself for him, if you know what I mean.'

Mr Jennings didn't. Not at all. Not in the circumstances.

'That's if I ever see him again. And what you and I did was most frightfully useful. Er … excuse me…'

She pushed past him, made a bolt for the door and was gone.

*

'I just dropped in to collect a few things.'

Suitcase in hand, Hugo looked decidedly uncomfortable as he faced his mother and his grandmother in the hall at Walton Mansions. Having slipped in unnoticed, they had appeared just as he was on the point of slipping out.

'Club 26' would be open for the evening's amusements in half an hour. The barman was crushing ice-cubes and slicing lemons.

Amaryllis and Emily looked at Hugo and waited for what he might have to say next. Neither seemed inclined to help him.

He waved the *Evening News*, 'They were advertising for a temporary junior salesmen at the Army & Navy Stores.'

'You've never sold a quarter of acid drops,' said Amaryllis.

'One of their department heads is off sick and everyone else has moved up a notch or something. Anyway, I was interviewed this afternoon and I've got a job for five weeks.'

The personnel manager had jumped at him. A presentable youth filling in time before university was exactly the ticket.

Hugo waved the *Evening News* again. 'I also have rooms,' he announced grandly. 'I shall be back in time to pack for Cambridge.'

'I trust your "rooms" will be up to scratch,' his mother murmured, 'Since you consider those here so far below.'

'And please. Don't try to find me,' Hugo had obviously rehearsed this bit and he was going to say it, willy-nilly, 'I've taken a different name. So as to avoid embarrassment.'

'Good evening to you then, sir,' said Amaryllis.

A few hours after Mr Jennings departed in his chauffeur-driven Wolseley, young Mr Somers presented himself at 26 Claverton Street.

Having unpacked in the first-floor front, he took himself down for dinner. He had been kindly invited for a drink beforehand by his landlady this first evening.

As he reached the bottom of the stairs, a strapping female loped in at the front door. For a long moment, she stood rooted. Young Mr Somers wondered if perhaps she was not quite all there.

Then, she flung her arms wide. He looked over his shoulder to see who else might be up on the landing.

'Hugo!' she cried. 'Oh … Hugo!'

She hurled herself at him. Thoroughly alarmed, he stumbled backwards into the newel post, his arms perforce encircling this extremely solid, totally strange young woman.

'You remember me!' The joyful conviction in Bunty's ringing declaration had Hugo Kilverston completely flummoxed.

Chapter Sixteen

September

London

'*... Other chaps' mothers meet for lunch at the Berkeley and take their dogs for walks in Shropshire...*'

This reproach, alone of the general assortment being bandied about when Hugo left home, had made a real impression on Emily. Not that she particularly wanted to join the complacent, back-biting sisterhood of 'Ladies Who Lunch' even if they deemed her acceptable, which was doubtful; nor did she envisage acquiring a dog as an accessory. The dogs of her acquaintance struck her as too intelligent to be so underestimated. But the idea of a weekend cottage began to wink like a beacon in her mind.

It was sound common sense. It would be good, sometimes, to get away from the scented, centrally heated box of 26 Walton Mansions; not to mention her mother. Valuable as Amaryllis might be as a business partner, personality clashes did still tend to be an ever-present hazard.

A review of her finances showed it to be a viable prospect. Nothing as remote as Shropshire, of course. Or even Hampshire. With the new Kingston Bypass, Surrey was the place. She could give the little red Morris its head and be there in no time.

Soon after coming back to London, Emily had bought a car. Like her mother before her, she learnt to drive by getting into it and going from Hampstead to Piccadilly, twice round the Circus and back again. There was talk these days of a driving test, but that need only worry any future aspiring motorists who might find themselves having to take it.

Before giving full attention to her intriguing new project, Emily felt it wise just to check that her son was not about to slide down slopes of despair to oblivion. Carefully avoiding all service counters, she strolled through the Army & Navy Stores.

She had to contend with an hors-d'œuvres of emotions as, from behind a pile of trunks in Leather Goods, she watched 'our Mr Somers' extol the attractions of a thirty-two-piece set of matched pigskin luggage to the shining faces of a keen young man and his fiancée.

Hugo appeared to be well scrubbed, well dressed and well fed. In deference to his stern injunction not to look for him, Emily forebore any further investigation as to his lodgings.

'You remind me of someone or other, Mr Somers.'

'Really, Mrs Grinling? I wonder who?'

'Ever since I first saw you, it's teased my memory. But I haven't fathomed it yet.'

'If you ever do, I shall be intrigued to know, believe me.'

It was Friday night. It was also Hugo's final evening at 26 Claverton Street and he was in the office, settling up. Tomorrow, he would go back to Walton Mansions; and next Tuesday, embark on a spot of Eng. Lit. at Cambridge.

As his mother had emphatically pointed out, she was paying for his place there and he intended, if possible, to make things up with her and let bygones be bygones. No doubt there was room for adjustment on both sides. But he, personally, was prepared to make allowances. He had experience, now, of some of the demands of making a living. More honest, probably, than that invented by his female relations, but he had no wish to leave London on a sour note.

Hugo was feeling magnanimous and in harmony with the world at present. Five weeks at the Army & Navy had been enjoyable but quite sufficient. Life at Claverton Street, which included a most invigorating relationship with the granddaughter of the house, was quite another matter.

At Bunty's boisterous prompting in the first ten minutes of his sojourn there, Hugo had recalled the day spent in her company on a Greenline coach during the General Strike which, with the return to routine tedium of school life, had pretty soon faded from his mind. Not so much the novelty of the excursion itself; that had been more than welcome. Just the annoying addition of some junior bruiser from Nunsfield galumphing after him the whole time. Bunty, on the other hand, had been gilding the memory for the past four years.

Once he recovered from the uninhibited display of muscle that went into the reunion, Hugo became aware of a swift and powerful attraction. She was everything his mother and grandmother were not. She exuded health and vigour, she was positive, she was uncomplicated, she was strong. She was wholesome.

Had he known how close the loneliness, the insecurity, the bewilderment of her growing up had been to his own, he would probably have gone off her straight away. Had he recognized the underlying ruthlessness of purpose common to them both, he most undoubtedly would.

As things were, the first-floor front at Claverton Street had never before seen such ebullient activity. Unless the late Dowager Countess of Heatherley, in her more mobile years, had set a rollicking precedent. Which was by no means unlikely.

Since Hugo's return to Walton Mansions the day before yesterday, he and Emily had achieved a sort of tacit truce. He made himself extremely pleasant in the card lounge and the bar; she expressed interest in his time at the Army & Navy, without a single enquiry about his living arrangements.

He would be off to Cambridge tomorrow. Emily came into his room, where he was filling his old school trunk rather more interestingly than for St Oswald's. She watched a set of wine glasses being carefully rolled in newspaper; two bottles of port in singlets. A few items of required reading were waiting to be pushed down the sides: *Decline And Fall*, *Silas Marner*, Spenser's *Faery Quean* and *Beowulf*.

After picking them up at Hatchards this afternoon, opening them gingerly and wishing he'd chosen Engineering, Hugo reminded himself that one wasn't really expected to work unless one wanted to and he probably wouldn't have to read them much. 'I'll get whatever else they tell me to in Cambridge,' he said.

Emily, having thumbed rapidly through *Beowulf* – in a Middle

English translation from the original Anglo-Saxon – handed it over without comment.

'I've bought a cottage not far from Leatherhead,' she announced instead, 'in an acre of garden with woodland at the back. It has a thatched roof with half-moon windows, three bedrooms and a well outside the front gate. It was one thousand, three hundred and forty pounds.'

'Isn't that rather a lot?' Hugo looked concerned. 'I mean, if you have to stagger about with buckets of water? Where's the lavatory? In the woods at the back?'

Emily hooted with laughter and explained that far from being a primitive wreck, the house was the first of a new development just off the London–Guildford Road. 'With all mod cons and a fitted kitchen,' she said. 'The old well just happens to be there on the green. More houses are to be built on the rest of the land in the next few years, but with an acre each and so many trees, nobody's going to be overlooked. All in the same cottagey style but all different. It's absolutely charming and it's a terrific investment, so there.'

Her enthusiasm was infectious. 'When do I get to see it?'

'When you come down for Christmas, I expect. If not before.'

'Oh, before. Definitely. You must tell me as soon as you're straight, and I might be bringing someone to meet you.'

This was the last thing Emily expected to hear. She had no doubt whatever that over the last five weeks, Hugo would have got well into his stride with girls. It was a state of affairs she assumed would continue for the next several years. That he wanted to bring one home to meet his mother, at this stage of his career, came as a complete surprise to her.

'I'm sure you'll love Bunty,' he fixed her with a smile that was gooey, keen, uncertain and bossy, all at the same time. 'She's the kind of girl who, if you don't, then you jolly well ought to!'

'He seems to be mad about somebody called Bunty,' Emily remarked later to her mother, trying to feel as casual as she hoped she sounded.

'How too excruciating. Where did he find her?'

'Goodness knows. The Army & Navy? Or his digs, perhaps? Wherever that was. It must have been fairly satisfactory, he looks quite blooming.'

'Well, everybody's called "Bunty" nowadays. Or "Toots". It could mean anything.'

October

'Please stop hovering with that gin just out of reach, Bunty. Thanks to you, I have a marked need of some in my tea.'

Priscilla had just been informed that not only was her granddaughter enamoured of their erstwhile lodger, but also that his name was not Somers but Kilverston and he was the son of Kate's old school friend Emily. Suddenly, the world was spinning much too fast.

'Poor darling Hugo,' Bunty was proclaiming, still with the gin decanter clasped to her chest, 'he left home and changed his name because no one understood him there, and he didn't want them dragging him back. Oh, sorry, here you are.' She plonked the decanter down.

'Are you having a cup of tea?' Priscilla vaguely felt the time might have come for a chat.

'Tannin's bad for you. I've just had a glass of milk and some carrot cake.'

'Isn't that more suitable for cows?'

'Dear old Gramps, you're thinking of cattle cake.'

As usual when thus addressed, her grandmother winced. 'You mean there's a difference?'

Lately, with her own congenital brand of grumpy resignation, Priscilla had begun envisaging an eventual match between Bunty and Jennings. A long way short of ideal, but what would you? His aspirations were painfully apparent, even to Priscilla's wearily remote perception. He was a respectable enough creature. Steady. Decent. Unlikely to go berserk and burn down the Army & Navy Stores. She could even feel that, in time, 26 Claverton Street would be passing into conscientious and capable hands.

This boy had only been in the house five minutes. Well, five weeks. At least she knew now who he reminded her of. Emily Kilverston, of course. And who else? Well, who indeed? She had no idea who his father might be.

'I rather wondered, when you had that day out with Mr Jennings...' she began, without much hope.

'Oh, Gramps!' Bunty gave a huge, ungainly shrug. 'He's as old as the hills! I expect Hugo and I will be getting married quite soon, actually,' she threw in with a kind of spuriously possessive, casual authority.

'Hugo has Cambridge to deal with,' Priscilla was brusque, 'and you have your Physical Training College.'

'I shan't be able to stay there much longer.'

'You've only been there three weeks!'

'I know, but ... well, this is the other thing I was going to tell you. I'm expecting.'

In the grip of understandable shock, Priscilla watched as her granddaughter, instead of looking suitably stricken, hugged herself with beefy self-congratulation.

Bunty knew quite well that by a stroke of rotten luck, she was landed with the result of an experiment in Battersea Park.

But nobody else did.

Cambridge

Hugo stared miserably at a University Library edition of Shakespeare, open at *Julius Caesar*. He had been told by his tutor only this morning that unless he applied himself more intelligently, his people would be advised that his place here could be filled to more productive advantage by practically any other young man in the British Isles.

Cambridge was not in line with his expectations, not at all. He had visualised a sort of perpetual river afternoon, lazy or bracing according to season; a fortnight's non-stop carousing known as 'May Week' to look forward to next June; the occasional appearance at a sleepily agreeable lecture, punctuated by sherry parties before lunch and dinners in Hall.

It was not that Hugo was workshy. On the contrary, he was willing. At the Army & Navy, once he knew exactly what they required of him, he had responded with alacrity and imagination. They were sorry to see him go, they said. They even offered him a permanent trainee position. But he felt the urge to explore what the world might have to offer besides sales-slips and a flair for handling customers.

When Emily undertook to subsidize him at university, he settled for English, as a subject not entirely foreign, to provide an undemanding breathing space in which to find a future direction. A modest degree might help. His so far unspecified goal was one of quiet achievement in an area offering respect and esteem; a properly run home with a place for everything and everything in its place; and in due course, a wife and at least three properly brought-up children. The precise opposite, in fact, of all that he had ever known.

Now, he was being asked to hand in, by tomorrow, a written comparison between the political causes behind the conspiracy to dislodge Caesar and the Bolshevik Revolution of 1917. He tried hard to concentrate on the text in front of him but his eyes insisted on glazing over all the time and the only words that kept leaping from the page were: 'A lioness hath whelpèd in the streets.'

His panic-driven trance was broken by a knocking at the door. At first he thought it must be his scout, but the sound was more peremptorily demanding than routinely brisk. He called 'Come!' and got up, glad of the interruption even though he could ill afford it.

A slightly built beige man of indeterminate age, sporting a toothbrush moustache and wearing black coat and pinstripe trousers, scuttled into his room like an aggrieved buck rabbit and hovered there, eyelids and nostrils pink and twitching.

'Am I addressing Mr Hugo Kilverston?' he enquired in a tight sort of muted bark. 'My name is Jennings…' he whipped out a handkerchief just in time to catch a monumental sneezing fit, 'I tend to hay fever when emotionally disturbed,' he added between bouts.

Hugo was totally mystified. 'You ought to wrap up, it's chilly for October.'

Jennings mopped his eyes. 'I'm a martyr to it.'

'Hard cheese. Er … have we met?'

'In a manner of speaking, no.'

'What brings you to Cambridge?'

'Miss Bunty Grinling.' He sneezed again.

Hugo brightened. 'Is she here too? Good egg!'

Jennings seemed to get a grip on himself. 'Regarding the first-floor front at 26 Claverton Street…' he began.

A shaft of enlightenment gleamed. 'So *you're* the unexpected vacancy!' Hugo smiled warmly. 'Very pleased I found it, to be honest.

Very agreeable.'

'That room, and all that went with it,' Jennings spoke with difficulty, 'was mine!' He clapped the handkerchief to his face again. This time, the sneeze sounded more like a sob.

Hugo was perplexed. 'You mean I took something with me when I cleared out? My dear chap, I'm frightfully sorry. What?'

A great deal of mopping and blowing went on before Wilfrid Jennings drew himself up to his full five foot eight and snarled, 'Miss Bunty Grinling!'

Hugo began to get the impression that there might be more here than met the eye. 'Jolly good sport, Bunty,' he offered warily. 'Are you an uncle or something? She never told me she had an uncle called Jennings.'

The set of Mr Jennings' chin became markedly bellicose. 'I have travelled up to Cambridge by train today, Mr Kilverston, for the express purpose of verifying that you are an unutterable...' a fresh threat of sneezing was brutally suppressed, '... cad, sir. And to punch you in the teeth!'

Hugo was taken completely off guard. The disgruntled buck rabbit suddenly lycanthropized – a word later adopted by Hugo with some pride – into a cross between a boxing wallaby and an embattled Yorkshire terrier. Arms extended, Wilfrid Jennings launched himself bodily through the air towards Hugo's face, both clenched fists landing with a crunch, somewhere round his chin.

Staggering slightly, Hugo was aware of at least three loose bottom teeth and the taste of blood.

'You aggrethive thwine!' he gasped, stung into injured ire. 'Take that!' He swung and thumped clumsily back, on reflex, without judging weight of impact.

Mr Jennings lurched sideways, knees buckling. With a sickening thud, his head hit the heavy brass knob at the corner of the fender. He lay very still.

'My God!' Horrified, Hugo approached the motionless figure. Crouching on one knee, he forced himself to look. He could not bring himself to touch. 'Er ... Mr Jennings?'

Mr Jennings just went on lying there, eyes closed, face waxen. A trickle of blood was seeping round into his stiff collar from the back of his head.

'Great Thcott!' Hugo whispered, 'What have I done?'

He stumbled away to find somebody.

November

Surrey

White roughcast walls gleamed in the chilly sun, waiting for wisteria to wander, suitably controlled, across their faces, under slightly raised thatch brows of half-moon windows. The carefully laid pink brick-path ran straight from the newly varnished oak front-door, down a gentle slope to the rustic gate, through unmade earth which would take kindly to being banked into step-terraced lawn with stone rockeries.

The house looked rather lonely in its fenced acre, set in the first corner of an expanse of well-wooded Surrey country which, over the next few years, was to find itself dotted with similar 'desirable residences of individual character within easy reach of London, Dorking, Guildford and Leatherhead'.

'Oh, Hugo, it's all too, too dinky!' Bunty squeezed his arm as they surveyed the scene from an upstairs window.

Hugo found himself unable quite to agree. The smell of new plaster was getting up his nose and the sight of what needed doing to the garden made him feel even more knackered than he already did.

It was over three weeks since he had been sacked from Cambridge. On his ignominious arrival back at Walton Mansions, at a time when his grandmother was mercifully absent, his mother had listened, stony faced, to his explanation. Halting and disjointed as it was, she could discern the ring of truth.

As an immediate, interim expediency, she sent him down here and told him to put his back into sorting out her new weekend bolthole. It would get him out of the way while she thought.

Bunty had come over for the day. Probably for the night as well, if the camp-bed could be made to hold them both. Her grandmother thought she was at college in Haslemere. College in Haslemere thought she was looking after her sick grandmother.

Studying her decidedly statuesque outline, Hugo was just a shade puzzled as to how this child of theirs could have come on to such proportions quite so quickly. Not that he knew much about these things, of course, but it did seem pretty rapid.

'First babies often show early,' she said airily, knowing full well from biology classes at college that the opposite was usually the case, particularly with stomach muscles like hers. She almost convinced Hugo that the load she carried had not had nearly a month's head start on their first rumbunctious coupling.

When he asked her about Jennings, she giggled loudly. 'Oh, the pathetic little man rogered me!' she admitted, disarmingly candid. 'I picked that word up at college, do you like it? Yes, well, I fought him off, but honestly! It was rape! I didn't actually think he'd managed to, you know, I mean, until you, Cuddlebun, I just didn't ... I mean I wasn't even sure what one did.' She bit her lip, blinked back tears.

Seeing her there, so temptingly earthy, so fecund, he became suddenly very decisive. 'You'll stay here tonight,' he told her in tones that brooked no argument. 'Phone College and tell them your grandmother's worse. Tomorrow, we're going to London.'

London

'Good gracious, I thought you'd gone months ago!' Amaryllis walked into the drawing room at Walton Mansions to find Hugo nursing a Scotch.

'He's come back,' Emily muttered.

'But he's up at Cambridge.'

'He's been sent down.'

She had not been expecting Hugo this evening. Not at all. Now, it would all have to be gone through again with Amaryllis. It was too, too bad of everyone to converge like this.

'How far down?' Amaryllis asked over Hugo's head.

'He's supposed to be in Surrey.'

'I *am* here, you know,' Hugo protested mildly into his glass.

'When you have no business to be, it seems,' Amaryllis snapped. 'What happened?'

'Not a pretty story,' Emily said.

'I'm asking Hugo. Well?'

Hugo related, as briefly as possible, the unprovoked attack by Jennings and his own natural retaliation.

Amaryllis asked if Jennings was dead.

'I thought he was at first. But then he came to and started storming about in a bate, demanding to see the proctors and telling everybody I'd seduced his fiancée and got her pregnant.'

'Had you?'

'I didn't know she was his fiancée. Nor did she. It was entirely his own idea.'

'How quaint.' Amaryllis raised a thinly pencilled brow, catching the effect in the mirror as she did so.

'He's an awful little tick, Gramaryllis, honestly. And Bunty's a ripping girl. He worked on her sympathies, weeks before I met her. It's just as likely to be his!'

'Is that what she says?' Emily asked.

'We … we haven't discussed it.'

'How can you not discuss a thing like that?' Amaryllis was consumed with interest at the idea of her grandson leaping into parenthood when she had assumed him still to be pounding his way through halls of learning. 'Do you do everything in silence at Cambridge? Like a Closed Order?'

Emily glared. 'Not, as I said, a pretty story.' She waited for her mother to offer appropriate support.

But Amaryllis was eyeing Hugo with a trenchant gleam akin to admiration. 'And we were wondering if he had it in him!'

'If you can't say something useful, Mother, please don't say anything at all.'

Suddenly, Hugo stood up. 'The trouble with you two is, you don't let a fellow get a word in edgeways. *I'm* going to say something! I *haven't* got it in me!'

They stared at him.

'I haven't got it in me,' he went on, 'to be as raffish, as self-seeking, immoral and unscrupulous as both of you. I hanker for a decent family life and a position of respect in the community.' He paused, looking from one to the other.

'Have you quite finished?' Emily enquired.

'Except to tell you this,' his voice rose half an octave and his face darkened as he thundered: '*I will stop at nothing to get what I want and I will ride roughshod over anybody who tries to gainsay me!'*

'Spoken like a Kilverston!' Amaryllis applauded.

'Bunty is a rattling good sort,' he continued more quietly, 'and we shall have children of our own, after this one, and enjoy a wholesome existence which will owe nothing whatsoever to your influence.'

'Who exactly is – er – Bunty?' Emily asked.

'Her grandmother rents out rooms near Victoria Station,' he replied, with a touch of defiance, 'and not that it concerns you, it's not as you assume. Bunty's grandmother happens to be Lady Grinling and the house is a family property which is all they had left after her grandfather went broke and shot himself. Her mother died of 'flu and her father was French.'

'Do you hap-happen to know his name?' Emily was clearly under some strain.

'She did tell me. Something to do with a knife. Couteau, that's it. Du Couteau. He was drowned on the *Titanic*.'

Out of frozen silence, Amaryllis drew a quivering breath. 'How utterly, utterly appalling!' Her voice was thin with shock.

'I suppose so, yes,' Hugo looked at her in blank surprise, 'but it was a long time ago. Anyway, he was a complete bounder. They weren't married.'

Both women looked at him as if he had horns and a tail. Also, they seemed to be struck dumb.

He grinned at them with definite bravado. 'Unlike us,' he said. 'Bunty and I got married this afternoon. If you'll excuse me now, my wife is waiting for me downstairs.'

He bowed to each of them in turn and left the room.

In the long silence that followed, Amaryllis poured two very stiff drinks and handed one to Emily. They both sipped for some time, listening to the ticking of the clock.

'They're under age,' Amaryllis said, hopefully, at last.

'No. They're both over eighteen.'

'Well, it must be illegal. It goes against the *Guinness Book of Records*.'

'What are you talking about?'

'*Old Moore's Almanac*. The Augean Tables of Kindling in Proximity. Whatever it is you break the rules of when you marry your sister.'

'Half-sister.'

'Like the Ancient Egyptians,' Amaryllis was well into her stride, 'only in those days, it was different of course. It was the thing to do, then. For anybody who was anybody. They all got fascinatingly inbred. They gave the Israelites hell.'

Half-listening, Emily assembled her facts in the light of Hugo's genealogical bombshell. As far as her mother was concerned, Etienne du Couteau, father of both Hugo and Bunty, was dead. And no connection of Roscoe's. Priscilla Grinling was unaware that Emily even had a son. Or if she knew by now, she was scarcely likely to question his paternity.

'What's all that got to do with anything?' she murmured when her mother stopped rabbiting on about the Pharaohs.

Amaryllis sighed patiently. 'She's going to have a baby! Hugo says it isn't his, but who can rely on arithmetic?'

Emily met her gaze. 'The Ancient Egyptians did,' she pointed out, 'quite heavily, when you think of the Pyramids. And Hugo was always quite good at figures. Give Mr – what was his name?'

'Jennings, I believe.'

'Give him the benefit of the doubt. But she mustn't have any more.'

Chapter Seventeen
1931

Hollywood. March.

'I know how you feel, Roscoe. Believe me.'

Siggy Lubin, Chairman of The Polyscope Picture Corporation, faced one of his earliest contract artists across the vast desk of his office in what had begun as a few ramshackle sheds on some land in an unmade suburb of Los Angeles and was now a complex of studios, back lots, workshops and administration blocks. 'I hear what you're saying, Roscoe. I sympathize.'

In the aftermath of the Monte Carlo train disaster in 1921, Roscoe's contract with Polyscope had, to his immense surprise and relief, been immediately extended. Siggy Lubin was not one to penalize his hottest property because of a misfortune involving a niece he barely knew.

The deliberate act of sabotage had been made much of by the sensationalist press at the time. Who? What? A Bolshevik plot? Why? Cloak and dagger speculations abounded, some lustfully implicating Roscoe Somerville, sole survivor, as an undercover agent; a sinister mole, perhaps? Activated during his frolics in the decadent playgrounds of Europe, either by Lloyd George or the Comintern, to wreak havoc on God's Own Country?

As far as Siggy Lubin was concerned, the incident had blown away a potential project, an expendable unknown and a couple of minor employees. It had spared his biggest male 'name', adding a whiff of spice to the drawing power. Did Siggy Lubin dump a capital asset in the teeth of cheap newshounds? He did not. Polyscope signed Roscoe Somerville for ten years.

That was ten years back. Roscoe had been thirty-one and in peak condition, 'leading-man material' well able to meet the challenge of the talkies without a hiccup. Polyscope built on Roscoe Somerville, churning out vehicle after vehicle; its publicity office feeding public interest with an ever-rolling supply of assorted leading ladies to melt his swashbuckling heart; its Chairman deliberately aiming studio policy at keeping the shine on a valuable image which, unguarded, would quickly have tarnished in the sticky hands of the gutter columnists.

Despite the presentation, no single Roscoe Somerville movie, silent or with sound, ever succeeded in matching, let alone topping, the attendance records set by *Phantom of the Box* or, in real terms, some of its predecessors. From 1926 onwards, Roscoe found himself being loaned out to other studios, playing 'as cast', without script approval or choice of co-star.

Now, his contract with Polyscope had three weeks left to run. He still looked good, with his own teeth and his own hair, as thick as ever; the odd strand of grey needed scarcely a touch. All the same, he was nudging forty-two. Ronald Colman seemed to be getting most of the roles he felt should be his at this time. He was weary of being expected to swagger through low-budget adventure romps with terrible scripts in the kinds of lead now being offered to Douglas Fairbanks Junior, aged twenty-four, in the higher-budget ones.

After persistent approaches, the need for which he found disturbing, Roscoe Somerville was here today to review his situation in the company and to discuss his future prospects.

'A... a little more authority? Maturity?' he was saying. 'I'll be honest with you, Siggy. I have no objection to – indeed, I should welcome – a new image. One which would develop me as a character actor. What do you say?'

That, he considered, revealed an attitude of far-sighted realism. Character actors were seldom billed above the title, although they could sometimes command even larger letters immediately below. Nor did they warrant inflated star salaries, although their value was well recognized and suitably rewarded. Character actors grew older with dignity and acclaim, in steady demand for richly varied roles of distinguished support. Roscoe waited for affirmative reaction from his Chairman.

Siggy Lubin rolled his cigar round and round between his thumb and forefinger for some time, without speaking. He was not enjoying himself. He had postponed this interview as often as possible, knowing it would have to happen sooner or later. He took a deep breath.

'I don't see you as a Melvyn Douglas,' he said, 'nor yet as a Boris Karloff.'

'I was thinking more C. Aubrey Smith,' Roscoe murmured. 'In time, of course,' he added, the actor in question being at least thirty years his senior. But he did feel the comparison invited the right kind of scope.

'You don't play cricket,' Siggy said, obscurely accusing, 'and you're not married.'

That was the crux, of course. Siggy Lubin was hot on family values. He himself was a grandfather now. His widowed sister, Mrs Krantz, had a nice apartment in his garage block. When her husband Nathan died, Siggy offered her a home, having greatly admired her fortitude over the loss of her daughter.

In Siggy's philosophy, his own relatives had been done by real handsome: his sister's little Tilly given a glamorous new name, promoted to unearned star status and as 'Rosa Delaney' flashed, untried, across the firmament with the world at her feet for a few giddy weeks before getting opportunely snuffed, instead of having to face ultimate, inevitable rejection by the punters. These days, he presided over a close-knit tribe, with two sons to succeed him and all his women kept well away from the motion-picture industry.

Unfortunately, scandal attached itself to Roscoe Somerville like bindweed to a gatepost. Not just trains blowing up, either. Years before that, in Polyscope's earliest days, tongues had wagged over Little Joyce, his first and youngest leading lady.

All talk, maybe, but ... Siggy seemed to recall her running off in the end with one of his own backers. And Roscoe, at that time, was living with another of his backers. Murky.

For nigh on twenty years, Siggy Lubin had been the mainstay of Roscoe Somerville's existence. Sure, he'd seen returns. But he liked his stars to have some substance in their private lives. He liked them married, with photogenic kids. So what if partners changed from time to time and kids got three poppas and four mommas, all marketable, all photogenic, all famous? Safety in numbers. But keep it legal. Set an example for the fans. Preserve the institution of family and stability. Something Roscoe Somerville had always been short on.

With discomfiture but no real regret, Siggy Lubin was no longer prepared to shore up a bachelor whose gaiety, to put it mildly, was starting to fray.

'You never get married,' he said reproachfully, 'not even once or twice.'

'I've never felt strongly enough on the subject,' Roscoe replied with truth.

There was only one woman in the world he would ever remotely consider marrying. And that, without a doubt, would be mutual annihilation. Since Emily Kilverston had made it abundantly clear more than once that she wished him dead, he could only oblige her by keeping out of her way.

He did wonder sometimes, with a pang, why she had not only thought it necessary to blow him to smithereens, but also enlisted the help of his eight-year-old son when it came to planting the bomb? That, he felt, was in truly diabolical taste.

'Word gets out, see, Roscoe,' Siggy was saying. 'I got word not so long since, I oughta tell you. About some wild crush at the Garden of Allah. Ain't you through with all that yet?'

Roscoe sat quite still; a mixture of bleak despair and cold, pointless fury stealing over him.

Home, to Roscoe Somerville, was a rented bungalow in the Garden of Allah, a residential development more or less exclusive to the Hollywood film community which catered mostly for the young and single on a roll to fame and fortune. Once into a first marriage, stars usually moved on to the more solid glories of Beverly Hills or Santa Monica. Roscoe was well suited there.

From time to time, the place hit the gossip headlines in connection with yet another gathering where the Prohibition laws, now limping towards extinction, were being blithely ignored, cocaine snorted, husbands and wives exchanged, relationships rearranged and heads broken.

A couple of months back, one such had led to a very young girl being chased through the bushes in the small hours by a man old enough to be her grandfather and flinging herself in a gale of shrieks on Roscoe's front porch. By chance, he was home that night, alone and fast asleep in bed.

Feeling none too sociable, he was less than enchanted, on padding out in his bathrobe to investigate the uproar, at finding what appeared to be the final stages of a particularly brutal rape in progress on his quarry tiles. With the advantage of relative youth, strength and sobriety, he pulled the man off.

He recoiled slightly from glowering, red-rimmed eyes in a face ravaged by over-indulgence, before shocked recognition hit. This was the bastard whom, in ignorance, he had once assumed to be Emily's husband. This was Franz-Clovis, Comte de Lavalle-Fontaine, way over sixty now and a lot the worse for wear.

Franz-Clovis raised an unsteady fist, but thought better of it and made off, muttering incoherently under his breath. The girl lay there at Roscoe's feet, whimpering. He picked her up, carried her inside, sat her on the sofa and made her a cup of tea. It seemed sensible.

As he watched her drink it, he realized two things. This was Belladonna, the current cabaret sensation at the 'Prince Nikolai' Supper Club on Hollywood Boulevard. And Belladonna was not a day over eighteen.

Rather surprisingly, as far as he could judge, she seemed not to be suffering unduly from outrage or shock. She was merely half-cut, sleepy and indisposed to conversation. Perhaps foolishly, he decided not to risk upsetting her by calling the police. Instead, he fetched pillows and blankets, tucked her up on the sofa and went back to bed.

A little later, he became foggily aware of a warm, female, naked form wrapping itself round him, accompanied by a breathy, lisping whisper of: '*I'th cold...*'

'She's pregnant,' Siggy's voice ran on relentlessly, 'the chick is pregnant. And she's been talking. Or her grandma has. Her grandma is the Princess Ivadnya Vishnevska. She owns the "Prince Nikolai" on the Boulevard. You know that?'

Roscoe nodded. He felt disinclined for speech. Not in competition with Siggy.

'Her grandma raised the chick, you know that? The chick has been raised nice. All she does is stand under a spotlight in a nice dress and the customers go wild. No touching.'

Roscoe nodded again. He had seen her in performance.

Performance? Belladonna, sheathed in couture, simply *was*. Against a background of subtly arranged music, she created an illusion of being in transit on this imperfect planet, poised for flight back to some enchanted paradise of origin. She simply hovered in repose there, appearing to search the audience with enormous, dark, inquisitive eyes brimming with untold promise for whomsoever might merit her recognition. Then, she simply went away. A little while later, she would return in a different dress and repeat the exercise.

She was naturally short-sighted. What with the drops in her eyes to increase their effect, the beam of the follow-spot and the total absence of any other talent, there was nothing else she could do. It was pleasant to be applauded just for standing about wearing lovely clothes. Nothing else was necessary. The men at the tables went weak at the knees at her beauty and ordered another drink. The women with them wanted to know more about her gowns.

All of which was excellent business for Princess Ivadnya Vishnevska. It was also excellent business for 'Ivy's', the exclusive dress shop also owned by the princess, which supplied Belladonna's costumes. Siggy Lubin had shares in both concerns.

'Belladonna has to be withdrawn in respect of her ... condition,' Siggy's tone dropped in hushed propriety. 'Hedda and Louella, they're gunning for you. You know that?'

Roscoe tried not to show that he was seriously alarmed.

Hedda Hopper and Louella Parsons, the two sizzling gossip columnists, vied to be first with the newest, niftiest innuendo. There was a third, who sometimes scooped them both, but had yet to pronounce on this current titbit.

Why bother, in Roscoe's view, if he was already dead?

Siggy, it seemed, had not yet finished. 'You know who Belladonna's mother was?'

Roscoe shook his head. It made a change.

'Little Joyce. You remember Little Joyce?' Siggy paused for the full implication to sink in before adding, 'Hedda and Louella, they're wondering if maybe Belladonna might be your daughter. You thought of that?'

'That is absolutely ... ludicrous! Disgusting!' Roscoe sprang up and stood quivering, rigid with shock.

'I've had them gagged for a while now, but they're pulling hard.'

Holding the talons of those two off Polyscope's good name had been costing Siggy a fortune. And the story was still hot.

Roscoe was lost for words; inarticulate at the prurient, slanderous injustice. 'It's not true! It simply is not true!'

There was a hint of genuine pity in Siggy Lubin's eyes before he swiftly lowered them to study his fingernails. When he faced Roscoe again, it was with a bland, glazed stare.

'*You* know that,' he reasoned gently, 'and even if maybe, I know that, it's still in the air. Floating like thistledown. Rolling along the sidewalks like tumbleweed.' He gazed out of the window for a moment, pleased with his poetic simile, seeing thistledown waft above boyhood fields round Hamburg.

Roscoe thought of dandelion clocks blowing across Hampstead.

'I guess I have to let you go, Roscoe,' the marble eyes swivelled back again. 'It hurts me. It cuts me deeply. But the truth is, your conduct of yourself is no longer in line with the aspirations of this organization.'

The truth was, Siggy Lubin was not inclined to sponsor Roscoe Somerville's transition from ageing Lothario to English gentleman.

If Princess Ivadnya Vishnevska was one to indulge in self-pity, which she was not, she would no doubt bemoan the way in which, without exception, the behaviour of her dependants brought scant returns for effort expended on their behalf. But Ivy preferred to review her life in terms of tit-for-tat; advantage gained from setback, profit pulled from loss, overall advancement maintained despite inadequacy in others.

She had, after all, collected a title from Heatherley, even though he was a dead loss otherwise; and a settlement for life from bloody Franz-Clovis, at a time when he'd had it to settle. That had enabled her to build a solid and substantial background in real estate and fashion, well able to withstand the crunch when paper fortunes blew away.

Not so Franz-Clovis, it would seem. He must have got his comeuppance good and proper. Serve him right. He was a sad sight these days, loafing about Los Angeles, gate-crashing dope parties, dazzling strangers with his tattered lineage. The regular monthly sums she paid anonymously into his bank account were more a tribute to her own abilities than a donation towards his welfare. Most likely, all they fed was a drug habit.

Had she known that the seedy image was a calculated choice, she would have been extremely surprised.

As for Vishnevski, the pet Russian bear with the sixty-carat bloodline, he'd had a sore head an' all. And a capacity for liquor that made him a damn liability as *maître* of the Prince Nikolai, let alone anything else. When, early on in the venture, he stumbled off into the night with the contents of the till, her relief was great, matched only by the news that he'd finished up under a streetcar in New Orleans. Still, due to his having existed at all, she had an even showier title and a classy joint which could only profit from his continued absence.

Most important of all, her relatively brief association with her own daughter, Joyce, had resulted in sole custody of Edith, apple of her eye. After the initial shock at being landed with a bastard granddaughter and no by-your-leave, Ivy had determined that this one, at least, should never have to fight for the right to survive. It would be brought up to expect the best of everything and be married, when the time came, to a carefully researched young man of Ivy's choosing. She never made any attempts to find Joyce. Why should she?

One way and another, Ivy Dibbins had been well pleased with the way her life had gone. Until now. Now, it seemed, all that she had hoped for, worked for, counted on for eighteen years, was being blown away with a random whisk of fate.

She paced tautly up and down Edith's room, fists tightly clenched to stop herself grabbing the snuffling figure on the bed and shaking it until its teeth rattled.

It's my fault, she told herself mercilessly. My fault for encouraging her to parade about thinking she's the bee's knees. Getting ideas and skiving off to try them out and fibbing to me about where she's going. 'Staying over at Milly's'? Pyjama parties with old friends from High? Ha! I need my head read.

It was only a few months back that Edith, trying on an evening gown from the new collection at 'Ivy's' boutique, had impinged on her grandmother as a superb natural model; five foot ten, willow-slim, with the gawky elegance of a top-bred yearling. It had seemed a good idea at the time to let her show some of the clothes as a kind of cabaret at the supper club. Edith, of course, was thrilled to bits.

The effect was sensational. As an addition to its already distinctive reputation, Belladonna sent the prestige of the Prince Nikolai into orbit.

Now this. When she could trust herself to speak, Ivy faced her granddaughter from the foot of the bed.

'How – how far on are you?' There was still a faint hope that it might be dealt with discreetly.

'Over three months.'

Too late. Anyway, what hope? Siggy had called this morning. The cauldrons of Hedda and Louella were bubbling. Even Siggy could no longer stop them boiling over, shares or no shares.

'Who? How? When?' she forced herself to ask.

Edith considered, damply, for some time. 'I don't know,' she replied eventually.

Ivy stifled a tearing, unbidden sob, reaching down from far-off times and places. What can you expect? It's Joyce all over again, isn't it? I should have told her. I should have taught her. But I thought ... I hoped...

Edith had, in fact, been kicking up her heels more often and for longer than her grandmother imagined. She had revelled in the adulation and the attention she seemed to attract simply by being herself. There had been so many wonderful parties, so many attractive men, she really couldn't say for certain.

There was one party in particular, though, at the Garden of Allah. When the old guy who said he was a duke or something cornered her and went on about his castles on the Rhine. He'd wept all over her and called her a Lorelei, whatever that was. So she'd flirted a little, to cheer him up, then he started groping her, so she'd run off and he'd come after her and caught her. So ... she'd let him. Anything to get rid of him.

She didn't want her grandmother to know about that. It hadn't been very nice. What came after was far more respectable. It would probably go down better. 'I did stay over at Roscoe Somerville's place one night,' she began, confidently truthful, 'in his bed with him. But he never once—'

'*What?*'

Edith had intended reassurance. Her grandmother's reaction scared the wits out of her.

'... *laid a finger on me*' was for ever left unsaid.

Ivy's head was spinning. Siggy had hinted at this. And she hadn't caught on. And those two vultures had the story ready to break. Who had given it to them?

Franz-Clovis de Lavalle-Fontaine had been badly hit by the collapse of the stock market, but by no means eliminated. Acting partly on occupational instinct and partly on personal whim, he invested heavily in Krupps, the engineering giant of the Ruhr.

He also followed, with intense interest, the techniques being practised on the depressed population of Germany by an obscure Austrian with piercing blue eyes, the magnetism of whose orations held the promise of a cure for all its ills.

Half Austrian himself, Franz-Clovis could identify with this man's aims and vision. He understood the uses of magnetism and the rewards it could bring. He was enough of an historian to recognize the course this rising leader's ambition might take, given no effective opposition.

He poured funds into the National Socialist Party of Germany. But he took care to keep his own name and presence far away. The Wall Street crash expediently allowed him to fade, unsought, from spheres of former activity.

Rejection by Emily Kilverston had impaired his dangerously volatile character more profoundly than he would admit. More, even, than he knew. Because of her he had, without pause, committed mass murder; destroyed innocent people, including his own mother. And still been deprived of his objective. He wanted revenge on all women; all people. He had no wish to examine the reasons why. For years he drifted aimlessly, following his corroding fancies; only regaining a dim sense of purpose at the notion of wielding influence, behind others' endeavours, over events which met with his approval.

He settled in Los Angeles and deliberately cultivated a seedy, undemanding image behind which he could behave exactly as he chose. It was amusing. He was tolerated as an eccentric by a wide assortment of groups. He used alcohol, stimulants, whatever would enhance the passing of time. He took what he wanted, when he wanted, from whomsoever he wanted, for transient excitement.

One night at the Garden of Allah, when his entertainment was rudely interrupted by Roscoe Somerville, he was quick to realize the opportunity of settling a very long-standing score.

'Uncle Roscoe! Uncle *Roscoe*!' Daphne Fitton, aged ten, came bounding ahead of her mother on to the front porch.

Roscoe was sitting there, nursing a Scotch. It was his first. He had spent the morning picking over various different options in the business of doing away with himself and had settled for a lot of drink followed by a lot of pills.

It seemed the least messy and the least unpleasant. He had written a whole stack of notes to whom it may concern. He was now ready to embark on the final project of his misspent life.

What the hell did Gertrude and Daphne want to come wading in for?

'Guess what? We're going to England!' She was jumping up and down in front of him, forcing him to focus again on the living.

'We?' He looked at her with pride. *This* was his daughter. He knew it, her mother knew it. His daughter called him 'Uncle Roscoe'. So what?

'Cool it, Daphne!' Gertrude hove into view. At fifty, she was still bony, still equine, tougher than ever. 'Go swim or something.'

'Okay.' Already in her swimsuit, Daphne pulled off her shorts and was gone.

'Time she was in school learning to be a lady,' said her mother.

'Hollywood High?' Roscoe sounded doubtful.

Gertrude brayed. 'I say "lady", I mean lady. English lady. Saltdean.'

'What?'

'Saltdean Ladies' College. Sussex, England. Where the nobs go.'

'Oh.' He was still doubtful. Daphne was an all-American kid. Gertrude's choice of name for her had always struck him as quaint. Well, if today went to plan, he wouldn't be here to see.

Gertrude looked at his glass. She looked at the bottle of pain-killers on the table beside him. She looked at the neat pile of sealed envelopes.

'You've been set up,' she said.

'Who'd believe it?'

'I don't believe it. I know it.'

He faced her, without much hope. Even if she did know it, what could she do? Now? He was washed out.

He was too low even to remind himself that Gertrude Fitton, as the third leading columnist in Hollywood, was a force to be reckoned with. It had not for a moment occurred to him that she might have taken up his cause. They were still friends, sure. But there were limits beyond which friendship, however solid, could not be expected to stretch.

'The dirt came from an unknown source,' she said, 'I haven't tracked it down yet.'

'I'm still dumped by Polyscope.'

'So you're available? Great.'

He peered at her stupidly.

'You've been exploited in rubbish too long,' she said. 'Now, maybe, you're free to consider a big-budget historical?'

What historicals were in production this year? He could only think of *Dracula* offhand, if that counted. Bela Lugosi was already cast. 'Who, er, who for?' he asked foggily, still halfway to the Styx.

'Me.'

Although her name never appeared, Gertrude Fitton had controlling interests in more than one of the bigger studios.

'*The Saxon Cometh*. Set in the Ancient British Dark Ages of England,' she explained carefully. 'You'll be playing King Arthur.'

He understood that he was being offered a lifeline. He tried to pull himself out of his daze.

'It sounds ... a unique opportunity, Gertrude old dear.'

'And another thing. You'll be the only one doesn't deserve to be dubbed. You speaking genuine Saxon.'

It must be born in England. That much, Ivy had decided. However it turned out. It might be monstrous, from what she'd been given to understand. It must all happen a long way from here. And it wouldn't do Edie any harm to get a taste of the rough underbelly of life, not after the way she'd been carrying on. Camberwell, that was it. The South Camberwell Hospital For Women. Serve the baggage right.

And what about Roscoe Sodding Somerville, then? How much truth was there in the rumours over Little Joyce? Ivy doubted if there was any, remembering the dates. But you can't take risks. He's a danger on this earth. He needs dealing with. He's a big star. A big name. How best to deal with him? How best to destroy him?

I know. I'll marry him.

Chapter Eighteen

April. London.

When Jason Kilverston was born, Bunty fancied the name because she liked the legend of the Golden Fleece; Hugo because he reckoned it summed up the whole situation pretty neatly.

Emily dropped in every day at the flat they had taken in Ebury Street, to monitor the baby's developing features. At thirty-five, looking about twenty-eight, she nevertheless pulled rank as devoted grandmother to do so; anxiously watching for signs that this was not her grandson.

There was absolutely no doubt, of course, that it was Roscoe's. Emily reflected sourly that Roscoe Summerfield's masquerade as a French con-man called Etienne du Couteau was casting uncomfortably long shadows.

July

'...*Brothers and sisters have I none*,' Emily crooned softly – the silly jingle came to mind every time she looked at Jason – '*but that man's father is my...*'

'Are we behaving ourselves with Grand Mumsie, then? Does Grand Mumsie want a cup of tea?' Bunty thundered in as if she were playing centre forward for Tottenham Hotspur.

Emily tried not to hear the revolting diminutive her daughter-in-law saw fit to use, lest silent cringe erupt into unbridled screech. She was perfectly well aware that Bunty disliked and disapproved of her. With instinctive accuracy, she also sensed that Bunty's fulsome exterior hid a truculent nature that disliked pretty well everybody, starting with her own grandmother. The exception would seem to have been Hugo. A schoolgirl crush had taken root, nurtured itself disproportionately for four years and became a fixation, crashing into rampant growth at a chance reunion which, to Emily, was a resounding example of Sod's Law.

Hugo had obviously been taken by storm. He was already showing signs of creeping disillusion. After the impulsive, appallingly mistaken wedding, there had been the business of finding somewhere to live; also, in view of the ignominious end to his academic career, some way of earning a living.

Thanks entirely to Priscilla's highly placed connections, Hugo was now working at the BBC as a researcher's dogsbody in the news department. His superiors were increasingly impressed by his zeal, which often outstripped the call of duty and Hugo took refuge there at Savoy Hill, relishing the irregular hours and coming home as seldom as possible.

Notwithstanding its acute irregularity, this union would be set to founder anyway in due course, Emily well knew. But time was of the essence. Future risk must be eliminated. She saw this as her urgent personal aim; to be achieved, moreover, without upsetting Hugo – or Priscilla, for whom she had a genuine regard – by the raking over of hair-raising 'causes and impediments'. Meanwhile, confirmation that Jason was not a genetic offence would be more than welcome.

'I wish to speak to the manager of this department.'

'I am he, Madam. I trust there's no cause for complaint?' Mr Jennings had his diplomatic skills at the ready.

The youngish woman in the sensible belted cardigan and the rakish beret smiled disarmingly and rustled the papers on her clipboard. 'I'm conducting a survey,' she confided, 'For the *Ladies' Home Journal*. On Department Managers at London Stores, starting here at the Army & Navy. Now you are … Mr Jennings?'

'I am indeed.' He straightened his tie and re-arranged his manner. 'How may I assist you?'

'Well, we're collecting material on you excellent gentlemen, to show our readers why some of you are where you are today. Mr Jennings, are you married?'

He sneezed.

'Evidently not,' Emily scribbled busily. 'Your wife would never let you come to work with a cold like that. I wonder if we could talk somewhere quieter? When we deal with persons of real standing, we do like our interviews to be confidential.'

Over the past year, Mr Jennings' self-esteem had become a little more than a façade kept grimly in place for working purposes. At these words, it flickered into faint renewal. He instructed his senior salesman accordingly and ushered his visitor towards his office.

In quite a short time, with a carefully devised list of questions and a cleverly judged approach, Emily not only had his confidence, but also an accurate impression of the cruel use made of his foolishness by her unappealing daughter-in-law. She listened closely to his tale of shattered dreams.

'So, Mr Jennings,' she observed finally, with compassionate warmth, 'I can't, in fact, put you down as a family man?'

'If you could only imagine how earnest was my wish … pardon me …' He sneezed several times.

'Courage!' Emily feared he was about to start again, 'you never know what's waiting for you, just round the corner!'

'But I do, Madam! The first-floor front at 26 Claverton Street. And loneliness.' In spite of the great sorrow in his life, Mr Jennings saw no reason to relinquish home comforts by taking his custom elsewhere. It was Bunty who had moved out when she married the cad.

Emily plunged. 'Had you thought of adoption?'

He was utterly astonished. '*I*, Madam? A bachelor, alone?'

'There's no law against it,' she smiled encouragement. 'Many gentlemen, after all, provide for their, erm, responsibilities. Without the tedium of binding themselves legally to the, erm, the responsibilities' mothers.' She watched him beadily for some kind of giveaway reaction.

'I confess myself at a loss to know, Madam, how you might form the impression that I…' He was torn over whether to ruffle his feathers in righteous indignation or preen them.

His dilemma was not lost on Emily. But she doubted if he would claim ownership of an infant palmed off on his lost love's preferred consort and demand its return forthwith. Well, it had been worth a try. One could still plant a seed or two.

'In your case,' she resumed, 'adoption might just be the means to a life of fulfilment. Without the emotional quicksands of a new relationship. After being so deeply wounded, I mean.'

The note of thoughtful authority in her voice melted his reserve yet again. 'I'd not have thought to encounter such wisdom in a market researcher from the *Ladies' Home Journal*,' he breathed, with a kind of awed wonder.

'I'm not on their staff,' she assured him quickly, 'I undertook this survey to oblige, only. My main interest is in social work. In my job, you see, Mr Jennings, one does sense unspoken disappointments, hopes ... I do trust you haven't found my questions intrusive?'

Mr Jennings was beginning to feel understood for the first time in his life. 'Not at all, Miss ... Miss...?'

'Mrs,' she beamed at him, taking a card-case from her bag and extracting one from a specially printed batch of six, 'Mrs Amelia Fibstock. Do think about what I've said. As a matter of fact, I happen to know of a dear little chap, nearly four months old now, in need of a stable home and a good, upright father-figure.'

She watched the interest flicker briefly, then fade at the preposterous idea. She got up. 'Do let me know if I can help.'

'I certainly will, Mrs Fibstock.' He flushed with gratitude.

She turned to go. Suddenly, out of sheer curiosity, she ran her pencil briskly down her questionnaire. 'Just checking, Mr Jennings ... you did say, didn't you, that you started here in Leather Goods?'

He smiled reminiscently. 'Right at the bottom of the ladder, yes; 1912, it would have been.'

Walking along the street, Emily contemplated the quaintness of life. The poor little man had seemed familiar the moment she saw him. Not only because of the obligingly strong resemblance to his son, either. Across the years, she saw herself persuading a young Mr Jennings to let her remove the cravat case from a set of luggage which he had just sold to a young Mr Summerfield.

'You'll be glad to know, mother, that your little great-grandson is the image of the Luggage Department Manager at the Army & Navy Stores.'

'All babies look alike to me,' Amaryllis was cautiously glum, 'Jason might be slightly uglier than most, but what a relief if you're right.'

'Oh, I am.' Emily's jubilation was positively reckless. 'Now, all I have to do is make sure that Roscoe's son and Roscoe's frightful daughter don't do any serious damage.'

Too late, she realized the slip.

Her mother stood very still. With that damned eyebrow raised. 'You do mean, "Etienne du Couteau" of course?' The correction came in tones of pure silk.

The time for bluffing it out was long past. Emily bowed graciously. 'If you'd been in my shoes at the time, I doubt if you would have admitted it, either.'

Amaryllis poured herself a drink. 'I think I've been remarkably tactful for almost nineteen years. When you look at Hugo.' She took a deep breath. 'May one ask what you propose doing now?'

'I wouldn't if I were you.'

September. Hollywood.

The owner of the Prince Nikolai Supper Club on the Boulevard preferred to maintain a low profile. She had an excellent team of professionals to run it properly and answer to her, or else. To them, on the rare occasions she entertained there, the Princess Ivadnya Vishnevska was incognito.

She did, however, keep a lively eye on who patronized her little goldmine and with whom. When it came to her notice that a party was booked to celebrate the 'wrap' of *The Saxon Cometh*, she chose to take a meal at a quiet corner table from which she could see without being seen.

The *Saxon* gathering was also by way of being a *bon voyage* for the producer and the male star. Gertrude Fitton and Roscoe Somerville would be leaving for England within the week.

Before undergoing the full glare attendant on any Hollywood spectacular, the film was to be given a preview as the opening attraction at a new cinema near Brighton, arranged by Gertrude to coincide with the settling in of her daughter at school.

Roscoe anticipated the trip with mixed feelings. Introducing Daphne to England would be great, but he knew too well that his intended triumphant 'Saxon Cometh Back' was going to be more of an open invitation to critical massacre.

During a lull in the music, Princess Vishnevska emerged from the shadows. Slowly, she crossed the empty dance-floor. Diners paused over their food. At fifty, Ivy looked magnificent. She was used to being admired. But she was not remotely prepared for her effect on the man she intended first to make mad and then to destroy.

Roscoe's face lost its colour. His mouth dropped open. He watched her advance as if dazzled by 200 watts. 'F-Flo?' he whispered hoarsely, 'Florence?'

Ivy stopped dead. This reaction, she had not envisaged. It added a dimension that must needs be explored. If only as a means to her self-appointed ends.

'Don't tell me you know my sister, Mr Somerville!' she exclaimed. 'Why, we lost touch about thirty years ago! How *is* Florrie these days?'

In her chosen role of observer, Gertrude Fitton tried to figure out the motive, since motive there had to be. Did the woman still blame Roscoe for her silly granddaughter's condition? In spite of all that evidence to the contrary being made public? In Gertrude Fitton's column, the truth – with Roscoe as hero of the hour – had clarioned forth and blown the other two harpies and their smut clean off their pages. Did little Belladonna's grandma prefer the idea of Roscoe Somerville as despoiler of her ewe lamb to that unpleasant old roué Lavalle-Fontaine? Why?

Lavalle-Fontaine had blown, months ago. Disappeared. Roscoe was still around. Was that it? So what was the lady up to?

Funny, Gertrude thought. Ivy Vishnevska's resemblance to that twin sister of hers, it never struck me before. But then, why would it? The tart making up to Pa on the *Titanic* is a world and a lifetime away. Roscoe-baby's a big boy now. He's on his own. What next, I wonder?

About an hour later, after much champagne on the house had been consumed and much conviviality exchanged, Roscoe found himself driving both Gertrude and Ivy home, at Gertrude's request. She also asked to be dropped off first.

When Roscoe was invited in for a nightcap at Ivy's house on Sunset, he was amazed to be greeted warmly by a heavily pregnant Belladonna.

'I never had the chance to thank you properly, even!' She turned glowingly to her grandmother, 'Like I said, Mr Somerville looked after me so good. Like the best sort of doctor!'

Having known quite a few sorts of doctor in her time, Ivy watched Roscoe's face as Edith again described her experience at the Garden of Allah. She also listened properly, this time. The cold-blooded aspects of her scheme began to waver.

Maybe I was hasty, she thought. Maybe I just didn't want to credit the counter-rumours about Franz-Fucking-Clovis. Maybe I was a bloody fool. And Roscoe Somerville knew Florrie. He even worked with Florrie. What at, we don't ask. But it must mean Roscoe's one of us, eh? Maybe it's time I got married again, anyway. I like him. Maybe that's a good enough reason, for a change. And a film star can't be bad for business, eh?

Got to sort Edie out in England first. Then, we'll see.

London

'One twothreefour, one twothreefour, stretch twothreefour, hup twothreefour…' Bunty was doing her exercises. What with Nanny on holiday and Hugo not coming home all night again, it was a very healthy way to pass the time.

It also took her mind off Jason, who was teething. Purple in the face, he was, yowling and gnawing ferociously on the bars of his cot. His mother considered aids like rings and rusks as effete as soothing his gums with gripe water. Better for him to develop his own resources. If he kept getting mouthfuls of shellac varnish, well, hard cheese on him.

Bunty had already shut the nursery door to keep the noise down. Now, she shut the sitting-room door as well. She wondered if Jason would improve at all. She certainly didn't like him much so far. He drove poor darling Hugo away for days at a time.

She was standing on her head for a count of a hundred and twenty when she realized the yelling had stopped.

'How dare you let him cry like that!' Hugo had come into the room. In his arms was a much mollified Jason, pulling on a bottle of blackcurrant juice laced with Drambuie.

'I never heard the front door,' Bunty replied as brightly as inversion allowed. Even upside-down, her husband looked cross. 'Fancy you being back, Cuddles! Hundred'n ten ... down in a sec. What have you been doing all this time?'

Hugo regarded her with thinly veiled distaste. He must have been mad. Stark, staring batty. He wished he could think of a reasonably humane, totally undetectable way to kill her. He was also exhausted.

'We've come off the Gold Standard,' he said. 'Income tax is up to five shillings and the dole is cut by ten per cent. I've been collating the news all night. I'm going to bed. I'll take Jason with me. We could both do with some sleep.'

Bunty stood up with a face like a giant tomato. 'Not before you've heard my news,' she cautioned archly. 'Mumsie has invited us down to Horsley. First weekend in October.'

Resisting the impulse to retch at Bunty's favoured sobriquet for his mother, Hugo was immediately suspicious. He could sense Emily's fancy for a couple more rockeries. 'I thought she'd taken on a proper gardener.'

'Oh, she says it's all looking splendid,' Bunty assured him. 'She just thought it would be nice for us to have a complete break. She, er, she doesn't mention Jason in her note.'

'What's the poor little blighter to do, cook for himself?'

'Silly old Cuddles! Gramps will have him. She'd love to!'

Hugo was assailed with extreme doubt. 'Have you asked her?'

'Not exactly. But I spoke to Mr Jennings on the phone. He's taking Gramps to the seaside the same weekend. It will do Jason the world of good!'

In the two months since his interview with that charming Mrs Amelia Fibstock, Mr Jennings had once or twice caught himself dwelling on the idea of becoming a family man. Without the unnerving complication of a wife. Was it really possible? Did he really wish it?

The whole business of Bunty Grinling's faithlessness had affected him more strongly than he realized. The conviction that he had fathered her son must, for obvious reasons, remain a sadly unacknowledged truth. In August, walking along the front at Saltdean, he had counted the number of fathers pushing prams. He found it obscurely encouraging.

It would mean leaving Claverton Street. Setting up a proper home. Well, he could afford it. But what an upheaval. What an unprecedented step. Come come, Wilfrid Jennings! You've been well suited at Claverton Street for fifteen years.

Somehow, though, since Bunty, it wasn't quite the same.

Back in London, he even began thinking of how, if he were to leave, he could best show his appreciation to Leedi Priscilla.

He wondered if it might be permissible to invite her, as his honoured guest, for a late-season weekend break at the Palm Gardens Hotel. Savouring the idea, his own audacity took his breath away. Wilfrid Jennings playing host to Leedi Priscilla? And yet, what more fitting tribute to the long-term comfort and security he had known under her roof? Would she accept? He might just ask her anyway. As a gesture. Regardless of any considered move.

When Priscilla eventually understood what he was trying to say, she was flabbergasted. No one in her whole existence had ever before offered her a treat. Or, for that matter, 'eagerly enticipated her greecious acciptance'. Her acceptance was more gruff than gracious; muffled with the incredulity of a street urchin given the run of a sweet-shop.

She was out when Bunty rang to billet Jason on her for the first weekend in October. To Mr Jennings, who happened to pick up the phone, the call acted as a catalyst.

This was almost certainly his own son. At a very vulnerable age, teething and such. To take care of him? For the very weekend just this moment booked at Saltdean? Aided by a senior legal relative? It was Fate. Not to mention a valuable test of his own potential as an adoptive parent in the future, surely? Whether or not it was ever acted upon?

In appropriately constipated tones, Mr Jennings informed Bunty that he would endeavour to prevail upon Leedi Priscilla in the matter.

October

The Registrar at the South Camberwell Hospital for Women had been understandably surprised to receive a letter from a Russian princess who, on strong personal recommendation, wished to book her granddaughter in for a confinement. Fairly certain that Her Highness had this institution confused with a posh private clinic in Camberley, the Registrar confirmed the reservation.

Who argues with Royalty?

Edith was taken straight there from Southampton and dumped. Outrage, hysterics, threats of suicide all to no avail. Ivy knew the care in this discouraging edifice to be basic but adequate. It also offered excellent opportunity for swift and discreet adoption. Edith had no interest in motherhood and Ivy was strenuously indisposed to raising another brat. Let alone one carrying the fermented genes of Franz-Clovis.

As to the surroundings, Edie had asked for this and she was getting it. She had about a week to go. She could sit it out.

Ivy did, however, intend to stay within reach. She was seriously considering buying a property in the country here. The whole sorry business of her granddaughter's predicament had left her feeling sick and tired of Hollywood. The Prince Nikolai was thriving. Maybe she'd sell. Maybe not. But a base over here was a priority. Something small. Have a look round, eh?

To this end, after installing Edith at Camberwell, Ivy went down to Hampshire and booked herself into a village pub.

Heatherley Racing Stables was among the most famous in the country now. The castle was an exclusive Girls' School with the added advantage of extensive grounds stretching away to the gallops. As the Heatherley land covered some 6,000 acres, 'tasteful' ribbon development on its perimeters by a speculative builder was not really too much of an intrusion.

The bright new bungalows were being snapped up, according to the estate agent. Even, he assured his new client, some of those not yet completed. But he still sensed a mood of disparagement as he conducted her round the third this morning.

Of course, she was a bit out of the usual run of young families with dads working in Basingstoke. Of a certain age, you might say. Elegant, with it.

He decided to try something else. 'The Dower House has just been converted into maisonettes,' he remarked casually, 'really charming. Quite unique. Naturally, they're rather more expensive.'

'Show me,' Ivy said.

Chapter Nineteen

Saturday, 7th October

Horsley, Surrey

It had been raining since yesterday morning. The ground at Emily's drive-in back gate, still waiting to be tar-macadamed, was a swamp. They played Mah-jong till they were dizzy, Hugo went to sleep on the sofa and Bunty complained that it wasn't at all what she'd been expecting.

'What were you expecting?' Emily asked.

'Well, jolly rambles. Blackberrying.'

'In this weather?'

'Perhaps it'll be better tomorrow.'

Things were livened up a bit by a totally unexpected call by the vicar, on his way home from a parish council meeting. With him in the Austin Seven was a Major Hope-Stukely, the treasurer. Emily, who had never met either of them, could not remember being more delighted to see two new human faces. She took their macs, sat them down and plied them with whiskies before looking at them expectantly to see what their business might be.

Saltdean, Sussex

Trevor Simpson, Manager of the Palm Gardens Hotel, would never know another weekend like this. It had begun with the wedding this morning. After the happy couple departed in a shower of boots, kettles and confetti, most of the guests carried on drinking at the expense of the bride's father while the staff tried to prepare for a batch of distinguished arrivals expected before dinner. It was not easy.

Trevor Simpson himself resorted to emptying, personally, all champagne bottles less than a quarter full, in the hope that the bride's father's hospitality would run out and everybody would go home. But they only went on to cocktails from the bar.

By five o'clock, Mr Simpson's demeanour had lost a good deal of its customary edge.

Horsley

In Emily's estimation, the vicar was a non-starter compared to the noisy maniac at poor old Lily's Chalk Farm conditioning unit. Mild and oat-coloured, this one delivered a lengthy discourse on not having had the pleasure before now of meeting his new parishioner, not in the whole year she had been resident, so elusive was she; well, of course, having to work in London all the week... 'But here we are now at last, are we not? Shall we be seeing you and your charming family in church tomorrow?'

Emily treated him to a smile of purest light. He was so blinded by it, his glass got topped up without him noticing.

'Actually, no,' she said confidentially, 'it upsets my metabolism. But it's so nice to welcome you both here.'

Glasses were topped up once or twice more, before Major Hope-Stukely mentioned that his wife thought he was being a 'funny uncle' at the verger's niece's birthday party and so, presumably, had the verger, until a couple of hours ago. Perhaps they should be getting along home now?

The vicar concurred, reluctantly. He rose rather unsteadily to his feet and they both prepared to brave the elements.

'Honestly, Mumsie, I don't think the vicar's used to strong drink.' Bunty's face was a mask of hefty reproof as the guests made off into the howling night.

'Stoke the poor blighter up a bit for driving that sardine tin,' Hugo observed, waving them off from the window. 'Poor old Stoop-Hokely's having to jack-knife to get into the thing, look!'

'His name's Hope-Stukely. You've had too much to drink, Cuddles! Honestly.' Bunty was on tomato juice.

They heard a rather sickening clunk. Emily peered out into the darkness. 'You may have a point, Bunty,' she conceded. 'The vicar forgot to open the back gate.'

Saltdean

Glassy-eyed, Trevor Simpson was attending to a daunting woman with an armful of loud baby.

'We need separate rooms, my good man!' Lady Priscilla tried to make herself heard over Jason's vigorous opposition.

'I can't say I blame you, Madam, with that racket going on. Do we have a booking for you?'

'My friend Mr Jennings and I—'

'Excellent choice. God gave us our relations, as they say, but we can choose our…'

Mr Jennings came in from tipping the porter. 'Now, Jason, who's a big boy, then?' He removed the bundle of wet fury from Priscilla before she dropped it. 'I'll take him a tata, shall I?'

Snatching up the baby bag from their pile of luggage, he startled her by disappearing into the cocktail bar. She was not to know that it opened on to the conservatory of potted fronds which gave the place its name.

As he fought his way through the wedding party remnants and their half-finished drinks, Mr Jennings managed with great presence of mind to lift a cherry on a stick, with which he tickled Jason's gums. The effect was instantaneous. He was able to retreat behind the greenery in peace and teach himself how to change a nappy.

Horsley

'Dear lady, your gate has just driven into my car.'

Once more, the vicar and Major Hope-Stukely stood, dripping, in Emily's hall. Once more, she unburdened them of their macs. Here at least was a possible diversion to fill the air space between herself and Bunty for the whole evening. Tomorrow was another day.

'You must stay for some supper,' she cried gaily. 'Only pot luck, I'm afraid. We brought a hamper down from Fortnums.'

They thought perhaps they should phone their wives. When they tried, they found the lines were down. 'Where's your car now, Vicar?' Emily asked.

'In your gate. And it will not, *will* not, get up out of the mud.'

'Then there's nothing else to be done.'

Saltdean

'All's well now, he's fast asleep in an aspidistra!' Mr Jennings came back from the conservatory, glowing with pride at his child-care skills; having also taken the precaution of equipping Jason with a few more cherries should he wake.

Trevor Simpson, in mid-remonstration with Lady Priscilla over the booking, barely heard him. 'It should have been in writing,' he insisted earnestly, absent-mindedly polishing off a tray of martinis left on the desk by a distracted waitress, 'did you put it in writing?'

'I amended it on the telephone,' Mr Jennings became suddenly sharp, 'last Tuesday, when we heard about the little stranger.'

'That's the first you knew? He's come a long way since last Tuesday.' Mr Simpson giggled foolishly.

Mr Jennings showed his mettle. 'I may tell you that I, too, serve in a managerial capacity. If you were in my department, you would have your cards in the morning. Leedi Priscilla—' he turned to her, 'I apologize. I have always found this a most agreeable place. Until today.'

The title penetrated Trevor Simpson's befogged brain. He lifted the desk-flap and propelled himself through. 'Please walk this way,' he wove a majestic curve across the lobby, 'I myself, personally, will conduct your lordships to your rooms.'

Horsley

'Would you be kind enough to open the wine for me, Major Hope-Stukely?' Emily was poised enchantingly in the doorway, a frilly apron over a hastily donned hostess-gown. Bunty and Hugo were squabbling upstairs; the vicar, after three more whiskies, was dozing by the fire.

Vernon Hope-Stukely rose in a cloud of euphoria. No verger's niece's birthday party could hold a candle to this. It was almost enough to make a feller cry.

'I'm going to tell you a secret, dear little lady,' he confided huskily, caressing the corkscrew from her hand, 'the name is Stuckle. Stuckle, yes. M'wife wanted it changed. Dunno why, it suits her very well.'

'There's always "Hope"?' she sparkled.

'I added that. It's forlorn.' Tears sprang to his eyes.

'Cheer up, supper's ready. Come along, Vicar.' Calling the others in, Emily thought how handy it might become to have two persons of standing in this village who would vouch for her.

Saltdean

A disturbance was going on at the other end of the lobby. Round-eyed spectators were gathering. Roscoe Somerville, the screen idol, had just come through the revolving door. On his heels were a horse-faced woman and a girl of about eleven.

At the sight of Priscilla Grinling, Roscoe stopped. There was nowhere else to go.

Trevor Simpson skidded to a dignified halt in front of him. 'Welcome to the Palm Gardens Hotel, Your Ladlesips,' he declaimed with an elaborate, courtly bow.

'I beg your pardon?' said Roscoe.

'Sorry. There's a Ladle close *behind* me, I should say.'

That bow had finished Trevor Simpson. Head spinning, he addressed the assembled lobby:

'Laid, Lordles and Gentlepeoples, As manager of this emporium, may I present you with actual, in-the-flesh…' he couldn't for the life of him recall the name, '… Hollywood Film Star, all the way from Hollywood. I will now repair smartish to somewhere else, because we had a wedding here this morning and there is a raucous baby asleep in a potted ipsidrasta and the situation has suddenly become too much for me and I feel sick. Your servant at all times.'

Launching himself bodily into the revolving doors, he was retrieved on the other side by a porter and manhandled out of sight.

'Do I know you from somewhere?' Priscilla studied Roscoe.

'I … don't think so, Madam.' Roscoe was banking on the years between.

'I'm Lady Priscilla Grinling.'

'No interviews now,' Gertrude's voice rose over the buzz, 'press call seven-thirty, Roxy Cinema. Admission by card only.'

'Pipe down, Gertrude,' Roscoe could see no alternative but to blaze it out. 'Lady Priscilla, may I present Miss Gertrude Fitton of Fitton's Fitness Breakfast Bars, who is also my manager? Gertrude, you are looking at a fine representative of what Daphne is here to learn how to be!'

Forcibly reminded, Daphne looked acutely miserable.

'Why do you have to be managed?' Priscilla enquired with interest. 'Are you savage?' A chord pinged faint in the depths of her memory.

'My public has been known to become so,' Roscoe beamed ready charm, 'Miss Fitton manages the behaviour of my public.'

'This is *Roscoe Somerville*!' Gertrude hissed.

Priscilla looked blank. 'Who?'

Gertrude was truly incredulous. 'The first English dame I meet doesn't go to the movies?'

'If you mean the Pictures, scarcely at all, it aggravates my migraine. Tell me, Mr Er, have you been at the Gaumont Victoria?'

'I'm afraid I've no idea.'

'How curious. I always know where I've been.'

'You two seem like old friends,' Gertrude observed. 'I'll go look for someone. We have to find our rooms. Nice meeting you, Your Lady. See ya.' She sashayed away to reception.

Mr Jennings had registered not a word of this. The sense of total devastation at the chaotic start of his brave enterprise was now giving way to concern for his infant son. 'Ay'll just get Jeeson from the conservatory,' he announced.

In the absence of any reaction, he scuttled away feeling vaguely *de trop*. Daphne, also at a loose end, followed.

Oblivious now of their audience, Roscoe and Priscilla faced each other. 'The Gaumont Victoria,' she resumed, 'I ask because I went there once with my granddaughter and her husband. I don't know what we saw. Evidently not you, since you don't recollect the occasion.'

As Roscoe burbled modestly about celluloid puppets not being masters of their fate, the ping in Priscilla's memory grew to a twang. 'I have it! It's because you bear a strong resemblance to my granddaughter's husband!'

Roscoe smiled politely, having no idea who that might be. Onlookers began drifting away. Let the film star deal with the garrulous old trout, then. No chance of an autograph, even.

Priscilla's memory was breaking into shards of pristine clarity. 'Now I think of it,' she said, 'you have quite a look of my granddaughter, too.'

Since Roscoe was unaware of Bunty's existence, let alone her marriage to Hugo, he was able to laugh with sunny relief.

Mr Jennings reappeared with Jason in his arms. Daphne was with him, clutching a bunch of cocktail cherries on sticks and looking a lot more cheerful.

'Sleeping like an angel,' Jennings cooed. 'Pardon me for abandoning yew, Leedi Priscilla, but he's really taken to that aspidistra.'

Priscilla turned to Roscoe, 'My great-grandson, Jason.'

Astonishment at such maturity was fleeting as Roscoe realized she was referring to the baby. 'And are you the happy father?' he enquired cordially of Jennings.

Jennings sneezed.

'He's real cute, Uncle Roscoe,' Daphne said, 'and he sure likes these cherries. I collected some more. Hey, Jason?' She shoved another gently into the baby's blissfully sagging mouth.

In an effort to retrieve his authority as Priscilla's host, Mr Jennings peered at Roscoe keenly. 'Have you been told, in the words of Edgar Wallace, haha, that you're a "dead ringer" for Roscoe Somerville, sir?'

Comfortably off the hook, Roscoe laughed long and hearty. 'Lot of it about, what? Lady Priscilla will be saying next I'm a dead ringer for her great-grandson, what!'

Priscilla looked at him very straight. 'It's a little early to tell. But now that you mention it...'

The opening of the New Roxy with the preview of a new film from Hollywood was quite an occasion. Polite enthusiasm for *The Saxon Cometh* was altogether genuine.

But Gertrude's battle cry, 'Today, Saltdean; tomorrow, the Empire, Leicester Square!' failed to dispel Roscoe Summerfield's gut feeling that Roscoe Somerville's roll was over.

On his return to the hotel, there was a note at reception from Lady Priscilla Grinling, inviting him to a walk before breakfast next morning.

Sunday, October 8th

Horsley

The weather had cleared. The telephone was still dead. The Kilverston residence, isolated on the edge of the village, was unlikely to get service restored before Monday.

The only person up and dressed at what she considered the wholesome hour of 7.15 was Bunty. The others, including two informal guests, were still incubating monumental hangovers.

Serve them right, in Bunty's opinion. They were disgusting. As for those two silly old men, what would their wives think of them? Singing and carousing and making up to her very unsuitable mother-in-law? Bunty would quite like to tell the vicar's wife and Mrs Hope-Stukely how idiotic their stupid husbands were. With an anonymous phone call or something. Now, while they were all still in their drunken stupors. If the phone was working. As it wasn't, they'd both go home and say anything they liked. And her decadent mother-in-law would get off scot-free.

Bunty hated Emily. Emily had ruined Hugo. And she hated Gramps, for knowing Sir John Reith and getting Hugo into the BBC. The BBC was only a new version of the Church, for sons one didn't know what else to do with. Everyone knew that. Now, they were egging him on to be an announcer when Broadcasting House opened in Langham Place next year. He'd never come home at all.

Actually, she was beginning to hate Hugo, too. He was no better than anybody else when you got to know him. Last night she'd locked him out of the room. She wasn't going to be fugged up with whisky fumes. The best thing about this horrible weekend was not having bloody Jason screaming the place down. She'd like to kill Jason. She'd like to kill Emily, too. She'd kill the whole lot of them if she could do it without getting found out.

On the way to the kitchen, she peeped contemptuously round the living-room door at the snoring heaps of the vicar and Major. Serve them right to leave them there. Let the vicar go missing and have the parish up in arms.

Except that she wanted to emerge as the only decent person in this madhouse. It might be useful, if she ever did manage to kill Emily.

At this actual moment, she was hungry. She looked in the larder, where she found a leg of pork. 'Today, we'll do things my way,' she switched on the oven. 'No more arty-farty bits from Fortnums!'

She rummaged about for liver salts. Well, it was a working day for the vicar. And not even a bicycle to get him to church!

Saltdean

'Wait, Lady Priscilla! Wait, please!' Roscoe felt like a straggler in the retreat from Moscow. They had marched at the double along the sea-front, with the dawn coming up like thunder, from Saltdean to Brighton's West Pier. He limped up, sweating.

Priscilla watched him with an expression of faint surprise. 'What is it, Mr Somerville? Have you a stone in your shoe?'

'I hadn't visualized a four minute four miles.'

'Outdoor exercise is detrimental to my health. I tend to get it over with as quickly as possible. Shall we stroll, now?'

She turned on to the pier. Side by side, they walked to the seaward end; beyond the theatre, out of sight of the front.

In the pocket of Priscilla's raincoat was the gun with which her husband had despatched himself almost twenty years ago. She took it everywhere, although she had never had occasion to use it. There was a first time for everything.

They leaned on the railing and looked out over a disgruntled sea which was beginning to heave itself choppily towards France.

Roscoe took a hip-flask from his pocket. 'Nip of brandy?'

'How very civilized.'

Unscrewing the measure-top, he poured her a double. 'I'm a whisky man myself.' He produced another flask from the other hip.

'You came well prepared.' She watched him pour his own.

'I did, yes. Cheers.' Several of Gertrude's sleeping pills had been crushed into the brandy. She knocked it back, not seeming to notice. He poured her another. 'Bottoms up, as Stanley Jellybean used to say.'

'Who?'

'An uncommon felon I used to know. He taught me a lot.'

'He sounds interesting. *Santé.*' She toasted him. She was appreciating this. She needed a spot of Dutch courage for what she was proposing to do. 'I was at school in France, you know.' She held out the measure for a refill. Roscoe supplied it.

'For one of your background, it's not unusual,' he said.

'Many years past, in other circumstances, we held a hunt ball in the castle where we lived.'

He topped her up again. 'The glories of yesteryear?'

'You could say so. My debutante daughter was partnered by a dashing young Frenchman. A certain Comte Etienne du Couteau.'

'Steve the Knife?'

'You're a linguist, too.'

'Within limits.'

'Jus' like M'sieur du Couteau. He spoke impeccable English with a charming accent. When I addressed him in French, however, I was startled at the panic in his eyes. Any more brandy?'

'For you, Lady Priscilla, this flask is bottomless.' Not entirely true, she'd had the lot now. 'Your guest's lack of proficiency in his native tongue must have puzzled you rather?'

'For twenty years, yes. Until you walked into the Palm Gardens Hotel last night.' After carefully balancing the empty measure on the railing, she took the gun from her pocket and pointed it at him, holding it with both hands. 'Please don't move, because I have one thing more to say. I bear no particulic-icular aminosity towards you. Indeed, I never had much time for my daughter. But this has been my declared intention since nineteen hundred and twelve and I never go back on my word.'

The gun was drooping at much the same angle as her eyelids. Gently, he relieved her of it. He held her close until he knew she was deeply unconscious. The massive piles of the theatre, the concert hall and the rest of the West Pier architecture hid them most effectively from the shore. With regret and utmost respect, he tipped her over into the strongly ebbing tide. It would carry her swift and far.

Horsley

Hugo was feeling ghastly, what with last night and now Bunty's home cooking. Supine, he yearned for the BBC newsroom.

'We need a nice tramp in the woods,' Emily said brightly.

'I doubt if you'll get one. They're mostly drunk, dirty and rude,' Hugo quipped sourly.

Bunty looked blank. After laborious explanations, she blamed the BBC for making Cuddles as brittle as Noel Coward. But she was all for a brisk walk. Especially when Emily suggested picking mushrooms. With luck, they needn't talk to each other much.

They left Hugo on the sofa and trudged off. At Emily's prompting, Bunty rooted with more enthusiasm than knowledge. They were back by teatime with a haphazardly assorted wild fry-up.

After the roast pork and college pudding for lunch, no one but Bunty could face eating any.

'Lucky old me!' she gloated cheerfully, piling them on her toast, 'You don't know what you're missing, honestly!'

Saltdean

'Lady Priscilla Grinling was an old and valued friend...' And he himself had been no more than a moment in the Gentlemens' Retiring Room, only to find her gone on his return.

Roscoe Sommerville was profoundly affected as he gave the police a detailed description of the early morning walk. He could only guess as to its tragic conclusion. He had left her watching the swell of the water. Had she leaned over too far? He readily outlined his movements for the next few days and was given clearance to return to London tonight, as planned.

Lady Priscilla's son was telephoned, but they were unable to contact her other relatives in Surrey. Mr Wilfrid Jennings, her travelling companion, undertook to return the baby to his mother in London this evening and break the news; life must go on.

It was a sad aspect of the case that owing to the heavy sea, recovery of the body was a matter for doubtful conjecture.

Horsley

'Bearing in mind the dangers of natural fungi in the hands of the uninitiated…' Doctor Galsworthy looked up, pen poised over the death certificate.

'But we *all* enjoyed the mushrooms she picked,' Emily, though very distressed, was adamant. 'She cooked them herself for tea.'

As lies go, would that be white, black or … Hugo settled for mushroom-coloured. He stood stiff and mute, still a bit puffed from his walk to the doctor's house.

'I feared the stomach-ache might be appendicitis,' Emily was elaborating, 'so I sent my son for you. No car, no phone. It took him some time. I gave her laudanum to soothe her. I was so glad at first when she dropped off to sleep, but then her colour and her breathing frightened me…' She seemed near collapse.

For one reason and another, Hugo preferred not to speak until he was spoken to, although he did manage to nod in support of what his mother was saying.

Ever susceptible to the fair sex, as he liked to put it, Desmond Galsworthy hated to see a woman cry. There was no reason to increase the anguish of this charming family by doubting the simple facts they had given. it was an unsuspected allergy. A tragic accident, by no means unusual. He signed the certificate.

Saltdean

Daphne Fitton had developed a touching affection for Jason. When the time came, that heavy day, to be delivered by her mother to her fate at Saltdean Ladies' College and bid him a tearful farewell, she handed Mr Jennings as many cocktail cherries as she had been able to pinch from glasses by lurking about in the bar while everyone was occupied with the police.

Gertrude Fitton and Roscoe had kindly offered Mr Jennings and Jason a lift to London. Jennings was very concerned to be at Walton Mansions to meet Emily, Bunty and Hugo. He felt it was only fitting, having no inkling of the day's events in Surrey.

Horsley

Doctor Galsworthy was disturbed at Emily's insisting that they return to London. In the circumstances, it was extremely irregular. The ambulance had removed the body, but that was by no means the end of the upsetting formalities.

'Have you tried ringing the hotel at Saltdean?' he asked her.

'My phone is dead,' she reminded him, 'and that poor little baby was to be brought back to his mother at my flat tonight.' She drew a shuddering breath, 'And my car is still barricaded into my garage by an Austin Seven that's tangled up in my back gate. Dr Galsworthy, what am I to do?'

He understood her situation and was touched by her manner, which suggested that he might be Sir Lancelot in person. He came to a swift and heady decision. 'If the widower were to remain…'

Emily stared blankly for a second before realizing he meant Hugo. 'He's under twenty-one.' She was glad Hugo was making tea in the kitchen.

'He's still the husband. And a father, I understand? If he were to stay here, I am prepared to drive you to London myself.'

Jason Kilverston was as good as gold in the back of the chauffeur-driven Bentley. Gertrude Fitton even remarked on it.

Mr Jennings glowed. 'Your young Daphne, Miss Fitton, she really took to him. Like he took to her cherries.' Despite his shock over Priscilla – about whose end he felt by no means sanguine – he was deriving much comfort from his own emerging bent for baby management. It had not for a moment occurred to him that Jason was being lulled on Sidecars, Stingers and Manhattans.

North of Croydon a large tree, blown down in last night's gales, was still causing delays. The chauffeur said not to worry, he'd get 'em there in no time. A Dulwich man himself, he veered away into the jungle of West Norwood and Herne Hill.

'Walton Mansions, Knightsbridge,' Emily and Galsworthy were making quite good time on the Kingston Bypass, 'just a block of these little modern boxes, you know? Mine is twenty-six.'

*

'Poor Leedi Priscilla, I can't credit it. She was my … my landlady.' In grief, Mr Jennings craved a listening ear.

Roscoe's was right there. 'You surprise me, Mr Jennings.'

'Always seemed frail. Not a day's illness in her life, that I remember. Robust, with it.'

'I'm sure she went as she would have wished. Robustly.'

'And you would know, Mr Somerville. You being there at the – th … gh!' Mr Jennings went a very strange colour. His breathing took on a frightening shallow rasp. He clutched at his chest.

'My God, is he having a heart attack?' Gertrude banged on the dividing glass, 'Driver! Driver!'

'Well, we seem to be the first, Doctor Galsworthy. Thank you. More than I can say.'

'It was a pleasure, Mrs Kilverston.'

'My name is Emily. And it's Miss. I chose not to marry.'

'Ah.' Doctor Galsworthy found this admission the very peak of clear-eyed modern womanhood. He was starstruck.

'Can I offer you a drink?'

I seen in the mirror, M'm. Not to worry,' the chauffeur was equal to any emergency at all times.

Mr Jennings, *in extremis*, was trying to say something. 'I have to get him back to Kilverston,' he gasped, 'Kilverston, twenty-six, Walton Mansions, Knightsbridge. Jason…'

'Take it easy, there. I'll see to it,' Roscoe assured him.

The car braked swiftly but smoothly to a halt. 'Here we are, then!' the chauffeur announced, with justifiable pride in his own quick reactions. 'Port in a storm, innit?'

They were outside the South Camberwell Hospital for Women.

Chapter Twenty

Camberwell

Edith Dibbins lay back after an intensely unpleasant three-hour climax to a week compared with which she imagined Alcatraz might seem like a vacation. She had no wish to look at it, even once. In case it might remind her of the nasty old foreign creep who she knew must have been its father. She neither knew nor cared if it be girl or boy. She rolled over and went to sleep.

As the baby was taken away, there was some kind of emergency that sent all the nurses scuttling.

Edith was in a semi-private cubicle just off one of the main wards; the sole concession to her comfort, arranged by Ivy – using an accent as thick as a Carpathian forest for the purpose – on a monetary basis with the registrar. Papers had also been drawn up for adoption at birth, sex immaterial.

Now, Ivy was once more in the registrar's office. The adoptive family – decent, God-fearing folk, she was assured – had already been contacted. The prospective father would be round to take delivery tomorrow.

After signing the necessary document, Ivy walked deep into the bowels of the fortress, up echoing stairways and along grim corridors reeking of Jeyes Fluid to see her granddaughter. She recalled her own enforced sojourn in this place. It hadn't changed a bit. How much simpler life might have been if Little Joyce'd been dealt the same hand as Edie's nipper'd just got.

Deep in personal reminiscence, Ivy barely noticed that most of the nursing staff were going the opposite way.

In spite of its name, the South Camberwell Hospital for Women was not unused to male invasions of the casualty department by drunks, fight victims and the like. It was less prepared for the spectacle of a uniformed chauffeur and a famous film star, supporting between them the sagging form of a well-dressed man apparently in the throes of a coronary.

Attention was fast and efficient. Nurses flitted in from the furthest reaches for a glimpse of Roscoe Somerville. On examination, Mr Jennings turned out to be suffering an acute attack of asthma, no doubt brought on by the stresses of the day.

At Mr Somerville's request, backed up by a substantial donation cheque, it was agreed that the patient should stay in overnight at least. At the same time, Roscoe was feverishly addressing the question of how on earth, without the hazards of a close encounter, he could best return the baby from Saltdean to Emily, since Emily it seemed to be.

Is Jason Kilverston my grandson? How? The question flashed through his racing brain without time for any sort of answer. He sent the chauffeur to bring in Jennings' belongings and applied his native wit towards an interim solution.

In the Bentley, Gertrude had just finished changing a nappy on the sweetly sleeping Jason. The baby bag (more accurately a carrying-cradle with room for baby, bottle and general equipment when properly packed) was in some disarray on the seat.

The door was flung open. 'Gentleman's overnight stuff! This it?' the chauffeur's manner had reverted to that of the sergeant-major under fire he once had been. Seizing the basket – nappies, talcum powder and all – he began strategic retreat. Gertrude, immobilized by Jason, could only shout 'In the trunk!' and hope he heard. To her relief, he opened the boot, pulled out Mr Jennings's very superior soft suede zip-up from the Army & Navy's top range and hurtled back inside.

Surrounded as he was by hospital personnel, autographing anything from treatment notes to temperature charts, the welcome sight of the assorted baggage in the chauffeur's arms caused Roscoe's wildest contingency measures to snap into gear.

In what doubtless appeared to his fascinated audience as a display of bohemian flamboyance, he unzipped Mr Jennings' bag and disgorged its contents in a heap on the floor. Selecting a scalpel from a tray of instruments someone had set down in the excitement, he perforated it with a series of neat incisions and stuffed it with the contents of the baby-carrier, into which he then piled Jennings' belongings. On completing the switch, he asked to see the patient.

Mr Jennings, sleepy and reasonably comfortable, lay on a curtained-off trolley, awaiting transfer to one of the few single wards.

'Here we are, old chap,' Roscoe said brightly, 'sorry it's all a bit untidy. Bit of a fracas in the foyer, dontcherknow.' He set down the baby-carrier which, overflowing with Jennings' personal effects, now looked like a basket of laundry.

'Uh?' Jennings attempted to stem the tides of sedation. 'Ma'y thank…' he pushed a paper into Roscoe's hand, ''S Admithon for … mm … mm. I signed it—' He was asleep.

Admission form? It didn't look like one. Still, no time to lose! Roscoe handed the paper in to the office and told the registrar that he would enquire for Mr Jennings tomorrow.

Knightsbridge

At 26 Walton Mansions, a warm friendship in the making between Emily and Doctor Galsworthy was rather nipped in the bud by the ringing of the doorbell. Desmond Galsworthy was much discomfited, Emily much relieved; having done no more, so far, than she felt necessary for the establishing of an ally.

Whatever had kept Priscilla and Mr Jennings with Jason so long? They should have been back by seven-thirty and now it was almost nine. Well, here they were at last. And she had the doctor to help her break the tragic news of Bunty.

The last thing she expected was to be confronted by a uniformed chauffeur in a tearing hurry.

'Charing Cross Station. Straight away. Gentleman says it's very urgent. The nipper's fine.' He thrust a left-luggage ticket at her and was off down the corridor and into the lift before Emily could collect her wits.

Utterly bemused and thoroughly scared, she went back into the drawing room. 'What's happening? What am I supposed to do?' She glanced at the clock. 'I'd ring Saltdean, but they must have left hours ago, surely? What did he mean, "the nipper's fine"? What's going on? Is it kidnap?'

The doctor, who had been thinking perhaps he should get back to Mrs Galsworthy in Surrey, was far too caught up in this drama now to do any such thing. 'Shall I call the police?'

'No!' Some sixth sense warned Emily that such a move would be both uncalled-for and undesirable. 'I'll get a taxi,' she said. 'Whatever it is can't possibly take very long to pick up. If perhaps you'd stay here? Just in case? Ring Saltdean maybe? If, between us, we can sort this thing out...? I'd appreciate your continued support so very, very much.' Her voice was husky, dangerously near breaking.

He agreed. How could he not? The mixture of gratitude, fortitude and promise in her eyes as she left the flat would often return to warm him in the course of a mundane future.

He lifted the telephone and quoted the number of the Palm Gardens Hotel, Saltdean. This time, the lines were free.

Charing Cross

After supervising the careful placement of the suede zip-bag and instructing the luggage clerk on no account to touch it until the lady arrived, the tall man with the beard and the tinted spectacles backed off into the shadows. If that splendid driver fellow did his stuff, Emily should be here on curiosity alone, never mind honest worry, inside twenty minutes.

She was. On surrendering the ticket, she watched with growing apprehension as a strange suede bag, which appeared to have been slashed all over, was slid towards her across the counter. It was unexpectedly heavy. When the luggage clerk demanded three-and-six, she almost dropped it.

'Steady on, there!' A figure leaped out of a dark archway and caught the handle.

Vaguely surprised not to be hit on the head or feel a chloroform pad being clamped on her face, Emily looked up in a daze of terror quickly superseded by focused wrath.

'If you really think a beard and glasses disguises you from me, Roscoe...'

He had intended merely to check safe delivery. Breaking cover had been entirely involuntary. 'One forgets. It serves as a rule.'

'Why is this so heavy? More important, what is it?'

Hows, why's and wherefores aside, she had a pretty good idea. When Roscoe opened the zip she was proved right. A well-grown six-and-a-half months, Jason was sleeping like an angel; an ineffable smile on his face, cherry juice trickling down his chin, snugly packed in assorted nursery paraphernalia.

To face each other on the station concourse had not been Roscoe's intention. Now that they did, better get it over with.

'Lady Priscilla Grinling fell off the pier this morning,' he said flatly, 'she's dead.' That was all she needed to know.

'So is Bunty.' That was all he needed to know.

'Who?' Roscoe's total bewilderment was genuine.

For Emily, memory floundered in competition with the events of this ghastly day. Of course, he had no idea.

'Daughter of the late Kate Grinling and Etienne du Couteau,' she replied quietly, watching the shock creep over him, 'also mother of Jason Kilverston here, and wife of your son, Hugo.'

She watched the implications sink in. 'Then Hugo is the father of...?'

'I didn't say that. Looking at this baby now, and looking at you, even though he's not wearing glasses and a beard...'

Whatever she was saying, it only added to the tide of torrential relief, crashing down across the last ten years and more. 'Hugo survived? Hugo wasn't – the train at Monte Carlo didn't...?'

'You seem to have missed your objective,' the observation was iced. 'He's big enough to look after himself now.'

Roscoe was stunned. '*You* tried to kill *me*!'

Emily hadn't the first idea what he was talking about, but no matter. 'I wish I had,' she said, 'long before Monte Carlo. It would have saved a great deal of complication. But I assure you I will, if ever I possibly can. Meanwhile, there's this little chap...'

'He's three-and-six,' the luggage clerk reminded them neutrally.

Emily lifted the suede bag, preparing to hand it to Roscoe. 'Perhaps you'll be good enough to take us home?'

But Roscoe was no longer there. She heard the slam of a car door. Furiously, she slapped down the money and got a taxi.

*

Desmond Galsworthy was a good deal better informed about the day's events elsewhere by the time Emily returned. Wondering how best to present the appalling facts to her, he was a little disconcerted at her apparent preoccupation with the peculiar bag she had lugged into the flat. She seemed less interested in what he had to impart than in his opinion of its contents.

'Well, it's a baby. Roughly six months at a guess.' Desmond Galsworthy's professional reflexes had difficulty in surmounting basic venal curiosity.

'Is he all right?'

'He looks all right.'

'Are you sure? He's unusually fast asleep.'

Through the exchange at Charing Cross, the taxi-ride, the bumping of the lift, Jason had slumbered, pink and motionless. In view of his current teething troubles, Emily was worried. This day, surely, could only get worse. 'Is he dead?' she asked.

Galsworthy leaned over the bag and sniffed. 'Not in the least. He's drunk. And up to the axles in cocktail sticks.'

After Galsworthy finally left, Emily cleaned up the now snoring baby and thought of poor Hugo, coping alone in Surrey. It might assist his growing up. Well, we're landed, aren't we, Hugo and I? With this little sozzled perisher. So, what next?

I brought it on myself. All of it. Jason will be better off without that ghastly Bunty. Everyone will. Especially Hugo.

And I'm still here. I'll always be here for Hugo.

Heatherley

Ivy had been working like a Trojan for a week, getting her newly acquired personal portion of the Dower House kitted out for her granddaughter to come back to. Now Edie'd dropped it, that was punishment enough. And the place was looking a treat.

Ivy's new domain was one of four self-contained divisions of a rambling Jacobean gem, each with a quarter of the garden. Never one for auctions or antique shops, she had furnished it by the simple expedient of going to Maples and buying the displays as they stood. The effect was *nouveau-riche*, a touch over-matched and very comfortable.

Two of the units were still empty. The conversion as a whole had been finished less than a month ago. Ivy's only neighbour so far was Ed Heatherley himself, now one of the leading racing trainers in the country. A sinewy little chap whose slight limp seemed not to stop him moving like quicksilver, with a sensible sort of wife and a cheerful daughter who rode as part of the horse. Since Ivy moved in, she had been up and out early every morning just to watch Ed and young Maudie riding.

The family was friendly and frankly thrilled to have a Russian princess moving in on them. Ivy could see no reason at all for telling Ed that 'once-upon-an-earl', in another world, she had been his aunt by marriage.

She was really sorry when word came that Ed's mother had met with a fatal accident on holiday at Saltdean. She would have wished to help in any way she could, if it hadn't been the very day she was a bit taken up at Camberwell.

London

'So you want to stay, Roscoe-baby? You really do?'

'Yup.'

'They'll go crazy for it over there. Believe me. It'll put you right back on top, over there.'

'You made a great American movie, Gertrude old thing. If my name helps it, I'm glad as well as grateful. But I reckon I belong here, now.'

The lounge at the Savoy was as good a place as any to come to momentous decisions. Critical reception after the high-gloss premiere of *The Saxon Cometh* was, as Roscoe had foreseen, a mixture of toffee-nosed scorn at the treatment and envy at the size of budget Hollywood could play with. Of course, it should never have opened in England first. That had been a whim of Gertrude's to coincide with putting her daughter in school here.

He was not copping out. His input to this epic would help swell the profits from sea to shining sea. It was just that one way and another, it was time for Roscoe Summerfield to come home.

'I'll be here for Daphne,' he said. 'Bit of a facer, banged up at school in a strange country, what?'

'She still thinks her Pa threw himself off the Empire State Building. You aiming to correct that?'

'It's up to you.'

She considered a moment. 'Maybe. When the time's right. You be the judge.'

'Fair enough. And … thanks.'

But it was more than Daphne. Daphne had been the product of Gertrude's own personal choice. The encounter with Emily at Charing Cross had shaken to its depths his hitherto unbreachable citadel of self-preservation and advancement.

The long-term consequences of his youthful apprenticeship on the wrong side of the law had brought him up short, to put it mildly. How much harm had he caused? And to whom? Kate Grinling? And this other, unknown daughter, who was now dead?

And look what he had just done to Lady Priscilla!

Well, maybe. But Lady Priscilla, however justifiable her reasons, had been bent on cold-blooded murder herself. The duel on the West Pier at Brighton was an even match, although he bitterly regretted the need for it. In the event of an enquiry should her body be recovered, he would be willing to answer.

It had never been Roscoe's nature to wish misfortune on anyone. Quite the reverse, as long as he himself was thriving. In his present frame of mind, it began to look as if, single-handed, he had caused the downfall of the entire House of Heatherley.

There was no redressing the balance. He would have to live with the weight of knowledge. It did occur to him, however, that minuscule as it might be, there was at least one insignificant atonement he could make. Anonymously, for preference.

The following week, after seeing Gertrude off on the boat train, he took definite steps towards implementing it.

London

Forty-eight hours of sedated rest in one of the few single rooms at the South Camberwell Hospital for Women had stabilized Mr Jennings' asthma quite nicely. The information that, due to a groggy signature on a mistaken form, he had become adoptive father to a male infant whose natural mother had left the building was almost enough to bring it on again in decibels.

Almost. He sat up in bed and gave the matter his serious consideration. He was well aware that the error was not irrevocable; that either the expectant parents first notified, now disappointed, no doubt far more suitable, could be recalled and apologized to, or that others could be selected.

He thought of that nice young Mrs Fibstock and her kind concern for his welfare. Fate had clearly taken a hand here. Fate had placed him in this situation and ridden roughshod over all his misgivings. Did one fly in the face of Fate?

He decided to name the boy 'Gilbert'.

Back in the first-floor front with his alarming acquisition, he set about finding a more fitting home. Within a few days, however, he was contacted by Lady Priscilla's lawyers.

To his astonishment, they advised him that in the likelihood of Lady Priscilla being officially declared lost at sea, he, Wilfrid Jennings, was nominated under the terms of her Will as trustee for life of the property known as 26 Claverton Street, in the Borough of Westminster, London SW1.

In due course, it was evident, he would be taking honourable retirement from the Army & Navy Stores. With the confidence born of new authority, Wilfrid Jennings assumed his altered status.

Heatherley

Enquiries in the village confirmed that the family now lived in the Dower House. Unaware of their prevailing circumstances, uncertain as to what his approach would be, Roscoe walked up the drive through the park, with a briefcase containing *Old Woman with Stocking*. How he would return it or to whom, he had no idea. But to return it was his avowed intent.

He reached the stables and paused, mystified and impressed by the high-class activity there. The Dower House looked to be in mint condition: paintwork gleaming, stonework sound, gardens perfectly maintained. It also appeared to have several front doors. Well, you have to start somewhere. Roscoe approached the nearest and rang the bell.

It was opened by Ivy.

Disorientating, rather. He stood mute.

'Well, there now!' she said, no less surprised. 'What brings you here?'

Whatever bearings Roscoe might have been getting as to his business in these parts dissolved with a puff. He laughed in helpless confusion. 'And you?'

'I live here,' Ivy replied, 'as of last week. With Edie. She's having a sleep just now. Why don't you come in?'

Amid the lush comfort of the Maples showroom, Roscoe explained that he had been hoping, on the off-chance, to catch an old friend. 'Teddy Grinling, actually. Lord Heatherley, I think he is, now. He does live here, doesn't he?'

'He's down in Sussex at the moment,' Ivy said. 'His mother died. Nasty accident.'

'I know,' said Roscoe, 'I was there.'

As close to the facts as possible had always been Roscoe's maxim; nor did it fail him. He presented a colourful abridgement of events at Saltdean, in which Priscilla – lustily fortifying herself from her own flask whilst holding him at gunpoint – had sportingly allowed him to answer a call of nature. Managing, on his return, to divest her of the gun with a gentlemanly tackle, he had yet been unable to prevent her over-balancing into the sea.

This version, which would in time become rooted in Roscoe's memory as the simple truth, was a riveting tale, expertly told.

Ivy's pre-conceived view of Roscoe Somerville had changed quite a bit lately, anyway, in the light of Edith's accounts. She listened without stifling her natural inclination towards liking him. 'Ed will be sorry to have missed you,' she said.

'Who?'

'Ed Heatherley. You a racing man?'

'Not so's you'd notice.'

'If you were, you'd know Ed Heatherley.'

Ivy herself always enjoyed a flutter; always followed form, whichever side of the Atlantic she happened to be. The prospect of settling into her own loose-box, as it were, at one of the country's leading training stables had made investment in the Dower House quite irresistible. Now, she recounted what she had gathered of Teddy Grinling's progress since 1916.

Roscoe felt more ashamed of himself than ever. Upright, decent little Teddy, dropped in the deep end at seventeen, collecting a gammy foot in the service of his country, joining forces with his own head groom and achieving all this? Amazing!

He started having second thoughts about producing a water-logged scrap of canvas with any sort of flourish. It smacked of condescension now, somehow. In the circumstances, it might well be worth hanging on to and getting renovated at a very much later date. For the time being, it had better stay where it was.

'Nice lot they are, too,' Ivy was saying with enthusiasm, 'no nonsense about 'em. And that daughter rides like an Indian. So tell me, what's next for you?'

Roscoe realized that beyond the fast-fading aim of somehow or other restoring *Old Woman with Stocking* to hands more deserving than his own, he had very little idea. 'I'm, er, I'm thinking of staying in England for a while,' he said vaguely.

'Like me. Whereabouts?'

At which point, Edith drifted in. For someone pretending not to have given birth last week, she looked pretty good, Roscoe thought. She was overjoyed to see him. She had regarded Roscoe as a kind of honorary senior relation throughout this unspeakably horrid time, in spite of her grandmother's darkest speculations.

The next couple of hours saw some new beginnings. Edith needed a future, according to Roscoe. Not merely a past.

'Standing about in frocks is fine as far as it goes,' he pointed out, 'but if you like the spotlight, you'll need to do a bit more than that.'

Belladonna had liked the spotlight very much. It was a proven fact that she could hold an audience with a quality that was both totally natural and, as yet, totally unconscious.

'You must learn how to use it,' Roscoe said, 'how to use your voice. How to move. Not as a singer or a dancer. You'd be lost, I fear. But as a personality, my girl. A technician who knows exactly why and how she is unique. Follow me?'

It had never occurred to either of them that Edith might have the makings of a real performer. It opened up whole new vistas. Stage schools were discussed. Roscoe himself undertook to make enquiries as to the most suitable.

By the time he booked into the Heatherley Arms that evening, he was of the opinion that this was a most delightful spot and that the recent conversion of the Dower House could turn out to be a very opportune arrangement.

With a shimmer of unaccustomed foresight, Roscoe Sommerfield began to wonder if, perchance, he might have come home.

Chapter Twenty-One
1933

When Franz-Clovis de Lavalle-Fontaine quit Hollywood, leaving anonymous tip-offs to both its high priestesses of sleaze, he went to ground in order to fight another day.

A clinic high in the hills above Lake Geneva worked wonders for health and appearance. Six months later, looking at least a decade younger than his sixty-one years, he travelled on into Germany for closer study of the man whose ambitions he found it stimulating to support.

Watching the Nazi Party sweep into power, he came to the conclusion that his investments had been justified and that Adolf Hitler could lead the country wherever fancy might dictate.

Franz-Clovis had no wish to be at the forefront of any new order. Twitches on an invisible string and subtle influence exerted at a distance held more appeal now. As a hobby, gently pursued, occasionally to liven a leisurely private existence.

In London, he looked about for a home base well removed from haunts like the Ritz Hotel and the Carlton Club. He preferred not to be hailed by old companions.

As soon as he saw it, the first-floor front at 26 Claverton Street seemed ideal. A gracefully furnished, spacious service-suite with kitchenette was exactly what he had in mind. On his first evening, a wary descent to the dining-room reassured him of an excellent cuisine and a clientele not of the kind to claim unsought acquaintance.

He installed himself and stayed, in moderate contentment, for almost a year.

One small factor of no apparent moment to other inmates, casual or permanent, grew steadily for Franz-Clovis into a disproportionate irritation. This took the form of a toddler, evidently belonging to the proprietor. As it developed, it seemed to gain the run of the place. At just over two, it was adept at giving its nursemaid the slip, harassing its pre-occupied father and his staff, sweeping anything within its reach off low tables, sliding downstairs and getting its head stuck in the banisters.

It answered – or not, as it chose – to the name 'Gilbert'.

It looked like a Botticelli angel. Fallen, Franz-Clovis reflected sourly, from a dizzy height. He wondered idly about its mother, presumably dead; and about what hidden fires prissy little Wilfrid Jennings must possess to have achieved a coupling at all, let alone begotten such a spark.

The forty-odd years since relinquishing his own son – with relief at the time – to the care of his wife's family disappeared in a wrenching echo for Franz-Clovis every time he looked at Gilbert Jennings. It was uncannily disturbing.

One October morning after breakfast, he walked into his own bathroom to find four stiff collars and a tooled morocco stud box being floated in ten inches of water, with an armful of silk ties about to join them. Gilbert must have come in with the maids and got left there.

In a red mist of fury, mixed with an obscure sense of bleak loss, Franz-Clovis tipped the boy into the bath as well. And held him under.

The mist cleared only just in time to forestall infanticide.

After handing the snivelling bundle over in the office downstairs with a clipped account of misadventure and timely rescue, Franz-Clovis de Lavalle-Fontaine drove down to Brighton and booked himself in at the Metropole Hotel.

Edith Dibbins had worked very hard at the Italia Conti Stage Academy for over a year. Most of the other pupils were kids, hired out under supervision as child artistes. In Roscoe's considered opinion, the training offered there was what Edith needed most: co-ordination of movement and just enough voice production to enhance a woefully inept but somehow fascinating treatment of a song. A proper acting-course, he felt, would only dissipate her fragile talents in self-conscious confusion.

Managers and agents came regularly to view the Conti crop, particularly at the start of the Autumn term, with Christmas in the offing. Doing little more than adorn the stage at one of these concerts, her main contribution being to render a few lines of *Look For The Silver Lining* in slumberously uncertain tones, backed by a clutch of small children, Edie was amazed to find herself surrounded afterwards by shining faces and offered a bewildering amount of employment.

It seemed self-evident that the Italia Conti Academy had served its purpose. With the agent whom Roscoe judged the most suitable, Edith's new career was planned. From carefully placed promotion of appearance at exclusive country clubs came engagements at private functions; progress to the bigger hotels being only a question of not much time. Belladonna's future on the cabaret circuit looked promising indeed.

In the interests of useful experience, it was decided to put her in an out-of-town stage show for a season, with contractual agreement for a solo number.

Belladonna's agent duly accepted a casting offer for her as Principal Girl in *Jack and the Beanstalk*. Rehearse London from November 30th; open Boxing Night for six weeks at the Theatre Royal, Brighton.

November

An unconvinced father, Hugo Kilverston relied quite heavily on his senior female relatives over the upbringing of his legitimately documented son. At two and a half, Jason alternated merrily between Hampstead with Amaryllis and Knightsbridge with Emily, whose concession to the situation had been to disband 'Club 26' in favour of a more proper ambience for the young. The flat was quite large enough to take a nanny as well as the current cook-handyman couple; what had once been the card lounge became a nursery; Hugo himself left Ebury Street and moved back into his old room. The arrangement suited him admirably.

Hugo's career at the BBC was going rather well these days. With the opening of Broadcasting House in Langham Place, he had progressed from junior news-researcher to fledgling announcer. Over the past six months, indeed, continuity and shipping forecasts had led to compèring Variety shows and even reading the nine o'clock news. Photographed at the microphone in a dinner-jacket by the *Daily Express*, the resultant fan-mail caused his superiors to regard him as a definite corporation asset.

Hugo was not slow to seize the moment.

'Brighton for Christmas!' he announced ebulliently, erupting into the flat for a few free hours one evening. 'What do you think of that?'

'Brighton in winter? What on earth for?' Amaryllis looked at him as if he were a firing-squad detachment detailed to escort her to the wall. She had just had two days of concentrated Jason in Hampstead and was feeling rather old.

'Very bracing,' her grandson said briskly. 'It's high time you got braced.'

'If you're hell-bent on the seaside, what's wrong with Bermuda?' Emily asked.

It appeared that a suggestion of Hugo's, aired at a BBC planning meeting a while back, had caught the attention of the powers that be. 'They don't have panto in Bermuda,' he replied.

In London's theatreland, for at least two months from Boxing Day onwards, the great English tradition of Christmas pantomime held sway. Competition would be hot this year between the Lyceum, the Coliseum, the Adelphi and Drury Lane to provide the most glittering, the most spectacular, the most star-studded seasonal treat. Excerpts would be broadcast, with commentaries to woo audiences and let provincials hear what they were missing.

Even though, as Hugo had pointed out, the provinces staged equally lavish pantomimes of their own. He formally recommended that the BBC widen its scope by promoting some of these, as well as West End productions. His original idea, with himself as a modest roving reporter doing a few interviews, was now expanded into an operation of vast proportions, involving technicians and compères in the South, the Midlands and the North, to mount a massive 'Panto Round-up' of two whole evenings' listening during the holiday period. Hugo himself had been delegated to the south, to co-ordinate a radio spectacular combining the King's Southsea, the Bournemouth Pavilion and the Theatre Royal, Brighton.

'I'll base us in Brighton,' he told his startled family, 'you two, Jason, Nanny, the lot. I'll come and go from there, and you'll all have a jolly good time. We'll do the thing in style and stay at the Metropole Hotel.'

New York. December

Gertrude Fitton was quite well aware of being in the thick of what, in America anyway, was beginning to be known in rarified quarters as a 'mid-life crisis'.

The hell with that! I know what I'm in the thick of! Who needs to stick a label on it? She poured herself another Scotch as she indulged the doubtful luxury of self-analysis: Stinking rich, sound of body, individual of mind, I go as I want, do as I choose, and where does that leave me? With a financial interest in three Hollywood studios, a newspaper column, a house on Long Island, an apartment on Park Avenue, a daughter three thousand miles away at school in Sussex...

... And no Roscoe.

Relentlessly, over twenty years, Gertrude had sculpted her feelings towards Roscoe with the precision of a Michelangelo into a unique monument to friendship. She had, on the whole, approved his decision to settle in England for a while. A couple of years back, knowing what she did of his youthful buccaneering, she had relished to the full the impudent irony of his buying a share of the Dower House at Heatherley. Besides, it made an ideal background for a schoolgirl, between trips home to the States. The bond of having a mutual daughter had become oddly stronger since Daphne's father no longer masqueraded as Uncle Roscoe.

Yesterday, however, a torpedo thumped through the mailbox in the form of a letter from Roscoe with the news that he was giving serious consideration to marriage. The lady was a fellow Dower House shareholder. Namely, Princess Ivy Vishnevska.

As food for thought, Gertrude was finding this stubbornly indigestible.

But she had to swallow it, didn't she?

Hell, who needs a husband anyway? Friends are best.

Besides, he's not married yet. He only says maybe.

Hey, how about I go over for Christmas? An old-fashioned English country Christmas could be real stylish. For all of us.

As she lifted the phone to make a booking with Cunard, the doorbell rang. A moment later, the butler handed her a cablegram.

It was from Roscoe. Daphne had run away from school.

Brighton

At thirteen, Daphne Fitton gave the impression of being older. Tall, a little gangling, certainly; but with assurance of manner from an inbred sense of security and a carefree sense of humour presenting an image far removed from that of most English girls her age.

Saltdean Ladies' College was doing its best to cram her into accepted middle-school mould with about as much success as it had once known with a scamp called Emily Kilverston, twenty-five years ago. The few (now ageing) members of staff who recalled Emily agreed that Daphne Fitton might not be as pretty but displayed, if anything, even saucier airs. It came of being American, of course. And so rich. During her two and a half years at Saltdean, Daphne had emerged as ringleader in assorted escapades of the kind to vex authority.

Ten days short of the end of this Christmas term, she decamped after a Saturday hockey match with three intrepid chums. They cycled into Brighton, where Daphne bought frocks and make-up for them all at Hannington's in order to go dancing at Sherry's Ballroom, a haunt of mildly raffish reputation.

The four of them were spotted on the floor by one of the school janitors, out on the town himself. After trying his luck on them with spectacular lack of success, he got his own back by reporting them instead. And making sure their re-entry to school ran into the teeth of a reception committee.

Gamely but fairly, Daphne took full kudos for blatant subversion. Her copious residue of pocket money was confiscated and she was removed forthwith to the San. Where, she was told, she would remain, to write end-of-term exams in solitary confinement. Uniform and washing things to be collected in the morning. It was too late now to disturb the dormitory.

As soon as she was left alone, Daphne slithered down a rope of knotted sheets, which she was prudent enough to take with her as minimal protection for sleeping under Brighton's Palace Pier.

The following day, she set about finding a job.

Harry Coates, Stage Manager for *Jack and the Beanstalk* was in several places at once in the Theatre Royal, supervising the get-in. Flats, cut-cloths, lanterns, ramps and rostrums were being manhandled in through the huge, open dock doors.

This was one of those Sundays. The company would be down tomorrow for the final week of rehearsals. He'd been expecting to get the scenery up and the lights placed by the end of today. Some hope, with the skeleton staff he'd been allowed! Bloody management, they had no idea, did they? Three crew and no electrician? What were they expecting, then, bloody Scrooges!

Splitting himself into four, he yelled directions for the stacking of each flat, the hanging of each cloth. Not to mention the beanstalk, which arrived in segments and had to be assembled under the stage to rise via the trap on lines attached up in the flies and thus grow by magic to dramatic effect. All the while, he himself was changing the gelatines on the floats: pink in some, blue in some, amber and green in others. There was the whole front-of-house battery to be dealt with, too, and no one else to do it. The lighting plot was complicated on this show.

'I can do that,' said a voice behind him, 'I guess you're more important everywhere else.'

Harry looked round to see a bony girl in a candy-striped dance dress. 'Who the hell are you?'

'Does it matter? You need the help, I need the work. This the plot?' She took it from his hands before he could stop her, 'Those the gels? I'll finish down here then go up in the circle, right?'

'What do you know about it?'

'More than you think. Scram!'

It was true. From the tenderest age, Daphne had been tolerated by Hollywood studio technicians. She had absorbed a good deal about the lighting of musicals, historicals and spectaculars; swinging across grids like a monkey when allowed, tightening nuts, focusing floods, operating booms.

There was a crash from the direction of the dock doors and a frantic shout of 'Harry! Over 'ere!' A section of the Giant's castle battlements had slipped its moorings and would now need running repairs. 'Don't move, I'll be right back!' the Stage Manager hissed with dire threat. It was ten in the morning.

Thirteen hours later, the crew long departed, Harry Coates and Daphne sat in the wings nursing mugs of black tea, the milk being long departed, too. The cast would arrive tomorrow with the bones of the production in place. The job was done.

'Well,' Daphne said, 'am I hired?'

There had been little exchange since the collapse of the battlements. Now, he looked at her as at a seasoned colleague who was suddenly questioning the status quo. When his shredded brain reconnected, he felt unequal to pertinent enquiry.

'See you tomorrow?' He had never had an assistant like her.

'When do I get paid?'

'I'll sort it out with head office in the morning. Better let me have an address.' Then something made him ask, 'How old are you?'

This was all a slight facer. For a split second only. 'Seventeen,' she replied, daring him to disagree, 'and the Hotel Metropole will find me.'

Franz-Clovis sipped a brandy and watched the world go by. It was pleasant to take a nightcap here in the vestibule, he found. Always something to look at. With idle curiosity, he noticed a very young girl with a dirty face, wearing a torn dance frock, stalk through the revolving doors and up to reception like a queen.

'I need a room, please,' she said.

The night porter regarded her with fatherly amusement. 'Do you have a reservation, Madam?' he asked smoothly, partly to let her down as lightly as possible and partly to gain time.

'I'm making one now,' Daphne said. 'My name is Fitton.'

Franz-Clovis stiffened with interest. To be sure, the child looked as if she had got the worst of a severe brawl. But hadn't he read somewhere that Gertrude Fitton's daughter was at school over here? This might be a diversion indeed! He got up and strolled casually across an expanse of marble floor.

'That's as maybe,' the porter was saying, 'but I've a girl your age and I reckon you oughter be in bed. Come along now, and I'll put you in a taxi home. Otherwise it'll have to be the police.' His hand was on the phone.

Daphne noticed it. She was very tired now. Not at all inclined to face the sort of thing the porter seemed to have in mind. 'S-surely you've heard of the name Fitton?' she stammered, attempting haughty surprise.

'Who, indeed has not?' Franz-Clovis hove to beside her. 'Gertrude Fitton is a name I am acquainted with over many years.'

'She's my mother. Truly, she is!' Daphne was not far short of tears.

'I shall be honoured to assist in any way, Miss Fitton,' said Franz-Clovis.

By radio-telephone from the Cunard office in New York to the *Aquitania*, Siggy Lubin was able to bathe Gertrude Fitton in a vast, warm tide of relief with the information that her daughter was safely and respectably installed at the Brighton Metropole. To his intense surprise, Siggy had been contacted to this effect by a certain Comte de Lavalle-Fontaine. Who, it was long since assumed, had quit the scene for good; if not the planet.

Gertrude cabled Roscoe at Heatherley.

As Daphne's legally appointed guardian in England, Roscoe immediately rang the hotel. On grasping the gist of an entirely disinterested, chivalrous intervention to salvage a grubby truant, he turned to Ivy in utter bewilderment. 'A highly distinguished gentleman has saved the skellum's bacon,' he said. 'With the same name as the old wreck who messed Edie about!'

'Maybe you got it wrong?' With life on its current track, Ivy was disinclined to muddy any waters. Her own memories of Franz-Clovis suggested this might well be one of his whims. If he were still alive. Which was very unlikely. 'Or maybe it's some upright distant relation? Families do have 'em.'

'Maybe,' he was still mystified. 'What's more, I gather the child's got herself a job backstage at the Theatre Royal. How's that for cheek?'

'Chip off the old block, eh?' Ivy commented. 'You'd better get down to Southampton tomorrow and meet her poor mother off the boat. Think she'll be coming to the panto in Brighton?'

The entire population of the Dower House – Roscoe and Ivy, with three fascinated and totally untheatrical Heatherleys – was to descend on Brighton's Theatre Royal for Edith's opening night.

Ivy had renounced the Edwardian dignity of the Metropole in favour of the wedding-cake façade of the Grand next door.

It reminded her of Monte Carlo.

Chapter Twenty-Two

Brighton

After dress rehearsal on Christmas Eve, the cast of *Jack and the Beanstalk* dispersed on the strict understanding that it would reassemble at 2 p.m. prompt on Boxing Day for a final run-through.

Roscoe and Gertrude parted company. He, to drive Edith up to Heatherley; she, to stay on at the Metropole with Daphne. As stage staff, Daphne would be required on Boxing Morning. No question of leaving town. Besides, she was far too proud of the job she was holding down to want to.

She was, she insisted, 'crucially indispensable' to Harry Coates. Even if no longer quite the case, Harry had certainly appreciated his timely interloper that deadly set-up day. When apprised by her legal guardians as to her true age, identity and felonious nature, he earned her undying devotion by offering to perjure himself with the management over the details on her employment card and keep her on for the season.

No one had the heart to refuse her. Not after showing such form. In spite of getting herself expelled at last by Saltdean Ladies' College for her pains. Gertrude reckoned she'd outgrown the place anyway. In the New Year, she'd think again.

Monsieur le Comte de Lavalle-Fontaine, saviour of the hour, was off on the right foot with Daphne's mother straight away. Which was no less than his intent. For one to whom beauty in a woman was the driving factor of any new quest for domination, it made a bracing challenge now to be pursuing an outstandingly plain one. Of an age, moreover, not far short of his own.

The rewards could be great. To contemplate eventual control of the Fitton empire was to gaze into a beckoning and limitless future of command over destinies undreamed of.

All too well aware of the sinister hearsay attached to the Lavalle-Fontaine name, Gertrude had never met Franz-Clovis. Meeting him now, the very suggestion that he might be the same man was ludicrous.

Anyway this one, she soon discovered, was called 'Fitz'.

Roscoe was unreservedly flummoxed. The lean, fit, bearded stranger with silver hair and ready smile was as far removed from the shambling rapist of the Garden of Allah as from the arrogant Riviera playboy with the cold eyes. And yet…

What was it exactly? The tilt of the head? The walk? Not the voice, not the manner. To hell with it! The man might just be a distant connection, no more.

Franz-Clovis felt no such uncertainty about Roscoe. Only a few years ago, this flashy upstart had ruined his enjoyment of a squirming nymph in Hollywood; and further back, infinitely more importantly, cut him out with Emily Kilverston. And lived.

He kept his hands off with the greatest difficulty. In the cause of his present objective, revenge must be deferred.

And contrived for extracting the utmost of its sweetness.

Boxing Night

'Overture and Beginners, please! Overture and Beginners!'

Daphne banged happily on dressing-room doors in her capacity as callboy. At the Metropole with Mom and 'M'sieu Fitz', as she was invited to call him, Christmas Day had been jolly. Crackers and dancing and kissing total strangers in paper hats. But it was good to be back at work.

She poked her head in at the one labelled 'PRINCESS/FAIRY' with an injunction to 'Slay 'em, Team!' The Fairy was a po-faced cow, but she was sharing with Edie, so what?

The Fairy went on blacking her eyelashes. Edie said, 'Thankth, Daph, have fun. Exthiting, hey?'

Daphne hoped very much that the show would do Edie some good.

She doubted it. All the Princess did was stand about and look loopy, in Daphne's opinion. And she couldn't even sing. But all the stagehands gathered to watch, so you never knew.

The house lights dimmed; the orchestra struck up the Debroy Somers Christmas Medley; a breathless rustle ran through the auditorium. The pantomime season of 1933 was under way.

The first performance went on much too long. At least fifty minutes would have to go by tomorrow's matinée, even to approach the attention span of the target audience.

The Heatherleys had a terrific time. Perpetually immersed in horselore, barely even aware of the theatre, they thought the show pure magic. They were spellbound at the effects, laughed immoderately at the comics, booed the Giant and roared the song-sheet at the tops of their lungs.

With professional insight, Roscoe had placed his party in the front row of the upper circle. He wanted them to look down on the full spectacle instead of craning upwards from the stalls and never seeing the whole stage. It commanded a good view of the audience as well. One could watch reaction. Also, as people in more expensive seats were not given to scanning the remoter reaches, one could see without being seen, if one preferred.

Roscoe soon realized that he did indeed prefer. He spotted his son, notepad in hand, immediately below in the dress circle. The curve of the balcony obscured a view of any companions.

Well, maybe Hugo was on his own, covering the evening for the BBC. He seemed to be doing pretty well, these days.

In fact, Hugo was flanked by Emily and Amaryllis, Nanny and Jason. His preliminary sortie tonight was a family outing. Even at two, Jason exhibited huge enjoyment, squealing at the fast and funny bits, falling asleep during the slow ones. The rise of the beanstalk nearly had him toppling over the edge.

Hugo's brief tonight was to assess what he might use and which artistes he might interview. He had marked Jack, played by a well-known, lithely attractive light opera soprano, along with the Dame and the Giant, if time.

His pencil hovered over the Princess. She did nothing at all, really. And her one solo number, with a few minimal dance steps, was breathed like a secret surprise. Yet, when she was on stage, it was hard to look at anyone else. He noted that she was billed simply as Belladonna.

Inarticulate, probably. His pencil moved on.

So far, he was enjoying his self-instigated assignment very much. Bringing them all down here for Christmas Day had been a brainwave. It had made a change to celebrate in a smart crowd of affluent strangers.

There was that moment, too, over the *petits fours*, when his mother had suddenly exclaimed, 'Good God! Franz-Clovis!'

Effcee? Never! Following her gaze across the restaurant. Hugo saw a tall white-haired man with horn-rimmed specs and a neat beard, sitting with a buck-toothed middle-aged woman.

Amaryllis looked as well. 'Oh, no, it isn't,' she asserted with conviction.

'Oh, yes, it is,' said Emily.

Positive and not to be shaken, she had nevertheless refused point-blank when challenged to accost him at his table.

This evening, Franz-Clovis sat in the stalls with Gertrude. Never having seen an English pantomime before, it was a puzzling experience. Musicals they knew; Burlesque they had heard of. But this wild mixture of vaudeville, operetta, transvestism and nursery-tale was totally foreign. Gertrude loved it. Franz-Clovis, bored beyond measure, pretended to. His mind explored some elegant notions for bringing Gertrude Fitton to heel.

Briefly focusing on the stage during a scene between Jack and the Princess, he realized he was looking at his erstwhile plaything from the Garden of Allah.

A current of eerie shock zigzagged quite disagreeably through him. *Merde*! What was this place, this Brighton? A salutary dreamscape by Bunyan in which to be forcibly confronted by past misdeeds? First Roscoe Somerville, now this girl! And yesterday he thought he saw Emily Kilverston stepping into the hotel lift. He dismissed it at the time, as he still inclined wishfully to see Emily Kilverston in every crowd on every street. Now, though, he was beginning to wonder. Who next?!

He would doubtless have to brazen this one out. Daphne expected them backstage afterwards. Ach … *Merde*!

Roscoe surveyed the tops of their heads from his dizzy perch. Was he or wasn't he? Well, whoever he was, old Gertrude seemed quite smitten. The bloke had better be worth it.

There was quite a crush in Belladonna's dressing-room afterwards. The Fairy, who had a ten-minute acrobatic spot of her own – which, did she but know, would be cut to three tomorrow – wriggled anonymously out and trudged sulkily off to the party at the Clarence, wondering what the hell the soppy creature had that pulled them in like flies.

Ivy had no wish to come face to face with Franz-Clovis. For he it was, without a doubt. She knew, just as Emily had known.

People who went to bed with Franz-Clovis remembered him.

Despite Daphne's efforts, Franz-Clovis and Belladonna did not come face to face. Probably just as well.

With so much milling about, eluding anyone was easy. Ivy gathered that Franz-Clovis was at the Metropole. She was even gladder now she'd picked the Grand.

Hugo and his family did not go backstage. There was no need. After seeing *Dick Whittington* at Southsea and *Cinderella* at Bournemouth, he would rough out a plot and convene the directors of all three productions. Anyway, Jason was getting fractious. They all went straight back to the hotel.

Emily and Roscoe had each spent a most enjoyable evening at the theatre, quite unaware of it being the same one.

In the foyer on the way out, Emily caught sight of Doctor Galsworthy, somewhat harassed, marshalling a sour-faced wife and an assortment of children through the melée. As soon as he saw Emily, he whispered to his wife, handed her the car keys and ducked away towards the cloakroom. Emily murmured vaguely to Nanny and did likewise.

'Happy New Year, Desmond,' she said brightly. 'Fancy bumping into you here. Splendid show, don't you think?'

He was in no mood for small talk. The advantage he held over Emily had given meaning to his life for the past two years. 'It's months since I've seen you,' he muttered urgently, his eyes moistening, 'I can't live without you, Emily!'

It was in fact about six weeks. Emily tolerated the mildly clandestine arrangement for reasons of precautionary common sense. 'Poor Desmond,' she smiled, 'what to do?'

'Come down here to Brighton with me? For a weekend?' he implored recklessly. 'Soon?'

'That sounds delightful,' Emily said agreeably. 'When?'

'I'll let you know,' he hissed conspiratorially, starting to scuttle away. Then he stopped suddenly and turned, adding far too loudly, 'I'm insatiable for you!'

Startled theatre-goers looked round, hoping to spot the siren. But Emily had disappeared into the ladies room.

Chapter Twenty-three
1934

February

Roscoe booked into the Metropole for the last night of the show, having sampled the splendours of the Grand on the first. It had been a productive few weeks. Cabaret dates for Belladonna already extended into the summer, but the kid needed a break.

It looked as if he might be taking Daphne, too. The original plan had been for her to go back to the States with her mother, but now there were some unforeseen developments.

For the first time in her life, Gertrude Fitton had been made to feel beautiful. No other man in all her fifty-five years, including Roscoe Summerfield, had exerted such an effect upon her. With the rashness of a dewy adolescent, she scaled the heights of rapture over Fitz Fontaine. If a tiny portion of her brain sneered that he was manipulating her, she did not listen and she did not care.

When he suggested New Year in Paris, Gertrude paused only to move Daphne into Edith's theatrical digs before following her Pied Piper to the mountain. They stayed at the Crillon for over a month. After about two weeks, Gertrude began to feel unwell. It was an outrage. She had never been unwell in her life; never so much as bought a bottle of medicine. In deference to the pressurized life she led, she was in the habit of swallowing one mild sleeping pill every night, but that was all.

At first, she put it down to something she had eaten. But it persisted. She had a natural aversion to doctors and simply kept hoping she would be better in the morning, but she grew steadily worse; weaker, paler, more listless.

Fitz was a tower of strength. His patience seemed limitless. Apologies for her frailty were brushed gently aside. To care for her, he said, was all he wanted in the world.

Before this miserable thing happened, they had talked of marriage. Gertrude had refused, a little ruefully, unable to believe he could possibly mean it. Now, as he repeated his heart's deep yearning, as he put it, she began to see the prospect as a haven. A safe harbour at last, after a lifetime of administering a fortune, which had once been a source of proud stimulation and was now a crushing burden. To hand over, as he suggested, to concentrate on getting well again seemed, in Gertrude's sick perception, an irresistibly soothing idea.

Paris. Monday.

Franz-Clovis could move fast. Transfer papers and an ante-nuptial contract were prepared almost before she realized it. When he suggested a wedding now, here in Paris, Gertrude suddenly rallied enough to disconcert him a little. 'Don't rush me, honey,' she pleaded, 'you must realize I couldn't do a thing like that without telling Daphne. Let's go back first, just for a day or two? My daughter's entitled to that, you surely agree? Then, I'll marry you wherever you want. I'll off-load Fitton's damn Breakfast Bars with all my heart.'

There was no way he could refuse her.

'You never know,' she added with a gleam of her old spirit. ' "Kind, merry Doctor Brighton" might even do me good!'

Brighton. Saturday.

Emily beguiled her companion over dinner at the Metropole and watched him wax progressively sillier. He was reasonably presentable to look at, she supposed. But if only she could have got herself blackmailed by someone really attractive!

Still, Desmond Galsworthy had to be kept sweet. For the rest of both their lives, if necessary. There was no doubt whatever about that.

Gazing morosely across the room, listening with half an ear as he whinged on about his wife and family, she noticed the buck-toothed woman who had been with Franz-Clovis at Christmas. Only tonight, she was dining alone.

I suppose she must live here, Emily thought. My God, she looks terrible! No oil painting to start with, of course. But she looks really, really ill! 'Desmond,' she said, 'don't you think that woman over there might be on the point of collapse?'

Galsworthy hoped not. He had enough of collapsed people every day. Reluctantly, he glanced where Emily indicated.

Gertrude had just about finished picking her way through the endless menu. She had eaten scarcely anything. Fitz was staying overnight in London on business; to be conducted out of office hours, today and tomorrow. So he had told her.

That he was in Berlin, in conference with party lawyers, was better for her not to know.

On Monday, he would be here with documents that needed her signature. Then, back to Paris. By Wednesday afternoon, she would be Madame la Comtesse de Lavalle-Fontaine. The ring of the name was a thrill in itself. Even in her present useless state.

She would get better as soon as she was married to Fitz. Marriage to Fitz was what she craved; had craved all her life without knowing it. Fitz would take care of her. And of all the hassles that had become so heavy lately. How lucky she was to have found him at last!

She touched the gold bracelet he had given her. Of an unusual link design, it had no clasp. It would never be taken off. Almost as good as a wedding ring, huh?

But not quite. That was to happen Wednesday.

Tomorrow, she would tell Daphne.

Right now, she was very tired. Right now, she'd go to bed.

As she rose from the table, the whole restaurant dissolved before her eyes in a cloud of tiny black spots. Stiffness gripped her throat; roaring filled her head. For a moment she stood tall and straight, but quite unable to move. Then she crashed forward to the floor.

Galsworthy and Emily were there before the staff had time to react, before the buzz of consternation even collected impetus. They had been watching it happen, second by second.

Unobtrusively enough to limit attention to about four tables, Galsworthy and the Head Waiter carried Gertrude swiftly from the restaurant. In a corner of the vast foyer, they laid her on a couch and drew a screen across.

Her face was waxen, with a bluish tinge; her eyes not quite closed; her breathing shallow and rasping. Having established that she was staying in the hotel, Desmond Galsworthy summoned the manager. 'I'm a doctor,' he said. 'Can we get her up to her room, please?'

Now that Emily knew this was Gertrude Fitton, the heiress, it intrigued her greatly that Gertrude Fitton should have been spending Christmas with Franz-Clovis. The connection with Roscoe, way outside her cognizance, would have intrigued her even more.

Once in bed, Gertrude began to come round. She threw up a small amount of dinner, apologized, thanked them all and asked for her pills. 'I always take just one sleeping pill,' she said with querulous finality.

The silver box on her bedside table was empty.

'Bathroom cabinet,' she waved a shaky hand. 'New lot. I'll be just fine.'

Franz-Clovis had taken to keeping the antique pillbox – one of his presents to Gertrude – topped up from a bottle she had never so much as looked at. He had neglected to check her supply before leaving, his mind being too much occupied with mergers.

Emily went to get it. She handed it to Galsworthy.

He read the label. It would have meant nothing to Gertrude, anyway. 'Sleeping pills?' he queried. 'These are low dose arsenic compound.' He turned to the manager. 'An ambulance at once, if you please. Emergency. It's imperative to get this lady to hospital without delay. I take full responsibility.'

Emily found him rather impressive, suddenly.

At the Theatre Royal, *Jack and the Beanstalk* romped to its riotous finale. To Roscoe, it had tightened nicely, over the run. He discerned pace and polish, despite the last-night horsings-around. Afterwards, he took the girls to supper at Wheelers and then back to their digs.

Daphne was to come over to the hotel the following morning after breakfast. 'Your mother phoned me from Paris,' he said, 'she has something of great moment to discuss with you. Don't ask me what, because she didn't say.'

Nevertheless, troubled guesses were teasing his mind. That voice on the phone, give or take the atmospherics, hadn't sounded like the Gertrude he thought he knew. Not at all.

He arrived back at the Metropole as the ambulance was moving away from it. As he walked up the steps he was startled, to put it mildly, by the sight of Emily Kilverston standing at the top with her arm through that of a rather nondescript man whose dinner-jacket could do with a press.

Roscoe had not seen Emily Kilverston since the night at Charing Cross two years back. It had been too dark and too fraught to study her then, anyway. He studied her now. She looked exactly the same as she always had, wearing a velvet dinner dress of the kind of tawny shade that became her so. She was paler than he remembered. And the light in her eyes, directed at the fellow beside her, was nothing short of nauseating.

Then she saw him, too. A wild sequence of expressions chased each other across her face. She seemed unable to decide which one to keep.

'Why, Roscoe!' she said.

'Hello, Emily.'

'Er, this is Doctor Galsworthy.' She paused and smiled vaguely, knowing that wouldn't quite do.

Roscoe waited.

'Desmond, this is a very old child friend of mine,' she burbled with a rush of bright invention, 'Roscoe Somerville. He's a famous film star, you know. I'm sure you must have seen him often.'

'Don't go to the pictures much. How d'ye do?' Galsworthy offered a hand.

Roscoe shook it. 'Very sensible,' he murmured, 'dreadful rubbish, most of 'em.' For the life of him, he couldn't figure this out. Were these two married? Engaged? Divorced? Just good friends? None of it seemed to fit Emily, not with this customer. 'Down here for long, are you?'

'Just the w-weekend,' Emily said, rather thinly.

'Break from routine,' her companion added, 'does us both good from time to time.'

Roscoe felt a chill creeping slowly all over him.

Galsworthy cupped a possessive hand round the back of Emily's neck. 'This little lady has had quite a day,' he said firmly. 'If you'll excuse us, sir, I think it's time we turned in.'

The chill broke into a gallop. They were married. Emily was a doctor's wife. Well, it was security, wasn't it? Stability? She'd always been a bit short of that. Good luck to her. To them both. I hope it chokes 'em.

He managed a grin from ear to ear. 'I'm, er, I'm getting married myself, pretty soon, dontcherknow.' Was he? A picture of Ivy rose in his mind. Warm and somehow very familiar.

'I hope you'll be very happy,' Emily sounded as if somebody was strangling her.

Roscoe glanced at Doctor Galsworthy's curving fingers. They seemed harmlessly slack.

He sketched a little bow to them both. 'I hope you will, too,' he said. 'Goodnight.' He took his leave.

They watched him stroll jauntily away across the hall.

Suddenly, Emily pulled her arm free. 'Desmond dear, did I tell you how wonderful you were tonight? If not, I will, I promise. In a minute.'

She hared after Roscoe and caught him up as he was about to step into the lift. 'Good luck, Roscoe,' she said, panting very slightly, 'and, well ... Toodle-oo?'

He took her hand and turned it palm up. He studied it very closely for a long moment. Rather as a fortune-teller might. Then he turned it over again and kissed the back of it lightly.

'Good luck to you, too, Emily. Always. Toodle-oo.'

Table of Kindling in Proximity

Jumping About

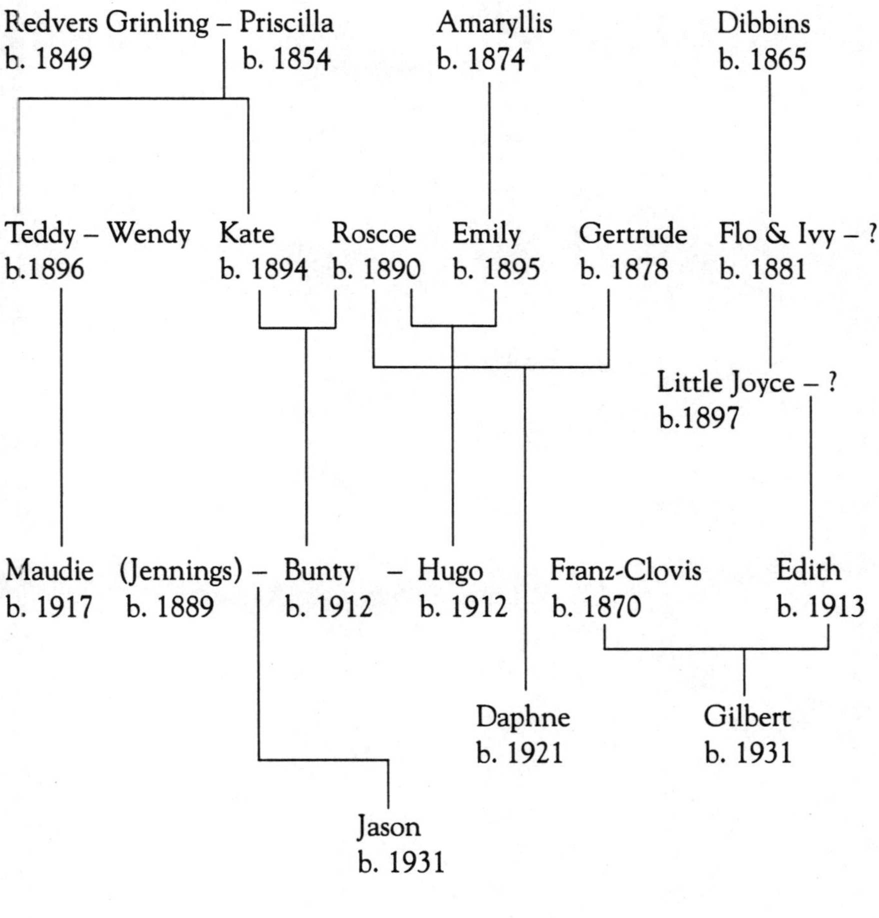